The Reluctant Contact

Stephen Burgen

Also by Stephen Burke

The Good Italian

Stephen Burke was born in Dublin, Ireland.
His first novel, *The Good Italian*, was shortlisted
for the Historical Writers Assocation Debut Crown award
and the Romantic Novelists Association Historical Fiction
prize. He is also a screenwriter and a director.

The Reluctant Contact

STEPHEN BURKE

HODDER &
STOUGHTON

First published in Great Britain in 2017 by Hodder & Stoughton
An Hachette UK company

2

A CIP catalogue record for this title is available from the British Library

Hardback ISBN 978 1 848 54919 7
Trade paperback ISBN 978 1 848 54920 3
Ebook ISBN 978 1 848 54921 0

Typeset in 12.5/16 pt Adobe Garamond Pro by Palimpsest Book Production Limited,
Falkirk, Stirlingshire

Printed and bound by Clays Ltd, St Ives plc

Hodder & Stoughton policy is to use papers that are natural, renewable and
recyclable products and made from wood grown in sustainable forests. The
logging and manufacturing processes are expected to conform to the
environmental regulations of the country of origin.

Hodder & Stoughton Ltd
Carmelite House
50 Victoria Embankment
London EC4Y 0DZ

www.hodder.co.uk

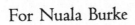

For Nuala Burke

Chapter 1

LUMPS OF ICE bobbed from side to side, disturbed by the swell from the boat. Within weeks this would all be ice, and the Billefjorden would be frozen solid for the whole winter. Then there would be no easy way in or out of here, except by helicopter. This was Yuri's favourite time of year. Others found it claustrophobic living up here, trapped in an icebox. But Yuri enjoyed being cut off from the rest of the world. It was peaceful. The only things that existed were what he could see around him. The chances of unwelcome surprises were slim.

He let the clean, glacial air enter his lungs slowly, savouring it. He felt alive, and renewed, after his trip back to Moscow. That was the city of his birth, but he returned there only when he had no choice.

Around him on the wooden deck were fifty burly miners, mostly Ukrainians and Belarusians. They had landed that morning at Longyearbyen airport on Spitsbergen, the largest island in the Norwegian archipelago of Svalbard. Numbering a hundred odd, they had split in two, with half making the journey south to Barentsburg, the other Soviet outpost here.

This would be the first time in Pyramiden for all of the men around him now, day one of a much sought-after two-year contract. Yuri was on his sixth, and if he had his way, there would be a seventh and an eighth. Pyramiden was his adopted home, one that he would not leave willingly.

There had been a flurry of excitement among the travellers a while back when they had sailed past a herd of walrus dining on a bearded seal, their long ivory tusks creating a bloody mess as they tore into their victim's blubbery flesh. Now the men smoked and chatted, and stamped their feet to keep warm. One passed around a metal flask of vodka to grateful hands.

They were all big men, made larger by their thick overcoats and cheap fur hats. There was something about their eyes, Yuri noticed. Spending so much time working underground, they might be expected to have narrow, beady eyes. Instead, for the most part, they shone wide and bright, with colours more vivid than the average surface dweller. Stunning emeralds and opals set in rugged, dark faces that could never be completely scrubbed clean of the black coal dust.

Yuri avoided going down into the lifeless darkness of the mine shaft as much as possible. As chief engineer for the whole town, he had more than enough work to do above ground to occupy his time. If something needed fixing below, in the bowels of the mountain, he would nominate his assistant, Semyon. The little Latvian weasel had been with him a year now. Previously, all of his assistants had been incompetents, content to do whatever they were told. Semyon, unfortunately, was smart, with notions above his station in life, which did not include being subordinate to Yuri for very long. However, Yuri had designed and built most of the systems in Pyramiden, and he was not about to share all of his secrets with anyone. As intricate and idiosyncratic as his systems were, he was still wary of being away, even for short periods. His greatest fear was that some day, someone would realise they could get by just fine without him.

Yuri felt a faint shift in the wind. Then everyone looked up as a large flock of black and white dovekies appeared from nowhere and whizzed by, just above their heads. One group of miners parted and Yuri saw a young woman sitting on her own on a bench. Pale. Twenty-five, or thereabouts. Not beautiful, but not ugly either. Foreign, he guessed. Proper foreign, not one of the skinny blondes from the Balkans. Her clothes were bright, in garish colours: an orange bubble coat, a striped woollen hat with hanging bobbles, as if she were going skiing. She was looking around, taking everything in. He felt her nervous excitement. She turned in his direction and their eyes locked for a moment. She smiled briefly before their view of each other was blocked once more.

The town came into view as the inlet reached a dead end. On one side stood the sprawling mine, nestled below Pyramiden mountain. On the opposite shore, across the fjord, was the Nordenskjold glacier, stationary to the naked eye, as it caressed the water's edge. Some of the miners pointed to an opening halfway up the mountainside. The entrance to the underworld into which they would descend each day.

Good luck with that, thought Yuri; rather you than me.

The mine was linked to the ground by a railway enclosed in a wooden tunnel, which brought the miners up and the coal down. Several times a year, a ship arrived from Russia to haul away the fruits of their labour.

Long before the boat reached the jetty, Yuri spotted his assistant standing beside Timur, the resident secret service agent. Timur was always easy to pick out, with his tightly cropped red hair and military bearing. Semyon, in contrast, was a slight man with oversized glasses and a mop of unkempt black curls. The two of them were waiting for him, no doubt. Trouble.

Theoretically, Timur was here to monitor NATO activity in this part of the Arctic Circle. In practice, he spent his days looking for ways to make the other residents' lives miserable. He and Semyon made a fine pair.

As the boat crew tied up the mooring ropes, Yuri stepped on to land and immediately went on the offensive.

'What have you done now?' he barked at Semyon as the two of them made a beeline for him.

Timur gave him one of his cold stares that gave the impression of being able to discern lies from truth. 'Semyon has made a serious accusation against you, Yuri, of sabotage.'

Some of the new miners, overhearing, turned their heads. The foreign girl looked over too. So, she speaks Russian, Yuri thought. Sabotage was the dirtiest word in the whole of the USSR, worse than capitalism, and it got the convenient blame for a litany of problems that were usually just the result of incompetence and inefficiency. Yuri feigned an outraged expression for his audience.

'What is it I'm supposed to have done now?'

Timur turned to Semyon for the answer.

'I don't know what he did exactly, but he did something.'

Yuri threw his eyes up to heaven. 'I tell you, I go away for one week, to bury my dear departed brother, and this place falls apart.'

'He did it,' said Semyon, 'I know he did.'

'Did what exactly?' asked Yuri. 'Would someone like to let me in on this little joke?'

'The heating to the executive block is out,' replied Semyon. 'But you knew that already.'

'You mean to say it's broken and you don't know how to fix it. Correct? How long has it been out?'

'Three nights,' said Timur.

'Ooh, I bet the execs aren't happy about that,' said Yuri, with a grin.

'No, we're not,' said Timur. 'My balls have nearly fallen off. If they get any harder we can play snooker with them.'

'It's a good thing I came back when I did then. Come on, let's get to work so I can fix whatever it is. You'll really have to pay more attention, Semyon, if you're to replace me one day.'

Yuri started to walk away, but checked over his shoulder as Semyon turned to Timur for support. The secret service man just shrugged, leaving Semyon no choice except to traipse after him.

'What happened to your brother?' Timur shouted after them.

'He drank himself to death,' replied Yuri.

Timur nodded as if this was nothing unusual.

At forty-five, Yuri had lived through the craziness of Stalin, the slightly tamer craziness of Khrushchev, and now the 'big sleep' of Brezhnev. Of the three, he reckoned this was definitely the best time to be alive. Brezhnev understood what the people wanted. An end to high-pressure production quotas at work, and lots of cheap vodka. He delivered both.

The threat of war with the Americans was at an all-time low. The burning question of the day was whether Brezhnev really was the most boring man alive; or if, in fact, he was alive at all and not a mannequin as some suggested. There was also some heated bar-room debate on how many more self-awarded medals he would be able to fit on his bloated chest. However, despite the new stability in the country, for Yuri the old gulag-avoidance rules still applied.

Don't trust anyone.

Keep your head down.

Look after number one.

For the whole afternoon, Semyon followed Yuri around like a jittery hen as he attempted to decipher the problem. They rechecked the furnace, the pumps, dozens of pipe intersections and the exec block itself. After four hours Yuri threw his hands up and admitted that he was as clueless as Semyon had been. Everything seemed to be functioning, yet the hot water stubbornly refused to arrive in the executive apartment building. Semyon grudgingly parked his sabotage accusations and offered a few suggestions. Yuri humoured him by trying them out, but none delivered the desired solution.

'We'll have to tackle it again in the morning,' said Yuri, as the night-time freeze made continuing their outdoor work impossible.

'But that'll be four nights in a row!' protested Semyon. 'We'll get into deep shit. I'm already in the bad books.'

'Look, don't worry about them,' said Yuri. 'They've survived this long, and a little dose of hardship will do them good. Besides, they can pin all the blame on me now.'

Semyon was satisfied with the last part.

The heating system was Yuri's masterpiece. A thing of beauty. A quarter of the coal they dug out of the mountain went into Pyramiden's furnace, which heated the water, which was then pumped around the whole town through miles of piping. Outside, they ran above ground under wooden walkways, which were kept snow-free as a result. He liked to think of the power plant as Pyramiden's heart. The pipes were the blood vessels, keeping the organs, the living quarters and their occupants alive. Heating was no joke up here, eight hundred miles from the North Pole. Without Yuri, the 1,000 inhabitants would all freeze to death. Soviets prided themselves on being able to tame nature, enabling them to live and work wherever they pleased. Pyramiden was proof they could.

Yuri dined with the other workers in the canteen in the Cultural Palace, waited on by robust Ukrainian women. The menu for tonight was cabbage rolls stuffed with rice and meat. Semyon sat at another table, as always. They were not friends, would never be, and neither of them had the slightest problem with that. Yuri looked around the room. Apart from the miners, there were clerical staff from the office, cooks and cleaners, farmers for the livestock and greenhouses, a doctor and a couple of nurses from the hospital, teachers from the kindergarten and school, and two dozen kids of varying ages, from toddlers to teens.

The room itself was the grandest mine canteen in the whole of the Soviet Union. One entire wall was covered with a mosaic depicting an Arctic scene with snow-covered mountains and polar bears. Yuri never understood why they had decided to put it there. Wasn't the whole idea to keep the cold on the outside? If anyone wished to be reminded of an Arctic vista, they need look no further than the nearest window. The Kremlin had its own reasons for pumping millions of rubles into this place. It was their little patch of the west, and it was designed to give any foreign visitor a glamorous – and entirely false – impression of what daily life was like behind the iron curtain. Whoever heard of a mine with chandeliers in its workers' canteen? And a plush cinema. And a heated swimming pool. And a Yuri Gagarin sports centre. And a library with sixty thousand books. All for miners!

When word got out about the relative luxury that was on offer here, Pyramiden was inundated with eager transfer requests from every mine from Siberia to Chechnya. There were downsides of course. The isolation. The bitter cold. The three winter months of 24-hour darkness. And the same faces to look at every day for two years. All of these were positives for Yuri.

Especially the two-year contracts the others were on. It meant he could begin a relationship with a woman, usually a waitress or one of the clerical staff, knowing that she would be leaving in a maximum of twenty-four months. If a romance wasn't working out, no problem. Why bother going through the hassle of a break-up, when her departure boat was already booked? And the same fjord that had brought her would take her away again, with no tears shed. He had an aversion to hurting, because it made him feel guilty, and to being hurt.

Right now he was single, but on the lookout.

Across the room, he spotted that young foreigner again. English. Some sort of a space student he had heard. Catherine. Pyramiden being so small, everyone already knew something about her, or thought they did. For Yuri, foreign equalled exotic; however, she was not his type. She was too young, obviously. Just over half his age. But that wasn't it. When he looked at her there was no spark.

One of the more surprising things he found about getting older was the range of possibilities it opened up. When he was twenty, he was attracted to a narrow age group. But now, in middle age, he found himself drawn to all sorts of women from twenty to fifty. Thirty years of choice.

At another table, he noticed Anya. One of the school teachers. Late forties. Straight, dark hair to her shoulders. Delicate chin. Brown eyes. Beautiful. She had been here a few months already and Yuri had his eye on her. If he had to pick from the bunch, she'd be the one, though she hadn't shown even the slightest interest in him so far. To date, the sum total of their conversations numbered zero. She had given him a monosyllabic greeting on three occasions. But he wasn't disheartened, yet. Winter here was long.

After dinner, he made his way down through the main square, past Lenin's bust as it gazed sternly across the fjord. His apartment block was for the single men, and was nicknamed London. The block for families was aptly called the Crazy House. The one for single women was called Paris, perhaps because everyone dreamed of going there, one day. That's where Anya was, and Catherine now too. Yuri would never get to visit the real Paris. Foreign travel was not for a worker at his level. But he knew the Arctic Paris well.

Inside his modest apartment, he finally got to wash and put on some clean clothes. In common with other residents, he had decorated his quarters with whatever could be recycled. Strings of coloured beads made from plastic wiring, pictures cut from magazines and framed. None of the apartments had kitchens, since they all ate together in the canteen, and food was free. They did have fridges, metal boxes attached to the outside of the windows. No electricity required. Yuri reached into his and pulled out a half-full bottle of vodka. He poured himself a glass, drank it down in one gulp and then lay on his narrow single bed, fully clothed. He set his alarm clock for two in the morning, and closed his eyes.

An image of his brother intruded into his head, from when he was six and Yuri was eight. Both of them with shaven heads after their mother had found lice. His brother looked up at him, confident of his protection and guidance, as they played war with the other kids in the neighbourhood. That was before their innocent world collapsed, and they had to play the game for real.

He was in a deep sleep when the beeping roused him. He got up, put on his warmest coat and hat and walked silently down the unlit corridor.

There was no one about as he stepped outside, in minus twenty degrees. Everyone else had more sense. They were all tucked up in their warm beds, apart from the execs with their unresolved problem.

Moonlight bounced off the fresh pristine snow, so he did not need a flashlight to find his destination. When he reached the correct section of the walkway he stopped and stood still for a good two minutes, waiting and listening for any followers. Satisfied, he jumped down to the frozen ground and crawled under the walkway, out of sight. He turned on his flashlight and pulled out a wrench from inside his coat. Working quickly, he began to remove the section of pipe he had sabotaged the night before his departure for his brother's funeral. A bit of insurance, to remind them how indispensable he was. Once he had dismantled the pipe, he removed the faulty valve he had added to the system and replaced it with a new one. Then he reconnected the lot and immediately heard the hot water flowing freely once more.

'You're welcome,' he said, looking in the direction of the executive building. 'Don't mention it.'

He turned off his flashlight, climbed back up onto the walkway and went back the way he'd come.

There was a light on in a second-floor apartment in Paris as he passed. He wondered whose it was, and what she was doing awake at this hour. A figure appeared at the window and he stopped. He remained motionless and watched out of curiosity, as well as not wishing to be seen out and about at this hour.

The person in the window reached out to draw the curtains. It was a man. Timur. He looked up and down the street, in the same way that Yuri had scanned his surroundings moments earlier before jumping off the walkway. Yuri stopped exhaling in case his condensing breath might betray his position. He saw Timur look away and pull the curtains shut.

What poor woman is he visiting, and at three in the morning? Yuri wondered.

He watched for a moment longer. The light remained on, but he saw no further movement.

Chapter 2

THE NEXT MORNING, Yuri got out of bed, picked up a dry towel and wiped off the dripping condensation covering his window. Outside, the volume of ice in the fjord had visibly increased overnight, almost enough for a brave soul to try to skip across to the other side. Two more weeks and you would be able to walk straight over there and touch the glacier. He showered in piping hot water, making sure not to get his hair wet. Walking around outside with a damp head was a guaranteed ticket to a fortnight's stay in Pyramiden's hospital. It was possible to avoid getting ill here by constantly wrapping up for the outside, and then pulling off layers as soon as you got inside again.

As he dressed, he turned on his radio, a Yugoslav military receiver he had traded in return for adding an extra radiator to a family apartment. Yuri had arrived with few possessions but his technical abilities came in useful for bartering. While the radio was one of the best models in town, he still had to work hard to obtain an acceptable signal. He achieved this by connecting a length of copper wire to the aerial and wrapping the other end around his room's iron plumbing pipes. The clearest signal was a Norwegian station, with presenters who spoke Norwegian, which he didn't understand. And they played far too much Abba for his liking.

Legally, he should not be listening to western stations at all. Back home, the police checked roofs to see who had their antennas bent towards the capitalist half of the world. Up here, there was more freedom as long as you didn't flaunt it. As a rule, Yuri only listened to western stations. If he couldn't find one, he preferred silence rather than listen to the official voices from home. Not understanding what foreign presenters were saying added a sense of mystery. Though he guessed that their monologues were probably as banal as those on Soviet radio.

The Norwegian signal was lost momentarily and Yuri adjusted the tuning dial. He found himself on a different station, which was faint and unstable, but they were playing Bowie. Yuri mimed along, not knowing what most of the lyrics meant. He could tell that the man had attitude and that's what he liked about him. If Soviet censorship was actually working, he should not have known who David Bowie was. But everyone did. As with many western stars, his records were banned for being ideologically harmful compositions. You could get them of course, in Moscow, if you had money or something to trade. You could get anything you wanted in Moscow. It was just a matter of knowing the right person to ask.

Bowie was also famous in the Soviet Union because he was one of the few western musicians who had actually visited it. On the way home from Japan, he had travelled by train from Moscow to Warsaw because he had a fear of flying. He did not play any concerts but the trip had generated a song, 'Warszawa'. The Soviet Union had its own rock stars, such as the Singing Guitars, aka the Russian Beatles. But Bowie was special.

Even in the big cities, an original vinyl was a rarity. When

Yuri was younger, western music was bootlegged on to old X-rays. Bone records, they were called. But since cassette tapes had become available, it was easier to get the music you liked. Except in Pyramiden. This was another of the sacrifices one had to make on Svalbard. You had to survive with what you found around you. People here had little, and what little they had, they shared. This was the Arctic way of life.

When the Bowie song was over, a Russian voice said, 'Until next time. This was Seva . . . Seva Novgorodsev. The City of London. BBC.' Yuri turned and stared at the radio. A Russian on the BBC. And then the man was gone as quickly as he had found him. A new programme began. Who the hell was he? Yuri switched off the radio but decided to leave the dial untouched. This man needed further investigation. He left his wet towel on the radiator to dry. Then he prepared himself to face the elements.

He grabbed his cigarettes and matches from the table and left the room. Smoking was something he only did outside. It was too cold to open his apartment windows to air the place out. He had recently switched to Bulgarian light cigarettes, which the advertising said were better for you. Inhaling them gave him a false sense of heat, as though his lungs were a stove.

Leaving his apartment block, Yuri lit his first of the day and turned in the direction of the waterfront. Then he began the five-minute trek to the power station, which was located beside the coal deposit and the harbour. Pyramiden's miners worked almost every day of the year to fill the coal deposit in preparation for the next ship home. No Christmas break for the Christians nor Hanukkah for the Jews, except on their own time, and in private. Once the ship had docked in the harbour, a crane levered the black rock into the hold. And as soon as it had sailed away, sitting deeper in the water, the whole process started anew. Their outpost was kept going solely for this purpose. If the coal ever ran out, the town would die.

Long before he reached the power station, he smelled the smoke from the burning coal, rising out of the tall twin chimney stacks. The plumes of smoke were an ugly sight against the still Arctic landscape, but needs must. His arrival this morning was earlier than usual, but he was annoyed to find Semyon already settled inside the control room with his arms folded.

'Morning,' said Yuri, turning his back to take off his coat.

Five seconds inside the room and he had already started to sweat. The power station was the warmest place in town.

'So, any bright ideas?' asked Semyon, before Yuri even had the chance to hang his coat up.

'For what?' he replied, stamping the last of the snow off his boots on to the doormat.

'The exec problem,' said Semyon. 'We'll have to fix it today, or they'll put us both out of our jobs.'

'Oh,' he replied. He tapped the glass on a pressure dial on one of the floor-to-ceiling control units, as if he were concerned about the reading. 'I had a brainwave last night actually. Couldn't sleep. One of the junction valves. That was it. All sorted now.'

'You fixed it?' asked Semyon. 'By yourself?' His eyes, magnified by his thick glasses, were burning a hole in the side of Yuri's head.

'Yep, all back to normal, nothing more to worry about. You didn't think of those valves, did you?' he added, out of pure malice.

'Sure I did,' blurted Semyon, 'I checked some of them. I didn't find anything.'

Yuri thought the man might bust a blood vessel, he was frowning so much.

'How many did you have to check before you found it?' the Latvian asked.

'Oh, let me see,' replied Yuri. He made a show of silently adding up with his fingers. 'A dozen probably. That one was rusted right through. Could have gone at any time.'

'Can I see it?' asked Semyon, in a tone that Yuri did not like.

He turned and gave his assistant a cold look. He was a cocky little bastard. Most people would think twice about calling someone a liar. Especially if that someone was their boss. Yet he had known the Latvian would ask for proof. He would have done the same under the circumstances. He walked over to where his coat was hanging, pulled the offending valve from his pocket and looked at it. Then, without warning, he turned and threw it low and hard. The speed of Semyon's reaction was impressive and he just managed to grab it before it hit the wall.

Yuri smiled and shrugged. 'Good catch. You've been playing American baseball, haven't you?'

Yuri had fought boys with Semyon's physique at school. They looked like pushovers but turned out to be little wiry bastards that you could never get a good hold of.

Semyon lifted his glasses and scrutinised the metal object, holding it right up under his nose. But it backed up everything Yuri had said. He had held on to it for months for that very purpose.

'Satisfied?' asked Yuri.

Semyon didn't reply. He avoided making eye contact with

Yuri, and said nothing further. That's right, thought Yuri, you've nothing to say now. In Yuri's opinion, which he kept to himself, the glue that held the Soviet empire together was dishonesty. Corruption equalled survival, and potentially success and happiness, if you were very good at it. Honesty condemned you to a frustrating life. Within such a corrupt system, it was possible for anyone to bend the rules as they saw fit, as long as they did not allow themselves to get caught. That was the key.

At noon, Pyramiden's residents began to assemble outside for the official opening of the new street Yuri had walked to work on that morning. The wooden walkway, connecting the town square to the power station, had been built to celebrate the sixtieth anniversary of the Great October in 1917. 'Great' because it was the beginning of the people's revolution and year zero of the communist age. Nearly everyone was there to mark the day. An absence without good reason would be noticed, though the community here didn't need much encouragement; there was little else to do, so they liked to participate in any organised event. They could even be persuaded to assemble outdoors, and freeze their asses off, just for a bit of diversion.

The adults formed a large loose circle, and chatted giddily among themselves while they waited for the mine president to arrive. The children ran around and through the group, swaddled in layers of outdoor clothes like babushka dolls, their rosy faces and wide eyes peeking out with excitement from under their hats. Yuri had always considered it strange that their parents would bring them, by choice, to one of the harshest places on the planet. Svalbard had the distinction of having the northern-most human settlements in the world.

The younger ones did look happy, he had to admit. For them
it was probably an adventure. It was the teenagers who seemed
depressed. Suicidal, Yuri would say, by the looks of the spotty
ones in front of him, staring vacantly at the ground. But
dissatisfaction was what teenagers were good at, wherever they
were.

He scanned the faces of the women in the crowd as the
director's speech began. He spotted English Catherine again.
For some reason, she was positively beaming with delight at
being present for this occasion. Standing behind her right
shoulder was Anya, the teacher. Yuri waited an age till he
caught her eye and then gave her his best smile, but she looked
away as though she hadn't seen him at all. Yuri sighed. Perhaps
this wasn't going to happen, and he should move on. She had
airs, this woman, as though she was on a different plane of
existence to everyone else. Not a snob, as such. Her clothes
were no better than the next person's. Just, she gave the impression of being elsewhere.

For a moment, he tuned in to the mine director's voice. As
usual he was speaking at length about coal. How the town
was meeting its targets and more. How the five-year plan was
progressing according to the five-year plan. How when it was
successfully completed there would be another five-year plan
to take its place, and so on. The director told them they should
all be proud of their collective contribution to these achieve-
ments.

Am I, thought Yuri? Yes, he decided, he was. Not for the
mine director, or Mother Russia, or communism, or Emperor
Brezhnev. He was proud of what he had built here, with his
own hands. It gave him personal, individual satisfaction. He
did not care if anyone else noticed or appreciated what he had
done.

After the director's statement on the rude health of the mine, English Catherine started a round of applause, which everyone felt obliged to join in with. Then it was the turn of Grigory, Pyramiden's resident party man. Yuri had no time for party hacks but he and Grigory were friends, mainly because he was not an average politico. A short, portly man in his late fifties, he was out of place in this raw frontier, more suited to the intellectual cafe society of Leningrad. His wavy grey hair and matching bushy moustache made him resemble Albert Einstein. To complete the picture, the moustache was often dotted with the crumbs of whatever he had eaten last.

Yuri enjoyed his company. Their conversations were a step up from any other he was likely to have here. With some exceptions, miners tended not to provide the most stimulating encounters. The two men played chess sometimes in the library, though Yuri suspected his opponent was guilty of postponing his best moves in order to prolong the game and make him feel better about his limited abilities.

Stuck up here in the Arctic Circle, Grigory was probably the only party man in the whole of the Soviet Union who wasn't making a prince's fortune dealing on the black market. There was not much to trade in Pyramiden. No one coveted a new fridge, or a washing machine. The town provided for all their needs. It was the only place in the whole of the Soviet Union where communism worked as it had been intended. Almost.

Grigory dabbled in poetry and was an eloquent speaker, though, as the party expected, his orations were peppered with the limitless wisdom of Lenin. The great man's bust listened, unmoved, from its plinth nearby. Grigory knew his audience, and his speech was mercifully short, rounded off with one of his two jokes about snow, both of which Yuri had given him.

As the crowd dispersed, with smiles on their faces, Yuri walked over to greet him.

Yuri often wondered if Lenin would have remained so revered, and for so long, had he not passed away young. No doubt, had he survived he would have fallen out with younger men who were eager to take possession of his throne. Khrushchev had famously denounced Stalin, once the dictator was safely dead, and later Brezhnev had not waited as long before he took Khrushchev's power for himself. If Lenin had lived to old age, then his words might have become subject to censure, as had happened to so many other former heroes since.

'Nice speech,' said Yuri. 'Vladimir Ilyich really does have words of wisdom to suit every occasion. Unless you just made those up. Did you?'

Grigory smiled. 'Yes, he does. Aren't we lucky. By the way, I was chilly while you were gone, Yuri. I had to sleep in a chair in my office for two nights.'

'That's all sorted now,' Yuri assured him. 'You can go back to your own bed. Apologies for any inconvenience.'

'I'm glad to hear it,' said Grigory. 'Funny the way it happened while you were away. A word of advice between friends, with ladder-climbers like Timur around, it is best not to tempt fate too often.'

'I don't know what you mean,' said Yuri.

Grigory smiled and ignored his answer. 'Have you met Catherine yet?' he asked.

Yuri turned to find the young English woman standing directly behind him. Up close, her wide blue eyes seemed to hide nothing. And the light sprinkle of freckles on her cheeks, the same colour as her strawberry blonde hair, gave her a childlike quality.

'No, I haven't had the pleasure.'

Catherine offered her hand, which was small, but her grip was firm.

'Pleased to meet you, comrade,' she said, in quite acceptable Russian.

'Call me Yuri,' he said.

He reserved the word 'comrade' for people he was annoyed with.

'Yuri here is a fixer of all things. He has magic hands,' said Grigory.

Catherine's eyes widened further, which did not seem possible.

'Then he is a valuable asset to the Soviet people,' she said, with a straight face.

Yuri and Grigory grinned at each other. Yuri had not met many foreign Reds. The ones he had, he found to be idealists in love with just that – an idea. One they had never had to live through.

'He is indeed very valuable,' agreed Grigory. 'Precious I'd say. Why don't you wait for me in my office, Catherine, and I'll be along there in a moment.'

'All right,' said Catherine. 'I'm sure we will meet again, Yuri.'

'Nothing is more certain,' he said. 'It's hard to avoid anyone here, even if you wanted to.'

Catherine smiled and walked off in the direction of the administration building.

'How was Moscow?' asked Grigory.

'Same,' said Yuri. 'Too many people, too much traffic. I didn't see much, only the inside of the graveyard.'

'Your ex-wife come?'

'Ha. No. She didn't come, surprise, surprise. It's better that way, believe me.'

'You two were in love once, though?' Grigory asked. 'Weren't you? Or have you forgotten?'

Yuri frowned, wondering where this was headed. 'A distant memory, that's all. And for such a short time, between fights, I am not sure it can be classed as love.'

'Shame,' said Grigory. 'Too many women is not good for a man. Especially at your age. By the way, while we are on the subject, do me a favour, and stay away from her.'

'What? You mean the cosmonaut? Where did that come from? I have absolutely no intention. Did she—?'

'No. She did not say anything. I have just had to deal with the fallout from your affairs too many times. And this one is an innocent.'

'I can see that,' said Yuri. 'Well, thanks for the vote of confidence. Much appreciated, friend. Don't worry, Miss Innocent is not on my to-do list. What's she doing here anyway?'

'She's writing her university thesis on why the first human settlements in space will have to be communist.'

'Seriously?' asked Yuri.

'I think she has some very interesting arguments,' replied Grigory.

'I'll bet she does. But that still doesn't explain why she's here, in Pyramiden.'

'We were the closest thing she could find to a space-like living environment,' said Grigory.

'Well, she's got that right,' agreed Yuri. 'Ice cold and light years away from civilisation. Cosmonaut Katerina. Her application to come here must have been greeted with open arms. I suppose they are going to milk her for publicity.'

'No one is using anyone. We are going to help her, that's all. You know some day you are going to drown in that cynicism of yours.' Grigory walked on.

'I'm a good swimmer,' said Yuri. 'Chess soon?'

'If I'm free. Just come find me.'

It was true what Grigory had said. Sometimes his affairs had not ended as cleanly as he liked to imagine. One in particular, involving the wife of a miner, had been spectacularly messy. Threats, spousal violence and a couple of kids caught in the crossfire. The experience had made him avoid the extra complications of married women ever since.

For several days afterwards, Yuri and Semyon worked together on the dam system that prevented the town from flooding in the spring thaw. No water was running down the mountain now, but it would as soon as winter was over, and they needed to prepare in advance. The two men rarely spoke for the whole of this time spent in close proximity to one another. When they did it was short and to the point. Yuri didn't know, or care, what he did in his spare time, but having Semyon around kept him on edge.

After yet another day of sly looks and non-communication, Yuri decided he was spending too much time second-guessing his potential Latvian usurper, and that he needed to think more about himself. It had been four months since he had any female companionship and he resolved to take matters into his own hands the following morning.

Parents were still dropping their children off when Yuri arrived in the school lobby, carrying his metal toolbox. He explained to the headteacher that it was routine for him to check all the systems in every building at least once a year, and today was the school's turn.

'But the classes are starting,' she protested. 'Couldn't you come back in the evening when everyone is gone?'

'Oh no. It'll take me the whole day at least,' he argued. And when she was still reluctant, he added, 'Wouldn't you rather a little disturbance now, than allow a problem to build up and have to shut down the whole school for who knows how long?'

'All right,' she said, with a sigh. 'I suppose, if you think it's really necessary.'

'Don't worry. You won't even know I'm here.'

Yuri took a moment to check the electrical fuse box inside the front door, while casting a curious glance down the hall towards the classrooms. He could already hear her voice, addressing her pupils. He had planned to make more of a pretence about his presence here by visiting all the other rooms first. But he decided to hell with that – he wanted to see her straight away. Perhaps she really did have no interest in him, but he was going to aim high until there was a reason not to.

On his way down the corridor, he passed a long line of children's winter boots. Hanging above them on hooks were their thick winter coats, with gloves dangling from the pockets.

He knocked politely on her classroom door and entered, without waiting for permission.

'Good morning, Miss Anya,' he said.

She didn't reply, just looked at him, waiting for an explanation for his intrusion. He ignored her stare and headed to the back of the classroom, watched by many little eyes. There, he knelt at the radiator under the window. His being in her classroom didn't seem to disturb her too much; she continued without hardly missing a beat. She was teaching mathematics to a group of ten-year-olds. Her style was direct and no-nonsense. She wasn't harsh with the kids, but she certainly wasn't motherly either. Yuri liked that about her. He didn't trust homemakers any more. He listened to her for as long as he thought he could reasonably stay in the room. When she wasn't looking he watched her from the corner of his eye. His

opinion had not changed. She was the best-looking woman
he had ever seen in Pyramiden.

Suddenly there was silence, and Yuri looked up to see that
the children had been tasked to work on a problem on their
own. Seizing this opportunity, he quickly packed up his things
and walked to the front of the classroom.

'Are you finding everything all right in here?' he asked her.

Even though she was not actually doing anything at that
moment, Anya looked displeased at being addressed directly,
in a way she would have to respond to.

'Everything is fine,' she said.

'No problems?' he asked.

'If there is a problem, I'm sure someone will call you. I
already said, everything is fine.'

He smiled. Her expression didn't change.

'Yes, yes you did.'

He nodded once and walked out with the feeling that his
knuckles had just been rapped, like a schoolboy. A long bleak
season of solitude appeared to be stretching out in front of
him. There would be no more boats until March. Pyramiden
had reached its full winter complement of women. He could
of course, set his sights lower, but he was not in the mood
for that right now. He wondered if there were any good books
in the library that he had not already read.

Since Yuri had returned at the beginning of October, the hours
of sunlight had been getting gradually shorter until one day,
towards the end of the month, the sun did not rise at all. It
would stay that way for another 111 days exactly. For a few
more weeks there would be several hours of twilight each day,
when there would still be a perceptible light just below the
horizon at sunrise and sunset. Then that too would be gone

and all would be given over to darkness. It was a surreal time for everyone. Yuri had experienced it eleven times before, but the fresh arrival of endless night still had a tendency to push him closer to the edge of sanity. Each day ran into the next, and the next, with no visible difference. Time seemed to have frozen at the moment when night was at its darkest and light should have begun its return. Wearing a watch became both pointless and essential. He expected that for the miners, the tunnel rats, it must be business as usual, since they rarely saw the sun anyway.

The weather changed too. Without the sun, the cold became something sinister. A foe to be battled.

Two days after the sun went into hiding, Yuri ran into Catherine outside the swimming pool. She had another gleeful expression on her face.

'You see?' she said.

'See what?' he asked.

She waved at the darkness surrounding them, and the starry sky above. 'Space. Now my study can really begin.'

'Ah,' he agreed. 'So it can.'

'You're on my list to interview,' she said. 'I'll be tracking you down one of these days.'

As she walked away, he was pleased that his first impression of her had been incorrect. She was not such a ditzy cosmonaut after all. As the wind began to whip up around him, he gazed up at the Milky Way, which was as clear as though he were looking through a telescope. He felt a sudden chill. Not from the cold. It was the thought that Catherine's theory might come true and that busts of Lenin might one day find their way up to those stars too.

After doing thirty lengths of the pool, Yuri made his way to the canteen in the Cultural Palace. He was late and there were no other diners left, but the kitchen staff managed to rustle up a hot meal for him from the leftovers. A clear fish soup to start, followed by minced pork dumplings with sour cream. The chandeliers had been switched off, and the only illumination came from the fluorescent kitchen lights. It was peaceful having the place to himself. A tsar alone in his grand dining hall. But it didn't last.

Timur walked up the staircase and stopped before reaching the top. He nodded for Yuri to come down to him. Yuri hesitated. A private word with a KGB agent was never desirable; but this one seemed unavoidable. He put down his knife and fork and walked down to the first stairwell, to where Timur had retreated.

'How long have you been in here?' Timur asked.

'I just got here,' Yuri said. 'Now my dinner is getting cold. Why do you ask?'

'Do you know what Semyon was doing this evening?'

'Yes, I do actually,' replied Yuri. 'The mine reported a problem with the air ventilation. I sent him down to fix it.'

'Why didn't you do it yourself?'

Yuri decided not to admit that he didn't like it down there. It offered too much of a ripe excuse for demoting a mine's chief maintenance engineer.

'I was busy,' he said. 'And it seemed like a minor problem. Semyon's well able to handle stuff like that on his own. What's he gone and done?'

Timur paused before answering. 'The job wasn't so simple, as it happens. He's dead.'

Chapter 3

THE WHEELS ON the cable car squeaked in regular rhythm as it pulled Yuri and Timur up the mountainside. The steel tracks were enclosed in a wooden tunnel, which was the only thing preventing their faces being lashed by the icy wind. This was the second death in the space of a month of someone Yuri had known. News of the Latvian's death had come as a shock, but he knew he was not going to shed any tears for Semyon. Still, he had been Yuri's assistant, and therefore his responsibility, at least to some degree.

Yuri glanced over at his travelling companion, who was staring at him. He wasn't crying either. Although Yuri couldn't remember Timur ever showing any kind of emotion. When he had relayed the news about Semyon, he had done so as though it were an inconvenience.

'Looks like your job is safe then,' said Timur. 'Competition out of the way.'

Yuri didn't answer.

'I know you sabotaged the heating system, just like he said,' continued Timur. 'That was smart.'

Yuri looked away and remained silent. The KGB man tapped his fingers on the side of the metal cable car, to the rhythm of some unknown tune. Yuri had come across many officials like Timur in his time. From experience, he knew it was best not to deflate their illusion that they were the smartest guys in the room. When men like him were feeling confident, they were less dangerous.

The broad, hulking figure of Igor, the mine foreman, gradually came into view at the top of the tunnel. Even from here, Yuri could see that the big man was shaken. Igor was six foot four and as wide as a house. A rampant beard covered half his face, and he was wrapped in the great black overcoat he always wore. The man had not done any actual digging in years. Yet, he was in charge of everything that happened up here. Igor nodded as they climbed out of the cable car, and stroked his beard.

'This way,' he said, and led them into the tunnel.

Yuri took a last deep breath at the mouth of the shaft, but regretted it immediately as the cold mountain air stabbed his lungs. Then he joined the others.

They followed the mine's strip lighting through a bewildering maze of tunnels. To Yuri, every black shaft looked the same as the last. At least Igor seemed to know where he was going. They passed a few miners, who gave them that peculiar, silent nod of condolence usually reserved for family members at a funeral service. Yuri had gotten those looks from his brother's neighbours the previous month, and receiving them again so soon was disconcerting. On this occasion, Yuri was not a relative, or a friend, and so deserved no sympathy.

After turning another corner, Igor stopped without warning and Yuri banged into his back. Igor stood and waited for his two visitors to start the conversation. The light in this tunnel was dimmer than in the main channel. Yuri looked around but could not see Semyon.

'Where is he?' he asked.

Igor pointed to a tarpaulin on the ground that may have been white once, but had now taken on the same coal-stained hue as the rest of this underground world. Resting beside the tarpaulin was a bashed ventilation unit and a small pile of rubble. Yuri looked at the roof above them. It appeared intact.

'Is it safe in here?' he asked.

'Yes,' said Igor. 'It's safe.'

Yuri looked from the body-shaped tarpaulin to Timur, waiting for him to make an inspection of the remains. He was the agent in charge, after all; what passed for the force of law in this Soviet outpost. Igor, he saw, was expecting the same thing, but Timur appeared to have no intention of going anywhere near the corpse. He wasn't even looking at it. Instead, he started to order the contents of his engraved silver cigarette case.

'What happened?' asked Yuri, getting impatient.

'The ventilation unit. He was working on it and it seems to have come loose and fallen on him,' said Igor. 'Part of the wall collapsed too.'

'So it was an accident?' said Yuri.

The foreman paused and caught Timur's eye, before nodding without conviction.

Timur sighed. 'Get him out of here. I'll tell the Norwegians.' And he started to head back the way they'd come.

'Aren't you going to check him?' demanded Yuri. 'He could be alive for all you know.'

Timur shot him an angry glance. 'I already did. I want to see you in my office now.'

'That's it?' asked Yuri. 'I want to see for myself.'

Timur continued on his way. 'You can play doctor, and policeman, if you want. My office, ten minutes. Then get him up top, Igor. And I'll need a written report from you, by tomorrow.'

Igor remained silent and expressionless throughout this exchange, which was probably how he had gotten to the senior position of mine foreman.

'He was already down here?' asked Yuri.

'Yes,' said Igor. 'One hour ago.'

Yuri realised that this sideshow had been put on just for him, to see how he would react at the scene. Which meant Timur had put two and two together and had come up with a crime, with his name as prime suspect. So perhaps this wasn't the accident it appeared to be. At least, if Timur was really convinced he had anything to do with this he would already have locked him up. The KGB man was just fishing. Yuri hoped he hadn't unwittingly given him any encouragement in his suspicions.

He knelt down and pulled the tarpaulin up with one hand. The sight that greeted him was not pretty. He was glad he had not had the chance to eat much of his second course. Semyon had a deep, open gash on one side of his forehead, and smaller abrasions across both sides of his face. Judging by his pallor, there seemed to be no point in checking for a pulse. Unlike Yuri's brother, laid out at the funeral home in Moscow, Semyon did not have the expression of someone who was at peace. The man appeared to have suffered in his final moments.

'Maybe his skull cracked,' said Igor. 'Or his neck. That's usually what happens.'

'Usually?' said Yuri.

'When something heavy lands on a man's head.'

'How many mine collapses have you had here?'

Igor looked Yuri in the eye. 'Since I've been here, none. I put the safety of my men first. They know that and they trust me. You can ask any of them.'

'No one is blaming you,' said Yuri. 'So what happened? Did this wall give way?'

'No,' said Igor, taking the suggestion as a personal affront. 'The wall is strong. I don't let anyone work unless the walls are strong.' He slapped the side of the tunnel with his large palm to prove the point. The man did inspire confidence. Yuri could see the other miners putting their lives in his hands.

'How did this happen then?' asked Yuri. 'Any of the other men see, or hear, anything?'

The foreman shook his head and pointed at the bulging tarpaulin. 'He was down here alone. I met him when he arrived, up at the entrance. I offered but he said he didn't want any help.'

Yuri could well believe Semyon refusing assistance. He was the kind of person who thought he knew everything, and could handle things better on his own. Yuri walked around the body to the ventilation unit, which was lying on the ground where it had fallen. With two hands, he lifted one side of it in the air. He didn't get very far. It was certainly heavy enough to kill someone if it hit them in the right spot. One bottom corner had a large dent in it, and long scratches in the same place, as if from metal against metal. Igor saw what had attracted his attention, and he nodded.

'I saw that too,' he said. 'To me, it looks like he deliberately pulled the whole thing down off the wall on top of himself.'

Yuri stood up and brushed the coal dust from his hands.

'You putting that in your report?' he asked.

Igor stared at him for a moment. It was the familiar Soviet pause. The who-am-I-talking-to hesitation. Gauging how well do I know this person in front of me? Could he or she be a paid informer? It was impossible to tell for sure, even if it was your grandmother.

Igor shook his head. 'I will write "accident".'

Yuri was about to leave when a thought made him kneel

down again beside the body. First, he went through Semyon's pockets. Igor stared at him but did not interrupt. He found some keys and money in Semyon's trousers. At the bottom of the inside pocket of his jacket, he found a miniature notebook, the kind with only twenty or thirty pages in it. He opened it and saw some odd words written at the top of each page, with a list of dates underneath, all within the last year. He had no idea what the lists referred to, but he put it in his own pocket for later. Then, with two hands, he pushed the body on to its side. The dead man let out an eerie breath. Underneath was the usual black mine debris. And stuck to the back of his jacket were Semyon's glasses, bent and shattered.

Yuri had heard and witnessed many strange things in his lifetime, but suicide by ventilation unit seemed unlikely. It was true that he had never gone to the bother of getting to know the man, but he had not pegged Semyon as the self-harming, defeatist type. He was ambitious, with solid goals in life. And he was still young enough to harbour realistic expectations of achieving them.

An accident was the most likely possibility. Semyon could have discovered that he needed to get the ventilation unit on to the ground in order to work on it properly. At which point he might have found the fixings difficult to dislodge; the humid conditions in the mine rusted metal fast. So then he could have decided to use brute force to get the unit off the tunnel wall, at which point it had all gone unexpectedly and horribly wrong. Tragic but simple. That is what Yuri's report would say too. An unfortunate accident. No one's fault, just bad luck.

However, even though this explanation had a degree of logic to it, it didn't sit easy with him. And the alternative even less so. If Semyon's death wasn't suicide, or an accident, that left the involvement of a third party. Person or persons unknown. Part of him knew that was what had happened. Someone had gone to some trouble to try to make this look like an accident. Yuri's first instinct was to resist the temptation to delve any deeper, and instead walk away from the whole thing. Normally, he would have done exactly that. But if someone had killed Semyon, then there must be a reason. And not knowing what it was would keep him awake at night until he found out.

Against his better judgement, Yuri left the mine and obeyed Timur's summons. He made his way to his office, which was hidden away down a corridor in the administration building. When he arrived, he found the door wide open. Timur had just made himself a fresh coffee.

'Want one?' he asked. 'There's enough for two.'

'No thanks.'

Was he really going to offer him a coffee and then accuse him of murder?

'Sit down, Yuri.'

Yuri pulled up a wooden chair as Timur sat down behind his desk. He blew on the surface of his steaming cup and sipped. Yuri's stomach felt hollow and twisted. A combination of hunger and his reflex reactions to the sight of a bloodied dead body. Timur put down his cup and started rhythmically tapping his fingers again, this time on the table.

'You know why I've asked you here?' Timur asked.

'Not exactly, no,' said Yuri.

Timur looked as though he didn't believe his answer.

'This Semyon business stinks. If that was an accident, I'll eat my hat.'

'You think he was murdered?' asked Yuri, trying badly to sound surprised.

Timur shrugged. 'Doesn't it seem that way to you?'

When Yuri didn't answer, Timur stared at him for a long time.

'The doc is going to take a look. I told him to be thorough. If he tells me there's something to be suspicious about then you and me are going to have a different sort of conversation.'

'You can't think that I . . . I wasn't even down there. I was in the canteen. The waitresses will vouch for me. You can vouch for me, you saw me there yourself.'

'When we met he'd already been dead a couple of hours. Where were you before the canteen?'

'Swimming.'

'With?'

'On my own. But I'm sure people saw me about the place. The cosmonaut did. English Catherine. Ask her. I can tell you one thing for free, you won't find a single person who'll say they saw me down the mine tonight, because I wasn't there.'

Timur gave a half-grin and sipped his coffee again. They both knew he could get a dozen people to swear on their grandchildren that they'd seen him dancing in the mine in a red dress, if that's what he told them to say.

'He wanted your job,' said Timur. 'He made serious accusations against you. And you didn't like each other. Sounds like a strong enough motive to me.'

'I didn't need to kill him to keep my job,' Yuri protested. 'He wasn't good enough to take it off me. And no, I didn't like him. Did you?'

'He thought he was better than you,' said Timur. 'Maybe you two had a fight. Is that what happened? And you didn't mean for it to end the way it did? Now would be a good time to come clean.'

'This is ridiculous, and you know it. I never laid a finger on him.'

'Sabotage then,' said Timur. 'Maybe you did something to that ventilation unit. Left it unsafe, ready to fall. Then you sent him down there. It was you that sent him down there, wasn't it? I believe you already admitted that.'

'It wasn't a confession. It's my job to tell him what to do. I sent him down with an easy task that should have taken him ten minutes to finish. It wasn't supposed to be dangerous.'

Timur sighed and rested his chin in his hand, rubbing his day-old stubble with his fingers. To Yuri's relief, he seemed to have run out of questions. For the moment, there was no evidence of a crime, unless the autopsy threw up something.

'If there's nothing else, I'd like to go now,' said Yuri, standing up.

'Sure,' said Timur, without looking at him. 'Thanks for dropping by. I'll be in touch.'

Back in his apartment, Yuri leafed through Semyon's notebook. There was nothing in it other than what he had seen in the mine. One word, at the head of each page, with dates underneath. All the dates were since Semyon's arrival in Pyramiden. But the words made no sense. Fox. Bears. Spider. Eagle. Elk. Was he some sort of a wildlife enthusiast? If he was, he'd kept it to himself. He stared at the pages a while longer, but gave up trying to figure out what they meant.

The next day, Igor told Yuri that the doctor had found nothing to indicate foul play. No signs of a struggle. Just one single blow to the head, consistent with the ventilation unit falling on top of him. Case closed. Yuri still found the explanation hard to believe. And the doctor was not a crime scene specialist. He was young and had probably never encountered a murder in his life. But for the moment, Yuri was happy to be off a potentially nasty hook, and he wasn't about to go causing a fuss. Luckily, he had never gotten too far on the wrong side of Timur. If he had, he suspected this incident could have cost him more.

Where they were, Spitsbergen island in the Svalbard archipelago, was Norwegian territory. Russia only had mining rights here, which were enshrined in the 1920 Svalbard Treaty. And since it was their house, technically Norwegian law applied to all who lived there, whatever their nationality. As Timur had said, the Norwegian authorities would have to be informed of Semyon's death. But Yuri knew they were not going to cause any trouble over one casualty in a Soviet mine. One of their own Norwegian mines on Svalbard had recorded so many accidental deaths, seventy-one in twenty years, that the scandal, known as the King's Bay Affair, had brought down an entire Norwegian government in the sixties. Needless to say, in Semyon's solitary case they would not be throwing stones.

Yuri wondered if this was why Timur did not seem too eager for a serious investigation. His own interrogation had been half-hearted. There were reasons why Timur might be pleased to leave this alone – a suspected murder would demand a Norwegian police investigation. And the KGB man would certainly not want foreigners snooping around on his patch. Especially foreigners who were members of NATO. NATO equalled America, only nearer.

The bad news spread quickly around the town. Some people were naturally upset. There had been deaths in their small community before, over the decades, and they had built a small graveyard on the edge of town. But friendships here were so transient that few people would have had the opportunity to get to know Semyon well. By rights, as his boss and co-worker, Yuri should have known him the best. The other residents assumed he had, and for the whole of the next day he was offered unwanted sympathy, and confronted with concerned enquiries about Semyon's family back home. Yuri did not know any of the answers, so he made up some good lies, giving people the replies he figured they wanted to hear.

Two days later, a pair of tall blond Norwegians arrived by helicopter. They all saw the lights approaching through the darkness, long before the tak-tak sound of the propellers reached them. As a reception committee, Timur brought together the same trio who had been there on that fateful night – himself, Yuri and Igor – plus one other. The Norwegians spoke two languages perfectly, their own and English, but not Russian. Yuri had no English and Igor certainly did not. Timur had a couple of standard phrases, but being sent undercover to London was not on his career horizon any time soon. Yuri knew for a fact that Grigory spoke English, or at least under-stood it, because he had seen him reading English books in the library. But when Yuri suggested that he might help them out as an interpreter, he had offered them Catherine instead.

It had seemed a good idea at the time, and she was eager to help.

'Did you know him well?' she whispered to Yuri as they waited beside the helipad for their guests to disembark.

'Not so well,' admitted Yuri.

'Poor man. Such a horrible way to go.'

'Yes,' he agreed.

'Can you imagine a death at a space station?' said Catherine. 'Do you think it would be like this?'

'No,' said Yuri. 'I don't imagine any Norwegians would come.'

He heard her take a deep breath, getting herself ready for

what lay ahead. On her face was a look of exaggerated deter-
mination. She caught him smiling at her.

'What?' she asked.

'Nothing,' he said. 'You'll be fine.'

Catherine's first job was to translate the doctor's report for
the two visitors. His autopsy had revealed a skull fracture
caused by a blunt-force blow, leading to massive bleeding on
the brain. Death, he said, had been almost instantaneous.
Well, at least the bastard didn't suffer, thought Yuri.

And then they all viewed the body, after which Yuri held
Catherine's hair while she threw up her breakfast in a hospital
sink.

'I'm sure we can manage from here without you,' Yuri
offered.

'No, I'm fine now,' she said, wiping her mouth. 'I can do
this. I said I would help.'

'You're sure?' he asked. 'You're a little green.'

'A glass of water and I'll be fine,' she insisted. 'No need to
make a fuss over me.'

Next they made the trip to the scene of the accident, with
everyone now more concerned about Catherine than about
poor Semyon's demise. The location where he had met his end
had been cleaned up since Yuri had last been there. And why
not? No one had publicly admitted that they considered it a
crime scene that ought to be kept intact. At this point it was
showtime for Timur, who took to his stage with relish. He
gave the visitors a verbal and theatrically mimed performance
of Yuri and Igor's reports into how the accident had most
likely happened, all with simultaneous translation from green-
faced Catherine.

Suitably impressed with the thoroughness of what they had
seen and heard, along with assurances that such a thing would

never be allowed to happen again, the Norwegians declared the case closed. They rubber-stamped the death certificate, which Timur immediately took possession of. He folded it and put it in his inside pocket.

'You must be pleased,' said Yuri. 'No outside investigators meddling in Pyramiden.'

'Like the paper says, it was an accident,' replied Timur. 'Nothing to investigate.'

'And you're just going to leave it at that?'

'For the moment,' said Timur. 'If I was you, Yuri, I would be pretty relieved at that news.'

It was a relief, but Yuri expected that he had not heard the last of it.

Just as the two Scandinavians were on the verge of departing, Yuri made the mistake of inviting them for a drink in the glass bar. They wanted to leave, he could see, but politeness made them accept. Yuri caught Timur's incredulous gaze. Obviously, the official policy of the day was to get rid of the foreigners as quickly as possible, but Timur had neglected to mention this to him.

The glass house was the closest thing to a tourist attraction that Pyramiden had to offer. Built entirely from empty red, green and white glass bottles, it had been erected by the residents as a special place to unwind. Inside, the motley group drank a glass of vodka and toasted to their mutual cooperation, and regrets were expressed that their visit had to be under such tragic circumstances. Then the Norwegians gave up on second-hand conversation, and spoke exclusively in English to Catherine. Yuri could see that she was enjoying being the centre of their attentions.

Timur opened his silver cigarette case and offered one to Yuri. From the look of them, they were definitely not the

usual Bulgarian tobacco. He lit both Yuri's and his own with
a gold lighter that had a military insignia engraved on its side.

'What are they saying?' the KGB man asked as the three
foreigners talked and laughed together.

'I believe she is telling them about her space study,' said
Yuri. 'And the taller one, I think, is chatting her up. But I'm
just guessing. I really have no idea.'

Finally, to everyone's relief, the two men boarded their
helicopter again and left.

The list of people who might have killed Semyon included
every adult in town. Pyramiden was a peaceful place, and
violence here was extremely rare, but lots of the men had
killed before. Yuri himself had killed three men. It was not a
fact that he boasted about. He had been thirteen in the dying
days of the Great Patriotic War, and the men he had shot were
German soldiers. The first one had been armed, and it was a
case of kill or be killed. The other two he had executed in
cold blood as they tried to surrender to him. They had been
in a pathetic state, shoeless and starving. But by that stage of
the war, Yuri had lost all pity.

Many of the miners had a similar story to tell. The older
you were the more Germans you had killed. And killing a
man was not something you forgot. The first one was the
hardest. After that, it was not such a leap.

Yuri wondered if Semyon had any enemies in Pyramiden,
apart from himself. Maybe he secretly owed someone money,
or a grudge had followed him here from his home town in
Latvia. Or perhaps his death had really been an act of God
after all, and Yuri was just being paranoid. But he didn't believe
in God, or anything else.

He decided to give himself the rest of the day off. He

thanked Catherine for her help. She nodded, proud of herself for what she had done. For him, it had just been something to get out of the way, but she had viewed it as a challenge.

'You know I am more than happy to do anything like this any time,' she called after him. 'All you have to do is ask.'

He made his way back to his apartment block. Two deaths in quick succession had given him too many reminders of his own mortality and had taken a toll on his mood.

As he passed a parked snow truck, three men appeared from behind it and grabbed him. They pulled him to the side of his apartment building, out of sight. With one man in front and one behind, they proceeded to punch him repeatedly in the abdomen. The third one watched. All the breath left his body and he crumpled to the ground, gasping for air. Yuri recognised these men. He had seen them recently at Semyon's table in the canteen.

'Semyon was our friend,' said one, pointing his finger down at Yuri.

'Really?' said Yuri. 'How long did you know him?'

'One month,' said the other, before kicking him in the ribs. 'We are Lithuanian, so he is our neighbour. One of us.'

'We know you had something to do with it,' said the first. 'He told us you weren't to be trusted.'

'Listen comrades,' said Yuri. 'He was my friend too—'

Another kick hit him just below the sternum.

'Don't call me comrade, you Russian pig,' said one of his attackers, he wasn't sure which.

Just then a vehicle noise nearby disturbed them and they decided to leave.

'We're not finished with you,' said the first over his shoulder as he walked away. 'We'll be seeing you. It's not like you have anywhere to hide.'

Yuri staggered to his feet and continued his journey home. Once he was safely inside his apartment, he collapsed on to his bed. He held the ice-cold bottle of vodka in his hand, for pain-killing purposes, both inside and out. The Soviet dream of diverse nationalities working together under one communist banner had obviously not taken hold in the Baltics. But at least he wasn't the only one interested in Semyon's death.

That night, when all was quiet, Yuri exited his room and made his way up the stairs to the next floor. He had never visited Semyon's apartment when he was alive, and he felt bad about breaking into it now. He wished to avoid any visible damage, so he slid a thin piece of wood into the doorjamb and prised the lock open. Home security was not an issue in Pyramiden. There were zero burglaries. Few people had anything worth stealing anyway. No one would know he had been in here, unless he was seen going in or out.

He guessed Timur would already have paid this place a visit, so perhaps he was wasting his time. He started with the bed, checking under the pillow and inside the bedclothes. Under the mattress he found a magazine with black and white photographs of naked middle-aged women, which he put back where he had found it. Kneeling on the floor, he saw a suitcase under the bed. It was heavy; he had to slide it out with both hands. He clicked open the locks and found it full of engineering manuals. The poor guy really did want to better himself. Some of the volumes were beyond even Yuri's level of expertise. Inside them, passages had been underlined, with handwritten notes in the margins.

Next, he tried the chest of drawers. Assorted clothes, socks, T-shirts. On top was a wallet, which he opened. There were several hundred rubles and a photo of a woman in her sixties, presumably Semyon's mother. Yuri could see the family resemblance. Beside the wallet was a half-full bottle of red wine. He inspected the label. Georgian. He was tempted to take it, but then he noticed a scrap of paper stuck to the bottom of the bottle. He pulled it off and saw that the handwriting on it was the same as the notes in the engineering manuals.

'8 o'clock. The whaling house.'

The note did not say what day the rendezvous was to be. Yuri wondered if it could mean a day that had yet to come. The rest of the apartment revealed no treasure, and Yuri slipped back out the door as silently as he could.

Chapter 4

IN THE MORNING, the bruises on his abdomen had progressed to a tender and angry, multicoloured mess. Yuri self-prescribed ice, which he plucked from his windowsill. Given that several people were now connecting him with Semyon's death, he decided against reporting to the hospital with extensive, violent bruising.

Since they were virtually imprisoned for the winter, the decision was made to bury Semyon in Pyramiden's graveyard. If he had relatives who wanted him reinterred back home, they would face that issue in spring. Any request would most likely be denied anyway. He was not important enough to warrant the hassle of digging him up and getting his corpse home. A steel coffin was prepared in the mine workshop. Steel because the permafrost, which was three hundred feet deep, had an ugly habit of splitting wooden coffins and pushing them back up through the surface, with the deceased occupier on full view. Yuri had seen one of these before, an Albanian miner who had died of a heart attack. When his body reappeared above ground for an encore in this life, it was so well preserved the man looked as though he were sleeping.

Grigory put Yuri in charge of organising Semyon's burial since he was the man's superior. The truth was that no one else wanted to do it. Yuri reluctantly agreed, but doing it made him feel bad for other reasons. He had not done this much for his own brother. Nothing in fact. His brother's neighbours had made all the arrangements for his funeral. Yuri's single contribution had been to turn up at the appointed time. This he had managed to do. At the service, the neighbours had asked if he would like to say a few words, but he had declined. The audience was a small group of men and women he had never met before, and would not see again, so what was the point. Wherever he was, his brother would not be able to hear him. There was also the fact that he had not laid eyes on his younger sibling for years. Everyone else in the room knew him better than he did.

The Arctic topsoil was frozen so hard that a mechanical digger had to be used to prepare the hole, ten feet deep. The bottom kept filling with sludge but there was not much they could do about that. Yuri ordered the usual simple headstone, crowned with a red metal Soviet star. If Semyon had a personal religion, it would not be officially recognised on his burial plot. The state expected its people to be both communist and atheist.

The graveyard was thirty minutes' walk from the settlement. A compromise distance between not too close to town and not too far out in the wilderness. There was no electricity here, so they worked under the digger's headlights and an outdoor tungsten lamp connected to a noisy portable generator. Yuri moved upwind from the generator to avoid the noxious fumes billowing out of it. He looked around at the other graves, half-expecting the dead to wake with all the racket the digger was making. Happily, the deceased Albanian miner had stayed firmly interred the second time around.

When they had finished preparing the grave, Grigory came to inspect their work.

'All right?' shouted Yuri, over the generator's din.

'It's a good hole, yes,' said Grigory. 'It'll do the job.'

The party man looked around the barren graveyard. It was surrounded on all sides by a knee-high wooden picket fence, an unsuccessful attempt at giving the impression that this resting place for the dead was in some way protected from the elements.

Beyond the fence, the ice on the frozen fjord reflected the starlight in the dark sky above. Behind them, in the distance, lines of amber street lights glowed in town. Yuri checked his watch. It was two in the afternoon. Silence was restored as the digger driver switched off the generator. The man started to pack everything into the bucket of his digger for the journey back to town.

'Do me a favour,' said Grigory. 'If anything should happen to me, make sure they don't bury me here.'

'Will do,' agreed Yuri. 'In that case, try and take your last breath in spring or summer if you can manage it. We can put you on the boat while you're still warm.'

'I'll keep that in mind,' replied Grigory, with a smile. 'What about you?'

'Do what you like with me,' said Yuri. 'I'll be dead so what does it matter.'

Grigory sighed and shook his head.

'What?' asked Yuri.

'Sometimes I wonder if you actually do care about anything.'

'Sure I do,' said Yuri. 'While I'm still alive, I want to stay here.'

Grigory frowned. 'Why? There's nothing here except snow and coal. It's a desert with ice.'

'Exactly,' Yuri replied. 'I like it that way. I'm a simple man with simple needs.'

Grigory threw his hands in the air.

Behind them, the driver had finished loading up.

'You two want a lift?' the man shouted.

'Yes, we do,' said Yuri.

'You'll say a few words at the funeral,' said Grigory, as he climbed up into the digger's cab.

'Oh no,' said Yuri. 'You're not roping me in to that.'

Grigory stopped and turned to face him. He said the same words again, in the same tone, making it clear this was not a request. 'You will say a few words at the funeral.'

'Come on. I hardly knew the guy,' Yuri protested. 'I didn't like him and he hated me. He would turn in his grave if he knew. You're the expert speech-maker around here. Can't you do it? It would be better coming from you.'

'It'll be expected from you. And make an effort. I'll give you a few pointers.'

'Thanks,' said Yuri, not bothering to hide his displeasure. 'That makes me feel a whole lot better.'

When they arrived back in town, Yuri parted company with the two men and decided to make another trip. He borrowed the keys to one of the snowmobiles. Then, wearing goggles and gloves, he headed out again for a ten-minute drive along the western shoreline. He brought his rifle along strapped to his back, just in case. Only pregnant female polar bears went into their dens for the winter. Hungry adult males were a year-round danger. He was also unsure of what might await him at his destination.

He kept to a slow and steady pace, as the headlights of the snowmobile provided little illumination.

The whaling house was a simple wooden hut erected by whalers who had worked these waters in the last century. It was hard to believe that men had once gutted whales, right here, on the shores of this bay. The water's edge must have been turned red with blood.

If anyone in Pyramiden in modern times wanted a high degree of privacy for a meeting, this would be the ideal place. It was long abandoned and no one went there from one end of the year to the other. Yuri parked the snowmobile to one side and turned off the engine. He had a quick look around the outside. There was not much to see. Everything was hidden under a thick blanket of snow. The hut had accumulated banks of snow halfway up its exterior walls. But he noticed that the doorway had been cleared recently, with just a foot of snow in front of it.

Yuri forced open the wooden door, not really expecting to find any answers to his questions inside. He turned on his flash-light and entered. Inside, a mound of snow sat in the middle of the floor, stretching all the way to a hole in the ceiling, like a giant conical sculpture. On the ground, in a layer of snow, he saw a line of footprints in two different sizes. Semyon had not been a big man so perhaps the smaller set of prints were his. The other footprints matched Yuri's own size. Next to an old sink was some fresh orange peel, and a cigarette butt. If Semyon had arranged to meet someone here, in this out-of-the-way place, they had obviously wanted to keep it a secret. But why?

He pulled out Semyon's notebook from his jacket. He read the names of the animals again. Then he noticed that one of the dates on one page, under the word Spider, was the day after he had returned from Moscow. The day he had told Semyon that he had fixed the heating fault by himself. Could Spider refer to him? It would not surprise him if Semyon had considered him something that needed to be squashed under his shoe. He checked the other pages. The only date more recent than that one was a week before Semyon died, written under the word Eagle. Some of the animals had only one or two dates written underneath them. Spider had many.

Yuri shivered and wrapped his arms around himself. The old whalers were hardy men, who did not have the benefit of his central heating system. They must have found it almost impossible to stay warm here. There would have been little wood to burn, as there were few trees nearby and no coal at all at that stage; the mine had not even begun until decades later. They must have had to haul fuel for miles.

He stayed a while longer, looking around. But there was not much else to see and the hut yielded no more information. Semyon couldn't talk either. Yet someone in Pyramiden knew what had happened in here.

Yuri drove back the way he had come, parked the snowmobile where he'd found it and returned the keys.

The bare overhead light in his apartment blinked into life and Yuri stopped. The place was as untidy as he had left it, and nothing obvious was missing. But still, he had a feeling that someone had been in here while he was out. And then he saw it. The copper wire attached to his radio antenna was not the way he had left it. Someone had disturbed it, and rewrapped it around the radiator in a different way.

It was nothing unusual to have your home searched. This was something that had happened to half the population of the Soviet Union at least once in their lives. It had happened to Yuri in Moscow, in his younger, hellraising days, before he had learned to keep his mouth shut. That one had been an official search. They wrecked his stuff while he stood there watching, powerless to intervene. The more faces he made, the more of his stuff they 'accidently' smashed.

But who had done it this time? His money was on Timur, if it was an official search. At least, for once, he had nothing to hide. Plus, Timur had made it clear he wasn't interested in investigating Semyon's death. He turned on his radio and found that it was still tuned to the BBC. He could get into trouble just for that.

And if it was not an official search, then who? The Lithuanians? Would they have been so tidy? Right now he didn't care; he just wanted to get under his covers and warm the cold out of his bones. If anyone wanted to rummage around his apartment while he slept, he was not going to object.

As he undressed, and felt a sharp pain from the swollen bruises on his abdomen, he had second thoughts. He grabbed his wooden chair and jammed it diagonally under his door handle.

From a distance, through the morning fog, the graveyard seemed to be on fire, which was impossible since there was nothing there to burn. Yuri was in the passenger seat of the truck carrying his late protégé's coffin. As they drew closer, he saw that the graveyard had been staked out with six-foot-tall flaming torches. He guessed it was the work of the Lithuanians, giving their so-called friend, and Baltic neighbour, a theatrical send-off. The generator and the lamp they were transporting alongside Semyon would not be needed after all.

As Yuri jumped out of the cab, the Lithuanians brushed past him, giving him cold looks. They opened the rear of the van and took possession of the coffin. A bit late now to be looking after him with such care, thought Yuri. He followed the pallbearers to the hole they had dug the day before. The bottom was a mushy pool now, of mud, water and ice. But no one passed comment. It would be covered in soon enough.

Unlike the recent Great October anniversary celebration, this was not a communal event everyone wished to attend. Apart from the three Lithuanians, there was Timur, Grigory and Catherine, who was looking traumatised. She didn't do anything by halves, Yuri thought. Either up or down with no in-between. She was someone who could be hired out for funerals, to express just the right amount of sorrow. With a handkerchief she started to dab away tears for a man she did not know. Grigory walked over to her and offered some words of comfort, which she appreciated.

Also present were what seemed like one or two token representatives from each work group. Igor and another grim-faced man representing the miners. The young doctor for the hospital. The head cook for the canteen staff. None of the children were there, but Anya was. She had obviously drawn the shortest straw among the teachers. Yuri was glad that she had, though the circumstances were not conducive to romantic conversation. Had he known she was coming he would have put more effort into practising his speech.

The light from a flaming torch to her left was having such a dramatic effect on Anya's brown eyes that Yuri found it hard not to keep looking at her. He found it remarkable that no matter how long he stared in her direction, she still did not manage to acknowledge his presence. They were occupying the same space, only feet apart, but they may as well have been on different planets.

Spurred on by the desire to impress the teacher, and an equal desire not to rile the Lithuanians any more than he had already, Yuri gave his best speech ever. He borrowed liberally from Grigory's suggestions, quoting from Tolstoy about life.

'There is no greatness where there is no simplicity, goodness, and truth. And joy can only be real if people live their life as a service. Our dear friend Semyon embodied all of these things.'

Yuri spotted Timur, behind the others, suppressing a grin. The Lithuanians held on to each other in a line, with their arms around each other's shoulders, presumably to lessen the pain of their friend's parting.

Next to be quoted was Pushkin on death.

'Ever peaceful be your slumber. Though your days were
    few in number
On this earth, spite took its toll. Yet shall heaven have
    your soul
With pure love we did regard you. For your loved one
    did we guard you'

As he got into his stride, he could see the growing surprise on the faces of his audience. The Lithuanians began to look at each other, as though they were not quite sure what was happening. He was so eloquent that even Anya looked in his direction once. When he was finished there wasn't a dry eye in the graveyard. Then he stopped abruptly because he had run out of things to say. To his embarrassment, everyone stood waiting for more. He turned to Grigory for help.

'Aren't you going to say something?' he whispered.

'No. I can't follow that,' said Grigory. 'You did surprisingly well. I'm shocked and, I have to say, impressed.'

Then he turned and addressed everyone present. 'Thank you to Yuri for those moving words. I am sure we all appreciated them. And now if anyone would like to join us for refreshments in the glass bar, you are all very welcome.'

The small crowd began to disperse towards the various vehicles that had brought them here. Igor gripped Yuri's hand

and wiped the satisfied smile off his face by saying, 'A terrible business. I hope they catch who did it.'

To catch a murderer someone must actually look for one, thought Yuri.

The Lithuanians upended their flaming torches and extinguished them in the snow. They filed past Yuri on their way out. None of them shook his hand but when he caught their eyes, their cold looks had changed to more confused expressions. Yuri was hopeful they might desist now from using his abdomen as a punching bag. The bruises were only just beginning to subside.

He turned, looking for Anya, and saw that Timur was standing close behind her. He wondered for a moment if she could have been the one Timur was visiting that night when he had seen him standing in a window in the Paris apartment block. It would be a disappointment if she was. He hoped that she had better taste in men. However, when Timur walked around Anya, on his way out, neither of them acknowledged the existence of the other.

Nearly all of the funeral group ended up back in the glass bar, drowning their sorrows in the case of the Lithuanians, or just taking the rare opportunity to socialise during working hours for the rest of them. Yuri only drank at night as a rule. He hated the harsh effect of sunlight on drunken eyes. It pierced straight to his brain. But since there would be no sunlight here for another hundred days, he considered this rule to be breakable today. Unfortunately, Anya did not come to the bar. Nor did the cook, who had lunches to prepare. Grigory stayed for an hour, chatting with him. But he was not a big drinker in public, and he took his leave as the others started to get more boisterous. Yuri knew for a fact that the party man preferred solitary drinking, in the privacy of his own apartment. The evidence was the collection of empty whiskey bottles, which he later converted in to home décor.

The glass bar was small, and Yuri had some difficulty avoiding being seated too near to the Lithuanians. They did not seem to want to talk to him either. However, judging by their regular glances in his direction, they were talking about him.

As the end of the evening drew near, it was just him and them left. When Yuri realised, he stood up and made to leave but one of them blocked his path.

'That was a good speech,' said the one who had punched him in the kidneys.

'Yes,' agreed the one who had kicked him on the ground.

'I'm glad you liked it,' said Yuri. 'It was a bit nerve-wracking, I must admit. Always hard to get the tone of these things right. Semyon deserved a good send-off.'

'You did it, you did it,' said the first. 'No doubt about it. We've talked and we've decided, either you're a really good actor, or else you may not have had anything to do with what happened. For the moment, we are not going to kill you.'

'Though that may change,' said the third. 'We'll let you know.'

At which point they all laughed. Yuri did his best to see the humour. He smiled stupidly as they pushed him back into his chair and seated themselves around him, penning him in. Then he had to endure their off-key Lithuanian songs, and jokes, some of which were actually funny. It took him a full hour to extricate himself from their friendly attentions.

Outside, it was as dark as it had been when he entered the bar, eight hours earlier. Thanks to the vodka, he was not feeling the cold as much any more. He staggered home, fumbling for his keys. He had almost reached the front entrance to London when a figure stepped out of the shadows. For a moment, he feared he was in for another beating. But it was Anya. Her eyes fixed on his for longer than they ever had before, and she had an odd, almost desperate expression on her face.

'Are you the one I'm waiting for?' she asked.

Yuri swayed slightly as he paused to consider this peculiar question. To his disappointment, it did not seem to have a sexual motive. He smiled and said, 'I think that's highly unlikely.'

Her tears came quickly, and he did not know what he had done to cause such a reaction.

In the hope that she might stop, he said, 'Would you like to come inside?'

Chapter 5

A NYA LOOKED AROUND his apartment as though it were something alien and unhygienic. If he'd had advance warning that she was coming, he would have made an effort to clean it. He couldn't remember the last time he had washed the bedclothes. His apartment was dimly lit, so he hoped that might at least partly disguise the grubby state of the place.

He offered her the single chair he possessed, but she ignored it and stayed standing near the door. Gearing up to make a quick exit, he suspected. He poured her a drink, without asking, and pretended not to notice her unease. He held out the glass, and watched her hand as she took it from him. A pianist's long, slender fingers, well-manicured, without nail varnish or rings.

'So, what's all this about?' he asked, as he took a sip from his own glass.

Up close, she was even more beautiful than he'd thought. He felt his eyes widening, taking her in. Her tears had not been fake, he was sure, but there was no trace of them now. She brought her glass to her lips and Yuri recognised a fellow drinker. It was what he spent most of his free time doing, though the volume he consumed was a lot less now than before. Age had made it harder to recover the next day. Today he had gone way beyond his usual limit, and he was already half a bottle ahead of her.

He liked to go out with drinkers. A sober partner was just irritating for both sides, and rarely worked out. Alcohol was a journey. Your companion either travelled with you or pretty soon you were both in different places. The problem rarely arose up here anyway. In the Arctic almost everyone drank. Either to keep warm or to help them deal with daily life.

Anya began to look uncomfortable, as though it had been a mistake for her to come here. Whatever was bothering her, she looked worn out, and stressed.

'I am supposed to meet someone here, in Pyramiden,' she said.

'Who?' he asked.

'I don't know,' she replied.

He wondered for a moment if she might possibly be unstable, but apart from the brief display of emotion outside, she appeared to be as sane as anyone else in town. She caught his concerned expression as he studied her, and she did not like it. Her vulnerability seemed to disappear in seconds, and her usual icy demeanour returned.

'What do you mean you don't know?' he asked. 'Sounds very mysterious. What are you supposed to be meeting this person about?'

She fixed him with a hard stare, searching his face for something. He didn't know what she was looking for, but he wished that she might find it. Now that he had her here, he did not want her to go. She shook her head, not wanting to talk about it further, and obviously losing any interest in him.

'I'm leaving,' she said. And as an afterthought, she added, 'Thank you for the drink. I needed it.'

She put the glass on the nearest shelf and turned for the

door. There were old photos of him from his army days on that shelf, which usually attracted attention. But not hers. Another few seconds and the opportunity would be lost, and she would probably never set foot in his room again. He did not quite understand how he had managed to get her in here in the first place. And he expected that repeating the same feat any time soon would be beyond him.

'Wouldn't you like to stay for a while longer?' he suggested.

She looked back at him over her shoulder, surprised. He saw her realising for the first time that he wanted her. Despite his best efforts she had apparently never considered him in that way before. Now she was surveying him as if he were a second-hand Lada.

He had resigned himself to her imminent departure by the time she eventually said, 'All right.'

He smiled as she took off her coat and hung it on the door.

'What's funny?' she said.

'You are.'

He moved closer and kissed her. They both tasted of vodka. But having only just pressed his lips against hers, she pulled away without looking at him. She walked over to the narrow bed, and began to undress. He enjoyed watching her even though she had taken this job from him. She was totally naked in seconds and she climbed under the covers. He took his clothes off, and she spent this time pushing and prodding the coarse pillow underneath her head, trying to get comfortable. It didn't meet with her approval no matter what she did to it, but he had nothing else to offer. Then to his embarrassment, she sniffed the sheets.

Foreplay did not seem to be on Anya's agenda, and Yuri wished that he had not drunk so much. If alcohol had one flaw, it was this; its effects could not be undone in a hurry.

She moved over to make room for him, but only because she had to. He lay down beside her, trying not to lean on her long black hair, which was spread out over the pillow.

With one hand she checked that he was ready and then she pulled him on top of her. If he had moved things along so quickly with any other woman, she would probably have been insulted. She made love like someone with a dangerous need. He was already looking forward to her next visit.

'How am I doing?' he asked.

'Shut up!' she said.

'We are not in a church,' he added.

'You'd be doing better if you'd just stop talking.'

It was all abrupt and to the point, but for the few moments they were entwined it felt magical. Usually, it took Yuri months of getting to know someone before achieving this kind of physical harmony. He did wish that it might last longer but considering what he had consumed over the course of the day, he was relieved he could do it at all.

When it was over, he resisted the temptation to say, 'That was amazing.' Instead, he offered her a cigarette. He was pleased with himself for having chosen wisely. Or had she picked him? However, he already sensed her retreating into her own world, to which he was not invited. Even though the bed was tiny, she had managed to completely separate her body from his, so that they were not connected at any point. He obliged by not touching her again.

'So, what was all that about downstairs. Who is this mystery person you are supposed to be having a rendezvous with?'

'It's a private matter,' she said, without looking at him. 'Forget I mentioned it.'

She put out her half-smoked cigarette in the remains of his vodka glass, and climbed over him to get out of bed.

'Aren't you staying?' he asked, as she dressed quickly. 'It's late. You're more than welcome to.'

She kept on dressing, without pause. Her white skin and delicate curves disappeared underneath her clothes. He worried that he might never get to see her body again.

'No. I can't sleep here,' she replied. 'The bed's too small.'

He knew the size of his bed was not the real reason for her departure, but he couldn't think of a way to make her stay.

'What's your bed like, in your apartment?' he asked, fishing for an invitation across the square. He would have happily followed her anywhere.

'The same,' she said. 'Too small for two.'

It was true. All of the single beds in Pyramiden were too small for two. Yuri had been meaning to steal a double bed from the Crazy House for years. But it was not something one could achieve alone, or without attracting curious attention. This time he resolved to find a way.

'See you,' he said, as she buttoned her coat and opened the door.

'Yeah,' she replied, with little enthusiasm in her voice. And then she was gone.

She had behaved just like he had a dozen times or more, with women he did not really care about. It did not feel good to be on the receiving end. He got out of bed and watched her running across the road to Paris in the moonlight.

For days afterwards, Anya ignored him completely like nothing had happened. He found new excuses to turn up at her school but he barely got a hello. When they met in the canteen she would keep on walking, and she never stood still long enough for him to engage her in conversation.

She was using his own tactics on him. He tried to remember how many of his former lovers had gotten around this barrier.

But he couldn't think of one. Once he had decided he didn't want to pursue an affair further, that was that. There was no point in going back. Revisiting a dead-end encounter only created more bad feeling and made it doubly hard to extricate oneself from the relationship.

None of this was comforting. He tried to put Anya out of his head. But instead, he spent most of his waking day thinking about her. She appeared in his dreams too.

For a few days he decided he hated her. It was not that his pride was hurt. He did not care about that. He just wanted her again. When they saw each other, he tried ignoring her as much as she ignored him. However, he was not sure she even noticed, and he ditched this as an ineffective strategy.

On a particularly wet, depressing day, Grigory tracked him down in the power plant control room, with English Catherine in tow. Both of them appeared to have something important on their minds. Over the last few weeks, he had regularly seen the two of them engaging in private chats.

'Yuri, as you know,' said Grigory, 'Catherine is here writing her thesis.'

'Yes,' said Yuri, 'she's told me all about it. I think she's told everyone by now.'

Catherine smiled broadly.

'But she has also expressed a desire to contribute to the community while she's here.'

Yuri's visitors looked at each other and nodded in unison as though they were expecting him to know exactly what they were talking about. He definitely had nothing that he needed translated.

'I see,' said Yuri. 'That's nice.'

'So, we thought she could be your temporary assistant,' said Grigory, 'just for the winter.'

Yuri stood up. 'Oh no. I don't need any assistance,' he replied. 'Does she even know anything about machines?'

'I should hope so,' Catherine answered, 'I've an engineering degree. I was in the top six in my class.'

'Have you a degree?' Grigory asked. 'In anything?'

Yuri shook his head. 'I was too busy learning my trade to go to college.'

Grigory smiled. 'A qualification of any kind? No? Well, that's settled then.'

Yuri pulled Grigory by the elbow to one side, while Catherine stayed where she was, pretending she was not trying to eavesdrop.

'What are you doing?' asked Yuri. 'I have enough things on my plate without having to babysit your pet foreigner.'

'I'm helping you,' Grigory replied. 'Couldn't you do with an assistant?'

'No, actually. They just get in my way. And look what happened to the last one.'

'You've been looking a bit down lately. What's that about? Snow fever? Missing the sun?'

'I'm not down,' said Yuri. 'You're seeing things. I'm fine.'

'Give it one week with her, that's all I ask, and we'll see how it goes. It will be good for her, and for you too, I think.'

'Do I have a say in this?' asked Yuri.

'Sure,' said Grigory. 'Up to a point.'

'Then no. Absolutely not.'

Grigory turned to Catherine. 'All right. Good. Catherine, you can start today. Yuri is going to show you the ropes.'

Catherine beamed. 'Oh terrific. Thank you. I hope it's not too much of an inconvenience.'

Yuri resisted the temptation to strangle Grigory for this favour.

'No,' he said. 'No trouble. Glad to have you aboard.'

Reluctantly, Yuri spent the day showing Catherine around his domain. To his surprise, she did seem to understand most of what he was talking about. Unlike Anya, she was not difficult to figure out. And on the job, she was easy company. The only disconcerting thing about her was that she peppered their conversations with questions like, 'Comrade, you must consider it a great privilege to be able to work for the glorious revolution?'

In his entire life, no one had ever asked him questions like that. He had the option of crushing her childlike naivety but instead, he buried his cynicism and just answered, 'It is a unique privilege, yes.'

This woman deserved the Soviet Union, but it did not deserve her.

'You're so lucky to live here,' Catherine said. 'I'd do anything to stay here. I'm not looking forward to going back to the evils of capitalism in three months' time.'

When she was not talking to him, he would occasionally hear her voice mumbling behind him. He caught her from the corner of his eye a couple of times, and realised she was speaking to herself, in English. He did not understand but she seemed to be giving herself words of encouragement.

For a second, a thought entered his mind: that she was the one who had killed Semyon just so she could get his job. A ridiculous idea. No one loved communism that much. Although, apparently she loved it quite a lot more than he did.

'I bet the boys in my engineering class would be jealous of me now,' said Catherine. 'Look at me, a worker in a proper Soviet mine.'

'You don't like it over there in England?' he asked.

'It's fine really. My family are there, of course. But for some reason, I always thought I would feel more at home here. You know what I mean?'

He did not, but said nothing.

'Just, I love the sense of community here. Like the way all those people turned out for that poor man's funeral. Simon, wasn't that his name?'

'Semyon,' said Yuri.

'Yes, Semyon. I spoke to people at the graveyard, and some of them didn't even know him that well. But there's such a bond between all of you, that they felt they had to come out in the freezing cold to pay their respects.'

He did not have the heart to tell her that half of them had been told they had to be there.

'Will that be going in your thesis?'

'Yes,' said Catherine. 'Probably. Can you keep a secret?'

Yuri considered saying no, before reluctantly saying, 'Sure.'

'Between you and me, I don't really care too much about my thesis. I've no interest in space at all, in fact. I wrote first saying everything I'd done. Miners' strike organiser '74, then gay rights, then civil rights, and so on. But I did not get an answer. Not one. I figured I needed something special to get noticed, so they would let me come here, and that was what I came up with. You won't tell on me, will you?'

'You asked to come here, to Pyramiden?' said Yuri.

'Yes,' she replied. 'I was so happy when they said yes.'

'But why Pyramiden? Why not Moscow, or one of the other beautiful cities?'

'Because, I read somewhere that this place showed the best of what the Soviet Union had to offer. And you know what, it's true.'

'I thought young people dreamed of getting away from isolated places, not the other way around.'

'Oh, I don't mind being alone,' she said, with a serious expression. 'Not at all.'

Later, Yuri found Grigory and asked him whose idea it had been for Catherine to work with him.

'It was hers actually,' said Grigory. 'She called by my office this morning. Something wrong?'

'No,' said Yuri. Nothing he could put his finger on.

Yuri returned home to find his apartment door ajar. He pushed it open quickly, hoping he might find Anya inside. Instead, sitting on the chair, the bed and the table, were the three Lithuanians. And they were helping themselves to his vodka, swigging straight from the bottle.

'Let ourselves in, Yuri,' said the tall one. 'Hope you don't mind. Drink?'

'No thanks,' said Yuri. 'Can I help you boys with something?'

Since all the available seats were taken, Yuri stayed standing, leaning against the door. He watched the level of his bottle dwindling as the men passed it around among themselves.

The tall one cleared his throat. 'The thing is Yuri, Semyon, before his untimely passing, mentioned to us that he had something on someone, and he was going to take advantage of it.'

Yuri had no idea what he was talking about, but he had a sinking feeling that this was not going to be good for him.

'Is that so,' he said.

'Yes,' the tall one continued. 'He never did get to tell us who or what it was. But we were thinking maybe that someone was you.'

'I've nothing to hide, guys,' said Yuri. 'It must have been someone else that he was talking about.'

The tall one shook his head.

'I don't think so. He did tell us that you were a saboteur. We've done a bit of that ourselves back home. We don't like you Russians in our country.'

People could get into a heap of trouble spouting nationalist rhetoric like that. The fact that the man was doing it in front of him, without a hint of fear, made Yuri doubly nervous. He didn't fancy getting any new bruises just for being a Russian, so he kept his mouth shut.

'So,' said the tall one. 'What had he got on you? And how much were you paying him? Whatever it was, we want the same.'

'I'm sorry,' said Yuri. 'You've lost me.'

'How much were you paying Semyon to stop him shopping you as a saboteur?'

'Nothing,' said Yuri, trying not to laugh. 'He never had any problem accusing me of that. He even said it to Timur. Why would I be paying him when he was already shooting his mouth off about me?'

The three of them looked at each other, apparently confused by this new piece of information.

'And what happened with Timur?' asked the short one.

He could see that, at least, they were afraid of the KGB man.

'Absolutely nothing,' said Yuri. 'Semyon had no proof. I'm a good saboteur, I don't get caught.'

The three of them smiled.

'Maybe we'll take him to Lithuania,' said the short one. 'He can blow up his own Russian tanks.'

Yuri joined the others with the best fake laugh he could manage. The tall one took the bottle, brought it to his lips and found it empty. He looked at it in disappointment, then put it on the table beside him.

'Come on boys, we have disturbed poor Yuri in error. Thanks for the drink. We'll replace that some time.'

'No problem,' said Yuri. 'Come again, any time.'

Just as they were almost out the door, Yuri had a thought. 'Hey fellas, any chance you'd give me a hand with something?'

Chapter 6

H E FOUND THE note pushed under his apartment door the following evening.

'Come to dinner. Paris. 8 p.m. A.'

She had ignored him for a full two weeks. No words. No smiles. Nothing. If he had any self-respect, he should have set fire to her invitation. But he did not.

It was already 7:45, so he jumped in the shower and did a speed wash. He wrapped up warm and made his way to Paris. The exterior of the building could not have been more different from the real Paris. It was a classic, large and ugly Soviet block. He wondered what kind of reception awaited him inside.

When Anya opened the door of her apartment, she looked him straight in the eye, smiled and said hello. Normal behaviour from anyone else, but from her it was new and startling. She had dressed up for the occasion, and was wearing a knee-length black dress with ankle boots. Her cheeks showed signs of a little make-up, he was sure, and she had moulded her hair into a long plait.

'Sit, sit,' she said, as she fussed over dinner.

She seemed pleased to see him, and he wondered what had

changed for him to deserve this reception. The only thing he could think of was that he had stopped trying.

As with the other apartments, hers did not have a kitchen. But unlike his own place, she had not engaged in Pyramiden's DIY decorating habit. The room remained exactly as she had found it when she arrived. She had managed to cajole two dinners from the canteen, and she had reheated them by placing the dishes on top of two bowls of boiling water poured from her electric kettle.

'Takeaway,' she said.

'It smells nice,' he said.

'Well, I can't claim to have cooked any of it. I can cook, you know. I used to cook all the time back home in Moscow.'

'Me too,' he said, 'though I think I've forgotten how, I've been here so long.'

While they ate, she quizzed him about his background, which she had never done before. He did most of the talking. He could tell it was a strain for her to make this effort at interpersonal communication, but he appreciated it. When they were finished, he washed up and dried.

Beside them the whole time was her narrow single bed. It was the same size as the one he had recently disposed of, though it was older and in need of repair. He pondered when would be the right moment to announce that he was now the only single man in London who was the proud possessor of a king-size double bed. He hung the damp tea towel on the radiator to dry. Then he turned to face her, and found her zipping up her coat.

'Let's go outside,' she said. 'Get your coat.'

'Where are we going?' he asked.

'For a walk.'

'It's freezing out there tonight.'

'You don't say,' she said. 'When is it not? We're not going far.'

Yuri did as she asked, and followed her down the stairs. They walked side by side, through the square, before she led him off the path, crunching across the snow-covered grass to the Lenin monument. The grass had been specially imported from Ukraine. Every winter, the weather tried to kill it off but to no avail. It sprouted again each spring after the big thaw. Indestructible Soviet grass.

She leaned her back against the pedestal, and pulled him close. They kissed, and she started to undo his belt. He looked around nervously, but no one seemed to be about. The lights were on, behind them, in the Cultural Palace.

'Here?' he said.

'There's an Eisenstein film on,' she said. 'I've seen it before. It's endless. They won't be out for another hour.'

She was not like any school teacher Yuri had ever met. He was glad he was sober this time. They made love in the freezing cold, supported by the founder of the revolution. Perhaps he had a saying for this kind of occasion. He did for everything else.

Afterwards, as they adjusted their clothing, he saw her shivering. Standing still in one spot allowed the Arctic cold to take hold of you, and being semi-naked made it downright dangerous. He wrapped his arms around her and held her close.

'Thank you,' she said after a couple of minutes, before breaking away.

He was determined not to let this moment of closeness slip away, like last time, and allow her to drift away from him again.

'I have a bigger bed now,' he said. 'Would you like to see it?'

'Really?' she asked, not believing him.

'I do. Come on, I'll show you.'

'You're lying,' she said.

'You'd better come and see for yourself, then.'

'Where did you get that?' she asked.

'I stole it,' he said. 'With a little help from some friends.'

They were standing inside the door of his apartment, staring at his new double bed. There was a reason the single beds in London were so narrow. This bed took up nearly all of his apartment's floor space.

The Lithuanians had helped him carry it across, the night before. They had not taken much persuading to commit an illegal act. The hardest part had been getting it down the stairs of the Crazy House without waking all of the sleeping families. The four of them had been like a circus-clown act, running across the square with a bed leg each.

'And why did you get it?' she asked. 'Are you thinking of getting married?'

'I got it for you,' he said, without any embarrassment at his admission.

She looked surprised. Maybe a little flattered.

'How did you know I'd come back?'

'I'm irresistible,' he said. 'OK, I didn't know. But I'm really glad you did. You want to try it out?'

This time, he undressed her. He took his time doing it, one button at a time, even though he could sense her impatience. They made love again on his new bed, making full use of the room to manoeuvre that had been sadly lacking in the one it had replaced. Despite the extra space, her long hair still managed to be an attractive nuisance, getting in the way when it was least wanted.

The old single bed was now sitting pretty in a vacant apartment in the Crazy House. An unpleasant surprise awaiting some newly arrived married couple.

Afterwards, instead of shifting away from him, she curled her body into his. Everything was going very well, he thought, until he said, 'So tell me more about you.'

It was a reasonable question since he knew almost nothing about her. She sat up and hesitated, and her familiar searching expression returned. For a moment, he feared she was going to make another bolt for the door. And then he saw her relax, and make the decision to stay.

'I'm not really a teacher,' she said, putting her head back on his chest. 'I'm a physicist. At least that's what I used to be. But teaching kids is the only work they'll let me do now.'

Yuri began to have a sinking feeling. This promising relationship of course had to come with a catch. And here it came. He wished she would stop talking now, and he could go back in time and not ask any questions. He didn't need to know her past.

'I used to work alongside my husband on the Soviet's third idea, that was until he defected five years ago.'

Wow, thought Yuri. Three things he didn't want to hear, all in one sentence. Husband. Defector. And the third idea, which he knew to be the Soviet nuclear weapons programme. The latter two should have troubled him the most. But the first, husband, was the one he liked the least.

'I didn't know you were married,' he said.

'I used to be,' she said. 'Well, technically, I suppose I still am. But he's gone.'

'He defected,' said Yuri. 'On his own?'

'Yes. On his own,' she said, evidently still finding it hard to believe herself.

'Why didn't he take you?'

'Good question,' she said. Although, she made it sound like the worst question in the world. 'I haven't seen him in five years, so I haven't been able to ask.'

Yuri was jealous of this man he'd never met, who must have touched her before he did. And what a fool he was to leave her behind. Some people did not know what they had.

'Why didn't you go with him?'

Anya shrugged. 'I didn't get to choose. I didn't know he was going. He didn't say a word. Not one. He must have known for months beforehand. We ate together, worked together, slept together. And nothing. All that time he was planning, and making arrangements. None of which included me. A husband should tell his wife something like that, shouldn't he?'

'He should,' agreed Yuri, as he tried to erase an image in his head of her naked in bed with this man. It would not go away.

'He went. He defected, but I was the one who got interrogated for days by the KGB. I told them I didn't know anything, but they didn't believe me. Not until much later.'

Yuri found it hard to believe too. How could she not know her own husband was defecting? Surely there must have been signs. It was not as if she was not an intelligent woman.

'In the end they couldn't prove I was involved,' said Anya. 'Not that that would have stopped them throwing me in prison if they wanted. But I think they did finally accept what I was saying. Though I didn't get off for free. They said my old job was too sensitive for someone who was tarnished with collateral suspicion. That life was finished for me, and they let me become an overqualified teacher of ten-year-olds.'

Alarm bells rang continuously in Yuri's head. She is trouble and you should just walk away. But he ignored those thoughts.

'We're connected, in a way,' he said. 'I worked at a uranium mine once, in the fifties. We supplied the raw material for you lot.'

She did not seem impressed by the correlation between her science job and his mining past. He had never actually been directly involved with the extraction of uranium. He had only installed showers for the poor bastards who had to dig the stuff out of the ground.

'It wasn't pretty what they did to those men,' he said.

The men, mostly convicts, had scrubbed the radioactive dust off every night, but it was already killing them. They knew it too. Daily exposure took its toll all too quickly.

'You want to blame me for that?' she asked.

'No,' he said. 'Why, do you feel guilty?'

She shook her head. 'I've said too much, I should go.'

'No. Not again,' he said, firmly. 'Just sleep, OK. You don't need to go running off every time. You told me your story, and it's safe with me. I won't tell anyone else. I want you to stay.'

She looked at him again with surprise in her eyes, as if real affection was not something she came across much. He could understand why. Her husband was a lying bastard. Although he was glad he had done him a big favour and left her behind.

She nodded her agreement and turned her back to him and faced the wall. He watched as she started to push and pull the pillow, to make it more comfortable, until she realised she didn't need to. He smiled to himself. He had searched high and low for a soft feather pillow, eventually stealing one from an executive apartment.

He began to massage her shoulders, brushing her long hair to one side. As soon as he touched her, he could feel the build up of tension, waiting to be released.

'Stop,' she said, without turning around. 'I'm going to sleep.'

Despite himself, the colder she was the more he wanted her. He didn't tell her that the uranium mine was where he had allowed himself to be betrayed for the one and only time in his life. Someone he had considered a friend had stolen his promotion, his ticket out of there, with a bribe to a party official. As a result, he had been stuck in that hellhole for a year longer than he should have. Since then he had been constantly on the lookout for deceivers, and he had never let it happen again. He knew how Anya felt. They had both been betrayed by someone they trusted. Although admittedly hers was on a scale well beyond his own.

He lay down beside her, close enough to feel the warmth of her body without touching it. The curves of her back were inviting but he resisted. He was afraid that, if he touched her again, this might be the impetus for her to get dressed and leave. He turned out the lights and watched her for a while. Her pale skin was ghostly in the moonlight coming through the window. He was happy she had stayed, even though she had taken some persuading. That would change in time, he was sure. Her breathing became slow and regular. And he too fell asleep.

When he woke at six in the morning, her side of the bed was empty. All her clothes were gone too. As much as he found her behaviour frustrating, she did make him smile. He could no longer say that she did the unexpected. Instead, she consistently did the opposite of what he wanted. She must have been as quiet as a mouse to sneak out of the bed without waking him; that would not have happened in the narrow cot he had gotten rid of. Maybe I should go and get it back, he thought, or find a padlock for the door. In that case, she would probably have climbed out the window.

He showered and shaved. Then he dressed and made his way to the canteen for breakfast.

The first mine shift of the day had already started. So when he reached the top of the stairs, only two tables were occupied, one by Catherine, who smiled and gave him a little wave. And at a table at the far end of the room was Anya. She did not give him a greeting of any kind, even though she saw that he was there.

He decided to put the boundaries of their new relationship to the test. He hoped they were making some progress, but it was hard to say for sure. After collecting his breakfast, a black coffee and some bread, he headed in Anya's direction. Politeness made him pause at Catherine's table on the way. She was having a proper Soviet breakfast of buckwheat kasha.

'Please sit,' said Catherine. 'We're both late this morning, aren't we?'

'Actually, I need to talk to someone,' he said.

The only other person was Anya, and Catherine turned and looked at her. He could see that she was disappointed he was not joining her. She did not hide any of her emotions.

'We can walk together to the power station after, if you like,' he offered.

'All right,' she said. 'I'll wait for you.'

He walked on to Anya's table and stood in front of her for a moment.

'Sit down, if you're going to,' she said, in a sharp tone, and without looking up.

'I don't mind if I do, thanks for asking,' he said.

'It's too early in the morning for smiles,' she said.

'Really, what time should they start?'

Outside, through the window, the morning was pitch black.

It must be cloudy, he thought, blocking the stars, because he could not even make out the glacier across the bay.

He sat down opposite her, and she looked at him for the first time.

'What I said last night . . .'

'Yes,' he said, wiping the grin off his face.

'You won't tell anyone about any of it, will you?'

'I already said I wouldn't, didn't I? You don't need to ask me again.'

'Yes, yes you did,' she said.

'I am keeping secrets for lots of people,' he said. 'Can I ask you something else? Has all of what you told me got anything to do with the person you're supposed to be meeting here?'

She shook her head. 'No, it has nothing to do with any of that. I was just explaining how I ended up being a teacher. You wanted to know more about me. You're probably regretting asking.'

'No. I did want to know about you, and I still do. So, what about your rendezvous?'

Anya frowned. 'I don't know, maybe it's not happening. I don't care any more.'

She shut off the conversation there and looked out the window.

'Will I see you later?' he asked.

She shrugged.

'Did you not enjoy last night?'

She turned, looked him in the eye and nodded.

'Well then, you should do what you enjoy. There's little enough to do here. I'd like to see you more often.'

'You see me every day.'

'You know what I mean,' he replied.

'We don't need to set a schedule,' she said. 'Do we?'

'No. You're right, we don't.'

A schedule sounded like a great idea to him. But he decided to let her set the parameters of their relationship. Not that he had much of a choice in the matter.

He glanced over at Catherine, whose patience, he could see, was wearing thin. He drank the last of his coffee and tucked the bread into his coat pocket.

'Well, you know where to find me,' he said. 'If you want.'

He stood and started to walk away.

'Maybe I will see you tonight,' she said, after him.

He smiled and kept on going.

Outside, Yuri and Catherine set off on foot in the direction of the power station.

'So, why were you late this morning?' asked Yuri.

She looked embarrassed. 'Promise not to laugh?'

Yuri smiled. 'I promise.'

'I was exhausted. This is my first real job since I graduated. Before that I was more of an activist. New Left and all that. Politics. Agitation. Part-time. Unsuccessful. Frustrating really. But I want to make a success of this. I've such a good feeling about it. And don't worry. I'll be fit as a fiddle in no time.'

'Sounds like you were a bit of a rebel back home,' said Yuri.

'I guess,' said Catherine. 'If you want to call it that.'

'And now that you're in the Soviet Union, what are you planning to rebel against?'

'Ha,' she replied. 'Now that I am here, I was hoping those days were over. You're lucky, you've already won that battle.'

For some reason, Yuri did not feel like a winner.

'She's one of the teachers, isn't she?' said Catherine. 'The one you were talking to.'

'Yes,' he replied. 'Anya.'

'She's beautiful,' she said, managing to make it sound not like a compliment.

'Very,' he agreed.

'Are you two . . .?' she asked, with a clouded expression.

He smiled. 'It's hard to know. You'd have to ask her.'

Catherine nodded and let the subject go.

In the afternoon, the two of them worked outdoors under floodlights, replacing a forty-foot length of pipe that had seen too many Arctic winters. As they carried the old pipe out of the way, Catherine's strength surprised him. Not because she was a woman – there were plenty of tough Soviet women workers. But her frame was slight and it did not seem likely that she would be packing much muscle underneath her clothes.

'I think you're fitter than me,' he said.

'I've four brothers,' she replied. 'So it was kill or be killed, when we were growing up. And at uni, no one takes you seriously as an engineer if you can't pull your share of the load.'

They dropped the pipe on the frozen, impacted snow, to be collected later.

A car pulled up nearby and Yuri saw Timur watching them through the windscreen. After a moment, he got out and signalled for Yuri to come over to him. Yuri had an unpleasant déjà-vu feeling. The last time Timur had done that it was to tell him that Semyon was dead. And he looked equally serious on this occasion.

'I'll be back in a second,' Yuri said to Catherine. 'Wait for me. Don't try lifting that new pipe on your own.'

'I could do it, you know,' she said.

'I'll bet you could,' he said, over his shoulder. 'But wait for me. Where would I be if you put your back out? I won't get another assistant for three months.'

'And you'll never get one like me,' she shouted after him. 'Not in a million years. I'm special.'

Yuri smiled as he crunched his way across a patch of hard snow to the waiting KGB man. He could see that Timur was in a bad mood.

'What are you doing?' the KGB man demanded.

'Working, what's it look like?' he replied.

'I mean with her. What are you doing with her?' said Timur, losing patience with him.

'She's my new assistant. She's good,' he replied. 'She knows her stuff.'

'Who said you could hire her?'

'I didn't. Grigory suggested it. Is there a problem?'

'Well, he should have cleared it with me first,' said Timur, his face flushed with anger.

'Why? She just wants to make a contribution,' said Yuri.

'She's a foreigner, that's why. She's not one of us. She hasn't been cleared. Don't take her anywhere sensitive.'

'Sensitive?' said Yuri. 'You mean your office. That's the only sensitive place in town. The rest is a coal mine.'

'If there are any issues with her,' said Timur, 'I'm going to blame you, so you better just make sure there are none.'

Timur got back in his car, slammed the door and drove off. Yuri turned and looked over at the waiting English woman. He wondered whether she had managed to overhear any of their conversation. If she had, she was not showing it.

'Come on, comrade,' she shouted. 'This pipe is not going to move by itself.'

Chapter 7

T HE EXTENDED PERIOD of endless night was a time when tempers became frayed, and depression could easily become an unwelcome guest, wearing people down. Yuri knew from experience that the solution was not to drink more, but to become more active. One of the problems was that the day lost its natural structure. For the rest of the world, the sun came up, and you got up shortly afterwards. You did a day's work and then went home. After sunset, the sun went to sleep, and most people did the same. And so on. When the sun did not show itself for one hundred days, it was up to each individual to impose a rhythm on their own day. If you wanted to stay sane.

In winter, Yuri swam in the swimming pool almost every day before work, and sometimes after work too. Anya tagged along sometimes, depending on her mood. She didn't swim, just sat in the viewing stand watching him go up and down.

'Why don't you get in,' he shouted.

'Too much effort,' she replied. 'My hair takes forever to dry.'

Yuri did it as much for the heat as the exercise. The pool water was heated like a hot bath. It was a tonic for bones that had difficulty shaking off the cold after a day spent outside in thirty below. When he had Anya for an audience, he pushed himself harder, just to impress.

Their peculiar romance continued. They sought each other out most evenings, without prior arrangement. They had become a couple, even if they did not acknowledge it in so many words. But their easy lifestyle had become a little too easy. He had started to notice her drinking more, and with a capacity well beyond his own. Every meal was accompanied by alcohol. If they met after dinner, they would still always have a glass in their hands. While intoxicated, she was at first high as a kite, seemingly in love with life, and him. Then a darkness could come over her in a flash, one which it was difficult to get her out of.

'Hobbies,' advised Catherine. 'That's what everyone needs.'

She continued to study the other residents' behaviour in this sunless environment. When she was not working with Yuri, she wandered around accosting people with her questionnaires. Yuri had never thought about Pyramiden in this way before, but he had to compliment her on her choice of town. In winter, they may as well have been living on another planet.

'Why are you bothering with this thesis?' he asked. 'I thought it was just an excuse to get here.'

'Oh, it was. But I always finish what I start,' said Catherine, as she flicked through a bundle of questionnaires. 'Try to anyway. I tried to turn England in to a socialist society. Still working on that one. The happiest people here, from what I can tell, are the ones who have hobbies, who stay active. That's what I'm doing anyway, and it seems to help.'

'You don't seem like someone who suffers from depression,' said Yuri.

'Oh, you'd be surprised, believe me,' said Catherine. 'I can go to some pretty dark places.'

He could see she was not joking.

'What about you?' she asked.

'Ha. No,' he replied. 'Is this one of your questionnaires? You don't catch me out so easily. I am not making an appearance in your thesis.'

'Oh. But it's all anonymous,' Catherine insisted. 'Really. There'll be no names.'

'No,' he said.

Catherine sighed. 'A man of mystery.'

'That's me,' he agreed. 'You won't be short anyway. There's plenty of people here who are more than willing to talk about themselves. Getting them to stop will be the hard part.'

'Isn't it amazing the way the sun controls our lives. Like we're still some primitive Neanderthals excited by shadows on a cave wall.'

'Yes,' he said. 'We have not moved on very much from that.'

When Yuri noticed that he had not spent a sober night with Anya for seven days in a row, he decided to take the unprecedented step of removing all alcohol from his apartment, before her drinking got out of hand. It had gotten to the stage where the telltale signs were starting to show. Red river lines in her eyes and dark shadows under them.

He had already witnessed some of the schoolchildren's parents giving her sideways glances and whispered words in the canteen. Small towns were the same everywhere. Everyone knew everyone else's business, and gossip at other people's expense was the norm. Not that the others were not a hard-drinking bunch themselves. It was part and parcel of the Arctic way of life. However, most made sure that they stayed on the right side of the danger line.

It hurt him to throw away good vodka, so he hid all he had behind a control unit at the power station. He did not consult Anya about their change in lifestyle. He knew what she would say. On the first dry night, she arrived at his apartment unannounced and opened his door with her own key, which he had cut for her himself. She kicked off her boots and made herself comfortable sitting on the bed. After a few moments she began to fidget with her hands, and started unconsciously biting her nails. Every now and then she glanced over at his fridge on the window ledge outside.

'Aren't we going to have a drink?' she asked, finally.

'No. Not tonight,' he said. 'I don't feel like it. Is that OK?'

She did not look as though she thought it was OK, but she nodded. 'All right. What will we do then?'

'We could go to a movie,' he suggested. 'Or for a swim.'

Neither of those ideas excited her. She thought for a moment and then said, 'Are they working in the mine tonight?'

'No, I don't think so. This is their night off.'

'Will you take me there?' she asked. 'I've never been.'

'Now? It's the middle of the night.'

'It's the middle of the night all day, every day. If you're not going to give me a drink, that's what I'd like to do. Are you going to take me or not?'

'All right,' he said, with no enthusiasm. 'But you'll have to change into clothes you don't like, it's a mess down there.'

'I only have clothes I don't like now. I dress like a school teacher. I used to be able to buy nice clothes, silk and cashmere, and wool. Everything I have left from those days has holes in it.'

'I like your clothes,' he said. It wasn't a lie. She was more stylish than anyone else in Pyramiden. And her figure made everything look good. Women here who were half her age admired her with envy. He did not know how she managed it, with her fiftieth birthday on the horizon, and partaking of almost no physical exercise.

As they walked past the mine bathhouse, he tried to talk her out of going up the mountain. But she had set her mind to doing it. And once she had done that, it was difficult to talk her out of anything. At the bottom of the railway, he helped her into the open carriage. Then he turned on the power and jumped in beside her as it moved off. She held on to his arm on the way up as if they were on a carousel ride. Above them, the mine shaft opening came into view and he was reminded of the night they had found Semyon's body.

At the top, he asked her once more, 'Are you sure you want to go through with this?'

'Yes,' she said. 'Don't you like it up here?'

'No actually,' he replied. 'It's my least favourite place in the world.'

'But you've always worked in mines, haven't you?'

'No. I've always worked *at* mines,' he corrected. 'I don't go in them, if I can help it. People are not moles. We are meant to live above ground.'

Anya smiled. 'Are you scared, is that it?'

'No. I am not scared.'

'You are scared. You big baby. Come on, lead the way. I'll protect you.'

He switched on the tunnel lights and led her down the principal pathway, so that they would not get lost trying to find their way back. One straight line down meant one straight line back up.

She looked around with interest for the first five minutes, before the black walls began to merge into one another and boredom set in, as Yuri knew it would.

'I see what you mean,' she said. 'I don't much like it down here either.'

Yuri stopped walking.

'You want to go back up?' he asked, hopefully.

'No,' she said. 'Turn out the lights.'

'What for?'

'Just do it. I told you I'd protect you, didn't I? Baby.'

Reluctantly, Yuri located the nearest wall switch and turned out the overhead strip lights. The entire mine shaft went black. He couldn't see a thing in any direction; neither sunlight nor moonlight could penetrate this deep. Immediately, his other senses took over, and the dank smell of this underground world seemed to become stronger.

'Now find me,' she said, laughing, from somewhere in front of him.

Yuri still had one hand on the wall and was in no hurry to let go of it.

'But what if I can't find the switch again?'

'Baby,' she whispered. 'Baybeeeeee.'

Between the first and second word he heard a change of direction, and he realised she had moved further away from him.

'Baybeeee,' she said, once more.

He turned his head in her direction, or at least where he thought she was. Then, against his better judgement he let go of the wall and hoped for the best. With his arms out in front of him, he moved forward, trying not to stumble over the loose lumps of coal that littered the ground.

'Where are you?' he asked.

She did not answer. For a moment, he feared she had gone even further down the mine shaft, and that he might not find her until the miners arrived for the morning shift. The thought occurred to him that Semyon could have been surprised in this way. With the tunnel in pitch black, he would not have seen his killer coming.

'Talk to me. This isn't funny,' he said. 'We could be stuck down here all night, you know.'

She still did not reply, but he heard her suppressing a laugh. She was within thirty feet of him, but in the darkness that may as well have been one hundred.

He adjusted his direction and swung his arms around in a semicircle. But he didn't make contact with a wall or Anya. He didn't like this game.

'Psst,' she said.

'Can you see me?' he asked. 'How can you do that? What are you, a bat?'

'No, I can't see you, but I can hear you moving around. You're like an elephant.'

She was very near now. He could smell her perfume in the air, mixed with the thick ever-present coal dust.

'You know, sometimes I think you have a death wish,' he said.

'Maybe I do,' she replied softly.

Following her voice, he kept in a straight line as best he could. He located her warm body six feet in front of him. Once he had her within reach, he wrapped his arms around her and held her tight. He didn't like the dark, or enclosed spaces, but he was not going to admit that to her. She leaned in to him and pressed her lips against his.

'Really?' he asked.

'Yes,' she said. 'Why do you think I asked to come up here?'

They made love in total darkness. Even when her face was an inch from his own, he still could not see a thing. Not even her eyes. He wished he could. Seeing her was part of the pleasure of making love with her. He liked watching her expression change when he did something she enjoyed. At least he could hear from her breathing that she was having a good time.

When it was over, he said, 'Now, I hope we can find the light switch.'

She took hold of his shoulders and turned him around.

'It's fifteen steps, that way, on your right.'

'You counted before I turned the light off?'

'Sure I did,' she said. 'You think I want to spend the night down here, even with you?'

Yuri walked forward, counting under his breath, and found the switch where she said it would be.

'It's not working,' he said.

'What! Oh no,' she said, with a hint of panic in her voice. 'What will we do?'

'I don't know. Maybe if I actually press it this time,' he said.

The tunnel flooded with light as the bulbs came to life one after the other. They both took a moment to adjust their eyes to the brightness.

'Very funny,' she said.

Back at the apartment, they showered together, and scrubbed the coal dust off of each other's body. He made her promise that they would never do that again.

When they were wrapped up warm in bed, he said, 'Tell me about your husband.'

From her expression, he immediately realised he'd walked on a landmine, again. He should have learned his lesson, not to ask her questions about her past. But he could not help himself; these were things he was curious about.

'Why do you want to know about him?' she demanded.

'I don't mean to intrude,' said Yuri. 'I know it's a sore subject for you. It just interests me, I guess, the sort of man that would leave you.'

She smiled. 'You will leave me too, some day. You'll see.'

'That's not fair. How can you say that?'

'This is my life,' she said. 'Bad things happen.'

'Well you shouldn't expect them to.'

Anya made a 'what-do-you-know' face.

'So, go on, tell me about him.'

She sighed before speaking. 'He was, I mean is, a scientist like me. I am sure he is still working, wherever he is. That's why they wanted him, to work for them in the west. We met in a research study group, when we were young. He was the star student. He had this confidence about him. He believed in himself, and so did others. We both got picked for the third idea programme. We had already started dating by then, but we kept it a secret. I was afraid if they found out, then I would be kicked off the programme. They'd never do that to him.'

'And you made bombs together,' said Yuri. 'How romantic.'

She looked annoyed at his cynicism.

'I loved working there. It was the best time of my life. I was good at it. I still am. It wasn't just about weapons. The future will be nuclear, you'll see. One day there will be no more need for your coal.'

'I presume you've tried to get them to take you back?' he asked.

'In the beginning. I thought they would see reason. It was so unfair to blame me for what happened. I tried to be good. I did every job they found me, with no complaints. But there was no reward for doing that. They just wanted me out of the way. To be forgotten.'

'And you loved him, before, I mean?'

'Yes. I did.'

'And he you?'

Anya shrugged. 'I thought so. It's not every day you have your world completely turned upside down by someone you trust. It's hard to take. I've been trying for years to make sense of it. Sometimes I wish I'd never met him.'

'Look at the bright side,' said Yuri. 'If he hadn't done all of that to you, you would never have come to Pyramiden and met me.'

She gave a wry smile. 'True. Beautiful Pyramiden. And what would my life have been without you!'

He had a strong desire to tell her that he loved her. But he kept this feeling to himself. He took her hand in his and noticed something.

'You don't wear your wedding ring?'

She looked down at her bare finger.

'No,' she said. 'I took it off because I did not want to be reminded of him. Then, I lost it.'

Timur's insistence that he keep English Catherine away from sensitive places had put an idea into Yuri's head. He knew that every worker in Pyramiden had two files related to them. One was in the main administration office, and listed each person's wage history, work record, personal details, merit badges and so on. The second file was under lock and key in Timur's office. This one, written by a stranger, documented your commitment, or lack of, to the advancement of the communist project. It would include your profile, affiliations, relationships and friendships, crimes committed, and anything informers might have said about you, whether they were true or not. Suspect people would have thick files, with many entries. Loyal communists would have thin files, but there would be a file nonetheless, even for the staunchest.

Yuri decided he would like to take a look inside Semyon's file. The one in Timur's office. He hoped it might provide some information about any trouble he was in, or the names of any enemies he might have. Unfortunately, this room did not operate like a library, with files that could be checked in and out. To view it, he would have to commit a crime.

The KGB man had regular habits. Every Monday, Wednesday and Friday, at 7 p.m., he could be found in too-tight shorts and a vest, gambolling around with a basketball, along with the other enthusiasts in the Yuri Gagarin sports centre. Timur always wore the same all-red outfit that the Russian Olympic team had worn in '72 when they had beaten the Americans and won gold. Like them, he played to win. Nobody liked playing against him or with him. But no one would tell him that to his face. His office remained locked and empty during game time. Yuri did not possess a key, but he knew where a set was kept for every office in town, in case of emergency.

On a lazy starlit afternoon a few days after his trip to the mine, he spied on the custodian of all key copies, the chief accounts clerk. A large lady from Georgia, she was also a creature of habit. She could be found at the head of the lunch queue on most days.

When she left her office, Yuri entered the building and liberated the key. Then, later that evening, he hung around outside the administration building until he saw Timur leaving. In the corridor, he made sure no one else was about. Then he unlocked the secret service office door, stepped inside and locked himself in. The office consisted of two rooms. The first contained Timur's desk, two chairs and not much else. Beyond that, there was an adjoining room, which Yuri had never been in before. He turned the door handle, and found it unlocked. Inside was a small iron stove and a dozen tall, alphabetised gun-grey metal filing cabinets.

If he had not recently eulogised Semyon, he would not have known that his surname was Gulbis. He tried the corresponding filing cabinet, but found it locked. As were all the others. He wondered if Timur would go to the trouble of carrying around a dozen keys all day long.

He walked back in to the main office and tried to guess where Timur might hide them. He paused as he heard a woman's quick footsteps outside in the corridor, followed by a knock on the door. Yuri stared at her stationary shadow under the door frame. Only the outer office had a window, and it had bars on the outside. If she came in through the door, there would be nowhere for him to hide. It would be difficult to explain why he was on the wrong side of a locked door. The woman tried the handle once more and then walked on.

While he was waiting for her to leave, Yuri spotted the silver ring of small cabinet keys. They were standing in plain sight, sharing a fruit bowl with a decaying banana. He grabbed them, hurried back to the other room and unlocked the G–H cabinet. He located Semyon's file and pulled it out. It was an inch thick.

'My, what a bad boy you've been,' Yuri said to himself.

However, when he started to flick through it, he discovered something entirely different.

'The little shit,' he said, out loud.

Semyon had been operating as an informer for Timur, and had been the whole time he had lived in Pyramiden. He had made detailed reports on a dozen or so individuals, including Yuri, several times. He quickly scanned the ones that were about him. It was the usual stuff: accusations of sabotage, self-interested, not a team player. Nothing he hadn't heard before, and definitely nothing he was going to be in trouble for in the future. All the reports were dated, and the most recent report about him was from the same date as the one he had noted in Semyon's notebook. He pulled out the note-book from his pocket. All of his reports in the file matched the dates on that page in the notebook. So he was Spider.

Semyon had kept a record of the dates of all his reports to Timur. And he had given each person a corresponding animal name in his notebook, in case anyone ever caught sight of it, Yuri supposed.

He wondered if one of the others mentioned in the file could have found out that Semyon was spying on them. Most people would not be too happy to discover that. Men and women had been killed for less. He considered writing down the other people's names, and what the Latvian betrayer had said about them. But he worried he had already been in here for too long.

He hesitated a moment before stuffing the whole file inside his coat. It was a further risk to take it, and he would have to replace it soon. He should really have left then. But as an after-thought, he decided to look up Anya's file. He expected to find one several inches thick, given the stories that she had told him. However, when he searched for it, he found that she didn't have one. Perhaps, he thought, she has been here such a short time, Timur hasn't gotten around to opening one yet. The other possibility was that she was just a teacher, and she had made up all the rest of it. He checked his watch, and decided to go. After replacing the cabinet keys where he had found them, he left as quickly as he could.

When he returned home, the first thing that hit him when he opened his apartment door was the overpowering smell of alcohol. Anya was lying fully clothed, but semi-conscious, on the bed. An empty bottle of vodka lay on the floor beside her. It wasn't his, so she must have brought it with her. He hoped it hadn't been full when she had started drinking it on her own. He brushed away the matted hair covering her face and she stirred. She half-opened her eyes and closed them again.

'Why do you think he hasn't come for me?' she asked. 'The one I am supposed to meet.'

'Him again? I don't know. I thought you didn't care any more.'

'I lied,' she said, half-asleep. 'You don't understand. How could you?'

'What don't I understand?' he asked.

She started to retch, and he helped her up on to her feet and into the bathroom.

'How much did you drink?'

'Quite a bit,' she said. 'Hard to say. You were late. What was I supposed to do?'

'In future you could just wait for me, how about that.'

She slid down the wall and slumped against the toilet. Somehow she managed not to be sick. When it came to drinking she was not a delicate flower. But she was so drunk, if he left her here she would pass out where she was.

Her body was completely limp, and he almost put his back out lifting her off the floor.

'Just leave me,' she slurred. 'I'm fine.'

He ignored her protests and made her walk beside him to the edge of the bed. The only thing keeping her upright was his arm around her waist. When he let go, she crumpled in a heap on to the bed.

He began to undress her. There were no more complaints. She would not speak again, or open her eyes, until the morning. He pulled her left arm gently, encouraging her to move on to her side. She settled in that position and started to snore. His brother had died like this. Such a stupid way to go. Unfortunately for him, he had no one watching over him to make sure he did not choke in his drunken slumber.

He had noticed the familiar signs of winter depression in her, but he suspected the cause of tonight's behaviour was not just a lack of sunlight. He wished this mystery visitor of hers would show up so that he could beat the crap out of him. If he existed at all. The man, imaginary or not, had become an obstacle in their relationship.

Chapter 8

I N THE MORNING, he left Anya sleeping peacefully exactly where he had left her, on her side in his bed. On his way across the playground he saw a dozen kids, carrying flashlights, on their way to school. He dropped in to the principal's office on his way to the power station and told her that Anya was feeling under the weather. Despite his best lying face, she gave him a knowing look of disapproval, which he did not think was fair. How the hell could she know that Anya had drunk herself into unconsciousness? She could have been sick. He resisted the temptation to start a row with her.

He guessed that Anya would surface around lunchtime, with a sore head. Coffee and a light meal would fix her. He resolved to check in on her at one o'clock.

Around mid-morning, Timur walked into the control room, without knocking, and looked at Yuri with a loaded expression. Yuri wondered if he could have discovered that Semyon's file was missing from his office. It had been stupid to take it on impulse, without having thought the risks through. He hadn't even hidden it well in his apartment. He had been so distracted by Anya's state when he got home that he had just kicked it under the bed. It would take a good lie to explain how it got there.

'Catherine,' said Timur, 'would you mind if I have a private word with your boss here?'

Catherine turned to Yuri for his approval.

'Of course,' she said, after he raised no objection. She walked by Timur to grab her coat and hat.

'You're very kind,' said Timur, with an annoying smirk.

'Shall I come back in half an hour?' she asked.

'No, five minutes is all I need.'

Yuri's heart rate quickened as he foresaw the end of his life here in Pyramiden. He could only guess what the punishment might be for the burglary of a KGB office and the theft of a confidential file. Murderers probably got less.

Timur looked around at the various machines and dials.

'Quite a system you've built here, Yuri. You must be a clever man. Do you agree you are a clever man?'

He thought it best to give a non-committal shrug to this one.

'Am I in trouble for something?' he asked, after losing patience waiting for Timur to spill the beans.

'Not really, no,' said Timur. 'At least not for anything you've done. Your girlfriend, Anya. Her drinking has become a problem.'

So everyone knew about them, Yuri realised, even though they had been discreet when other people were around. Nothing stayed secret for long in Pyramiden. And especially not from Timur, whose job it was to keep tabs on them all.

'A problem for who, exactly?' Yuri asked.

'For me, and therefore you. She had to be sent home from the school today after making some sort of a scene in front of the children. There were tears apparently.'

Damn it, thought Yuri. She must have woken and gone to work after all. No doubt she smelled like a distillery. And he had set her up for a bigger fall with the story he had told the school principal.

'The parents were none too happy,' continued Timur. 'If anyone is going to shout drunkenly at their kids, I think they would prefer if it was them.'

Yuri wanted to find her straight away, but Timur was enjoying taking his time. He wished there was some sort of test that people had to go through before they were given power over others. Anyone considered likely to abuse that power should automatically fail.

'Are you going to get to the point of this any time soon?' Yuri asked. 'Because if not, I'd like to go and see how she is.'

Timur was not pleased about being rushed.

'All right,' he said. 'Here's the deal. From today, I am making Anya your responsibility. If she shouts at a kid again, I am going to blame you. If she comes to work smelling of booze, I am going to blame you. If she gets out of line in any way, I am going to blame you. Got it?'

'That's not exactly fair,' said Yuri. 'Maybe she had one too many last night. She's not the only one who drinks in this town.'

'No,' agreed Timur. 'But the miners can drink all they like. She works with children. So she can't just do whatever the hell she wants. Let me put it like this, if you can't control her, I will. Now you can go find her, if you want.'

Yuri did not move. He waited for Timur to leave so he could gather his thoughts. He had known from the beginning that Anya was going to be trouble, so none of this came as a surprise. But now, if he was to keep her, this situation would need careful handling.

Yuri found her in the canteen drinking coffee. Her face was colourless, and she looked shaken. She was staring up at the mural on the wall, the Arctic scene with its large yellow sun beaming down. Yuri sat down beside her.

'I don't know how you stand it without the sun for so long, every year,' she said. 'I think I'd lose my mind if I had to ever do it again.'

'What happened at the school?' asked Yuri.

She turned to face him and he saw that she was ashamed. 'How did you know something happened?'

'Timur paid me a visit,' he replied. 'I have been tasked with keeping an eye on you.'

Anya laughed. 'Weren't you doing that already?'

'Not well enough, apparently.'

She held her cup in both hands. Despite her best efforts to control them, they shook as she brought the coffee to her lips.

'I'm fine. It's just something that happened once. It's not a big deal. I don't need looking after.'

'I think you do,' he said. 'It's my fault too. I need to try harder.'

'And what do you care, Yuri?' she asked.

Her raised voice made the waitresses look over in their direction.

'I care,' he said. 'You know I do.'

She looked at him strangely, like she had that very first time.

'It isn't you . . . is it? You're not the one?'

Yuri sighed, and touched her hand.

'You've got to stop this. It isn't healthy. No one is coming to meet you.'

Anya gave him an angry glance, and pulled her hand away from his.

'They told me to come here. For nothing. Three months I've been waiting.'

'Who told you?' he asked.

'Do you know why they've ignored me? Because I am a nobody – nothing. I used to be someone. Now look at me. Look where I have ended up.'

It occurred to him again that maybe she was crazy, and her obsession with this absent visitor was all in her head.

'You're with me. Isn't that something?'

She shook her head. 'You're a good guy, Yuri. But I am not what you need. Maybe we shouldn't see each other any more.'

'I am afraid that's not possible,' he replied. 'You are now officially my responsibility. If we stop seeing each other, I will be in trouble. We are stuck together.'

'You would be better off without me. And you have your little foreign dolly bird, don't you?'

Yuri smiled. He was pleased to detect a hint of jealousy in her tone.

'I work with her, that's all. Catherine is not my dolly bird. You still haven't told me what happened at the school.'

She closed her eyes for a second, the memory of the incident obviously raw.

'I was still drunk from last night. And this morning when I went in, they wouldn't stop talking. Yak, yak, yak, in their little high-pitched voices. I told them not to. I didn't shout. But it was going right through my head, and when they kept on doing it, I just lost it. I shouldn't have. Poor little things. I don't think they knew what hit them. They are good kids really. I'm going to apologise to them tomorrow. I didn't get a chance to do it today because the headteacher came in when she heard them crying and she ordered me out.'

Yuri was thankful he had not witnessed this scene.

'How many of them were crying?' he asked.

'All. All of them. One started, and that set them all off.

Like a choir. The more I tried to calm them down, the louder they got.'

Yuri sighed. 'I want you to promise that you'll stop drinking. If you don't you'll lose your job at the school. Do you want that?'

Anya looked over at the waitresses, who were still watching them from the far side of the room.

'I hate my job,' she said. 'But no, I don't want to lose it, it's the only one I've got. I will stop drinking. For you. Because you are the only one who likes me.'

Yuri smiled, even though he knew she did not mean it. At least if he could get her to stay dry for a while, that would be something.

'More coffee?' he asked.

'Yes please. Keep it coming.'

'And something to eat?'

'Yes, I probably should. Though I'm not sure my stomach will agree.'

Yuri loaded a tray for her, with fresh coffee and potato pancakes. Then he sat and watched her eat.

'I've been a bad girl,' she said, between mouthfuls, 'but the punishment is not so bad, being looked after by you.'

'My pleasure.'

'No, I mean it,' she said. 'Thank you, Yuri.'

He shrugged. 'Less talking and more eating. The food will help.'

He wanted to think that this incident was the start of a turning point for her, and for them. But he didn't really believe that. Not yet anyway. There was still something in her eyes that said she was not at peace with herself.

The next morning, Yuri escorted a nervous, sober Anya through the lamp-lit streets to the front door of the school.

They had rehearsed what she would say, both to the principal and to the children. It would not be acting. She was genuinely sorry, and wanted to put it behind her. Between themselves, they had made a pact to avoid alcohol completely for a whole month. This was not something he would have chosen for himself, in December of all months, but it certainly would not do his body any harm. And he reckoned she needed as much support as she could get. As she said herself, he was the only one who seemed to take an interest in her. She had no friends among the other women. He had even heard one of them calling her the ice queen behind her back. He could understand where they were coming from. She was not open or welcoming, until she got to know people, which her closed manner made almost impossible. As far as he was concerned it was their loss. And he liked not having to share her with anyone.

Having deposited her safely at work, Yuri headed for the power station. He found that Catherine was not there. This was unusual as she was more diligent and conscientious than any Soviet worker he had ever come across. She even put the great Stakhanov, the originator of mine hand-drilling, in the shade.

Yuri was not in the mood for doing any work. He was sitting in a chair, thinking about Anya, when he noticed a note stuck to one of the monitoring machines.

Fire in back-up generator. Gone to investigate. Catherine.

He grabbed his coat and bolted for the door. Outside, he skidded on ice but managed to right himself and kept on going. Grigory waved him down as he passed.

'Do you have a minute, Yuri?' he asked.

'No. Sorry. Later,' said Yuri, without stopping.

'What's wrong?' Grigory shouted after him.

'Nothing. I hope.'

Yuri barged in the door of the shed that housed the back-up generators. Catherine was standing with her back to him, screwing the front cover back on to one of the machines. The smell of burning lingered in the air, but whatever fire there had been was now out.

'What are you doing?' he demanded.

'There was a bit of a blaze in here,' she replied. 'Nothing major. Although, it could have been if I had arrived any later. I put it out.'

'On your own?' he said angrily. 'You don't do something like that without calling me.'

'I didn't know where you were,' she said, her tone rising to match his own. 'And why can't I do it on my own? Because I'm a woman?'

'No,' he said. 'Because you are a temporary trainee. What happened?'

'A short-circuit, I think. One of the wires burned right through. I think there must have been dust underneath, and it just took off.'

Yuri stared at her with suspicion. Since he had been here, he had never had a fire in any of these generators.

'It was just getting going when I arrived,' she said. 'If I hadn't, the whole place might have gone up.'

Yuri calmed. A genuine saboteur would have let everything burn.

'You can leave that off,' Yuri said. 'I want to have a look.'

'You don't believe me?' she asked.

Catherine pulled off the metal cover once more and Yuri spotted the unmistakable mark of a fresh burn on the back of her hand.

'You're injured,' he said.

'Oh, that. It's nothing.'

'Show me,' he insisted.

He held her hand close. She winced when he touched the scar.

'I'll get you some cream for that,' he said.

'It's fine. Really.'

Yuri looked inside the damaged generator, and it was as she had described it. A short-circuit more than likely, and the inside, underneath the motors, was filthy. They would all have to be cleaned to prevent the same thing happening again.

'From now on, we need to stay in contact,' he said. 'I am going to get us each a radio. And you will keep yours with you twenty-four hours a day. All right?'

Catherine smiled. 'Am I allowed to turn it off when I go to sleep?'

'Yes, you can do that,' Yuri agreed. 'But that's the only time. And promise me you will not try to put out any fires without me, or do anything else dangerous.'

'I promise, I will try and find you first, with my radio,' she said.

'And if you can't?'

'Then . . . I'll put out the fire by myself.'

'No,' he said. 'You will try me again on the radio, and you will keep trying until you get me. OK?'

'OK,' she said with a sigh. 'I don't see what the fuss is about. I'm a big girl. I'm more than capable of handling myself.'

'Tell that to your hand,' he said.

This was exactly the kind of thing that Timur had warned him about. Suspicious fires in an essential piece of equipment, only witnessed by a newly arrived foreigner. He would not be mentioning any of this to the KGB man. For now, he believed her. But he knew from personal experience that a good sabo-teur could cover their tracks.

He dined with Anya in the canteen, without their customary drink beforehand. And there would be none to follow. The whole thing was a source of amusement, at least for the first day. He saw her looking longingly at a bottle of red wine on a nearby table. And when she looked back, she caught his stare and smiled. He knew this honeymoon wouldn't last and there would definitely be harder times ahead. Her return to the school had gone better than expected. The principal had been understanding, and the children had behaved as if nothing had happened.

'They've got short memories, for some things,' said Yuri. 'And they don't hold grudges, not like adults.'

'I hope so,' said Anya. 'I don't want them to hate me.'

'Did you ever think about having any yourself?'

Anya smiled as if the idea were ridiculous. 'Kids? No.'

'What about your husband?' Yuri asked.

'We were too busy, in the programme. He was all about the work. We never had enough time for each other, let alone to spend raising children. How about you?'

Yuri paused before answering. No one in Pyramiden knew about his family history, except for Grigory. No one knew because it was not something he had ever told anyone.

'I have a son,' he said.

He waited for her reaction as she took in this news.

'What!' said Anya. 'Why didn't you tell me before?'

Yuri shrugged. 'I don't see him. I married young, and me and his mother aren't on exactly friendly terms.'

'Well, when was the last time you saw him?'

'Twenty years,' said Yuri. 'When he was six. He'd be the same age as English Catherine now.'

'He's a grown man?'

'Yes,' said Yuri. 'Old enough to have had kids himself. He could have for all I know.'

'Maybe he'd like to see you?' said Anya.

'I doubt that very much,' said Yuri. 'After twenty years, don't you think it's a bit late?'

'No. You're his father. You should write to him,' said Anya.

'No.'

'Don't you want to see him?' she asked.

'I was never a part of his life, so why start now. Just to make me feel less guilty? I do feel guilty but his mother didn't want me to see him, so what could I do.'

'You give up too easily on things, don't you?' she said. 'Is that why you're here, so you can put everything difficult in your life behind you?'

Yuri stared at her. He didn't disagree with anything she had said. It was just unnerving the way she had figured him out so soon. Abstinence had already made her sharper. A noise from his coat pocket saved him from further personality dissection. He pulled the two-way radio out and put it on the table. They could both hear Catherine's voice talking into hers.

'I'm switching off now, Comrade Yuri,' said Catherine. 'Getting an early night. See you tomorrow.'

Anya glared at the radio. 'What the hell is that?'

'I got them for English Catherine, so I can keep track of her.'

'Why do you need to keep track of her?' asked Anya.

'Her' was said with a touch of venom.

Yuri smiled. 'She got herself into a spot of bother today. I can get one for you too if you like. Maybe I should.'

Anya shook her head, and Yuri put the offending radio back into his coat pocket.

That night, as Anya slept beside him, Yuri lay wide awake, staring at the ceiling. The last time he had seen his son he had not known it would be for the last time. He had taken him, at a prearranged time, from his mother's apartment to the local park. They chatted and fed stale bread to the ducks beside the frozen pond. They had a brief disagreement when the boy had wanted to skate on the ice; it was early winter and it was still too thin. Apart from that they had a pleasant day together. When he dropped him home, it was the usual wordless exchange with his mother. She didn't even bother to make eye contact with him any more.

Two weeks later, he called at the door to arrange another visit, and a stranger told him that they had moved. It took him three months to find them. She had found a new man; they were living together. He was going to be a father to the boy, and neither of them wanted Yuri to be part of the equation. Yuri and the boy had no say in the matter.

He objected, of course, but he had little power to change the situation. And as days turned into weeks, he got used to the idea. It meant he was free, with no ties to anyone. He walked away, without looking back.

When he was six the boy had looked just like his mother. Straight fair hair, with two-tone eyes that were green on the outside and brown in the middle. Yuri wondered if he had grown up to look anything like him.

There was no chance of him falling asleep now, so he reached under his bed and his hand found Semyon's file. He carried it over to the table and opened it. The early pages contained official typewritten reports. It was clear from these that Semyon had been an informer going all the way back to his student days in Latvia. He had even received several commendations for the diligence of his work for the state. Who knew what havoc he had sown over the years among friends, teachers and relations? Some people ended up being informers after being caught committing an offence. Faced with the choice of punishment or telling tales on their friends, most chose the latter. However, Yuri suspected it was Semyon's ambition that had marked him out as a suitable candidate for recruitment.

None of Semyon's Latvian reports were in the file, only the ones he had written since he had arrived in Pyramiden. The first bunch made Yuri laugh out loud. Anya stirred in the bed behind him, so he kept quiet. He turned the pages as silently as he could. If she had been drunk, as usual, she would have been sleeping more soundly.

The subjects of these first reports were Semyon's Baltic buddies, the Lithuanians. Yuri compared the report dates to the ones in the notebook, and he discovered that Semyon had given them the coded name Bears. In his reports he had faithfully catalogued a litany of their drunken boasts about sabotaging Soviet interests in their homeland. However, in fairness to the little weasel, he did remark that he was not sure whether to take any of their claims at face value or whether it was all bar talk. Yuri had to agree. The Lithuanians had a high opinion of themselves, and a chip on their shoulders as big as the Berlin Wall. If they had found out that Semyon was informing on them they certainly would not have been pleased. Perhaps they would have been angry enough to commit murder. He imagined the three of them surrounding Semyon in the mine shaft, and having a row about his betrayal. One blow from the tall one with something heavy, and that would have been that.

But then why had the Lithuanians threatened him, and

beaten him up, claiming to be Semyon's best friend in the world? Unless that was a show they had put on for his benefit to keep him guessing.

He had another look at the pages that Semyon had written about him. A more thorough read confirmed his first impression. There was nothing in it that Timur would not have said to his face. And any accusations of sabotage or individualism, however merited, fell flat when set against the fact that this lauded Soviet outpost only functioned because of him. He didn't give a shit about communism, or Soviet ambition, but he worked hard. Until now, this much had protected him.

The pages were handwritten by Semyon, and in the margins, here and there, another hand had made a few notes. Timur. Fuck him, thought Yuri. If he wanted to make trouble for him, he could give plenty in return.

Another report documented various conversations Semyon had had in the bar with a miner from Chechnya. Yuri remembered him. He had left on the last boat before winter, after his contract had expired. The man obviously had a loose tongue while drunk, as he had made a litany of comments about named party officials in his home town. For the most part, they were accusations of financial corruption. All of them were probably true. A non-corrupt party official in the Soviet Union was a rarity.

Timur had written a note to self at the end of this report.

Have this joker arrested as soon as he gets home.

The poor guy was to travel all the way home, oblivious to any problem, with his wife waiting at the dock. And he would be arrested in front of her for speaking the truth to someone who pretended to be his friend.

All of the reports had corresponding entries in Semyon's notebook. Except for one. The Latvian had apparently done three reports on Eagle. But whatever these were, they were not in his KGB file.

The other reports were of minor interest, apart from one. For some reason, Semyon had made six short reports on Grigory. In the notebook he was Fox. Yuri read each report word for word. There was nothing in them that he could see. They were all innocuous conversations. Semyon had attempted to draw Grigory out on various contentious issues. But true to form, Grigory had replied with intelligent, philosophical answers. How peculiar, thought Yuri. Why had Semyon continued to approach Grigory, and to write reports about him, when he never once said anything incriminating? Perhaps Timur had made him do it. But what was so interesting about Grigory? And who did Eagle refer to?

Chapter 9

'THE VERY MAN,' said Grigory, as he stood near the exit door in the foyer of the Cultural Palace.

Yuri looked around. He had been so immersed in his thoughts that he had walked right past without noticing him.

Grigory closed the out-of-date edition of the *Izvestiya* newspaper he had been reading and slipped it into his blazer pocket. It was quite a trick to have one eye engrossed in political propaganda and the other on the lookout for people he wanted to talk to.

'You've suddenly become a hard man to pin down,' said Grigory. 'In a hurry?'

'No,' said Yuri. 'I've got time. What is it?'

'Let's walk,' said Grigory, pointing the way towards the film projection room.

Yuri pictured Semyon doing the same thing, walking, talking, only with an agenda of some sort. Semyon the weasel, and Grigory the fox. Grigory was a clever man, and Yuri wondered if he had known what the Latvian was up to.

'What was all that panic the other day?' Grigory asked. 'Where were you running off to?'

'Oh, Catherine had put out a generator fire, by herself.'

Grigory frowned. 'She's OK?'

'Yes,' said Yuri. 'Just a minor burn. She won't do it again. We have a new system.'

Grigory nodded, but his expression was still clouded.

'And it was an accident? The fire.'

Yuri looked him in the eye. 'Yes, it appeared that way. Is there something you are not telling me?'

'About Catherine? No. With her, what you see is what you get.'

Yuri did not entirely believe him. 'Is that what you wanted to see me about?'

'No,' said Grigory. 'You've had some trouble lately, I hear, with your new lady friend. Anya, isn't it?'

Yuri sighed. 'This place is too small.'

Grigory smiled. 'I was under the impression you liked living here. Have you changed your mind about that?'

'No. And there's no trouble,' said Yuri. 'She just had one too many one night, that's all.'

'How is she doing now?' asked Grigory.

'She's not an alcoholic if that's what you're asking. She is being more careful, now that she knows her limits.'

Both men remained silent as the cinema projectionist came out a door and passed them carrying five reels in heavy metal cans.

'She is no more an alcoholic than I am,' continued Yuri, when the man had gone. 'She can handle herself. And besides, I am looking after her.'

'You're looking after her,' said Grigory, with a raised eyebrow.

'Yes, I am. What's wrong with that?'

'Nothing,' said Grigory. 'Would it be too forward of me to ask if this one is different from all the others?'

'Yes,' said Yuri. 'It would. Mind your own business.'

'As you wish,' said Grigory. 'I was only trying to help. If I can be of any assistance, you know my door is always open.'

Grigory turned and walked back the way they had come. Yuri felt guilty for being so cool with him.

'Thanks,' he said, after him.

The more he considered Semyon's reports on Grigory, the more he was convinced that the motivation behind them was professional jealousy on Timur's part. Apart from the mine director, Grigory and Timur were the two most powerful men in Pyramiden. Grigory, it had to be said, wielded his power with a lot more subtlety than the KGB man. And he was popular, which Yuri knew could be a strong motive for envy, especially in someone as immature as Timur.

As for Semyon, there was nothing in his reports that would have made Grigory angry, if he had found out about them. Apart from the fact that he had the cheek to write them at all.

Sobriety had its downsides. Sure, it brought a feeling of well-being, and increased energy. Mental agility certainly took a leap up too. But since they had both been on the wagon, much of the fun had fizzled out of his and Anya's relationship. Conversation now tended to be serious and considered, and laughter a lot less frequent. Her visits to his apartment were no longer every night. Alcohol, it seemed, had been at least part of the attraction. He hoped this was an adjustment period and that their relationship would find a new rhythm soon enough.

Knowing that she would not be visiting that evening, Yuri decided to follow a hunch on his new chief suspects in Semyon's death. After work, he left the power station and joined the miners coming off shift, as they made their way to the bath-house. Yuri went inside and took his turn at the showers. The

water ran black off the hairy miner beside him. Then he headed
to the sauna. The heat hit him in a rush as he opened the
door. Inside, he spotted the three of them, as usual, talking
conspiratorially in a corner on their own.

'My Lithuanian friends,' Yuri said. 'Long time no see. How
is the mine treating you?'

'It is breaking our backs,' said the short one.

The tall one stayed silent for a moment, looking him in the
eye. He was, Yuri guessed, trying to figure out what his
angle was. He planned to reveal that later. When he did, of
the three the tall one would be the one to be careful of.

'What can we do for you, Yuri?' the tall one asked, when
he had finished staring. 'We don't normally see you in here
with the little people.'

'Oh,' said Yuri. 'Semyon has been on my mind a lot lately.
I know they said it was an accident, but I don't believe that
and neither do you. I wanted to see if you had come up with
any more ideas.'

'Terrible business,' said the short one.

'You mean apart from thinking you did it?' asked the tall
one.

'Yes, apart from that,' said Yuri.

'Maybe we still think that,' said the tall one.

They all smiled, although it was already an old joke. Yuri's
money was on the tall one having done it. Or maybe all three
together.

'I have some new information,' he said, 'regarding Semyon
and the three of you. I think you might find it interesting.'

The tall one looked around to see whether other miners
might be eavesdropping.

'You'll come for a drink after, Yuri,' he said.

He had been dry for less than a week and he felt like saying no. But he wanted to follow this and see where it led. At least he would not run into Anya at the bar, so there was a good chance she might not find out. Yuri agreed and left the sauna first. He showered again to get rid of the sweat. As he was dressing, the other three passed the changing-room doorway on their way to wash. Yuri had not liked the looks the tall one had been giving him earlier. He decided he had better swing by his apartment on the way to pick up some means of protection.

The glass bar was empty when he arrived, but it would fill up soon enough after dinner. Yuri wanted the security of extra people around. He heard the door opening behind him, and the tall one walked in on his own. He got himself a drink at the bar and joined Yuri at his table.

'So, what's this new information you were on about?' he asked.

'Your friends aren't joining us?' Yuri asked.

'No. They're tired. They had a long day.'

Yuri wondered if the other two were outside, lying in wait. For once, he wished the bar was crowded.

'Go on. I'm listening,' said the tall one.

'What do you think of informers?' Yuri asked.

'Informers.' The Lithuanian almost spat the word. 'I think they should have their tongues cut out. And that's when I am feeling generous. Why do you ask?'

'Because our mutual friend Semyon was one.'

The man looked at him with what seemed like genuine surprise. He leaned back in his chair and took a slow, deliberate sip from his glass.

'How do you know this?' he asked. 'What evidence do you

have? You can't just go around making accusations like that against people. Especially the dead. Not without evidence.'

'I read some of his reports,' said Yuri. 'From his personal KGB file. He has been an informer for twenty years.'

The man's eyes widened. He turned around as two miners entered the bar. They sat at the furthest table away from them. The Lithuanian moved closer and lowered his voice to a whisper.

'You read his file? How? Maybe you are working for them too?'

'Let's just say I didn't get it legally,' said Yuri.

'You still have it then?'

'I didn't say that,' said Yuri, even though it was still under his bed. 'I had it for a while. Long enough.'

Yuri kicked himself. He had not foreseen that the where-abouts of the file would be important. He had lied badly, and the man knew he had it now.

He wasn't sure yet how smart this guy was, but he was intelligent enough to know that Yuri held all the cards. And he didn't like it.

'So he wrote stuff about me?'

'Yes. You and your friends. I was in there too. He was a busy boy, Semyon. Quite the writer. I obviously gave him too much spare time.'

Yuri allowed him a moment to digest this information.

'You don't seem too surprised that he was an informer.'

The tall man shrugged. 'I'm not as good a judge of character as I used to be. But I thought he was one of us. A patriot. Not a dirty Russian lackey.'

'You never can tell,' agreed Yuri.

'What did he write about me?'

The more the man spoke the stronger his tone became. He

did not seem to care any more that the other drinkers might overhear. Yuri had told him too much already, and he was looking for a way to gain the upper hand.

'Well, you can imagine,' said Yuri. 'Pretty much everything you ever said to him since you got here is in that file. You call it patriotism. The KGB has another word for it. I'm surprised you haven't been arrested already.'

'They can't prove a thing,' the man blurted out, too loudly. The other two drinkers looked over briefly and went back to their conversation.

The man's eyes narrowed. 'How much do you want for it?'

'For what? The file? I'm not here to blackmail you, if that's what you're thinking.'

'Then why are we both here?' he asked.

Yuri was here to see whether the man had known what Semyon was up to. But from his reactions he was pretty sure he had not. He regretted having mentioned the file to him at all. From the look on the Lithuanian's face, he was not going to let it go.

'I just thought you should know, that's all,' said Yuri.

He made his excuses soon afterwards and left. The Lithuanian was not happy letting him go, but the bar was half full now, with too many eyes and ears.

Yuri had made sure not to get drunk. He expected he would need his wits about him before the night was over.

It was three in the morning when he heard his apartment door being tampered with from the outside. Here was the answer to his earlier question. The Lithuanian was not going to win any prizes for brightness. He entered silently and walked towards the bed. In his hand he was carrying a wooden club. Yuri wondered whether he was going to wake him and demand the file, or hit him and search for it himself.

He watched the club being raised, silhouetted against the moonlit window. Then it came down hard on where his head might have been on the pillow. At the same moment, Yuri jumped up from the chair he had positioned behind the door. Before the man could turn, he stabbed him in the arm with a two-inch blade. His original intention had been just to threaten him, but that plan had changed when he saw what the Lithuanian was prepared to do to his skull. The man dropped the club and held his arm, which was pouring blood.

Yuri held the blade against the man's cheek.

'I told you I didn't have the file. It's back where I found it,' he lied. 'If you really want it, you can ask our KGB friend for it. And if you ever come back to visit me again, I will use this on your throat. Now get out.'

The Lithuanian did not say a word. He just left, still holding his arm. There was only one way to deal with men like him. He was afraid of Yuri now.

Before he met Anya the following evening, Yuri brushed his teeth a half dozen times, trying to eradicate any lingering smell of booze. When they kissed he watched her reaction, but she seemed not to notice anything. They made love in his apartment. An act that sobriety and familiarity had enabled them to refine into something approaching an art. Hers was a body he knew well but never tired of.

Afterwards they chatted about this and that, but he could see that tonight she was bored with his company. He racked his brain for an interesting subject but nothing came. Finally, he decided to mention an idea that had been on his mind.

'Maybe we could come up with a way to extend your contract so that you could stay on here.'

She had said to him, after the episode at the school, that she did want to keep her job.

But now she laughed at the suggestion. 'I am not staying here. Wild horses couldn't make me. Once I meet my contact—'

This row had been brewing for a long time and Yuri finally let loose.

'I'm not listening to you any more about your ridiculous contact. Is there really someone you are supposed to be meeting, or did you just make all of that up? Because that's what I believe.'

'You think I'm crazy, is that it?' she asked, her nostrils flaring.

'Honestly, I don't know. You tell me. I don't know what to think. But if you want me to stick around much longer you better give me something right now, because I've had enough.'

He meant it and she could see it in his eyes. She paused for a moment, then sat up in the bed with the sheet wrapped around her.

'I haven't told anyone this before. I'm telling you now because you are the only one I trust.'

Yuri watched her and stayed silent.

'Six months ago, I received a letter in my apartment in Moscow. Unmarked. No stamp. It was his handwriting. My husband's. After five years of silence, he was making contact with me. He wrote that he had wanted to bring me with him at the time of his defection, but they wouldn't let him, the English or the Americans, I don't know which. But now they said they would take me to the west too, if I came here to Pyramiden.'

Yuri tried to hide his disappointment. She was here to leave, and he was not part of the plan. All this could have been plucked from her imagination. But as much as he wanted it to be a lie, he reckoned she was telling the truth.

'And you believed him?' he said. 'About wanting to take you with him, back then. It's easy for him to say it now.'

Anya shrugged and shook her head. 'I don't know what to believe. Why would he say it now if he didn't mean it?'

'And why here?' said Yuri. 'Why Pyramiden? Surely there are easier ways.'

'I don't know,' said Anya. 'I assumed they had some way out from here. But I've been here three months, and nothing. Where is my contact? Why doesn't he show himself?'

'Is this what you really want?' Yuri asked. 'To go there and be with him?'

'I think so . . . I am not sure about anything any more! But that's why I came here. They arranged it all. That's the part I don't understand. If there was to be nothing, then why bring me all the way here?'

Yuri was too angry to think about what she was saying. She had not mentioned their relationship once in all of this, as though it had not happened.

'He left you!' he reminded her. 'For five years, without a word.'

'I know,' she said, nodding. 'But what if what he says is true? That he couldn't take me. He's still my husband.'

'You want to be a traitor, like him?' asked Yuri.

'I am not a traitor. I don't know anything that they don't know already in the west. I haven't worked in a secure department since he left. I have no secrets to sell. It's not about that.'

It all seemed so far-fetched to Yuri. He had never heard

a story like it. As with everything, he tried to analyse it logically.

'So why now? Why is he contacting you now?'

'I was being watched for a long time. Everyone knew that. They thought I was in on it, they couldn't understand why I was left behind. I couldn't understand it either. But maybe it was only possible to contact me now, when they have stopped watching.'

'So he writes to you and you decide to drop everything, and do what he asks, just like that?'

'What everything? I have nothing. I am a school teacher. A bad one at that. I have no friends, no life, nothing.'

'And he's going to give you all that back?'

'I know he cannot fix everything. It's too late for that. But haven't you ever dreamed of going to the west? Even just to see something different. To experience a different life.'

'No,' he replied. 'I like it here, in the middle. This is my different life.'

She smiled at him and touched his cheek.

'You are the only person I know who actually likes the Arctic. Everyone else just does it for the money. But you can't get enough of it. Why?'

'It's clean. And empty.'

'Now there you go again, why do you like empty places?'

Yuri shrugged.

'You don't like people very much, do you?' she said.

'I don't need other people,' he agreed. 'I prefer to be on my own. Except when I'm with you. But it seems you don't feel the same way.'

'It's not like that,' said Anya. 'Meeting you was unexpected. I didn't plan for this to happen between us.'

'But it has,' he said. 'Does it change anything for you?'

She paused, then shook her head.

'But if I'm not going anywhere, as it seems, and I am to be stuck here, then I'm glad it's with you.'

Yuri stood up and walked to the window. Across the square, in the light of a street lamp, he saw Catherine returning to Paris. She waved at a man who had just left her. Yuri caught sight of him just before he disappeared around a corner. It was Grigory.

'I am not stuck,' said Yuri. 'I want to be here. I'd like you to stay with me. I don't want you to go. Especially to a man who obviously doesn't love you like I do.'

'You love me,' she said, apparently surprised. 'Since when?'

He turned to look at her.

'For quite a while. I thought it was obvious.'

'No,' she said. 'Not to me. You might have considered mentioning it.'

'Would it make a difference? I'm serious. I'm asking you to stay, and to forget about this man.'

She shook her head. 'I'm sorry. I can't do that.'

Anya stayed the night, and they made love again. But it was different, as though she was doing it out of sympathy rather than passion. His head told him to walk away before he got hurt even more. But he wanted her. And the pain, however bad it might get, did not matter. It was ironic, he knew. Since he first got here, he had counted down the days of every relationship he had, knowing he would be free before too long. And just when he had lost the desire to be free, the woman he had set his sights on only dreamed of escape.

The next morning, Yuri went to work early. But he had no interest in doing anything. He sat thinking about what had happened the night before. He had not lost his temper with

Anya. But now, in a split second, he exploded in a rage, attacking one of the metal and glass control units. He pummelled the glass with his fists, smashing them. And he left large dents in the lower part of the metal with kicks from his work boots. The storm subsided quickly, when his knuckles started to bleed. He was just catching his breath when Catherine entered. She looked down at the shattered glass on the floor and the bashed metal on the cabinet. This particular unit was not going to work again for a while.

They stared at each other for a moment, neither knowing what to say. Then they both surveyed the damage. Catherine turned, hung up her coat and grabbed a broom and pan.

'I get like that too, sometimes,' she said. 'I wish I could do some smashing as well.'

'Be my guest,' said Yuri. He took the sweeping brush out of her hand. 'My mess.'

Now that Yuri and Anya knew where they stood, sobriety seemed pointless. So they began to drink together again. Alcohol and sex became their routine, in that order. Not so much drinking that she caused herself trouble at work. But as close to that limit as she could get. Likewise, Yuri drank to lighten his mood, willing himself not to take their relationship seriously.

When he was sober, another factor weighed on his mind. As had been proven by Anya's personal experience, when someone defected, the person left behind paid a high price. Everyone knew that they were a couple. No one knew that he was just a stopgap for her until she was reunited with her husband. If she did manage to defect somehow, what would happen to him?

However, as the days passed without incident, Anya's suggestion that she had been dragged to Pyramiden for nothing seemed to become a stronger possibility. None of it made much sense to Yuri. And the more Anya tried to find the logic in it, the more irritable she became. And the harder she drank.

'You think it's funny what they've done to me, don't you?' she said late one night, her body gently swaying, her eyes unfocused.

'No, I don't think it's funny,' he said.

'But it makes you happy?'

'Yes, it does,' he admitted. 'The more time I get to spend with you the better. Although I prefer you when you're not so drunk and bad-tempered.'

Anya's drink spilled as she waved her glass at him.

'You don't want me to be happy. That's the truth, isn't it?'

'I think you would be happy if you stopped looking for what you are missing, and if you just lived for now.'

'It seems like I don't have much choice, do I? But I'm damned if I am going to pretend to be happy about it.'

When she had calmed, and was sitting in a chair, Yuri said, 'Tell me again how you come to be here.'

'I told you,' she said. 'My husband wrote in his letter that a plan was being put in place, and if I followed it, he would know that I wanted to be with him. Nothing happened for two months, and then the official letter came to say I had gotten the job here.'

'You didn't apply for it?' he asked.

'No, I'd never even heard of Pyramiden before that. Believe me, I would not have picked the closest town to the North Pole as my new home.'

Chapter 10

O N HIS WAY to work the next morning, Yuri came across Grigory and Timur standing outside the executive apartment block. They were both on the receiving end of a tirade from Cosmonaut Katerina. Yuri had never seen her so animated. The two most powerful men in Pyramiden looked as though they had not experienced anything quite like this in their entire adult lives. As he drew closer to the conversation it became clear that she had discovered that the two men lived in executive apartments in which the living quarters were larger than those for the ordinary workers. Everyone in their building lived under the same special conditions. Now she had the two of them cornered and looking for a way to escape.

'What would Lenin say about this?' she demanded. 'He'd be furious, wouldn't he?'

The two men looked sheepish. Yuri had to stop himself from laughing.

'He'd tear down those apartments, wouldn't he?' Catherine continued, waving her finger at the offending block.

Yuri was not so sure that Comrade Lenin would be as outraged as she was. He imagined that he would probably actually be settled in there, with his feet up, enjoying the relative luxury of the largest apartment in town. Brezhnev and his cronies had no problem with the perks that came with their positions. They all had dachas in the finest resort spots in the USSR. It was expected. Everyone knew that was what you got when you became a party boss. A different life from everybody else. A rich westerner's standard of living with a communist stamp of approval on its ass. It was acceptable because they didn't get it through capitalism. They got it standing on the broken backs of the Soviet workers. But the people didn't resent what they had, they wanted it for themselves.

'So, what are you going to do about this problem?' she demanded.

Neither of them had an answer. They looked to Yuri for help. He could have abandoned them to their fate, but he did the right thing.

'There you are, Catherine,' he said. 'There's a problem we need to attend to, urgently.'

The two men looked incredibly relieved. Yuri would store this credit away for later use. Remember that time I rescued you guys from a real communist?

Catherine reluctantly let them off her hook. Yuri could still feel her anger as they walked away. It was quite a fearsome sight from someone who was normally so calm. He looked back over his shoulder and saw Grigory giving her a look of admiration. Timur appeared to be still in shock.

'If you were looking for me, you could have got me on my radio. Isn't that what it's for?' she said.

'Yes, I forgot about that.'

'There isn't a problem, is there?' she said, after he had led her in no particular direction for a couple of minutes.

'No,' he confessed.

They stopped next to the livestock enclosures, where the pigs were just being fed.

'Look, you can't do what you were just doing,' he said. 'You can't question people who are high up in the party. And definitely not the secret service. That's called democracy. We are not in one of those.'

'But when there is obvious inequality it should be stamped out, shouldn't it?' she asked, with a completely straight face. 'That's their job, to look out for that kind of thing.'

Sometimes, what she said was so naive he had to remind himself that she wasn't making a joke.

'When there is obvious inequality,' he said, 'you either grab some of it for yourself, if you're able, or if you can't do that, then you do what everyone else does – just be jealous and bitch about it with your friends, when you're sure no one is listening. Although, I don't really recommend that because the odds are high that at least one of your friends is probably an informer.'

'You know, you have a very cynical view of your own country, Yuri. The Soviet Union would not have achieved all that it has if everyone had the same negative attitude as you.'

Everyone was accusing him of being a cynic lately.

'This is why I left England,' she said. 'People would say they believed in a just socialist society, but then when you put them to the test, no one had the bottle to follow it through. If it's to work, you can't compromise on anything. Why haven't the other workers revolted over this?'

It always amazed him how her questions could be like a sharp blow to the chest, knocking the wind out of you. Revolution was a word from another, distant lifetime. His grandfather's time. Leonid, his father's father, had, with youthful enthusiasm, taken a full part in the overthrow of the tsarist system. After a stunning victory that shocked the whole world, he had been hit by one disillusionment after another. The difference between Stalin and Tsar Nikolai II was hard to discern. Both were totalitarian rulers. However, as Yuri's grandfather was fond of pointing out in private, the latter interfered less in people's lives, and the former had managed to murder a lot more of his subjects.

Yuri sat Catherine down, deciding to give her some truths as he understood them.

He told her that the communist party, instead of being a revolutionary force as it was originally intended to be, had instead become the biggest criminal mafia organisation the world had ever seen. If there had ever been true ideals in the Soviet Union, which he seriously doubted, then they had all been trodden down by decades of corruption and abuse. Tears welled up in her eyes. He was having this effect a lot lately.

'I don't believe you,' she said. 'You are telling lies because you have lost faith, and you need to get it back. I'll help you.'

It was a dilemma, what to do with this woman. Crush her? Or lie?

He sighed. 'You're right. I am a cynic and I must try to fight it.'

'At least you know, Comrade Yuri,' she said. 'That's a good start.'

He knew it was only a matter of time before she would come to understand. The same way children eventually discovered that Father Christmas wasn't real. At some point, well before their teenage years, children were destined to discover two shocking truths: that the world was not as magical as they had been led to believe, and that their parents were capable of perpetuating a lie for years. In the Soviet Union, communism had replaced Father Christmas as the great fraud every child had to discover for themselves.

Yet, here was a grown woman who had never been through

the process of enlightenment that the average Soviet went through. She had missed the rite of passage from indoctrinated believer to non-believer who kept his or her mouth shut. This, he guessed, was where the Father Christmas myth and communism went on different paths. In the case of communism, you were expected never to admit that you didn't believe. And you took this secret to the grave. For those who insisted on professing their true feelings, an early grave might be arranged. Or there were other ways of silencing you, such as internal exile to somewhere like the city of Gorky. The only other option, as chosen by Anya's husband, was defection.

Not wishing to shatter Catherine's illusions too quickly, he said, 'You know, I think you had an idea of what we were like before you came. And maybe the reality is a bit different.'

'It is,' she agreed. 'It's so much better than I imagined. I can't believe how well you are all treated here. If our miners back home had any idea about all of this luxury, they would all be coming over.'

'Well, Pyramiden is not an average Soviet mine,' said Yuri. 'It's a one-off.'

'I guess it is,' she agreed. 'But what an example to set. I suppose the plan is that all Soviet mines will be like this some day.'

'I'm not so sure about that,' he said, fearing that he was fighting a losing battle with her. 'It's a showcase town, that's right, but the show is not really for us. The point is that it's in the west, and westerners can visit here and they are given this impression of Soviet life to take away with them. It's not real.'

'What's not real?' said Catherine. 'We're here aren't we? It's a working, fully functioning mining town. And one hundred per cent communist.'

Yuri decided to throw in the towel. She was unshakeable and would just have to find out for herself.

'Do me a favour,' he said. 'Lay off Timur and Grigory about their apartments. They were built that way, long before they got here. And it's not something anyone can fix.'

'All right,' said Catherine. 'If you say so. I'm glad we had this talk.'

'Me too,' he lied.

She walked on, leaving him feeling as though he had just done ten rounds with a better fighter.

Today, instead of working at Pyramiden, Yuri was due to accompany one of the resident polar researchers to a weather station they had set up a mile out of town. There were always scientists here, doing this and that. Mundane, everyday research. Not like Anya and her husband. His companion today was a bearded, outdoors type from Mongolia. Conversation was not the man's strong point, which suited Yuri. He was glad of the opportunity to get away from everyone and to clear his head.

They travelled by snowmobile for the first part of the journey, with their headlights on full. Usually Yuri led the way, but the Mongolian was someone who liked to be in charge and he sped to the front as soon as they left town. The last part of the trip required a twenty-minute hike up the side of a mountain. Yuri was sorry this climb had not happened during his recent dry period. The Mongolian took off on foot like a mountain goat, as Yuri huffed and puffed behind him. There was no way Yuri could keep up with him. When he broke out in a fit of coughing, the man paused and waited for him. Yuri, gathering his breath, took the opportunity to look back the way they had come. From here, you could see all the way out to open sea, beyond the frozen limit. It was strange to see waves moving in the moonlight, having been surrounded by nothing except rigid ice for so many weeks.

'You smoke?' asked the researcher as Yuri caught up.

'Yes,' said Yuri. 'You have one?'

The man shook his head. 'Bad habit,' he said, and took off again.

Yuri decided not to bother trying to keep up this time. He went at his own pace and let the Mongolian win the race to the weather station. This building, and a couple of others, had been built in the 1930s. They had recorded continuous weather data since then, except for a brief period during the Great Patriotic War. A British ship had sailed up the fjord one day, and had told everyone they had to leave. The Nazis were coming and the Allies could not protect all of these isolated outposts. Soviet mining and research only resumed after the war had ended.

His companion was already busy at work when Yuri reached the station. Yuri's job on these trips was to check that all the equipment was in good working order. Happily, this meant he had little to do. The monitoring gadgets the researchers left here were designed to be abandoned in the harshest of elements. A maintenance engineer like him was rarely required. He went inside the main building, a round brick tower. After lighting the wood stove, he made himself a black coffee. Through the window he saw the Mongolian taking notes outside before moving on to the next instrument. At the rate he was going, the man would be finished in no time, but Yuri was not in any hurry to leave.

He sat back in a chair and sipped the hot, soothing coffee. Then he rested his head against the back of the chair and closed his eyes. Thoughts of the war brought back memories. His brother had not wanted him to go and fight. They had been inseparable up to that point. By '44, it was just the two of them and their mother. Their father had died defending Stalingrad, along with countless others. A medal was posthumously awarded. But it wasn't enough for Yuri; he wanted revenge against the Germans. He was much too young to join up, but he managed to attach himself as a helper to a regiment that was heading west. Yuri confided in his brother, but he went straight to their mother and told her about his plans. She tried to stop him. He was headstrong back then, more so than now, and he ran away at the first opportunity.

He got his revenge but it did not bring his father back, or make him feel better. But to have won the war was a powerful feeling. One that still brought a smile to his face. They had faced the greatest evil the modern world had ever known. And they had crushed it. All the way to Berlin. After that came a feeling of emptiness. He had never found a purpose or cause in life since then that even came close.

When he finally returned a year later, he and his brother were both different people. Their mother said she had not seen her younger son for months. It took several days to find him, running with a gang of street kids in another neighbourhood. Yuri expected to resume his role as his brother's protector but his help was no longer wanted. When he tried to explain what he had been through in the war, and tell his stories, his brother would switch off. Then it would descend into a row, with his brother asking if he thought it was a picnic for those left behind.

He never said it in so many words, but Yuri knew he had never forgiven him for leaving. They were never as close again as they had been. And over the years they drifted apart more and more until they were strangers. Their mother, when she was alive, was the only tie that bound them. After her death they rarely communicated.

At the funeral, his brother's neighbours had spoken of an open and generous man. Sure, he had a drink problem, but if anyone needed anything he could not do enough for them. He always had time for a chat, and a joke. Everyone smiled when they told their stories about him. They seemed genuinely to like and miss him. Yuri did not know the man they were talking about. He wished he had.

He opened his eyes and saw that his coffee had gone cold. His neck felt stiff, and he realised he must have fallen asleep. He looked up and found the Mongolian staring in at him through the porthole window. The man said nothing and walked on. Yuri presumed this was the signal that he was done.

'Everything OK?' said Yuri, when he came outside. 'Did you get what you wanted?'

'Yes,' said the Mongolian. 'All done.'

'So what did all those instruments tell you?' he asked.

'They told me that it is very cold here,' the Mongolian replied, with perfect deadpan delivery.

The man walked on down the slope with his haversack on his back. Yuri took one last look at the sea, which was dotted with glowing icebergs. In the darkness it was difficult to tell where the sea and the starry sky met. Both looked the same. The white dot of an iceberg in the distance could easily be mistaken for a star in the sky. As he prepared to follow the researcher, a feeling of foreboding came over him. For the first time in his life, he was not looking forward to returning to Pyramiden.

After they had parked their snowmobiles, Yuri watched the researcher walking away. Semyon had done this job with the research team, several times. He wondered if the Mongolian could be the person called Eagle in Semyon's notebook.

Mongolians hunted with eagles, so it was not such a stretch. The problem was that it could also be anyone in town. Only Semyon could explain why he had picked a particular animal for each person. Yuri walked in the opposite direction, and as he turned a corner he bumped into Grigory.

Grigory smiled. 'Thank you, Yuri. Your arrival this morning was just in time.'

'You both looked in a tight spot,' agreed Yuri. 'Any longer and Timur might have had to shoot her.'

'She's right, of course,' he said. 'I didn't have the answers she was looking for. An idealist expects perfection but in the real world, things are sometimes not as they should be.'

'Most of the time, I would say,' said Yuri. 'Wouldn't you agree?'

'No, I wouldn't,' said Grigory. 'But then we are different, you and I. I was actually hoping to run into you today. Don't you think it's about time we had that game of chess? It's been a while.'

'What, now?' said Yuri.

He was tired after his trip, and hoped Grigory would suggest another day.

'I'm free now,' said the party man. 'How about you?'

Yuri sighed. 'All right. One game. Then I have to be somewhere.'

Grigory gave him one of his knowing smiles. They walked together to the library, where Yuri organised the table and chairs while Grigory set up the pieces. He had his own personal set, made of real moulded silver plough horses and workmen. Proletariat royalty instead of kings and queens.

They chatted idly for the first few moves, and then the reason for this hastily arranged rematch became apparent.

'How much do you think a person should drink?' asked Grigory.

Yuri didn't bother controlling the flash of anger in his eyes. Grigory saw it and ignored it.

'Should one set a limit, I mean, or not?' he continued. 'We are all drinkers, us Russians. Brezhnev has even made it easier for us, with the prices. But where should we draw the line between pleasure and problem? It's a difficult one. Don't you think?'

He had already had this conversation with Timur, and he was tired of their interference. But he knew that Grigory was generally well meaning.

'You're talking about Anya,' said Yuri. 'Just say what you want to say.'

'Am I?' said Grigory, playing all innocent. 'Well, let's take her as an example. Why not. A teacher has the right to enjoy herself, in her free time, like anyone else, as long as she is productive during her working hours. Yes?'

'Agreed,' said Yuri.

Grigory took one of Yuri's pawns, and placed it on the table in front of him.

'And if a person, Anya for instance, ceased to be productive, then we could say she has strayed over that fine line into the problem area. Couldn't we?'

'She is a good teacher,' said Yuri. 'The kids like her.'

'Ah, I'm not sure that last part is true,' said Grigory. 'I believe they call her the ice queen, for a perceived lack of emotion. But that's not important. They are at school to learn. They don't have to like their teacher. I didn't like any of my teachers. One maybe. But by the principal's account, she is an excellent teacher who elicits good grades from her students. Or at least, she did until recently. Round about the time she started seeing you, as a matter of fact.'

'So, it's my fault?' asked Yuri.

'Did I say that? Your move.'

'Yes, you did, I think, in your own roundabout way.'

Yuri moved one of his pieces without looking at the board.

'I thought you were going to take care of her,' said Grigory.

'I was. I did. She stopped for a while. We both did. But she likes to drink. She's happier when she's drinking. She gets depressed otherwise.'

'What has she got to be depressed about?'

Yuri studied his friend's expression and realised that, like Timur, he did not seem to know about Anya's background. It was quite a feat by whoever had organised it, to get the wife of a defector all the way here without the local bigwigs being informed about who she was.

'She has some family issues,' said Yuri, which was not quite a lie.

Grigory nodded. 'Divorced, like you?'

'Separated,' said Yuri. By the iron curtain and a few thousand miles.

'Has she any kids?'

'No, she has enough of them here.'

'That's true. All right. People are talking, this is the point. And they're talking to me. If we were back home in a big city her drinking would not be so obvious. But here, you can't hide a thing from anyone.'

'People should learn to mind their own business,' said Yuri.

'Let's hold our breath for that, shall we?' said Grigory.

He took another of Yuri's chessmen.

'Human nature is what it is,' Grigory continued. 'Look, she's here for the winter. We can't even think about replacing her until the spring.'

Yuri looked up from the board. 'She's going to be replaced?

When was that decided? How can you do that? She's on a two-year contract.'

Grigory shrugged. 'It doesn't matter about contracts. If things go on like they are, she won't leave us much choice.'

Yuri shook his head. It seemed there was a conspiracy to take her away from him, one way or another.

'Check,' said Grigory. 'It doesn't have to play out that way, of course. If sufficient change is demonstrated.'

Yuri had lost interest in the game. He sat back in his chair.

'Aren't we going to finish?' asked Grigory.

'I'm not in the mood. You always win anyway.'

Grigory did not look happy. He sighed and knocked over the remaining pieces. Yuri got up to leave as Grigory began to put the set back in its case.

'Usually you put up more of a fight,' said Grigory. 'If you don't mind me saying so, you haven't been yourself either since you started seeing her.'

'If you remember, you were the one who told me to stop sleeping around. Make up your mind.'

Grigory closed the chess case and held it close to his chest.

'This time it's serious, is that what you're saying?'

'Yes, it's serious,' said Yuri. 'So, I'd appreciate it if you didn't go transferring her out of here. I just met her, and I'd like to see a bit more of her if that's OK with you, and Timur, and the school principal, and the rest of this bloody town.'

Grigory nodded. 'I'll see what I can do. She can help herself, if she wants to stay. Is that what she wants, to stay here?'

Yuri sighed and looked away.

'Maybe it would be better for everyone if we did transfer her?' said Grigory.

Yuri shook his head.

'All right then,' said Grigory, as he stood up. 'We'll just have to find a way to keep her. If you're sure that's what you want.'

'That's what I want. Thanks, Grigory.'

'Don't thank me. I haven't done anything yet. If I do you can thank me then. We'll pick up this game another time, when your mind is not so occupied.'

Anya may have hated the winter darkness and being trapped by the ice, but it seemed this was the only thing keeping her here for now. If it was not for that, Yuri suspected he would not even be having this courtesy conversation with Grigory. The school would have resolved the problem themselves without seeking his advice. The alcoholic would already have received her marching orders. Perhaps they were bad for each other, as Grigory implied. They certainly weren't making each other happy, not like they had in the beginning. But he felt attached now, and he was set on seeing where their relationship would take them.

He thought about what he would do if she was still here in the spring and ended up being transferred back to Russia. Her dream of being reunited with her husband would be over. In that event, she would need him more than ever.

Chapter 11

ONCE AGAIN, YURI received a summons to Timur's office. The message did not say why he wanted to see him. The previous two times he had been there, he had gotten in with a stolen key. It was a strange sensation to return to these rooms and find someone inside. While Timur finished some paperwork, Yuri spotted the cabinet keys, still in their usual spot in the fruit bowl. Timur continued to make some notes on a page. Yuri guessed it was just a show for him. The man had little to do here. He glanced towards the inner door to the file room, which was ajar. Perhaps Eagle's file was in there somewhere, or in the pile in front of him now, on Timur's desk. The KGB man could have been reading it, which would explain why it had not been in Semyon's file when he had taken it.

He had managed to return everything to its rightful place in the file room, two nights previously. He was sure he had not been seen. So he expected this meeting would be about something else. Then he became suddenly nervous. The Lithuanian knew he had taken Semyon's file. What if he had seen some advantage to himself if he turned informer?

Timur looked up from his papers and waved for Yuri to sit. The secret service man put down his pen and sat back in his chair. Thankfully, there was no finger-tapping this time.

Instead, he picked an apple from the fruit bowl and took a bite out of it.

'Yuri, I want you to keep an eye on someone for me,' he said, while chewing with his mouth open.

'Anya is fine,' he replied. 'I've already talked this through with Grigory. I don't know what everyone is making such a fuss about.'

Timur smiled.

'That's good to hear,' he said. 'But no. I didn't mean her. I am talking about your assistant, the English woman. Catherine.'

'Her!' said Yuri. 'Why?'

'Her behaviour lately has been making me nervous,' said Timur.

Yuri stared at him in disbelief.

'She does have a habit of speaking her mind, but she's more red than any of us. We should be sending her into space instead of Gagarin.'

'She's an agitator,' said Timur. 'You heard her the other day, causing trouble over the exec building. She could have been sent here as a saboteur.'

The same thoughts had entered Yuri's head, after the generator fire incident. But he did not believe it.

'You don't really think that, do you?' Yuri asked. 'You seriously suspect her?'

'It's my job to consider all the possibilities,' said Timur. 'Enemy agents come in all forms.'

'It's not just an act with her,' said Yuri, 'Or if it is, it's a very good one.'

'You consider yourself a good judge of character?' asked Timur.

'Is that a trick question?' said Yuri. 'Yes, I do. For what it's worth.'

He always had the urge to shower after speaking to this

slime bucket. There was no way he was going to agree to be his informer. He liked Catherine, and felt responsible for her.

Yuri stood up. 'Sorry, but I am not doing this,' he said. 'You'll have to get someone else.'

He got the impression that Timur had been expecting this answer. The man did not seem at all ruffled by it.

'You've been in Pyramiden for a very long time, Yuri. Perhaps now is the moment for us to advertise for a proper replacement. Someone who values their position here. Or alternatively, you could just write down everything that Catherine says to you, and show it to me. Your choice.'

Yuri didn't like either option. Timur took another bite of his apple. He had a smug grin on his face as he watched Yuri running through the ins and outs of this dilemma.

'Let's be friends, Yuri,' said Timur. 'I don't see why we can't be.'

'I have enough friends,' said Yuri. 'My social calendar is full. Plus, you already have me watching out for Anya. Isn't some of this supposed to be your job?'

Timur shook his head. 'My job is to get other people to gather information, and then I will decide if it's useful or not. That is what I am doing in this case. As her boss, you have special access that no one else has.'

He had Yuri over a barrel and he knew it.

'No objections?' said Timur. 'Good. You are now officially a KGB informer.'

'I'm flattered,' said Yuri. 'Do I get paid?'

'No.'

'Why should I do it then?'

'For one good reason. Because it will annoy me if you don't. Is that what you want?'

Yuri shrugged.

'You know, I was half-thinking of reopening the Semyon case. There was something fishy about all of that. Even you thought so, as far as I remember.'

'OK, OK,' said Yuri. 'I'll do your dirty work for you.'

'Good man. That's more like it. Look at the bright side. We'll get to have more of these chats.'

Encounters with Timur would be much easier if he just cut to the chase, held a gun to Yuri's head and ordered him to do what he wanted. The more subtle power games were much more tortuous. They both knew there would be only one outcome if Timur threw his weight around. But making people squirm seemed to be an end in itself for him.

It was remarkable that Yuri had managed to get to his age without ever being asked to inform on a friend. He had heard endless stories from people he knew, but he'd never actually done it himself. Perhaps he had been considered someone to be watched rather than someone to do the watching.

When he met Catherine the next day at work, he felt bad about the whole business. He hoped it was all a sick joke that Timur was playing on him. A status game to show he was the one with the power. He had met officials before who pulled these kinds of stunts for pure malicious enjoyment. Himself and Timur were not competitors, so he did not know what might have possessed the man to torment him in this way.

Since talking to Catherine was like listening to a Lenin speech on a loop, Yuri didn't see any actual harm in relaying what she said to Timur. He had no intention of getting her into trouble, but it was not necessary to censor what she said in order to protect her.

Still, the fact that he was listening to her as an informant without her knowledge made him feel worse than bad about himself. Semyon had done the same thing to him, and the others on his list. He wondered if this had created self-esteem issues for him, or if he had taken pride in his work for the secret service. Nothing about this made Yuri proud.

He found himself staying quiet when he was with Catherine. Asking her any question, no matter how trivial, had all of a sudden taken on a more loaded and invasive significance.

'Are you feeling all right?' asked Catherine, when he had not spoken for hours. 'You don't seem yourself today.'

'I'm fine,' he said. 'Just things on my mind.'

He had a feeling she might understand if he explained. She would probably agree with the Soviet obsession with protecting itself from the west. Although, he knew she would not be pleased to learn that she was the one coming under suspicion.

'Anya?' she asked, with a look of sympathy that made him feel even worse.

To betray a friend must be the lowest of the low, he thought.

'Not Anya, no,' he replied. 'Just other things.'

'How is it all going there with her?' she asked.

'Up and down,' he said. He was not sure at which point of the rollercoaster they were right now.

Catherine nodded. 'I know what that's like. She's nice. I haven't spoken to her all that much, but she strikes me as a very smart lady. Not very teacher-ish is she? Whatever that is. Dowdy, I suppose. And definitely not glamorous like she is. Quite a catch you've got yourself there, Yuri.'

You don't know the half of it, he thought.

'What about you, you have a boyfriend back in England?'

Catherine frowned, for once, and he saw this was not a subject she liked.

'No. I'm single at the moment,' she said. 'Been that way for quite a while. Friends say I set the bar too high. But I do seem to send men running in the opposite direction.'

'I doubt very much that's true,' said Yuri.

'Oh, you'd be surprised. The last man I dated more than once was in 1973.'

'Four years ago!'

'Yes,' she said. 'A lot, isn't it. I was too busy, campaigning for this and that. No time for romance. That's what I tell myself anyway.'

'We'll have to find you someone here,' offered Yuri. 'If you're interested.'

Catherine's cheeks went bright red. 'Oh no, no thanks. I'm a firm believer in just letting these things happen.'

'This from the woman who has been alone for four years,' said Yuri.

'That is true,' she agreed. 'But really, no. I don't need a matchmaker. Thanks for the offer.'

'You don't find us Russian men attractive, is that it?'

'I didn't say that. Some of you aren't bad. Not all of you.'

'Well, what sort of man do you go for? Tall? Short? Dark-haired? Blond?'

The longer the conversation went on, the more uncomfortable she became.

'Just good-looking is fine,' she said. 'But I go more for the personality. And the right worldview, if you know what I mean. I found before if a boyfriend didn't share my politics, then it was just total disaster. My fault, of course. That bar again, I suppose. But I am open to the idea.'

She blushed again and started looking around the control room for things to do. When she couldn't find anything, she grabbed her coat.

'There's something I forgot to check,' she said. 'So, I'll just go and do that, and I'll come back later.'

She tripped over the mat going out the door, but managed

not to fall flat on her face. As she looked back at him, he saw that she seemed to be confused about something.

For Yuri's first debriefing as a dirty lowlife informant, Timur chose the sauna at midnight, when it would be empty. Yuri felt bizarre sitting there, naked except for a towel, discussing possible foreign espionage with a similarly undressed KGB agent. Timur was annoyingly fit-looking, but for some reason he was sweating at twice the rate that Yuri was.

Top of Yuri's agenda was to get this over with as quickly as possible.

'After this, I'd like to stop, if it's all right with you,' said Yuri. 'She's no more an agent than my granny is.'

Timur shook his head. 'Come on, what have you got?'

Yuri sighed and unfurled two rolled-up pages on which he had scribbled some notes five minutes before this meeting.

'Monday she talked about how she felt guilty that she had a privileged upbringing, and when she saw that there were other families around who were not as fortunate as her.'

'What sort of privilege?' asked Timur.

'She didn't say,' said Yuri.

Timur frowned. 'You didn't ask?'

'No.'

'These are the sort of important details you are supposed to follow up on.'

Yuri felt like saying why don't you do it yourself, but he held his tongue.

'Ask her next time,' said Timur. 'Go on.'

Yuri continued. 'Wednesday, she talked about how all workers in Pyramiden should get a pay rise, and bigger, equal-sized apartments. She did actually say that.'

'See. She's at it again, stirring dissent,' said Timur.

'That's how the glorious revolution started, didn't it? To

erase inequality. We call them heroes now, not dissenters,' said Yuri. 'Don't you feel the slightest bit guilty sitting over there in your oversized apartment while the rest of us live in shoeboxes?'

'No,' said Timur. 'I earned it. What else?'

'She doesn't want to go home. She wants to stay here.'

Yuri was glad to see that Timur had the same reaction as he had.

'In Pyramiden?' said Timur. 'Why in the world would she want to do that?'

'Because she thinks it's commie nirvana, and that she's died and gone to red heaven.'

Timur looked at him as if he was pulling his leg.

'I'm serious, that's the way she is. They should make a movie reel about her, and show it in schools. Forget Lenin, kids, be more like this girl. There are worse examples to follow.'

'Anything else?' asked Timur.

'Her favourite author is Tolstoy.'

'Good choice,' said Timur. 'Mine too.'

'Her favourite poet is Pushkin.'

'I haven't read him,' said Timur. 'I don't get poetry. Have you read him?'

'Not in several decades. My dad was a fan.'

Timur nodded, though it was plain he had no interest in hearing about Yuri's father.

'More?' he said.

'No, I think that's it,' said Yuri, looking through his disorganised pages again.

'You must have more,' said Timur. 'You spend all day with her, every day of the week.'

Yuri racked his brain and remembered. 'Well, there was one thing. She hasn't had a boyfriend since 1973.'

Timur turned and stared at him. 'Why not? What's wrong with her?'

'You can't ask a girl that,' protested Yuri.

'You're not supposed to be shy about this,' insisted Timur. 'It's not so hard. Be forward or you don't get anywhere.'

'See! You're trained in all this,' said Yuri. 'You'd be much better at it than me.'

But Timur was unmoved. 'She talks to you. She trusts you.'

She did trust him, Yuri knew. He hadn't done much that could be called a betrayal. But still, that's what it was. There were no degrees to it.

'You really want more of this stuff?' Yuri asked.

'Yes,' Timur said.

'In my humble opinion she is not trying to undermine the state,' announced Yuri, in a mock-military voice.

'I already told you. It is not your job to draw the conclusions,' said Timur. 'I will do that. Your job is just to provide the requested information.'

'You can't want me to keep doing this? For how much longer?'

'Until I tell you to stop. And judging by how unproductive you have been so far, that will not be for a good while yet.'

'I'm telling you, it's a complete waste of time. She thinks the moon should be communist for heaven's sake. I don't know what you're expecting from her.'

'I have my reasons, which you don't need to know about,' said Timur.

'What?' asked Yuri, his interest aroused. 'What are your reasons? You have some information about her?'

Timur shook his head and stood up. 'You ask too many questions, Yuri, when you should be listening, just listening.'

He walked over to the door of the sauna. Then he stopped and turned.

'Get more private stuff if you can,' he said. 'Family. Background. Friends. Boyfriends, before 1973. What she means by privileged. Anything. No matter how trivial it seems to you. And if she says something of interest, follow it up with another question. And another if necessary. No lead may be too small. You don't know until you follow it. You got that?'

Yuri nodded. 'Are we done?'

'Yes, we're done,' said Timur.

To Yuri's relief, he left finally, leaving him on his own. He looked down at the pages of his report, which were squashed tightly in his hand. They were complete nonsense and barely legible. Yet, he did not fail to notice that Timur had not asked to keep them for his files.

The smell of perfumed incense hit him before he opened his apartment door. All the lights were off inside, and Anya had placed some candles around the room. She was sitting on the chair near the window, with her legs folded underneath her. She had wrapped a white sheet around herself, and apart from that she was naked. Any thoughts he had about having a serious conversation with her vanished in an instant.

'Is it someone's birthday?' he asked.

'No,' she said. 'I just decided to make your place pretty, for once. How was your day?'

He scanned the room. There was no sign of a bottle anywhere, nor an empty glass.

'It was not great, if I'm honest,' he said. 'I've had better.'

'It isn't over,' she said. 'There's still time to fix it.'

He dropped his coat on the floor and walked over to her.

He grabbed her under her arms and lifted her off the chair, leaving the sheet behind.

'What's on your mind?' he asked, as he kissed her neck.

'How about we do whatever you want,' she whispered.

Yuri smiled. 'Be careful. I might want a lot of things.'

She started to unbutton his shirt. 'Well then, we'd better get started.'

When he was in his twenties and thirties, 'a lot of things' would have been achievable. But with fifty approaching like a freight train, and far too much binge-drinking along the way, he was content with quality over quantity.

'Sorry,' he said, when it became clear that his body was not up for round two.

'You're not interested in my offer?' she asked, looking insulted.

'I am,' he protested. 'My mind is willing. But my body is saying I'm older than I think.'

'Pretend it's your last day on earth,' she said. 'And you are never going to get the opportunity to do this again.'

Yuri laughed. 'Extra pressure is not the key to this situation.'

'What is then?' she asked, sitting up in the bed.

'Youth,' he answered.

Anya threw her eyes up to the ceiling. 'You are not exactly in need of a wheelchair just yet. Let me see what I can do.'

With much gentle and not-so-gentle encouragement from her, a sequel was successfully enacted.

Yuri collapsed on to the pillow, out of breath. His heart was thumping twice as fast as usual.

'Now that's definitely my last,' he said. 'If you want more you'll have to go and find another man.'

Lying down beside him, she appeared to be only half satisfied. But she could see that he would be of no further use to her. She sighed and left his body to recover. The candles flickered around the room as a gale buffeted the windows.

'Why don't you move all your stuff in here,' he said. 'Or even better, what if I asked if we could get a room at the Crazy House? We'd have more space.'

She watched him talking without giving away what she was thinking.

'I know there's one free,' he continued, 'because I liberated this bed from it. I would just have to move it back.'

Had she not been in such a tender mood, he suspected she might have crushed his suggestion out of hand. But today she seemed intent on not hurting his feelings.

'Half my stuff is already here,' she said. 'And I spend almost every night here too.'

'That's not what I'm talking about,' he said. 'I'm talking about really living together.'

'Like a family?' she said.

'Yes,' he agreed. 'Like a proper couple. Which I believe we are now. Wouldn't you agree?'

Again, she gave nothing away. But a subtle downward movement of her eyes said more than words. They could be a proper couple in another lifetime, but not this one. It was not a hard blow. The shock would have been greater had she agreed.

'Let me think about it,' she said, lying.

'All right,' he said. 'Don't take too long. I have other offers, you know. Lots of them.'

'You don't strike me as a home bird, Yuri. When was the last time you lived with someone?' she asked.

'Twenty years ago,' he admitted. 'When I split up with my wife.'

She raised her eyebrows. 'You haven't lived with anyone else in all that time?'

He shook his head.

'And what did I do to be so honoured?' she asked.

Yuri shrugged. 'I've never been with anyone like you before. It's not been easy all of the time, I have to admit. But the best things often aren't.'

She was enjoying his compliments, he could tell, but she appeared unsure what to do with them.

'You are good to me,' she said. 'I don't deserve it.'

She started to touch him again with her hands, and to his surprise they were able to make love again. The third time turned out to be the most tender of them all.

She went to sleep before him. Her breath rhythmic and peaceful, her brow unfurrowed. Yuri had gone beyond sleepiness and he lay awake beside her.

It was hard to believe this beautiful woman had chosen designing bombs as her career choice. He wondered if she had worked on the Tsar Bomba. The largest explosion the world had ever seen. So big they had decided never to repeat the feat. Thanks to her husband, the other side would already know how they had done it. It was a stupid game, wanting to have the power to destroy the most, in order to gain respect and instil the greater fear. When the world was run by morons, like Timur, what did you expect?

Apart from the guys with military secrets, such as Anya's husband, there were others who wanted to go west. Artists, for instance. Yuri had more respect for them. Stifled in the Soviet Union, they needed to go in order to thrive. Solzhenitsyn had hardly published a line in ten years when he was bundled on to an aeroplane to Switzerland. Rostropovich had gone in '74 and became the conductor of the National Symphony in Washington. Baryshnikov, lead dancer with the Kirov, also defected in '74 in Canada. Now he was a star in the west.

Those who didn't go found their anti-communist behaviour treated like an illness. Grigory had told him that Andropov, the KGB chief, had set up a chain of special psychiatric hospitals that were full of writers, Christians and Baltic nationalists like the Lithuanians. In these hospitals, you were supposedly cared for until you saw the light. They were run by the interior ministry, not the health department, which said it all.

Perhaps Anya was like an artist. Stifled. And what she needed was to get away. Or Pyramiden could be the answer for her, as it was for him. He guessed that she had never had nights with her husband to match the one they had just had. Physicality was not everything in a relationship, but when it worked like it did with them, it had to mean something. A positive to add to the others. When the physical side did not click, it was hard to fix. In those situations, Yuri had ended the relationship quickly, even if the attraction was there.

Anya opened her eyes and saw that he was awake.

'How was your last day?' she said.

'Pretty good,' he said. 'As end-of-the-world moments go, I've no complaints. How was your last day?'

'I liked it too,' she said. 'No complaints.'

She closed her eyes again and was soon asleep.

In the morning they showered together. Then they lay for a while in the bed, wrapped in each other's arms, until it was time to go.

'Will I see you later?' he asked, as he put on his boots.

'I don't know,' she said. 'I might have to do something. I am not sure yet.'

'Oh,' he said, deciding not to pry. 'Come after then, if you like.'

'I'll see,' she said. 'No promises.'

From the ultimate in closeness to 'no promises' within the space of minutes. He stopped himself from sighing. And he resigned himself to the fact that he would probably never know what made this woman tick.

'Thank you,' she said.

'For what?'

'For not being angry with me. I know I don't behave the way you would like me to all of the time. But it's the way I am. It isn't you.'

Yuri had a horrible feeling he had said these same words himself, to other women. He hoped she had more respect for him than he had had for them. Although, he feared she didn't.

Chapter 12

Yuri stamped his feet as he smoked outside the front door of London. Light snow was falling, lit up by the street lamps. His face was getting damp as the flakes stuck to his skin. The end of his cigarette was soggy. It was ruining the enjoyment of it, so he stubbed it out on a wall.

The way Anya had behaved the previous night had been unusual. Gentle, philosophical, apologetic, concerned. None of her usual traits. He liked this Anya and wished he saw her more often. He had spent the day wondering what had brought on this sudden change in her.

She had said that she had something else to do that evening, but when she failed to appear at all he decided to go and visit her in Paris. As chief engineer, he had the key to the main entrance. He knocked on her apartment door and called her name. She didn't answer, and when he tried the door handle, it was locked.

He was going to leave and look for her elsewhere, but a feeling made him walk back and knock again. After calling her name once more, he was sure that he heard her voice inside. He decided to force the door. The flimsy lock broke on the second push. The room was in darkness but he saw her lying awkwardly on her bed. He knelt beside her. She was semi-conscious, and mumbling incoherently. She didn't smell of booze, but Yuri noticed a bottle of pills on the table. He put his hands under her back and pulled her up, trying to get a sense of how she was. Her head lolled to one side, and her eyes rolled back. After letting her down gently, he read the label on the pills. It was a name he did not recognise, and there was no description of what they were for.

He ran out into the hall and thumped on the nearest door. One of the women from the administration office answered.

'Get the doctor. Hurry,' he said.

The woman did as he asked, running down the hall in her slippers, with a coat thrown over her nightgown. Yuri went back into the room and tried to get Anya awake. He pulled her up towards him again until her head was resting on his chest.

'Let me sleep,' she murmured. 'I just want to sleep.'

Ten minutes later, although it seemed twice that, the doctor and a nurse arrived, dressed in their civilian clothes. They decided she would have to go to the hospital. Yuri helped to carry her down the stairs on a stretcher. She wasn't dressed for the cold outside so they wrapped her in blankets.

At the hospital, the nurse insisted that he wait outside in the corridor. Moments later, he heard Anya retching violently as they pumped out her stomach. It was hard to listen to. And then all was quiet. He eavesdropped at the door and heard the nurse trying to calm her. The doctor came out into the corridor, almost hitting him on the head with the door.

'She was lucky to survive,' he said. 'We managed to get a lot of it out of her system. Any later and who knows.'

'What was it she took?' Yuri asked.

'They are for depression. Did you know she was taking them?'

'No,' said Yuri. 'She never mentioned she was on medication, and I never saw her taking anything.'

'Well, she must have brought them with her from Moscow, because I didn't prescribe them. I think she is over the worst.'

'Thank you,' said Yuri. 'Can I see her?'

'Yes, you can. But you won't get much sense out of her for a while. She did it on purpose, you know. No one takes that many pills by accident.'

Yuri nodded. He did not need to be told. This had been coming for months, although he had never thought that she would actually do something as extreme as this. He thought it was just her thing to be down and then come out of it in an endless repeated cycle.

In hindsight, last night seemed to have been her way of saying goodbye. Their last night on earth.

He went inside the white-tiled room and sat beside her on a chair. She was a light shade of green but looked comfortable. The nurse had cleaned her up, and all evidence of what she had just been through was gone.

'How are you feeling?' he asked, when she opened her bloodshot eyes.

'Awful,' she said, with a half-smile. 'How did I get here?'

'My fault,' he said. 'I suppose you'd rather I had left you.'

She shook her head. 'I'm glad you didn't. Maybe you should have.'

'What were you thinking?' he asked. 'What if I hadn't come to find you?'

The nurse waved her finger at him to indicate that it was too soon for him to be interrogating her.

'Got tired of waiting,' she replied faintly. 'I'm glad you came.'

She reached out and squeezed his hand gently. Yuri heard

the door behind him, and he turned and saw Grigory standing in the corridor, looking in through the glass panel. Anya had closed her eyes again, so he got up and walked outside.

'The news has already spread,' said Grigory. 'The parents are up in arms. They won't let her teach their kids again.'

'How nice,' said Yuri. 'Did any of them ask if she was alive?'

'What do you expect?' asked Grigory. 'She's unstable. This is the end of it. She's finished at the school.'

'She'll be sent home in the spring?' Yuri asked. 'It's decided?'

Grigory paused, and looked up and down the corridor. 'No, I'll get her away sooner than that. On one condition only. If you'll help.'

Yuri was confused. It took him a moment to understand. When he did, he grabbed Grigory by the shirt and yanked him into an empty room.

'It's you! You're the one she's been waiting for? All this time, it was you.'

'Keep your voice down!' said Grigory.

If it had been anyone else, Yuri would have punched him.

'Why the hell didn't you tell her before?' he demanded. 'You've left her dangling on a hook for months.'

'Because she's a drunk, that's why!' said Grigory. 'I didn't trust her to keep her bloody mouth shut. And I was right. I bet she's already told you her whole life story, about how her partner defected and never told her. But now wants her back. I didn't get into this game to reunite Romeo and Juliet. If I'm going to stick my neck out for her, it's going to be my way. Rule number one is that she doesn't get to know that it's me. Otherwise, you can forget it.'

'Oh no. You're going straight in there and you're going to tell her.'

'Let go of my shirt,' said Grigory.

Yuri allowed him to push his hand away.

'If you want me to help her,' said Grigory, 'we do things my way, or not at all. You'll have to do most of it.'

'Me?' said Yuri, 'I'm not getting involved in a defection. Are you kidding? They shoot people for less. Besides, I don't even want her to leave.'

'Selfless to a fault, as always,' said Grigory. 'I thought you liked her.'

'I don't like her. I love her,' protested Yuri. 'You get it?'

'But not enough to give her what she wants,' said Grigory. 'Fine, if you don't want to help her, then we'll forget the whole thing. Believe me, I'd much prefer it that way.'

The nurse opened the door and looked at them.

'Everything all right in here?' she asked.

'Yes,' said Grigory. 'We were just leaving.'

The nurse left them alone again, and Grigory tried to follow her. Yuri grabbed hold of his arm.

'We're not finished.'

'Tonight we are,' said Grigory. 'Let's talk again when you are less emotional.'

Grigory walked out the door and back down the corridor, adjusting his crumpled shirt on the way. Yuri returned to Anya's bedside and sat watching her sleeping as monitors beeped around her. He was afraid to leave her alone in case she decided to finish what she had started, although in her present exhausted state she didn't look capable of very much.

And when she woke, would he tell her he had met her contact? Not yet. Not until he had figured things out with Grigory. Of all people he would never have guessed that it would be him. He supposed that was part of the job of an agent, to seem like the last person in the world who could possibly be one. For Yuri to get involved in this in any way would put at risk the life he had established for himself here. He would do it for her. But was it the best thing for her? He didn't know the answer to that question.

He had considered Grigory a friend, up till now. That man didn't exist any more. Perhaps had never existed. He guessed that in this matter, which would put them all to the test, their past friendship could not be relied upon to count for much.

He fell asleep in the chair, and woke in the early morning to find the nurse had put a blanket over him. She was now checking the monitors on the other side of the bed. Anya was still out for the count, but some of her former colour had returned to her cheeks.

'Morning,' said Yuri. 'Thanks for the blanket.'

'Good morning,' said the nurse. 'She woke up for a while in the night.'

'Oh,' said Yuri. 'Did she say anything?'

'Not much. She just lay there looking at you. You should probably go and get some proper rest. She's not going anywhere today. Why don't you come back later?'

Yuri nodded. He did need to get some proper sleep. But he also wanted time to think, alone.

'If there's any problem, can you get someone to find me?' he asked.

'There won't be any problem,' said the nurse. 'It's all under control.'

Yuri believed her. If he was ever sick, he wanted her looking after him. He decided against returning to his apartment; he knew he wouldn't be able to sleep with so much on his mind. Instead, he arranged to meet Grigory at the Blue Lagoon reservoir.

The reservoir, a man-made lake just outside town, provided all of Pyramiden's drinking water.

He arrived first, on foot. Grigory had chosen the meeting point. There were no buildings or workers stationed here. Yuri heard a noise behind him, but he didn't turn around. Below a thin layer of ice, the fresh water shimmered in the darkness, even though it was three in the afternoon.

'I like it here,' said Yuri. 'I don't want to be sent away.'

'You won't if we do this right,' said Grigory, from ten paces behind him. Yuri half turned, but Grigory did not come any closer. His eyes were scanning the terrain in all directions. Was he really checking to see if Yuri had sold him out so soon?

'How?' Yuri asked.

'I don't know yet,' replied Grigory.

'You don't have a plan!' said Yuri. 'But you've had months to organise it. Who's in charge of this?'

Grigory frowned, 'There was only me, and now there is you. Anya has not been a priority for anyone, except her husband. Apparently, he's been hounding them for this for five years, and they finally gave in.'

'Who's them?' asked Yuri.

Grigory smiled. 'The other side.'

'And are you one of them?

Grigory did not reply and his expression gave nothing away.

'How about by land?' Yuri suggested.

It was fifty miles south-west to Longyearbyen, the nearest Norwegian town, but it may as well have been a hundred. There were no roads between them, just snow and ice. The boats would return in the spring, but the arrivals and departures of Pyramiden staff were closely watched by Timur.

'The land route is risky,' said Grigory, 'but possible. So you're going to help her?'

'Somebody has to,' replied Yuri, 'and you don't exactly fill me with confidence.'

He looked back in the direction of the southern end of town where the helipad was located.

'I can fly a helicopter,' he said.

'Can you?' said Grigory, with a complete lack of excitement. 'You see the trick with this is to do it without anyone knowing that you've done it. She has to disappear as if by magic. If you make an unusual trip the same day she's gone then Timur will have your head on a chopping block before you know it. Unless, of course, you want to go with her and not come back. Why not do that, if you love her, as you say?'

The thought of going with her had occurred to Yuri, but now he dismissed it immediately.

'Anya, her husband and me, one big happy family. No thanks. What'll I say to her?'

'We could not tell her anything,' Grigory suggested. 'And wait till the last moment.'

'No,' said Yuri, shaking his head. 'I'm not doing that to her. She needs to know.'

'Fine,' said Grigory. 'Tell her the bare minimum then. But don't tell her it's me. Tell her I've made contact, and that we're putting a plan in motion. Most of all, tell her I said it would help a lot if she stayed fucking sober.'

Yuri studied Grigory for a moment. 'Why are you trusting me? How do you know I won't inform on the both of you?'

'Because you like her,' said Grigory, 'More than like.'

'But I'm not in love with you.'

Grigory smiled. 'To harm me is to harm her. Go ahead if you want.'

Yuri nodded. He was new to this game.

'You ever hear of Flight Lieutenant Belenko from the Soviet Air Force?' asked Grigory.

Yuri shook his head. 'No, why?'

'Last year he was testing one of our new planes. The MiG-25. It goes at Mach 3, three times the speed of sound. Had the Americans scared shitless. They've been dying to get their hands on one. Anyway, last September Belenko takes off from Chuguyevka airbase, and instead of the mission he was supposed to do, he flies 400 miles straight to Japan. He was going so fast nobody knew where he was. Until he crash-landed at Hakodate airport, and defected.'

'Nice story,' said Yuri. 'And your point is?'

'My point is,' said Grigory, 'that he did it all himself. And he didn't put a whole bunch of other people in danger by asking them to help him. Unlike Anya.'

'We're short on MiGs around here,' said Yuri. 'So how did you end up involved in all this?'

'Which answer are you more comfortable with?' said Grigory. 'The one where I do it for the money. Lots of it? Or the one where I believe the world we live in is wrong and that I want to do something about it? Take your pick.'

Yuri nodded, 'Money then. The wages of sin.'

As Grigory walked away, a thought occurred to Yuri. He turned and shouted after him.

'Timur is interested in you. He had Semyon informing on you.'

Grigory nodded. 'How do you know that? On second thoughts, I don't want to know. I remember those conversations. I imagine they didn't make for very exciting reading.'

'You think he suspects you?'

Grigory shook his head. 'Probably just looking for information to use against me, if he needed to. He's ambitious, that one. Be careful around him.'

'My late assistant was ambitious too,' said Yuri. 'You didn't by any chance kill Semyon, did you?'

'I thought that was an accident,' said Grigory.

'Unlikely,' said Yuri. 'So it wasn't you?'

'I don't kill people,' said Grigory. 'I'm not that sort of spy.'

Yuri lingered on his own at the lagoon for a few more minutes, giving Grigory time to get back to town first. He had never been here with Anya, even though it was the most romantic setting in Pyramiden. He resolved to bring her here when she had recovered. It seemed that they had little time left together and he was determined to make the most of it. What an idiot he was, looking forward to telling his lover that he had found a way for her to leave him.

Anya was released from the hospital after five days. Being out was not easy for her. People stared, and avoided her company, particularly the irate parents of the children she had been teaching. She was annoyed to have lost her job, insisting she was fine now. But after what had happened there was zero chance of a reinstatement any time soon.

Yuri considered not telling her anything about meeting her contact, but it was not long before she sought solace at the bottom of a glass. Hoping to avoid another self-destructive breakdown, he told her in the way that Grigory had instructed, while they were out getting some fresh air. He had been approached, the contact wished to remain anonymous, he would act as go-between.

To his surprise, her face flushed with anger.

'What are you doing? You think it helps me to give me false hope like that?'

'But it's true,' he said. 'I was contacted while you were in hospital.'

'By who?' she asked. She searched his face to see if he was lying.

'I can't say,' said Yuri, realising how ridiculous it sounded. He regretted agreeing to Grigory's condition.

'They want to keep their identity secret. They'll only talk to you through me.'

'Why? Why won't they talk to me?' she demanded. 'I have to meet them.'

'Sorry,' said Yuri, shaking his head. 'This is the only way it's going to work. If I hadn't agreed, the deal would have been off.'

'What deal?' she said. 'You made a deal about me?'

'Look, they are going to try and get you away. If I agree to help.'

She digested this information for a moment. 'And did you agree?'

'Yes.'

'You're not making all of this up?'

'No.'

When he eventually convinced her he was telling the truth, her mood changed completely to a mix of relief and elation. She bombarded him with questions.

'When am I going? And how? Why won't they speak to me in person? It's her, isn't it? That English woman. Your friend.'

He supposed it was a natural conclusion to reach. A foreigner, newly arrived in town, had spy written all over her.

'I can't answer any of your questions yet,' he said. 'But I will soon, when it's all in place.'

He could see that the arrangement was frustrating for her.

'You trust this person; I mean with me?' she asked.

Before Grigory had revealed his secret to him, he would have considered him to be one of the few people he could count on in the world, if he needed help. Now he was not so sure. Nothing had been as it seemed.

'As far as it goes, yes,' he said, 'but I make a habit of not trusting anyone too much. Life is easier that way.'

Anya frowned. 'If I'm going, I might never see you again.'

There was no 'might' about it. They would never lay eyes on each other again for the rest of their lives. Unless they were caught, and sent to the same prison.

'I know,' said Yuri, 'but this is what you want, isn't it?'

She thought for a moment before saying, 'Yes, it's what I want.'

'Perhaps we should stop seeing each other now then?' he suggested.

She shook her head. 'Not yet. I don't want to. Do you?'

He pretended to consider the question before answering.

'No,' he said. 'I want to keep seeing you.'

He knew he should probably tell her that it was a good idea. A clean break for both of them would be the best thing. And he knew it would certainly save him from a lot of pain, which he knew was coming down the track.

Anya froze when she saw a group of schoolchildren with flashlights approaching them across the playground. They stopped in front of her, and a girl stepped forward and handed her a bunch of tiny yellow flowers.

'We hope you get well soon, Miss,' she said.

Anya took the flowers and held them close to her chest.

'Thank you. That's very sweet of you.'

'When will you be coming back?' asked a boy.

Anya looked to Yuri for help.

'That's up to the doctor,' lied Yuri. 'Right now she needs lots of rest.'

The children nodded. They looked expectantly at Anya but she seemed lost for words. They turned and shuffled off.

'See,' said Yuri. 'They like you.'

Anya seemed genuinely surprised. When they eventually found out that she was a defector, they would probably send special teachers into each classroom to stop the traitor virus spreading among these impressionable young minds. Yuri could already see the look of horror on the parents' faces. Not only was she a drunk, and suicidal, but an enemy of the state too.

'I've had enough air,' said Anya.

They walked back to his apartment together. Inside, she put the flowers in a jar of water. They had obviously been cultivated by one of the parents in an apartment. Nothing grew outside at this time of year.

Yuri helped Anya undress and got into bed beside her.

Despite the fact that he was now planning their eventual separation, he was pleased their affair would continue for the time being. In the meantime, he thought, circumstances might change, which would mean she could remain with him. This was only partly selfish on his part. He considered that staying with him really was her best option; the one that would bring her happiness.

If she was really going, then the clock had already started ticking.

Chapter 13

EVER SINCE THE dramatic night at the hospital, Yuri had known this moment was coming. He was not looking forward to it, but at the same time, he did not care much about what Timur had to say on the whole business. However, he was aware that it was not a good thing to be getting so accustomed to sitting in Timur's visitor's chair. One of these days, questions and requests could easily turn into an interrogation, with greater consequences at stake.

Timur entered from the file room, sat in his chair and slammed his hands loudly on his desk.

'I asked you to watch out for her,' said the KGB man, in an angry tone. 'And now I hear she almost died. Would you call that looking after her? I don't think it qualifies, do you?'

Yuri had an overwhelming desire to tell him what he really thought of him. But that would have to wait for another day. For now, they both knew the balance of power was weighted in only one direction. It was also unfortunately true, what he was saying. Regardless of what role Timur had given him, he was supposed to be looking after her. He had failed. And he did feel guilty about it.

'I saved her, actually,' said Yuri. 'She mightn't still be with us, if it wasn't for me. What do you call that?'

'Lucky,' said Timur. 'For you, as well as her. Did she say why she did it?'

Yuri wondered if he really did suspect something. But he was pretty sure nothing had changed, and that Timur knew nothing more than that she was a teacher who drank too much. Whoever sent her here would not be pleased with how much attention she had drawn to herself since her arrival.

'No,' he replied. 'Just winter depression, I'd say, like we all get.'

'We don't all try to top ourselves,' said Timur. 'We have never had a suicide here. She didn't say anything about anything, beforehand I mean?'

'No,' said Yuri. 'I think I might have taken notice if she had. There were no signs.'

The secret service man was clearly not impressed with his powers of observation, but he didn't press the matter further.

'If you don't mind me asking, were you two having problems in your relationship?'

He did mind him asking. A lot. But an answer was unavoidable.

'No more problems than any couple,' replied Yuri. 'You know how it is.'

From the confused look on Timur's face, he apparently did not know how it was. For the first time, Yuri scanned the room looking for personal items. There was no photo of a wife or girlfriend anywhere. And since he had been in Pyramiden, Yuri had never seen him in a relationship with anyone. He doubted whether his personality was a huge attraction for the women in town. Although there was that time, a few months back, when he had spotted him at a window in Paris. That had been too late at night for an official visit. He guessed he could figure out whose room it was if he tried, but he did not care enough about the man's private life to go to the bother. They were so far from the rest of civilisation here that sometimes people hooked up with partners they would never dream of going near if they were back home.

Yuri noticed a few new brown files on Timur's desk. He wondered if the KGB man had finally gotten around to opening a fresh file on his lover. There was certainly lots to write about now.

'I want you to keep a close eye on her,' said Timur. 'And do a better job this time, will you? We don't need another unfortunate death this winter. Moscow would call that careless.'

'You never know what is going through people's minds,' said Yuri. 'But in my opinion I think she's not going to try it again. In any case, I will not let it happen. You don't need to ask me to watch her. Plus, she's talking about her future. She has things she is looking forward to.'

Timur nodded, without pretending to set too much store by Yuri's opinions.

'What has she to look forward to?' he asked, as though it would surprise him to hear she had anything positive on the horizon.

'Life without me, for one thing,' said Yuri. 'When she returns to Moscow in the spring.'

Timur smiled. And life without you meddling KGB bastards, thought Yuri, if she makes it to the west. That would be nice. He would not mind that himself.

'I will be busy, keeping an eye on her, to do the job properly,' said Yuri. 'So what about the other thing? Can I stop doing that, now?'

Timur looked momentarily thrown.

'Oh. You mean Catherine?' he said eventually, when he understood. He paused for a moment to consider the request.

'No. I want you to keep doing that too. You see her at work every day. It's not like you have to go out of your way to find her.'

Yuri felt like arguing, but he knew it was pointless; he was not going to win. The man had a bee in his bonnet about Catherine for some reason.

'It won't be for much longer,' said Timur, reading his mind. 'One more report should do it. Perhaps. We'll see. You better make it a good one.'

Yuri nodded, relieved that his brief stint as an informer was almost over. It had been a distasteful experience so far and he would be glad to see the end of it.

Another issue was also looming large in his mind. The KGB man was linking him with Anya's continued well-being, which was not such a problem. But what would Timur do if they managed to get her away? The post-escape conversation would begin as usual with the words, 'Did I not tell you to keep an eye on her?' He would have to ensure, as Grigory had said, that there was no provable connection between him and her defection. Questions would be asked, for sure. And he would be under suspicion. He was her lover after all. Everyone knew that, even the schoolchildren. He could understand how suspicion had so easily fallen on Anya after her husband's disappearance. Yet, she had the luxury of being able to argue her innocence without lying.

He had a good argument, at least, to defend himself. She had attempted suicide without his prior knowledge. It was not such a stretch from there to say he knew nothing of her plans to reunite with her husband.

The doctor insisted on doing a psychological evaluation of Anya, which was annoying, but understandable under the circumstances. Anya refused to do it unless Yuri was present with her. The doctor did not agree that this was a good idea, but he relented once he realised this was the only way he was going to get to interview her.

Yuri accompanied her to the hospital, and sat beside her on the other side of the doctor's table. Anya held his hand tightly throughout. She glared at the doctor as though he were the enemy, even though the man had saved her life only a week before. The doctor did not want Yuri there, and Yuri did not want to be there either. But Anya was setting the rules, not them.

First, he checked her heart rate and blood pressure. All was normal. His only concern was some weight loss that she could not afford, given her slender frame to begin with. The doctor advised regular meals, three times a day, every day. She was not to skip any of them.

Then he asked whether she regretted what she had done. The answer came back straight away, as though she had prepared it beforehand.

'It was a mistake,' said Anya. 'I wasn't myself. I didn't know what I was doing.'

When asked she denied ever having had suicidal thoughts before. There was something about her over-insistence on this point that made Yuri not believe her. He could see that the doctor was thinking the same thing. Yuri wondered if she had tried it after her husband had left her. This man really did have a lot to answer for.

The doctor opened the top drawer of his desk and pulled out an empty bottle that Yuri recognised. It had once contained the antidepressants with which Anya had recently tried to kill herself.

'Who prescribed these for you?' the doctor asked.

'My doctor in Moscow,' she replied. 'Can you get me more of them?'

Yuri and the doctor shared a look. Anya saw it, and she let go of Yuri's hand.

'They help me,' she said.

The doctor shook his head. 'These are very strong. We don't even keep this type. I can give you something milder, if you like?'

Yuri turned to Anya. She was never pleased when she did not get her own way. Eventually, she nodded that she was willing to accept whatever meagre offerings he was willing to give.

The doctor stood and walked to a wooden unit against the wall. He pulled out a wide, flat drawer, on which were many types of medicines. He picked up the bottle he was looking for, and returned to the table. Then he opened Anya's empty bottle and dropped a handful of tablets into it, one at a time, from the second bottle. He closed the second bottle and placed it in his top drawer.

'I've given you enough for one week,' said the doctor. 'When that's finished, come back here and I will give you another week's supply. And so on.'

Anya glared at the bottle, and then at the doctor.

'You don't trust me?' she said.

The doctor did not answer, though he seemed surprised that the question even needed to be asked. She had no credit with anyone now, and she would have to earn it back.

'This is the way we are going to do it,' he said. 'When you are back in Moscow, you can do what you like. But here, I am the physician in charge. All right?'

Anya nodded. However weak these new pills were, she wanted them. The doctor moved on to more probing questions

What had been going through her head when she had taken so many pills? Was she glad when she woke up, knowing that she had survived? Or did she feel she had failed in something she had set out to do? A failure to be rectified later?

These were not places Anya was willing to go with him. She gave yes and no answers to them all, and she added nothing more. By the end of the interview, the doctor was frustrated. He was none the wiser about her mental state, apart from that it was not good. Yuri was glad he had come, though; for him, it had been a very revealing conversation. When it was over, Anya reached across the table to retrieve her newly replenished bottle of pills. The doctor watched her taking it, and for a moment, Yuri was sure he was thinking of taking it back off her. She quickly put the bottle away in her coat pocket. She seemed relieved to have the pills in her possession.

'One a day,' he said. 'At most. So, I won't be seeing you before next Monday.'

When they walked outside into the afternoon darkness, Anya was furious.

'Who does he think he is, talking to me like I am a child. I said it was a mistake, didn't I?'

Yuri expressed sympathy, but he was with the doctor, one hundred per cent. In fact, he wished he could get him to interview her once a week. Anya pulled open the bottle containing her weekly ration of seven pills exactly. She plucked one out with her fingers and placed it on her tongue. It made Yuri nervous that she had managed to hide this habit from him for so many weeks.

'You really need them?' asked Yuri.

'Yes,' she said. 'I can live without them. But it's better with.'

'How long have you been taking them?'

Anya shrugged.

'Five years?' he asked. 'Since he left you?'

'No,' she said. 'Longer than that.'

Yuri turned to look at her.

'You were depressed before he left?' he asked. 'Why were you depressed before?'

Anya did not answer, and kept on walking.

The first Yuri heard about it was from listening to two waitresses gossiping in the canteen. One of the miners had been arrested for burglary, and was being held in the single available jail cell in Pyramiden. When he questioned the women they had no further details other than the bare facts. It was most unusual news. A winter of strange events. Yuri went looking for Grigory to find out exactly what was going on. As it turned out, the tall Lithuanian had been arrested by Timur. Yuri knew what had happened without having to hear the rest.

'Timur found him in his office. He had broken the lock on the door, and apparently he was searching the place for something,' said Grigory. 'I don't know what.'

'Semyon had informed on him to Timur,' explained Yuri. 'Him and his friends are Lithuanian nationalists. He was looking for the file.'

'How on earth do you know all of that?' asked Grigory.

'Because I told him it was there,' replied Yuri.

'And you knew this because . . .?'

'Same way I knew Semyon had informed on you. Because I took the file myself,' he admitted. 'Don't worry, I put it back. I went in with a key too. That man is more of an idiot than I thought.'

Grigory walked quickly from behind his desk and closed his office door.

'Damn it!' said Grigory. 'You are supposed to be keeping a

low profile, until we can get this job done. What were you thinking?'

'It was a couple of weeks ago. And I wanted to see if the Lithuanians had anything to do with Semyon's murder.'

'Semyon's murder? What are you, a policeman now? Everyone thinks that was an accident except you.'

'It was no accident,' said Yuri. 'Someone killed him. I know it.'

'You have some evidence to support this?'

Yuri looked away, knowing the answer was going to sound stupid.

'A feeling,' he said.

'A feeling!' said Grigory, throwing his arms in the air. 'That's just great. A feeling. What if this Lithuanian starts blabbing about you? What will we do then? You are putting this operation at risk. I already told you that I am not doing it without you. If you get arrested, then Anya stays here.'

'He won't say anything,' said Yuri. 'He's scared of me.'

'I'll bet he is,' said Grigory. 'Right now, I'm scared of you. OK, from now on, no more Mr Detective, all right. No more taking files that don't belong to you. No more giving information to people who don't need to know anything. Just keep your nose clean.'

'Agreed,' said Yuri.

Grigory poured himself a glass of whiskey and drank it in one go. Yuri declined when he offered him one too.

'And pray tell, what has your detective work uncovered about Semyon?' asked Grigory.

'Nothing,' said Yuri. 'Absolutely nothing.'

'Perhaps because there is nothing to be found. Did you ever consider that?' asked Grigory.

Yuri was beginning to come round to that way of thinking.

Surely if Semyon had been killed, the reason would have revealed itself by now. Perhaps it was just a ridiculously simple accident, after all.

At least he didn't have to worry about the Lithuanians any more. The tall one was the leader. Without him the other two were unlikely to cause any trouble for anyone. Besides, they would be keeping their heads down, hoping that Timur would not be arresting them too. The KGB man would not be releasing the tall one in the meantime. He would be the first passenger on the spring boats. Until then, he would be out of Yuri's way, under lock and key. The man would be no loss to the Lithuanian nationalist movement either, if he could not carry out a simple burglary without getting caught. And he had done for himself now. A spell in one of the interior ministry's psychiatric hospitals would be considered too lenient a penalty for this crime. A more likely sentence for the burglary of a KGB office would be a long holiday in a penal prison, if he was lucky. Yuri was not going to shed any tears for him. The man had it coming.

'From now on, I want you to look on me as your boss,' said Grigory. 'In future, if you want to do anything other than your normal work routine, I want you to clear it with me first, OK? And I mean everything.'

'OK, fine,' said Yuri. 'Whatever you say, boss.'

His life was becoming one long round of reporting to other people. To Timur about Catherine. And now to Grigory about everything else. He decided not to let the party man know what he was doing for Timur.

He was tired of playing detective too. Life would be a whole lot easier if he allowed himself to accept that no one else had been involved in Semyon's death. Right now, he had too much in his head. He needed to make his life simpler. Although, he considered it unlikely that was on the cards until Anya was out of his life.

The next day, Yuri worked with Catherine on an electricity junction box. He allowed her to take the lead on the work, because he was too distracted. The way her technical skills had come on in just a short space of time impressed him. And he no longer had to double-check anything she did.

He was juggling so many things that for the first hour he hardly said a word. But then, with his last conversation with Timur in mind, he began to ask Catherine a series of personal questions. His hope was that one last thorough report would see him released from any further informing about her. This is what Timur had implied, and he intended to hold him to it.

He quizzed her about her early boyfriends. College life. Her family circumstances. How she had become interested in communism. The various other English communists she had met. These turned out to be mostly fellow students and union organisers, none of whom seemed to live up to the high standards she expected of them. Her stories of her time in the New Left movement always ended with words of disillusionment. He expected she would feel the same about the USSR, as soon as she got to know it.

He asked her anything and everything and, as instructed, he followed the trail of her answers to see where they led. After an hour of this, he was confident he had built up a large enough store of harmless details to get Timur off his back for good. He would have done his bit for the secret service, with no real harm done. And he intended to never breathe a word about it to anyone else for as long as he lived.

Catherine had been behaving oddly all morning too, he

thought, answering his questions in short sentences followed by long pauses. She had also been giving him long searching stares. He had smiled at her when their eyes met, without being quite sure why she was looking at him in that way. He wondered if what he was doing was obvious to her. But then, he thought, it was really just idle chit-chat. The only unusual thing about it was that he had never shown so much interest in her before.

Now they were working side by side in a cramped space, and he found her staring at him again. He turned and held her gaze, expecting she was about to ask him something important. When she leaned in to kiss him on the lips it caught him completely by surprise. He stepped back, almost falling over in the snow, and she flushed with embarrassment. He had never witnessed anyone's cheeks going quite so red so quickly.

'I'm sorry,' she said. 'My mistake.'

He considered saying something, but nothing appropriate came to him quickly. And he guessed whatever he said might only make the situation worse, so he remained silent until she spoke again.

'You're still with her?' she asked. 'With Anya.'

Yuri nodded. 'Yes, I am.'

She avoided his eyes, trying to hide her disappointment. Yuri was surprised at how many signals from other people he was managing to miss or misinterpret at the moment.

'I'm sorry,' she said. 'You wanted to know so many things about me, my boyfriends, I thought . . .'

'I didn't mean to give the wrong impression,' said Yuri. 'Really. I was just being curious about you. I didn't mean to pry so much.'

He wished he was brave enough to tell her the truth. It should not be her apologising to him.

'No. No. It's not your fault,' she insisted. 'Just me being stupid. Again. I've gone and made a mess.'

'No,' said Yuri. 'Forget it. Please. It was nothing.'

Both of them looked for things to do, so they would not have to look at each other.

'I thought you two might have split up after what happened,' said Catherine. 'You know how rumours start here. People were saying this and that. By now, I should know better not to listen. It wasn't to do with your relationship that she did that thing . . . putting herself in hospital?'

'No. Did someone say that? That incident was nothing to do with me and her. Nothing at all, I hope,' said Yuri. 'No. Me and Anya, it's complicated. But she needs me now, more than ever, after what happened.'

Catherine nodded. 'I can see how she would. She is lucky to have you. What a fool I am!'

She was eager to get away, he could see, but they were stuck together until the junction box was fixed. Another hour's work, at least.

If ever there was a time when he should come clean to her about what he was doing for Timur, this was it. He took a deep breath.

'There's something I should tell you, Catherine—' he said.

'You don't need to explain,' she interrupted. 'Just me being an idiot. Not for the first time. Let's just forget it happened. Can we?'

The opportunity was lost in a moment as his courage left him. He had guessed she liked him, but not in a romantic way. She was only slightly more than half his age. He was sure he had not given any fuel to the notion that something might happen between them. As if his life could not get more complicated.

Sentences entered his head that might mend the situation, and make her feel better. He rejected all of them, and the best he could come up with was, 'I hope we can still be—'

'Of course. Of course. We are friends. Just friends. Aren't we?' she said.

'Yes,' he agreed. Although he knew that she was a better friend to him than he was to her.

'I hope this won't change anything between us,' said Catherine.

'Why would it?' said Yuri. 'I've already forgotten it, like it never happened.'

And that was that. They carried on working in silence, and spoke no more about it.

Secrets were a burden. Yuri did not want to learn any new ones. He was already overloaded. The more secrets he came across, the more he became convinced that this was how Semyon had met his end. Informers traded in secrets after all. It was their currency, which they exchanged for money or favour. There was one clear option that could have led to the Latvian's early death, as far as he could see. A person Semyon was informing on found out, and was not happy. Unhappy enough to murder. He wondered whether Semyon had known that he was in danger.

Yuri woke to a morning sky that was the same deep black it had been the previous night. He longed for the time when he could open his curtains and see the dawn light over the fjord. In this midwinter period, he did not close his curtains at night. There was no light to keep out. Today, he did not bother drying the river of condensation on his windows. It formed a pool on the windowsill and dripped slowly on to the floor.

He sat up on the edge of the bed and rubbed the sleep

from his eyes. Then a folded piece of paper in front of the door caught his eye. It was tempting just to ignore it. What people could not say to your face was better left unheard. But he walked over and picked it up. The message was short and to the point. And it sent a shiver up the back of his neck.

Whaling House, 8pm tonight.

He could not go. It was his choice. Whoever had written this had some connection to Semyon. If he went there, he could easily end up having an Arctic funeral too. It would be stupid to even consider it, but he knew he would.

The moon was bright in the sky as he drove out there on a snowmobile. He stopped several hundred yards away on a ridge, and watched the whaling house for signs of life. There were no lights, nor smoke from the chimney. And no vehicles outside. He checked his watch. He was on time. The minute hand had just passed the hour.

He decided to leave the snowmobile where it was, and to approach the hut on foot. He soon regretted his decision as his legs sank deep into fresh snow. A thought occurred to him, that perhaps he should have told someone where he was going in case he did not come back. Inside his coat, he had a hunting knife, which he hoped not to have reason to use.

The wood hut was ten yards away. Last chance to turn around, he thought. He felt the knife through his coat, and then he pushed open the door. The first thing he noticed was that the pile of snow in the middle of the floor was gone. Someone had obviously had the stove going in here, and recently. The second thing he noticed was a sharp pain on the back of his neck, and then the floor approached much faster than he would have liked.

He woke sitting in a chair to find two Lithuanians looking at him. The short one and the one who never said much. The tall one was, as far as he knew, still in Timur's jail cell. He would not be getting out again until it was time to put him on a ship to a jail back home. The short Lithuanian was twirling something in his hand. The hunting knife Yuri had brought in his jacket.

'Sorry we had to hit you, Yuri,' said the short one. 'Can't be too careful. Our friend Jonas is in jail, you probably heard.'

'Yes, I did,' he said, rubbing the back of his neck. 'Sounds to me like it was his own fault.'

'We think you informed on him,' said the silent one.

Yuri sighed. 'Is that why you brought me here? I didn't know he was going to go breaking in to the KGB office. If I had known, I would have told him not to do it. Besides, he didn't think it through, it was a waste of time.'

The two men looked at each other, neither understanding what he was talking about.

'Why do you say that?' asked the short one.

Yuri stood up, and the two men both took a step back.

'Easy,' said Yuri. 'Just keeping warm. How long was I out?'

'Five minutes,' said the silent one. 'That's all.'

'Go on,' said the short one, getting impatient. 'Why was he wasting his time?'

'Because,' said Yuri. 'Timur has already read the file about you guys. He obviously decided not to do anything about it, for whatever reason. What was the advantage to stealing the file now?'

The short one shook his head. 'Jonas said, now that Semyon is dead, without the file, there would be no evidence of what he had written.'

Yuri accepted that there was some truth to this, although

not much. If it came down to one man's word against another's, Timur would be believed ahead of anything the tall Lithuanian might say.

'It doesn't matter now,' said Yuri. 'The milk is spilt.'

He sat down on the chair again, still feeling dizzy after the blow.

'Funny place to have a meeting, fellas. Why here?'

'This is our unofficial clubhouse,' said the short one. 'When we want to get away from Russians for a while.'

Yuri nodded. 'I like what you've done with the place. You ever bring Semyon here?'

'Sometimes he was here,' said the short one. 'We thought he was one of us. Why?'

Yuri shrugged.

'Is that the only reason you brought me out here? To see if I had informed on your friend, Jonas?'

The men looked at each other nervously.

'No,' said the short one. 'Jonas said you would have an excuse for everything we asked you. He said no matter what you said, we should mess you up anyway.'

The silent one took out a short club from his pocket. The short one seemed intent on using the knife that Yuri had helpfully provided.

'Now listen boys,' said Yuri, as he got up and brandished the chair lion-tamer style. 'What's the point in doing that? You'll only end up in the same cell as Jonas. Is that what you want?'

The silent one moved forward slowly. Yuri did not fancy his chances of taking the two men at the same time. He made a quick movement towards the short one, and smashed the chair over his head. The man collapsed to the ground, groaning. Yuri still had a broken leg from the chair in his hand.

'You want some too?' said Yuri.

'You shouldn't have done that,' said the silent one, who was now talking too much.

He picked up the knife off the ground and held it in one hand, with the club in the other. Yuri backed away while the man advanced towards him, one step at a time. The short one was recovering now, and was starting to stand. Yuri began to have a sinking feeling. It appeared that Jonas was going to get his way.

The silent one lunged at him with the knife. Yuri swung the chair leg against his arm, which was enough to make him miss his target. The two of them grappled with each other, neither allowing the other to strike a blow. Yuri headbutted the man's nose and heard it crack. Behind them, he saw that the short one had regained his senses enough to rejoin the fight. He was almost on top of them when the door opened. The three of them turned to see Grigory standing there, with a rifle in his hands.

'What's going on here?' said Grigory.

Yuri caught his breath as the silent one put his weapons away. The short one had a bloody diagonal gash across his forehead, and the silent one's nose was gushing like a tap.

'Chess club,' said Yuri. 'Sorry we didn't invite you.'

The two Lithuanians did not say a word as they prepared to leave.

'I hope that business is cleared up now,' said Yuri. 'And we don't need to have another meeting about it. What do you say, fellas?'

The short one looked at him and nodded. Grigory gave them both a cold look as they stepped past him on their way out the door.

Yuri bent over with his hands on his knees and got his breath back.

'Not as young as I used to be,' he said. 'How come you're here?'

Grigory put the rifle over his shoulder.

'I saw you leaving town,' he said.

'Spying on me?' asked Yuri.

'Someone needs to, obviously,' said Grigory. 'Do I need to take you to the hospital?'

'I'll have a pain in my neck tomorrow, that's all.'

Grigory shook his head. 'You want me to do something about that pair?'

'No,' said Yuri. 'Baltic stuff. It's done now. I hope. You know how to use that rifle?'

'A little,' said Grigory. 'But it's not loaded. I could have hit them with it.'

Chapter 14

WHENEVER THEY COULD find inconspicuous time together, Yuri and Grigory met at the Blue Lagoon and went through the options for getting Anya as far as Longyearbyen. The journey could be made by snowmobile, but she could not travel alone, so someone would have to go with her and get back without being missed. This presented a major difficulty since in the midwinter conditions of ice, snow and permanent night, it could take two days to get there and two days to get back.

'We'll have to wait until the sun returns,' said Grigory. 'Going now, with just headlights all the way, would not be a good idea. Suicide more like. I presume you don't want to die just yet?'

There was an unspoken assumption that the someone who would accompany Anya would be Yuri, since Grigory had already made it clear he was not going to stick his neck out too far for her.

Apart from the light problem, if the weather got bad they could be in bigger trouble.

'Are you sure she wants to risk her life for this? It's no joke out there. Nobody makes that kind of a trip at this time of year unless they have no choice,' said Grigory.

'I'll talk to her,' said Yuri. 'Make sure she knows what she's getting in to.'

Then there was the helicopter, which Yuri was more than capable of flying. The problem with this, as Grigory pointed out, was that it could not be taken without people noticing. For a start half the town would hear the engine warming up, which would be essential for de-icing before take-off.

The third possibility was to wait until the spring and find a boat that would take her.

'It's too long a wait,' said Yuri. 'I think she might crack up before then.'

Snowmobile seemed the least bad option, and they began to think of ways that Grigory could cover for Yuri's absence. Catherine would know he was not around, since he spent time with her every day, so she would have to be dealt with in some way. Grigory laughed when Yuri told him Anya was convinced that Catherine was the secret contact.

'Good,' he said, 'maybe you could encourage that?'

'I'm not sure I need to do anything,' replied Yuri. 'But if we get caught I don't want her pointing the finger and calling Catherine a master spy. What would happen to her if they did suspect her? She'd be OK, wouldn't she?'

Grigory threw a stone across the thin frozen layer on top of the lake. It bounced once, then slid another twenty feet before coming to a stop.

'Are you asking if the fact that she's a foreigner would protect her?' said Grigory. 'I think if they suspected she was really an agent, nothing would keep her safe. In this game, no one behaves by gentleman's rules.'

'And Anya?' said Yuri. 'What about her? She is not selling secrets, or spying on anyone. She is just a wife who wants to be with her husband.'

Grigory paused and gave him an odd look. 'She is no ordinary wife. She worked on a restricted programme. Love is not a valid excuse for defecting with a head full of secrets.'

'I'm not so sure it is love,' said Yuri.

'Is that not what all of this is about?' asked Grigory. 'Why is she doing it then?'

'I am not a mind-reader but I think she is trying to recapture something she lost, to get her life back like it was before. But that old life is gone, and there is no way to get it back. Not now.'

'You've told her this?' asked Grigory.

'Not in so many words, but yes, I have tried,' he replied.

'Let me guess, she doesn't believe you.'

'No. She's determined to follow it through. She thinks I'm biased because I don't want her to go.'

'Is that true? You still don't want her to go?'

'Isn't that obvious?' asked Yuri. 'We are great together. And her husband is a liar and an idiot.'

'Oh,' said Grigory. 'I thought this might be another version of your "put them on a boat and wave goodbye" routines, just a bit more complicated.'

'Just a bit.'

Grigory looked confused. 'So why are you doing it then, if it's not what you want?'

Yuri shrugged. 'It's not for me to choose. It's what she wants. She wants to be with him more than she wants to be with me.'

Grigory stopped talking for a while, and stared at the frozen water. A large air bubble erupted under the surface of the ice as drinking water for the town was extracted from a pipe deep underneath the surface.

'I might have another idea on how to get her there to Longyearbyen,' said Grigory 'Leave it with me for a while.'

'Something you'd like to share?' asked Yuri.

'No,' said Grigory. 'Not yet. But it might just work out for all of us. Right now, I don't like the other options. They are too risky. For you especially.'

He turned and walked away, leaving Yuri wondering what this sudden brainwave was all about.

'Why is she a communist?' asked Timur.

Yuri was sitting in the sauna again with the KGB man, despite his best efforts to have their meeting moved to a location that required clothes. Being half naked with Timur was not an experience he looked forward to. But he hoped that this would be their last time. He had even gone to the trouble of preparing thorough notes in order to seal the deal.

'She believes in communism as the fairest system for people to live under,' he began. 'One in which everyone is valued equally, and no one gets left behind. She believes the world would be a better place if the communist system spread everywhere, including England.'

Timur raised his eyebrows.

'That's what she believes,' said Yuri. 'Unless it's a brilliant act, which I don't think it is.'

Timur nodded, and added as an afterthought, 'Of course, it's true.'

'Of course,' agreed Yuri.

For the likes of Timur, the Soviet system was indeed perfect. Not for any of the positive reasons that Catherine had outlined. Not for fairness, or equality, or any of those noble ideals. Instead, the system gave men like him power over others, power to enrich themselves, power to do what they wanted. All with impunity, because the party protected its own. One of them could not be condemned for corruption without endangering the whole house of cards. So they closed ranks around each other at the first sign of trouble. And it was not unusual for the accuser to be the one who was punished.

'Boyfriends?' asked Timur. 'Before 1973. Who were they?'

'I did ask about them,' said Yuri. 'But there really doesn't seem to have been much action there. She said that boys in school and college found her a bit odd. That was her word.'

'Odd?' asked Timur.

'I think she means she was a bit of a misfit,' said Yuri. 'Which she is, but in a good way. I think she is quite inexperienced when it comes to romance.'

Two large miners walked in the door, naked, with towels draped over their shoulders. Timur scowled at them and they stopped in their tracks.

'We're having a meeting here,' said Timur. 'You'll have to come back later.'

The miners looked from Timur to Yuri. They were not about to argue with the KGB man, but they reserved most of their displeasure for him. Great, thought Yuri, now they will think I'm an informer. It was true. He was. But with any luck he was about to be retired from that low profession. However, if a rumour was started about him, in this little town it would be hard to shake off, no matter what the truth was. This was another reason why he had wanted this meeting to happen in a less public place.

'So no boyfriends at all?' asked Timur.

'None really,' replied Yuri. 'Just a few brief encounters. If she met someone she liked, which she seems to have seldom done, they usually did not return her interest for very long. And for her, there was always something missing.'

'She's choosy then?' asked Timur.

'Oh yes. I should think so,' said Yuri. 'That's probably part of the problem. She also mentioned that some men had found her politics to be off-putting.'

Timur nodded. Yuri had studied all of his reactions. It was hard to know what the man wanted to hear. If he had known he would have tailored his report to satisfy him. As it was, he was throwing information at Timur, hoping that he would somehow cover what was required of him. All of it seemed to be useless gossip. The subject of her past relationships seemed to interest him the most, but there was precious little material on this topic to go on.

Yuri could imagine Catherine's male contemporaries finding her off-putting. She did come across as strange, at least until you got to know her.

'And when this space study of hers is finished in the spring,' said Timur, 'what will she do then?'

'It's actually a bit of a fraud' said Yuri. 'She isn't really interested in how we might live in space. She only thought it up as a way to get here.'

'She lied to us?' said Timur. 'We gave her permission to come here on the basis of her thesis work.'

'Well. Yes,' said Yuri. 'But she lied in the best possible way. She wanted to come here. She has no more interest in space than you or I do.'

Timur considered this for a moment, before smiling. 'That was clever.'

'She's very resourceful,' agreed Yuri. 'I think she might take over my job some day. She is certainly capable enough. She keeps me on my toes.'

Yuri looked away as he noticed beads of sweat trickling down Timur's hairless chest. Almost there, he kept telling himself, and you'll never have to do this again. He looked at his handwritten pages, searching for anything he had forgotten.

Timur watched him and waited, but he could not find anything other than what he had mentioned already.

'I think that's all,' said Yuri. 'I went down every avenue, like you said, and followed each one as far as it went.'

The secret service man did not look satisfied, but he said nothing.

'You want my opinion?' asked Yuri.

Judging by his expression, Timur definitely did not care to hear what Yuri had to say for himself. But he replied, 'Go on.'

'Catherine is a good person. She is no more an enemy of the state than I am. If you would just talk to her yourself, I am sure you would come to the same conclusion.'

To his surprise, Timur seemed to be taking on board what he had said.

'I might just do that,' he replied. 'I don't think it can do any harm. Sometimes it is good, at a certain point, to gauge these things for oneself. There's only so much you can get from reports, after all.'

Job done, thought Yuri. He folded up his notes until they fit in the palm of his hand.

'I hope this was useful,' he said. 'Better than the last time?'

'It wasn't bad,' said Timur, with a shrug. 'You are improving.'

'So, I can stop, as we agreed?' asked Yuri.

'We didn't agree anything.'

'But you said if—'

'No, I didn't, I said maybe. You can continue, as normal, for the time being. After that, we'll see.'

Yuri felt like stuffing his notes down Timur's throat and holding his mouth shut.

'What are you waiting for?' asked Yuri. 'There isn't any more. She's clean.'

'It takes time to make a thorough evaluation of any individual,'

said Timur. 'I cannot say when I will have enough information. I'll let you know when you can stop.'

Yuri calmed himself, and shrugged. 'Fine. Whatever you
think.'

The door opened again, and this time four miners entered,
chatting to each other in what sounded like Chechen. Timur
didn't object to them coming in. Yuri took that as the sign
that the meeting was over. He took his pages, and held on to
his towel as he stood up. Two of the miners took Yuri's place
on the wooden bench, and the other two sat on either side
of Timur. Unlike the earlier two miners, these men obviously
did not know who they were sitting next to. If they had they
would not be crowding him like that. Yuri made a quick exit
before Timur had time to follow him.

He dressed without showering, and walked straight out of
the building. He was not happy about what appeared to be
his open-ended engagement as an informer. No matter that
Timur wanted it to continue; there would be no more reports
from him, he decided. If Timur pulled his threat again, about
replacing him, he thought he could ask for Grigory's support.
Then the two of them could fight it out together.

At his apartment, to his disappointment, he found that Anya
was not there. He was about to go looking for her when there
was a knock on the door. He smiled, pleased that she had
sought him out first. But when he opened the door he found
Grigory standing in the hallway. Grigory grinned at the oversized double bed squashed into the tiny apartment, but he said
nothing about it.

'Come with me,' said Grigory. 'That thing I mentioned is
coming together.'

Yuri just wanted to rest and recuperate. Timur had drained
the life out of him. But he put on his coat and followed the

party man down the stairs. It had been two days since their last meeting at the Blue Lagoon, and they had not spoken since.

'Where are we going?' he asked.

'You'll see,' said Grigory. 'Your lady friend not around tonight?'

'No,' said Yuri. 'I'm not sure where she is.'

When they stepped outside Yuri expected Grigory to turn right and head for his own apartment building, or to his office, which lay beyond that in the administration building. However, instead, Grigory went behind the London block and walked across the snow-covered school playground.

'Would you like to tell me where we are off to, and why?' asked Yuri.

'No, I wouldn't,' said Grigory. 'Be patient.'

Soon they reached the greenhouses, which served as the all-year-round kitchen garden for the canteen. Grigory opened the door and went in. Yuri followed. The inside of the green-house was in semi-darkness, lit only by stray amber light from the street lamps outside. Yuri reached for a light switch.

'Don't,' said Grigory. 'Leave it off.'

Yuri was about to question this when he saw a shape approaching them through the shadows from the other end of the greenhouse. The bulky figure made him nervous, but he could see that Grigory was calm. A bearded, rugged man stepped into the light in front of them. He was not a resident of Pyramiden and Yuri had never seen him before in his life. A Norwegian by the look of him. Middle-aged, but fit, and more at home outside than in.

'Yuri, this is Bjorn,' said Grigory. 'I asked him to come and see us.'

'Who is he?' asked Yuri. 'And how did he get here?'

'Bjorn is an old friend,' said Grigory. 'He has proved useful to me before.'

Bjorn nodded his agreement.

'And he got here by helicopter,' continued Grigory. 'He's a trapper, but he flies too. Not many of them left nowadays.'

'I didn't hear a helicopter!' said Yuri.

Bjorn laughed. 'I landed outside of town. Far enough away so no one would hear. And I hiked the last part of the way. Grigory said I should not be seen by anyone.'

Yuri turned to Grigory for an explanation.

'Bjorn here is going to deliver our package to Longyearbyen.'

Yuri pulled Grigory to one side. 'I can't send her off with someone I don't know, just like that. Who the hell is he?'

'He is our guarantee that this is not going to rebound on us. He takes her, and as soon as she's gone, the two of us will make ourselves as conspicuous as possible around town. Then after a day, you can be the one to raise the alarm. Your beloved has gone missing, and you have no idea what's happened to her. We can even organise a search party.'

'But who is he? asked Yuri. 'He works for them?'

'No,' said Grigory. 'He is exactly what I said, a trapper. He works for himself. He spends most of the year out in the wilds. Nobody knows these islands better than he does.'

'I don't know about this,' said Yuri. 'I can't just hand her over to anyone.'

While they spoke, Bjorn busied himself looking at the plants that were growing in the greenhouse beds. He pulled a carrot off a bunch beneath the soil, brushed it clean and started eating it. He seemed to have no interest in what they were saying about him.

'He can be trusted. You can take my word for that. This is not the first time I have employed him for this kind of work.'

'What exactly has he done for you before?' demanded Yuri.

'The same. Delivering packages.'

'People?'

'No,' said Grigory. 'Not people. But it isn't any different. One package is the same as another.'

Yuri did not like the way this conversation was going, nor the abrupt manner in which this new plan had been dumped on him. He turned to leave but Grigory grabbed his arm.

'He is your ticket to safety. I thought you would be glad.'

Yuri turned to look at the Norwegian.

'He is a stranger,' said Yuri. 'How can I give Anya to him? She trusts me.'

'Out there, I would trust him with my own life,' said Grigory. 'I will vouch for him.'

Yuri calmed, and Grigory let go of his arm. The trapper sensed they had finished their private chat and walked over to them.

'Is she ready?' he said. 'I will take her now.'

Yuri held up his hands. 'Hold on. She is not going anywhere tonight. I thought the plan was to wait until the sun came back.'

The Norwegian shook his head. 'I do not need the sun to find my way. And right now, how many people know I will take her?'

'Just us three,' said Grigory.

'That's good,' said the Norwegian. 'But the longer we wait, the more chance others will find out. We should go now. That's what I recommend. If not now, then soon.'

Yuri shook his head. The man did exude confidence, he had to admit. Perhaps he could trust him to get her there safely. But he was not ready to let her go.

'I need a week to prepare her,' he lied. 'Minimum.'

The Norwegian was not happy. He looked to Grigory for help, but the party man remained silent. Yuri felt Grigory studying his expression, and he wondered if he knew what was going on inside his head. He suspected he did, as Grigory started nodding his head, accepting the situation.

'Can you come back in a week?' asked Grigory. 'It seems we need this extra time.'

'To wait means more danger, for you and for me,' said the Norwegian. 'Why would you do that?'

'We have no reason to believe we will be discovered,' said Grigory. 'We are prepared to take the risk of a few more days. Are you?'

The Norwegian rubbed his beard, thinking this through.

'For more danger, I will need more money,' he said.

'Yes, yes, whatever,' said Grigory, dismissing all talk of cash with a wave of his hand.

'Then I will meet you, outside of town, this day next week, at six in the evening, OK?'

'You know the weather station, north of Pyramiden?' asked Yuri. 'We could meet you there.'

'I know it,' said the Norwegian. 'I will be there. Make sure the woman is too, and on time. I will not wait long on the ground.'

He offered his hand to Yuri, and they shook on their agreement. Then he nodded once at Grigory and left.

Yuri did not speak for several minutes afterwards. He was still annoyed that Grigory had made arrangements like this in the first place without consulting him. Most of all, he was annoyed that his new plan was cutting short his last few weeks with Anya.

'He's right, you know,' said Grigory. 'Sooner would be better.'

Yuri nodded, but he didn't care.

'Does she really need a week to prepare, or is that for you?' asked Grigory.

'For me,' he admitted. 'I expect she would probably have gone now if I had asked her.'

Grigory did not look surprised. He put his hand on Yuri's shoulder. 'Enjoy your last week. Then deliver her to Bjorn.'

When Yuri failed to show any enthusiasm, Grigory added, 'Don't forget the last part.'

To Yuri's surprise, Anya seemed more nervous than thrilled when he told her she would be leaving in a week's time. This was the news she had been waiting to hear since she arrived in Pyramiden. He was glad that she was not jumping up and down with delight, but he had expected a little more gratitude.

'Don't you want to go?' he asked.

'I do,' she said. 'Of course I do. Just, now, it seems very sudden. I spent so many months thinking it wasn't going to happen at all. It's hard to get my head around that it's actually real.'

She was pleased to hear that the journey would be made by helicopter, and she would not have to endure the hardship of an arduous trip on land through the snow and ice. This part of Grigory's plan was a relief to Yuri too. Regardless of Anya's hardiness when it came to alcohol, he thought she was far too delicate for the real Arctic that existed beyond the edge of town.

She wanted to know about the person who was taking her, and he lied, saying the Norwegian was someone he knew to be trustworthy.

'Is he here now?' she asked.

'No,' he replied. 'But I have met him, and discussed everything. He will return here in seven days' time.'

'You mean he was here, in Pyramiden?' she asked.

'Yes,' Yuri admitted.

'When?'

'Yesterday,' he said. 'He's gone. You will meet him yourself soon enough.'

'Will you be making the trip with me?' she asked.

'I'm afraid not,' he said. 'I will take you to the rendezvous, but then you will be on your own. Is that all right?'

She nodded her head, but he could see she was nervous about the idea.

'So, it seems we have only one week left together,' said Yuri. 'How would you like to spend it?'

'With you,' she said, far too slowly, as though she'd just realised it was the answer he probably wanted to hear.

'You know you can back out of this at any time, if you want,' he said. 'It's your choice.'

'I know,' she said. 'And I appreciate everything you are doing for me.'

He waited for more but she sank deep into her own private thoughts.

'How about one drink to celebrate, or drown your sorrows?' he asked. 'We could go out if you like?'

She smiled briefly before her frown returned.

'Would you mind if we skipped it tonight?' she said. 'I think I need to think things over, alone, if that's all right.'

In his mind, he crossed off one of their last nights together. Now there were only six.

'Sure,' said Yuri. 'Whatever you want. I'm here if you need me.'

She hugged him, and left without another word. He waited a moment and then looked out the window down into the square. She walked over to Paris, across the snow. Then she stopped before the doorway as though she had forgotten something. She looked back towards his first-floor apartment. He was standing away from the window, and the only light on was in the bathroom, so he was not sure if she could see him. After a moment, she turned and walked along the walkway in the direction of the port. He did not know where she was going. Perhaps she needed a drink after all, and was headed to the glass bar without him. After another thirty seconds she disappeared out of view.

Chapter 15

I T TOOK QUITE a lot of persuasion but Anya finally agreed
to accompany him to the variety show taking place in the
Cultural Palace on Saturday night. This was an annual midwinter
event. An attempt to raise everyone's spirits, halfway between
when they'd last seen the sun and when they were due to see
it again. For weeks in advance, many of the residents took their
minds off their troubles by preparing for their part in the show.
Costumes were made, sets were designed, jokes were written
and songs rehearsed. Had Anya not been relieved of her teaching
duties, she would no doubt have spent part of every day preparing
her pupils for their party piece in the opening act.

If they did not go, they would have spent yet another evening
in his apartment, hardly talking, and having sex. The latter was
easily the most successful part of their relationship. But even
Yuri had begun to find the same routine becoming a chore,
regardless of the fact that it was all about to end soon. He
knew why Anya had been initially reluctant to go. Attendance
would require sobriety until at least the first interval. Not so
easy for a woman who was habitually well on by eight o'clock.

'Look on it as a date,' he said. 'I don't think we've ever had
one of those. Not a proper one. Come on, you'll enjoy it.'

'Do I have to dress up?' she asked, with a sigh.

'Arctic dress-up, that's all,' he said. 'Nothing special. It's not like the opera back home.'

'You went to the opera?' she said, with an annoying look of surprise on her face.

He may have been a maintenance engineer, but he liked to think he was not completely uncultured.

'No,' he admitted. 'But I've seen people going in their finery. And I fixed the lights once, in a theatre, when the performers were practising.'

She nodded as though this was the answer she expected.

'I used to go to the theatre all the time,' she said, with a glint in her eye. 'I did acting classes when I was young. Hard to believe now. Look at me.'

'No. I believe it,' said Yuri. 'I bet you are good at pretending to be somebody else. You have an actress's face. Good for lying.'

She threw a book at him, and laughed freely in a way he had not seen in weeks.

'I played the lead in Chekhov's *Three Sisters* in my final year.'

'You remember it?' he said. 'I'd like to hear some.'

'No,' she said. 'You'll only laugh at me.'

'I promise, I won't,' he insisted.

She stood in the middle of the floor, in her bare feet. The oversized bed allowed her a limited stage to perform on, of six feet by six. She paused for a moment, prepared herself, and then recited an impassioned monologue by heart. When it was over, Yuri applauded and she tumbled on to the bed into his outstretched arms.

'Bravo,' he said, as he began to undress her. 'I've never made love to a famous actress before.'

On Saturday evening, Yuri put on his best clothes. A clean, ironed blue shirt, buried under his winter layers. He also shaved and polished his black work boots. He did not possess normal shoes any more. There was no point. The snow would climb over the edges and drown his feet in seconds.

He called at Anya's door in Paris, and had to wait while she made some finishing touches in the bathroom. Yuri checked his watch. The show was due to start in ten minutes' time.

'Hurry up,' he called. 'Or you'll miss the schoolkids. You want to see them, don't you? They're usually the best part.'

The bathroom door opened a few seconds later and Anya stepped out.

'Wow. Look at you,' said Yuri. 'That's a sight you don't see every day on Svalbard.'

She was wearing a figure-hugging, knee-length black dress with broad-heeled black boots.

'Do you think these will be OK outside?' she said, raising one foot in the air.

'Yes,' said Yuri. 'They look ready to take on any weather. And the dress is stunning. Why did you bring that here?'

'I didn't expect to get to wear it,' she said. 'It's the only nice thing I have left. I like to look at it in my wardrobe. If anything happens to me next week on my trip, I'd like you to bury me in it.'

He stared at her stony expression until she broke into a smile.

'That's not funny,' said Yuri. 'Don't say things like that. Nothing is going to happen.'

'I know,' she said. 'I trust you to look after me.'

She reached up and touched the side of his face with her fingers.

'What did your husband wear when you went out?' he asked.

'How do you mean?'

'White shirt, black tie?'

Anya shrugged. 'Something like that, I suppose.'

'Don't you remember? Come on, let's go,' he said. 'We better not be late.'

They made their way, arm in arm, along the wooden walkway towards the Cultural Palace. On both sides of the square, most of the town was doing the same thing. As they entered the foyer, some people turned and stared at Anya. Ever since her suicide attempt, she had been keeping a low profile in order to avoid these looks.

'They won't let me forget,' she whispered. 'Will they?'

'They are not staring because of that,' said Yuri. 'The women are staring because they are jealous. You look like a million rubles. Look at them, they are all like Arctic babushkas. And the men are staring because they are jealous of me.'

Anya smiled, even though she knew he was making half of it up to make her feel better.

The theatre was packed with giddy residents as they entered. And the air was filled with the din of conversation. A row at the front had white pages with the word 'reserved' written on them. Yuri led the way up the aisle, and found two seats together at the back of the auditorium. Anya made herself comfortable as he began to pull off some of his outer layers. With his jumper over his head, he heard her say: 'Oh look, your dolly bird has found a mate.'

Yuri pulled his jumper off and followed Anya's eyeline to the front of the stage. Timur was pulling up two of the reserved signs from the front row. And standing beside him was his date for the evening, Catherine.

Yuri stared in disbelief. Timur had a smug grin on his face as he ushered Catherine to her seat. And what was worse, she seemed to be flattered by his attentions.

'I didn't know they were together.' said Anya. 'Why didn't you tell me?'

'I didn't know either,' said Yuri, through gritted teeth.

'Everything all right?' she asked.

'Yes, yes. Fine,' he replied, even though it was far from it.

All of Timur's interest in Catherine's private life suddenly became clear. What was worse was that he had played along with the whole sordid business.

His temper subsided when the lights went out and he did not have to look at the red-headed bastard sitting beside Catherine any longer. Anya held his hand as the show began. As always, the kids' song and dance number was the early hit. The crowd, many of them parents of the self-same progeny, applauded and cheered. Yuri turned to Anya, and could see that she was proud of her former charges.

After an hour, the first act ended and the lights came back up. An announcer, one of the waitresses from the canteen, said there would be a fifteen-minute break before the show resumed. Yuri and Anya followed the crowd back to the foyer where wine and soft drinks were being served.

'Drink?' he asked.

'Yes, a red wine, please' said Anya.

Yuri was already walking away before she had finished her sentence. Straight ahead of him, standing at the bar, was Timur. Yuri felt like hitting him, but he stopped short and kept his hands by his sides.

'What are you doing?' Yuri demanded.

Timur turned and gave him a sideways glance before turning away again.

'If you've something to say, Yuri, now is not the time or place.'

Timur looked behind them to where Anya was standing on her own on the other side of the room.

'Look,' he said. 'I do believe you are neglecting your girl-friend. Run along now, there's a good boy.'

'Not until you tell me what you are up to with her.'

Yuri could see that Anya was watching their exchange and getting uncomfortable.

'You are forgetting your station in life, Yuri,' said Timur. 'Myself and Catherine are having a simple evening together at the theatre. So if you don't mind, I am going to go back to her now. And I suggest you do the same.'

Timur walked away carrying two drinks. From where he was standing, Yuri could not see Catherine through the crowd. He wondered if she was deliberately avoiding him. He collected two glasses of wine and made his way back to Anya.

'What was all that about?' she asked. 'You two looked like you were fighting about something. Jealous?'

Yuri smiled. 'No, I assure you. It's not that. It's something between me and him.'

'You want to go?' she asked.

'No,' he said. 'This could be our last night out together. We're staying to the bitter end.'

On the way back in, Yuri spotted Grigory looking around the crowd and noticing Timur and Catherine together. He did not appear too pleased either. When he passed close to Yuri, he said; 'Interesting evening, isn't it? A lot going on. You'll have to explain it all to me tomorrow.'

While the second act unfolded, Yuri watched the silhouettes of Catherine and Timur instead of the stage. He did not believe the young English woman was anything other than what she appeared to be, as Grigory had said. But the sight of her laughing with the KGB man made him think of the missing file from Semyon's list. Eagle had three dates on its page, and the first one was before Catherine arrived in Pyramiden. So it definitely did not refer to her, unless that date referenced some long-distance communication. It was tempting to stand up in front of everyone now, and demand to know which one of them was Eagle. The most guilty face would put an end to the mystery. Perhaps Eagle was Semyon's murderer. He had ruled out most of the others. But, as yet, he had no idea how to find out who Eagle was.

In the middle of the night, Yuri left Anya sleeping in his bed. He went out into the corridor and pulled the door gently closed behind him. Outside the front door he put on his coat and walked across the square to Paris. Using his own key, he went in the main door. He walked up one flight of stairs and followed the numbers on the doors until he reached Catherine's apartment. Standing close to the door, he listened for a while, but there was no sound from inside. He looked through the keyhole but there was nothing to see. She could be asleep in there – but he knew she was not. His betrayal of her, which he had considered harmless at the time, had turned out to be greater than he could have imagined. He considered going over to the executive building and bashing Timur's door down. But he decided he would have to bide his time before he could attempt to repair the damage he had done.

He had just started to walk back across the square when he heard it. He knew what it was before he saw it. Behind him, about a hundred feet away was a large male polar bear, well over a thousand pounds. The bear was standing on two legs, investigating a stack of empty barrels. The animal turned and stared at him. Yuri knew it would be a mistake to run. He gauged the distance to his own door. He didn't fancy his chances if the bear charged him now. Keeping his eyes locked on the white giant, he continued to back away slowly. The animal dropped its front legs onto the ground, and started to walk in his direction. Yuri could smell its foul breath on the wind.

He hoped this bear had visited town before. He might remember warning shots being fired if he had ventured too close to humans. A polar bear that had not learned this lesson was stuffed and on display in the Cultural Palace. But Yuri had no gun with him now.

He was sure the gap between them had closed slightly, so when Yuri reached Lenin's monument, he said to hell with it, and ran. The bear let out a loud growl. He didn't look back to see if he was being chased. The trick was not to stumble in the snow. He already had his keys in his hand as he bounded up the front steps of London. His hand was shaking but the key went straight in. He pulled open the door and slammed it shut behind him.

He listened for a couple of minutes in the hallway. Then he cracked open the door a couple of inches and peered out. He saw the bear to his left, lumbering out of town. Yuri shook his head and smiled. Lucky.

'I like him,' said Catherine, when he questioned her the following day. 'We have a lot in common.'

The more she talked about how amazing it was how many shared interests and opinions they had, the more Yuri realised, to his horror, that the little shit Timur had used the personal information he had given him in order to seduce her. He felt sick to his stomach. It was beyond a nightmare. And it was one of his own creation. And the only way to undo it was to come clean about what he had done. But he was too ashamed to do that.

'You know you have to be careful with relationships here,'

he said. 'Everyone is just passing through so it's best not to take things too seriously.'

'Are you worried about me, Yuri?' she asked with a smile. 'You don't have to be, you know. I'm a big girl.'

'And you actually like him?' he said. 'I find that hard to believe. He is not exactly the most charming person I've ever met.'

By the look on Catherine's face, Yuri sensed he was already going too far.

'He's a nice man,' she said. 'And he has treated me well so far.'

His head raced as he tried to think up a silver bullet that would make her stop seeing Timur.

'You can do a lot better,' he said.

'Just because you don't like him, doesn't mean that I can't,' said Catherine. 'What have you got against him anyway?'

What he's doing with you, for a start, thought Yuri. And how he had tricked him into helping him.

'This is about him, isn't it?' said Catherine. 'I mean it's not actually about me at all.'

Yuri didn't know what she meant by that, but he tried to cover it by saying, 'It is about you. I don't want you to get hurt. I wish you'd listen to me. I've known Timur longer than you have.'

Catherine's nostrils flared and he felt defeat on the horizon.

'Look,' she said. 'I appreciate the advice, but I don't really need you telling me who I can and cannot see. You don't find me giving advice to you about Anya, do you?'

Yuri was drowning and he decided to make a tactical retreat, for now, before he made things worse.

'You're right,' he agreed. 'Of course you can do what you like. It's not my business to interfere in your private life.'

He felt twice as guilty after hearing the truth from his own mouth. Catherine softened after hearing his apology.

'Well, I appreciate you being concerned about me,' she said. 'But there is really no need.'

Some day soon she is going to hate me, Yuri thought, but not as much as he hated himself right now.

It was not a wise thing to punch a KGB man in the jaw, but that's what Yuri did the first chance he got.

'I am going to hit you now,' he announced, as they encountered each other in the changing room of the sports centre.

Timur was dressed in his red basketball outfit. He clearly thought it was a joke at first, until he saw that Yuri's fist really was approaching his face. He raised his arms in a late attempt to fend off the blow, but Yuri connected well with a jab with his right fist to the chin. Timur's head snapped straight back, and Yuri heard his neck click. It felt good. He wanted to hurt him. The man deserved it.

Yuri adjusted his footing and prepared for Timur's counter-attack. None came. Timur just took a step back and shook his head. Yuri lowered his fists from their defensive position.

'I am not going to inform for you any more, on Catherine, or anyone else,' Yuri said. 'And I don't want you messing with that girl again.'

Timur stared at him blankly, and then said, 'Of course, the job I gave you, in the service of the state, has nothing whatsoever to do with any recent personal developments between myself and Catherine. The two are completely unrelated.'

'I'm not a believer in coincidences,' said Yuri. 'Especially this one. You used me to get her into your bed, didn't you?'

Yuri felt his insides implode. He doubled over and had to force himself not to vomit on to his shoes. Whatever martial arts move Timur had just used, he had not seen it coming. All he knew was the man's outstretched fingers had hit him with tremendous force at a central point just below his ribcage. At least all of his secret service training had not been for nothing. Yuri was still bent over, looking at the floor, waiting for his body to remember to breathe. It could have been worse, he supposed. If the man had wanted to break any of his bones, he expected he could have with ease. Yuri righted himself, hoping there was no more of the same to follow.

Timur dabbed some blood from his lip with a handkerchief.

'Happily, Catherine is not present to hear your nonsense,' he said. 'This time, I am going to let this pass, but I'm warning you – do not overstep the mark again.'

Yuri was thankful that he had managed to land the first blow. He didn't fancy his chances of delivering another now that Timur was ready and waiting.

'If you leave Catherine alone, then we won't have a problem,' said Yuri.

'What are you, her father?' asked Timur. 'She's an adult. She knows what she is doing. And you should mind your own business.'

Yuri managed to stand upright again, by pressing against his stomach with his arm.

'So tell me,' he said. 'What service to the state was that information I gathered for you, exactly?'

Timur looked at him with disdain.

'Like I told you,' he said. 'You can't be too cautious with foreigners. Luckily my fears were unfounded, and I have found Catherine to be a solid supporter of the revolution.'

Yuri laughed. 'So you've ruled her out of your enquiries, have you? Funny the way, as she tells it, you like the same things. Music, poetry, literature. You're a dark horse, Timur.

Or else you're a lying little shit, one or the other. I know which one I'd choose.'

Yuri took a step backwards as Timur made another move for him. Timur saw the fear in his face. He smiled and relaxed his arms by his side.

'She's your assistant. I get that,' he said. 'You feel responsible for her. But if you ever do, or say, anything like this to me again, I will not be so understanding. I recommend you devote your attentions to Anya, as I originally requested. Your services as an informant are no longer required. And come the spring we will have to see if we really do still need you as chief engineer. I will be watching you between now and then.'

Timur stared at him, probably expecting a cynical reply. Yuri did not give him the satisfaction. The KGB man turned and left. Yuri did not feel up to walking just yet, so he sat down and waited for his body to recover.

The next time the subject of Timur came up at work, Catherine told him, 'He asks a lot of questions about you.'

'What kind of questions?' asked Yuri, alarmed.

'Oh, just what you're like, and what I think of you . . . I told him I thought you were an honest worker. He agreed. I think he likes you.'

Yuri buried a smile. He knew he needed help with this situation and he decided he had no option but to tell all to Grigory at their next meeting at the lagoon.

'What I did, I'm not proud of, but it's not so different from what you do, is it?'

'I am not an informant,' said Grigory. 'I'm a spy, or a double agent if you like to be more precise.'

'Oh no,' said Yuri, waving his index finger at him. 'Don't

come on all better than me. You inform on your fellow comrades for foreign countries. Enemies of the state.'

'It's called espionage,' said Grigory. 'There is a difference. Mine is an honourable, dishonourable profession. What you did to Catherine, which I frankly still find hard to believe, was just plain dishonourable. If you're feeling ashamed, that's because you ought to be. But don't try and drag me down there with you.'

'What am I going to do about it?' Yuri asked.

'If I was you,' said Grigory. 'I'd confess to her, and get down on my knees and beg for her forgiveness.'

'Is that what you would do? Really?' asked Yuri. 'I don't think so. You haven't lasted this long in your game without getting caught by coming clean to every person you've wronged.'

'That's my advice,' said Grigory. 'You can take it or leave it.'

Timur and Grigory had much in common, Yuri thought, including a high opinion of themselves. Hypocrisy seemed to be part and parcel of the spy game.

'Couldn't you do something?' asked Yuri. 'Aren't you technically his boss?'

'Technically,' said Grigory. 'In practice no one is superior to the KGB. And even if I was, this is your mess. You made it and you're the only one who can fix it. How could you agree to inform on her in the first place?'

'Don't you start,' said Yuri. 'I've enough of that going on inside my own head. I came here for your help, not abuse.'

'You could always shoot him,' said Grigory. 'One less problem for both of us, and Anya. Not to mention Catherine.'

'Not helpful,' said Yuri.

'Why not? Are you afraid of getting caught?'

'Just a little,' replied Yuri.

'In the war, self-sacrifice for one's comrades was the surest route to a medal.'

'As you can see, I survived the war. Self-sacrifice is not really my thing. What did you do during the war?'

Grigory looked reluctant to answer.

'You did fight?' said Yuri. 'Don't tell me you found a way out of that?'

'Not exactly,' said Grigory. 'At first, I was a spy for our side against the Germans. After we won the war, I was a spy against our allies. That's where I met them. First Berlin. Then later in Vienna.'

'And you were turned, isn't that what it's called?' asked Yuri.

'I did my own turning. I volunteered.'

Yuri nodded. 'Yes. For the money wasn't it?'

Grigory smiled.

'I would pay you to solve this Catherine problem,' Yuri offered.

'Time. Time will solve your problem, you'll see.'

Yuri sighed. 'How much time? I can't bear to think of him touching her. It makes my skin crawl.'

Grigory shrugged. 'I hope you've learned a valuable lesson. When you lie down with dogs.'

Yuri shook his head. 'Well I really appreciate us having this chat. You've been completely useless.'

'For what it's worth, I find that people like Catherine, who want to save the world, are often looking to be saved themselves. Perhaps she sees Timur as her rescuer?'

Yuri shook his head, not wishing to hear any more, and started to walk away.

'How's your defector?' Grigory shouted after him.

'She is ready and waiting,' said Yuri. 'She is being remarkably patient, considering she has waited so long.'

Grigory looked up at the black afternoon sky.

'You'll have more time for chess, I hope, once she's gone,' said Grigory.

Yuri was some fool, he reckoned, to have lived so long in Pyramiden and to know so little about its residents. Old spies and new ones. Defectors and informers. And a murderer. That person, whoever they were, was still walking around among them. Getting away with it. The more time passed, the less chance they would ever be caught.

He stood and watched dozens of miners coming off shift. They left the bathhouse in small groups and headed back towards their respective homes. It could have been any one of them. They all knew the mine well, and they were physically strong enough to make short work of the little Latvian.

Yuri blew on his hands and stamped his feet. Then he followed the miners into town. Several peeled off in the direction of the glass bar. Yuri would have done the same a few months ago. It seemed like another lifetime now. He guessed he would return to his old habits, as Grigory had said, once Anya was gone. Hard drinking and womanising too. It had been his routine for over a decade. He didn't miss it. But without her there would be little else to do.

As he reached the edge of the town square, he stopped. Up ahead, he saw Timur and Catherine walking towards Paris. He thought she was laughing at first, but he soon realised they were actually having a fight. Yuri could not make out what they were saying but they were both raising their voices. And Catherine seemed to be giving Timur worse than he was giving her. Someone should have warned Timur that she set the bar high for her boyfriends. It would not take her long to discover that Timur's politics were all about his own self-interest. Yuri hoped he was witnessing the demise of Pyramiden's first international romance. But it was not to be. Timur started to strike a more conciliatory tone. Unfortunately, he knew how to be tender, as well as malicious. After a few more minutes, they seemed to have patched up their differences and were heading for the Paris door. Yuri felt powerless to do anything about it. Timur did not see him, but Catherine caught his eye before looking away. There was no reason for it, but he had the strange sensation that she was doing this to punish him in some way.

He wondered if he really could get away with murder, like Semyon's killer had. Unfortunately, the demise of a KGB station chief would hardly be ignored in the same way that the Latvian assistant maintenance engineer's demise had been. Despite this, he contented himself by focusing his mind on the best fatal accidents he could come up with.

Chapter 16

WITH ONE DAY left before Anya's departure, Yuri decided to call to her apartment to see how her preparations were going.

'You haven't even started to get ready,' he said, when he saw all her clothes still hanging in her wardrobe.

'It will only take me five minutes,' she said. 'I brought everything I own here in two suitcases. What you see are all my possessions in the world.'

'I can take some now,' he offered. 'You can't be seen walking out of here with luggage in your hands. How would you explain that?'

'How about "I am going on a holiday to where the sun shines for at least part of the day".'

'Come on, this is serious,' said Yuri. 'What will I take?'

'Nothing,' she said. 'I want to leave them all behind. They remind me too much of my old life. Do you know someone who would like them?'

'I don't know anyone who would fit into these skinny things,' said Yuri. 'Well, you had better bring a few extra clothes. Who knows how long you'll have to stay at Longyearbyen before the next part of your journey. You'll need to be able to change.'

She nodded half-heartedly, appearing to have little interest in thinking that far ahead.

'I don't even know where I will be going,' she said. 'Did the contact tell you?'

'No,' said Yuri. 'I will ask. Would you like me to pick some warm things out for you? We can put them in a small bag, so it doesn't look like you are moving country.'

Anya folded her arms and did not even glance over at the clothes he was showing her.

'This is our last night together then?' she asked.

'So it seems,' said Yuri. 'Does that make you sad?'

'Yes,' she said. 'I wish it wasn't.'

Neither of them felt like making love. They slept together, wrapped in each other's arms in her narrow bed. Yuri dozed fitfully, and woke around two in the morning. He lifted one of her arms off his chest and laid it on the bed beside him. Then he dressed and crept out of the room.

He had a night-time arrangement to meet Grigory at the Blue Lagoon. These days, with darkness all around them, twenty-four hours a day, it didn't really matter what time of day or night it was. It still felt exactly the same.

Outside he followed the winding path that led behind the Cultural Palace to the reservoir, only using his flashlight when he had to. That was the problem with perpetual night. Any sort of light made you stick out like a beacon. Especially a moving one. When Yuri was a hundred yards away from the lagoon, he could already see where Grigory was from the glowing end of his cigarette.

'All set?' Grigory asked.

'I guess,' said Yuri. 'There is not a lot to do. She doesn't want to take anything with her.'

'She can get new clothes when she gets there,' said Grigory.

'Where is she going? Do you know?' asked Yuri.

'Yes,' he said. 'Didn't I tell you? She's going to England. Here. You'll need to take this.'

Grigory handed him a small, rectangular bundle wrapped in a plastic bag.

'What's this?'

He looked inside and found a sizeable sum of money in Norwegian krone.

'This is for Anya?' asked Yuri.

'No,' said Grigory. 'You have to give it to the Norwegian, or else he won't take her anywhere.'

'Aren't you coming with us as far as the weather station?'

Grigory smiled. 'No. I am not. My part in this is now officially over. Anyway, you don't need me. The Norwegian will do everything. You just need to get her there on time.'

'What was your contribution, exactly, to this whole enter-prise?' asked Yuri. 'I hope you will be telling your English friends how much I have done. Maybe they can start paying me when you retire.'

'I set the whole thing up,' said Grigory. 'Nothing would be happening without me, remember? I have done enough to get myself shot. I can tell them you would like to be a spy. Is that what you want?'

Yuri shook his head and laughed at the idea. 'I would be a good one. What do you reckon?'

'I believe you would,' agreed Grigory.

Yuri stuffed the plastic bag inside his coat.

'Any last-minute instructions?' asked Yuri.

Grigory turned and looked him in the eye.

'Just be careful out there. If anything doesn't look or feel right, just walk away, and keep on going.'

'Now you're making me nervous,' said Yuri. 'Is there something you are not telling me?'

Grigory shook his head. 'You'll be fine. There won't be any problems.'

'So, I have no reason to worry, right?'

'No. Not that I am aware of,' said Grigory. 'But in these situations, in my experience, it is best to be prepared for anything.'

The next day did not start well. At noon, when Yuri went to pick up one of the snowmobiles, he found that they were both gone. He kicked himself that he had not hidden one the night before. And it troubled him to be reminded how much of an amateur he was at this game. There was no way of getting to the weather station without one. He discreetly enquired who had taken them. It was the Mongolian researcher and another scientist. And they were not expected back until the early evening. All Yuri could do was wait and hope that they would return in time for them to make their six o'clock rendezvous with the Norwegian. Grigory had made it quite clear that the man was not going to hang about. He wondered how much grace time he would give them. He guessed it would depend on how much he needed the cash he was getting paid for the trip.

Yuri checked in on Anya but didn't tell her of their looming problem. She was already agitated enough. If she bit the nails of her left hand any lower she would draw blood.

Yuri spent the rest of the afternoon working with Catherine, but every chance he got, he went to check for the snowmobiles again. The English woman became increasingly frustrated at his lack of concentration on their work. When he went out to check for the fourth time, Catherine asked if he needed any help, and offered to accompany him if he wanted. Yuri declined the offer, and told her it was a personal matter he had to attend to.

'You don't have to hide things from me, you know,' she said.

Yuri stopped and turned to look at her.

'It's about Anya, isn't it?' she asked. 'Is she in trouble again?'

'No, no trouble,' he said. Although the day was not yet over.

'Good,' said Catherine. 'Well, I want you to know you can trust me with things like that. Just in case you are wondering, I don't tell Timur any of the things we talk about. That's strictly between us.'

'I'm glad to hear that,' said Yuri. He wished he could say the same.

By four o'clock, he was beginning to get very worried. The meeting with the Norwegian was in two hours' time, and it would take them forty minutes to get out to the weather station in the dark. By this stage he had deposited Anya in his apartment, with a small bag of clothes he had forced her to bring. He promised to retrieve her when it was time to go. She did not ask any questions, just put herself completely in his hands. He wished he had more control over the events that were about to happen. He wanted it done right, and it was frustrating that he was not the one in charge.

Yuri was relieved when Catherine went home and he did not have to keep up the pretence any more. The garage remained empty with one hour left before the rendezvous. He was beginning to think that he would have to call the whole thing off. He wondered how Grigory contacted the Norwegian, and whether he could get a message to him quickly. The trapper lived eighty-five miles away in a remote area in the south of the island, near the research station at Hornsund. If he was coming from there, he would already be in the air.

The sound of the two engines entering town, at just after five, was a relief. They would have just enough time, if there were no further delays. He waited until the two researchers had retrieved their belongings from the snowmobiles, and had walked out of sight. Then he took the keys to one of the vehicles and drove it to the edge of town, in case anyone else might decide to take it. After parking it behind the fuel depot, he walked back to get Anya.

She looked up at him from his bed, and he was conscious that it would be the last time he would see her this way.

'All set?' he asked.

'Yes,' she said, with a sigh.

'Come on then. It's time to go. If we are doing this, we have to move quickly.'

Anya climbed off the bed and zipped up her coat. Yuri grabbed her bag of clothes and led the way down the stairs. They were about to leave the building when he remembered something.

'Wait there,' he said.

He ran back up the stairs, taking them two at a time. From underneath his bed he retrieved the bag of cash Grigory had given him that morning. Then he ran back down the stairs to Anya.

'What was it?' she asked.

'Your bus fare,' he replied. 'By the way, I almost forgot, you are going to England.'

'Where in England?' she asked.

'That's all I know,' he replied.

They walked swiftly to where he had parked the snowmobile. Once he had started the engine, she got on behind him. Yuri drove slowly away from town, not wanting to make too much noise. If they were seen together, he would be immediately connected to her disappearance. But soon the town was some distance behind them, and he relaxed. It was dark, and they were so muffled up against the cold that even if they had been seen by anyone back there, it was unlikely they could be identified.

He picked up speed now that it was safe to do so. He felt Anya tightening her grip around his waist. The Arctic weather was being kind to them at least. There was just a light breeze blowing in their faces. Yuri was relieved that they were making good time. Even with the headlights on, he reckoned he would have had difficulty making out the route if he wasn't already so familiar with it.

Anya hardly said a word for the whole trip. She had not said much of anything since he had informed her that she would be leaving. He had no idea what was going through her head. He decided that when they reached the weather station he would give her one last opportunity to back out of the whole thing.

He drove as close as he could get to the weather station. Then he braked to a skidding halt and checked his watch. They had time to walk up the hill and still have fifteen minutes to spare before the Norwegian was due to arrive. They were far enough away from Pyramiden that no one would see the helicopter's lights or hear its engine. They hiked up the hill, using Yuri's flashlight as their guide. Luckily, the wind had remained calm, meaning the temperature was not as biting as it sometimes was.

Before they reached the summit, he turned to her and said, 'If you have any doubts, now is the time to say them. It'll be too late once you are on board that helicopter. He will take you all the way to Longyearbyen because that is what he is getting paid to do.'

Anya shook her head but said nothing. He could see that she was nervous.

'OK,' said Yuri. 'If you're sure.'

He pushed open the door to the round tower and they went inside. He lit the wood stove and used a piece of burning kindling to light a kerosene lamp. The smoke from the chimney did not worry him. There was no one else around for miles.

'You want something hot? Tea? Coffee?' he offered.

'No,' said Anya.

She stood at the porthole window at the front of the building, staring down the hill they had just walked up.

'All right,' said Yuri. 'Make yourself comfortable, and I'll go and see if he is here.'

Outside the front door, he checked his watch again. Six o'clock exactly. He scanned the southern sky but could see nothing except stars. The Norwegian would likely take a route that kept him well away from Pyramiden. In that case, perhaps he would arrive from the east or west. He turned and looked in the window, and saw Anya warming herself by the stove. He was impressed by her calm composure. She was remarkably together for someone who was about to start a new life with a man she had not seen for five years.

The Norwegian was now five minutes late, after insisting that Yuri be on time. He had a good mind to cut some money from his fee. Five minutes turned into ten, and ten into twenty, with still no sign of his arrival. Yuri heard the wooden door creaking behind him. Anya came out and stood by his side, and followed his gaze up to the sky.

'He's late,' said Anya.

'Very,' said Yuri. 'I'm sure he will be here soon.'

'Maybe he is not coming,' she said.

He turned to look at her and was surprised that she did not seem overly upset by this possibility.

After standing with him in the cold for a few minutes, Anya went back inside. He wished that he was as unperturbed as she was, because he was doing enough worrying for both of them. If only Grigory was here to tell him what to do.

Having listened for so long, he could separate any new sound from the ones that were present all of the time. Perhaps he was imagining it, but he was sure he could hear the faint tak-tak-tak noise of a helicopter some way off. The wind had carried it his way, and now it was gone. Either the wind had changed or else the helicopter had moved off in the wrong direction. He hoped the Norwegian knew the island's terrain as well as Grigory had said he did. Finding a town that was lit up like a Christmas tree was one thing, but how could he navigate his way to the weather station in this darkness?

Yuri went inside and grabbed an armful of wood blocks from beside the stove. Returning outside, it did not take him long to get a small fire going with the help of some lighter fuel. It wasn't much but it would be easily visible from the air. Nearly an hour had passed since they arrived. He turned his ear to the wind again. Nothing. All he could hear was the breeze and the hissing of the snow as it melted beside his fire.

'He isn't coming, is he?' said Anya, behind him.

'I don't know,' said Yuri. 'I did exactly what he told me to do.'

'I want to go,' she said.

'No. It's too early,' he said. 'We should wait. Maybe he got delayed.'

'It doesn't feel right,' said Anya. 'He isn't coming.'

Yuri had to agree. It didn't feel right. But he decided to

wait anyway. Anything could have delayed the Norwegian, and who knew how long it would take to set this up again. The minutes ticked by, without sight or sound of his arrival. Every time Yuri looked at his watch he became more and more pessimistic. The fire was burning itself out and he decided not to add more wood to it. A thought occurred to him – that by staying this late, he might be putting Anya in danger. But if their plan had been discovered, they should have been caught by now. They had a commanding position on the hill. There was no possibility of anyone surprising them. He would see or hear anyone coming long before they reached the summit. So if they had not been discovered, where was the Norwegian? Again, he thought of Grigory. He should be here dealing with this, offering solutions.

The sound of footsteps close by startled him. The noise was coming from behind the weather station. He walked around the side of the building, keeping close to the wall and holding his flashlight out in front of him. He regretted not bringing a weapon of any sort. Once again, he was reminded what an amateur he was. He heard the sound again, and spun his light in its direction. The sight of a six-foot-tall reindeer with huge antlers was as unexpected for Yuri as was the sight of him for the animal. Luckily, the reindeer spooked first, and it bolted away before Yuri had time to think about how he might defend himself.

He returned to the front of the building, just as Anya came outside again and closed the door behind her. She kicked snow into the fire, putting out the last embers. A line of smoke rose straight upwards and dissipated above their heads. Neither of them said anything as they set off down the hill in the direction of the snowmobile. When they reached it, he had a last, hopeful look at the stars.

'I hope you don't think I made it all up,' he said.

She smiled. 'I don't think that. But I don't trust him now, whoever he is. Please don't ask me to go with him again.'

'I won't,' he agreed. 'I'll think of something else. I don't know what yet. But I will.'

They drove back to town, and he walked her to her door.

'Aren't you coming in?' she asked, when he did not follow her.

'No,' he said. 'I need to deal with this. I'm sorry about what happened.'

'I know you are,' she said. 'Come up later, if you like. I don't think I will be sleeping much tonight.'

He was ready to kill Grigory. He wondered if he had known this was going to happen. Be prepared for the unexpected, he had said. Yuri thought he had been, but a no-show by the Norwegian was not one of the possibilities that had even entered his head.

Grigory was not in his apartment, or at his office. Yuri eventually tracked him down in the library. He was engrossed in a book as Yuri walked in the door. His chess set was laid out on the table in front of him. The party man looked up and smiled when he saw him.

'Problem solved?' he asked. 'I've been waiting for you. I thought we might celebrate with a game.'

'No,' said Yuri. 'The problem is most definitely not solved. She is in her apartment. Your Norwegian didn't show up.'

Grigory looked stunned. A genuine reaction, thought Yuri, but he did not give much credit to his own judgement any more.

'What do you mean he didn't show?' asked Grigory. 'You went to the right place? And on time?'

'Yes,' said Yuri. 'I was the one who picked the location. We waited over an hour.'

Grigory frowned as he bookmarked a page and returned the book to a shelf. Yuri threw the bag of cash into his arms.

'This is your responsibility,' said Yuri. 'You were the one who set this up.'

'I can't understand it,' said Grigory. 'He's never let me down before.'

'Well, he picked a fine time to do it,' said Yuri. 'She won't go with him now, even if you rearrange. She doesn't trust him, and I don't blame her.'

'This is very strange,' said Grigory. 'Something must have gone wrong. You didn't see any sign of anyone?'

'I thought I heard an engine once, just for a few seconds, but then nothing appeared.'

The thought that the Norwegian may have been nearby seemed to trouble Grigory even more.

'No one followed you?' he asked.

'I'm pretty sure not,' said Yuri. 'It's hard to hide out there. I think I would have spotted someone.'

'I don't know what to say,' said Grigory. 'I'll try and find out what happened.'

'You do that. In the meantime, what am I supposed to tell her?'

'I don't know,' said Grigory. 'Tell her what you like. But if she won't go with the Norwegian, then I think we should consider putting an end to it.'

Yuri shook his head. 'I've decided I'm going to take her myself, when the sun comes back.'

'I told you. It's too risky for you.'

'I know,' said Yuri. 'But that's what I am going to do.'

According to Grigory, despite repeated attempts he had been unable to make contact with the Norwegian in the two days that followed his no-show.

'It's not unusual for him to go off the radar for months at

a time,' said Grigory. 'But not without finishing a job he had agreed to do.'

'Maybe he got scared,' said Yuri.

Grigory nodded, but he didn't appear to believe that this was the reason.

The Norwegian brought to two the number of niggling questions that were regularly resurfacing in Yuri's mind. The first was Semyon. Grigory was tired of listening to his conspiracy theories about the Latvian.

'He was just an assistant maintenance engineer, as far as we know,' said Grigory. 'Nothing more.'

'I am a maintenance engineer,' Yuri pointed out, 'and look what I get up to. He was also an informer.'

'Half of the Soviet Union have been informers at one time or another, including you,' said Grigory. 'You're getting paranoid. Conspiracy theories are supposed to be my area. The Norwegian and Semyon have nothing in common.'

'Don't they?' said Yuri. 'Semyon worked for Timur, a Soviet secret service agent. The Norwegian works for you, an agent for the other side. That ring any alarm bells for you?'

'No,' said Grigory. 'The Norwegian and Semyon have never met. I am sure of that. And no one knows I am an agent, otherwise we would not be having this conversation.'

Yuri tried to put it out of his mind, but the thought that there was something very wrong somewhere would not go away.

'If me and Anya get caught, Timur and everyone else is going to think that I am the foreign agent. He already thinks I'm a saboteur. What do we do to foreign agents?'

'The lucky ones might get exchanged for one of ours,' said Grigory. 'But you are Russian so they will never let you go. Life in prison, I would guess. Or if they really take against you, a bullet.'

'Great,' said Yuri. 'That's comforting to know. And what are you going to do for me, if I get caught doing this?'

'Sending you a cyanide pill is traditional,' said Grigory.

'And if I should happen to mention your name?' Yuri asked.

'I'll call you a liar,' said Grigory. 'Who do you think they'll believe? You or me?'

'They will believe you,' Yuri conceded. 'Funny that, isn't it, that of the two of us you are considered more trustworthy, while you've been an enemy of the state for how long?'

'I am not an enemy of our people,' replied Grigory. 'Just of the criminals who pretend to govern us for our own good. It's an important difference.'

'I think most of our people would call you a traitor.'

'Unfortunately, most of our people are stupid,' said Grigory. 'Communism thrives on stupidity, as does capitalism. The people invariably get what they deserve.'

'I see,' said Yuri. 'If you are not a communist, and you are not a capitalist, then what are you?'

'I am a pragmatist,' said Grigory. 'Capitalism is the lesser of two evils. Both are tyrannies in their own way. But at least with capitalism it is possible to have some degree of control over your own fate.'

'Why have you never defected then?' asked Yuri.

'I have never been invited. I have no tradable skills in the west, unlike Anya's husband. There, it is all about market forces. Supply and demand. You understand? Here, I can supply what they need; inside information, local assistance. There is a demand for my services. Not much, but enough. When you take Grigory out of the Soviet Union, his usefulness disappears.'

'Ha,' said Yuri. 'You make it sound like you are a thing to be bought and sold.'

'That's exactly right. I have been bought. A long time ago.'

'You don't regret what you did, even a little?' asked Yuri.

'No. No regrets.'

'But some day you will go there? When you retire?'

'For what?' asked Grigory. 'Unlike Anya, I have nothing waiting for me in the west. I have my flat in Moscow. I will spend the remainder of my time there. There are lots of books I want to read, and haven't had the time to. This will be my last job for them. I have already told them. They don't mind. There are others they will use. Younger men, and women, who they have also bought.'

'It will be my last job too,' said Yuri. 'My life was fine until you and Anya came into it. When she is gone, I will just have you left to deal with.'

Chapter 17

THE LONG-RANGE WEATHER forecast had given notice of an impending storm, during which they would all be obliged to spend their days indoors. A sneak preview of the prison that awaited him, Yuri thought. Anya was the only person he would risk doing this for. It didn't make a whole lot of sense that a successful outcome would mean losing her. But that was how it seemed destined to be. For now, the sun's return felt like a long way off. Usually, the Arctic spring was a time of optimism and rebirth, but not this year.

The problem with storms was that they made outdoor work either dangerous or impossible. So once the forecast came in for a three-day snow blizzard, Yuri and Catherine set to work double-checking every system in town. If a pump was about to go, it was better to find it and change it now.

The storm would bring icy winds blasting up the fjord, which would lower the temperature even further. This meant that the coal furnace would need to be at full capacity for the duration. Breakdowns in the middle of a raging tempest, as Yuri had learned from experience, were a nightmare.

'Can't we just come outside and fix it, if something goes?' said Catherine.

'Sure,' said Yuri. 'If you want to lose a few toes and fingers to frostbite.'

'But nothing should go wrong, should it? We haven't had a serious problem in ages.'

'See,' said Yuri. 'I knew it. You are just a lazy capitalist, after all, trying to get out of extra work. A true communist never shirks her responsibilities.'

'I am not shirking,' protested Catherine, her face flushed with indignation. 'I am just asking is it really necessary, that's all.'

'Yes. It is,' said Yuri.

'Fine,' said Catherine. 'That's all you had to say. And I wasn't shirking.'

She caught him smiling, and he did his best to put on a straight face.

'You like making fun of me, don't you?' she said.

'Sometimes, yes,' he agreed. 'Sorry.'

'Don't apologise. That's why I'm here, isn't it? For your entertainment.'

When they had finished, late in the evening, they battened down everything that could move and hoped for the best. If they had done their jobs well, and nature was kind, a three-day holiday awaited.

Yuri collected a box of tinned food and biscuits from the canteen. In his time in Pyramiden he had seen many days when making the short walk from London to the Cultural Palace was suicidal.

Yuri encouraged Anya to stay with him full-time until the storm ended. She arrived just as the windows started to rattle with the first gales.

'This place,' she said, with barely disguised contempt. 'Tell me again why you like it here so much.'

'It's peaceful,' he replied.

'Yes, I can see that,' she said, as the whole building appeared to shake.

Yuri saw her looking alarmed as she put her hand on a wall for support.

'Don't worry,' he said. 'These blocks are built to last.'

It was true. A lot of thought had been put in to their design. Every block had rounded corners to deflect the Arctic winds. And buried beside the foundations of every building were Freon rods to stop the ground thawing out too quickly in spring.

She laughed at his collection of canned goods, which he had stacked on the table in a triangle.

'Oh, yummy,' she said. 'Is that what we are supposed to eat?'

'It's what I am going to eat. You can join me or starve. Your choice.'

Anya looked at the labels. 'Beef goulash. Chicken goulash. Lamb goulash.'

'Don't look down your nose at it. You'd be surprised what I can whip up with a can of ready-made food. During the war we lived on American spam.'

'You fought in the war?' she asked.

'Yes. Why do you sound so shocked?'

'I just didn't think you were that old,' she said.

'Thanks a lot. I am not that old,' he replied. 'And you are a few years older than me. I was young going. Underage. Though I think I was middle-aged by the time I came home.'

'My soldier boy,' she said. 'Where did you fight?'

'All the way to Berlin.'

'Ah. A hero. Why have you never said anything? Some people never stop with their war stories. You're a dark horse.'

'Believe me, I've never done anything heroic in my life.'

'I bet that's not true. And what you're doing for me is pretty heroic.'

'I think it would be more accurate to say that what I am doing for you is the stupidest thing I've ever done.'

Anya turned to look at him. 'You don't have to, you know.'

Yuri smiled and shook his head.

'What do you think England is like?' Anya asked nervously.

Yuri didn't know. He had been surprised that it was not the Americans who had taken her husband. He guessed they would have been the people who would have had the most use for him. But maybe the English had taken him in order to impress the Americans. They seemed to like doing that.

'What kind of life will I have there in the west?'

'I don't know the answers to any of these questions,' said Yuri, 'you'll have to find out for yourself. Are you still sure you want to go?'

'Do you think I should?' she said.

He wanted to say no. 'I can't answer that one for you either. It has to be your decision. For my part, I would much rather you stayed with me. I can make you happy.'

'Why are you helping me then?' she asked.

'Because it's what you want, isn't it?' he said.

'Right now, I want you,' she said. 'When I am with you I don't think about anyone else.'

Another lie to keep the others company. They made love in a half-hearted way. He sensed her mind was elsewhere, as it had been since the day he had told her that the Norwegian was going to take her to Longyearbyen. He couldn't remember the last time she had let herself go with him. It was no fun making love to a disengaged stranger. He woke in the middle of the night to find her side of the bed empty. Outside, there was a lull in the storm. She was sitting on a chair, looking out the window at the aurora putting on a green and red light show above Pyramiden mountain. Her pale face lit up in an ever-changing array of colour.

'What are you doing? Come back to bed,' he said.

'I want to talk to him,' she said.

'Who?' said Yuri, hoping she didn't mean her contact, Grigory. This was something he could not deliver, no matter how much she wanted it.

'My husband,' she said. 'I want to talk to him.'

Yuri was momentarily speechless, especially since she had never raised this issue before now.

'How the hell am I supposed to do that?' asked Yuri.

Anya shrugged. 'I don't know. But I think I need to do this before I go anywhere.'

'But it's all arranged. I really don't think talking to him beforehand will be possible,' said Yuri.

'There is a radio station here, isn't there?' she said. 'If I can't talk to him, then I want to call the whole thing off. I'm serious. How can they expect me to defect to be with someone I haven't seen or spoken to in five years? He could be completely changed. Maybe he doesn't even love me any more. This is the man who left me behind, after all. I have to talk to him. To be sure.'

For the first time she was talking sense, thought Yuri. And he had to admit that he had some sympathy for her position. He sighed and agreed at least to raise the subject with her mystery contact.

'Contact!' said Anya, with a derisive laugh. 'It's funny, isn't it? The definition of a contact is someone who makes contact. Except mine doesn't. He or she only talks to you. It's not really fulfilling the job description. If it was up to me I'd sack him.'

Grigory unfortunately would be only too delighted to be fired, if given the option. And Yuri would not be offering the idea to him. He fully expected that Grigory would dismiss out of hand the risky notion of a radio conversation between Anya and her husband. And he would use her obstinacy as another reason that they should forget about helping her at all.

Another thought entered his head. If he could set up this call, maybe it might all go wrong. After talking to her husband, Anya might decide that she did not trust him enough to drop everything, and join him in the west. This would leave her only one option: to stay with him.

'What was the last conversation you had together?' asked Yuri. 'He really gave you no sign at all that he was leaving? Even a hint?'

Anya stared into space, gathering her memories.

'We had breakfast together. It was a Sunday. We usually slept late at weekends but he was up before me, saying he had a meeting with our bosses. I didn't think anything of it. They were always having private conferences with him. The rest of us were excluded from those meetings.'

'No luggage in the hall?' asked Yuri. 'Empty drawers? Men with dark glasses at the door?'

Anya smiled. 'No. Nothing obvious like that. Believe me, I've been over and over it a thousand times.'

'So what did you talk about at this last breakfast?' he asked.

'I was asking where we might go for a summer break. I said I wanted to swim and get some sunshine. We spent so much time in the lab, we were pale as ghosts. He wasn't interested in talking about it. I didn't know it at the time, but he knew he wasn't going to be spending the summer with me. We used to go to the Caspian Sea for years. Have you ever been there?'

It annoyed him that these holidays were memories she cherished.

'No,' said Yuri. 'I haven't had much in the way of holidays. I take some days off here in the summer, and I go fishing. It's the opposite then. Instead of darkness all the time, the sun shines twenty-four hours a day.'

'I'd like to see that,' she said. 'It must be better than all this blackness.'

'And then what happened?' he asked. 'After breakfast?'

'He kissed my cheek and left. Just like any other day. Except then he never came home. I went to work the next morning and he wasn't there. By mid-afternoon I started to worry that no one seemed to know where he was. Then some men arrived. They spoke to our bosses. There was a lot of shouting. Then they brought me in and started asking me questions. I didn't know what they were talking about. Of course he hadn't defected, I said. I had never heard anything so ridiculous. He wouldn't go anywhere without me. I said they must be mistaken. I called the senior agent an idiot. That was when they arrested me. I was led out of my own building in handcuffs. The first place they brought me was to our flat. They asked me to identify what was his. We went through the wardrobes and his desk. Do you know what the funny thing was?'

'What?' asked Yuri.

'As far as I could tell, he had taken absolutely nothing. Just what he was wearing on his back.'

Yuri's eyes widened. 'I can see why you'd like to talk to him.'

As expected, Grigory blew a fuse when he heard.

'She doesn't get to make demands. Who the hell does she think she is? She is lucky we are helping at all. I hope you told her no.'

Yuri shook his head, and Grigory threw his arms out in frustration. The isolation of their regular meeting place, the blue lake, had the disadvantage of allowing the party man to vent his anger as loudly as he liked.

'It makes sense to me,' countered Yuri. 'Given the circumstances, it is a reasonable request. Would you give up everything to be with someone who left you five years ago without so much as a goodbye?'

'I wouldn't even consider getting back with them in the first place,' said Grigory. 'And what is she giving up? She has no life any more. She was a scientist, which she messed up by not keeping tabs on her partner. Then they did her a huge favour by getting her a job as a school teacher and now she has messed that one up too. If I were her I wouldn't be asking too many questions. I'd keep my mouth shut, thank my lucky stars and do as I was told.'

'Well then she'll be staying here. Because when she gets something into her head, there's no way to talk her out of it. And if she does stay, I can guarantee you that she's going to hit the bottle again, big time. Is that what you want? Her wandering around, shouting about the spy who wouldn't help her. The contact she never met, who is hiding among the good people of Pyramiden.'

'She doesn't know who I am,' said Grigory. 'For that very reason.'

Grigory took out a cigarette and lit it with what Yuri was sure was a shake in his hand. He did not utter another word until he had taken the first drag.

'No. But she knows who I am,' said Yuri. 'And I know who you are. She could tell that to Timur. How long do you think it would take to find you then? A week? Less? A day?'

Grigory cursed under his breath. 'I told you this bloody

woman would be nothing but trouble. I knew I should have stayed out of it. Why didn't I listen to myself?'

'Honestly, you should have,' said Yuri. 'I wish you had. Your intervention has not been helpful for anyone. But now we're all in this together. So what do you say? Can you get her husband on the other end of a radio?'

Grigory sighed. 'I don't know. I can try. It'll take me a few days, at least.'

Yuri was intrigued and waited for more information.

'I'm not going to tell you how I contact them,' said Grigory. 'Are you kidding? I'll get a message to them. And we'll see. What about our end? I suppose you already have a plan.'

'I do. The radio station,' said Yuri. 'It's not manned at night.'

'Good idea,' said Grigory.

'Anya thought of it, actually,' said Yuri.

Grigory frowned. 'And you can get in there?'

'I have keys for nearly every building in town, including that one. And I know the layout. They ask me to fix their equipment when it breaks down. I can get us in no problem. We just have to do it without being seen. But the main thing is we need someone at the other end who is willing to take our call.'

'Let's talk again in a day or two,' said Grigory.

He still did not look happy.

'Tell her that if we do it, there will be this favour, and nothing else after that. OK?'

'I'll pass that on.'

'I mean it. She better not even dream of asking for anything else.'

'You really don't like her, do you?' asked Yuri.

'It's not about liking,' said Grigory. 'She's not to be trusted.'

'I trust her,' said Yuri.

'Yeah, well love is blind. Isn't it?'

'And you trust me?' asked Yuri.

Grigory paused for a moment before answering. 'Let's just say, of the two of you, I have more faith in you not to stab me in the back.'

Yuri laughed. 'I don't think this spy game is doing your blood pressure any good.'

The news gave Anya a visible boost, although the idea of finally speaking to her husband in person after all this time did make her nervous. Yuri assured her that she was right to do it, and that it couldn't do any harm.

'You must have questions you want answered?' he said.

'I do,' she agreed. 'Lots of them.'

'Maybe write them down,' he suggested. 'It will be a rush. We'll have to get in and out of the radio station without raising any eyebrows. So, you'll have to make the most of what little time you have.'

Anya nodded but she wasn't listening. She took his advice and started writing out questions on a piece of paper. The first leaf was full in under a minute, and then the second. On she went until it started to resemble one of Catherine's question-naires. He was not pleased that she had so much to say to this man. He tried to take a look over her shoulder but she hid the page with the palm of her hand.

Yuri decided he needed a break from her. He grabbed his coat, made an excuse and left.

Outside, a strong wind was blowing from the north, carrying any loose snow with it down through the town. He hurried across from one side of the square to the other, with the wind doing its utmost to knock him over. Keeping close to the relative shelter of the buildings along the way, he made his way to the wooden radio station. Lights were on inside and he could see two of the staff moving about. The main radio room was not visible from the outside, so the principal danger was being seen going in or out. On a night like tonight that wouldn't be a problem. The weather front was keeping everyone indoors. But he couldn't control the winds at will, so this sort of help was not something that could be relied upon.

The lights went out in the radio station, and the two staff came outside. They chatted on the doorstep as one of them locked the front door with a key. Yuri had one of those, on a ring with dozens of others, which he kept at the power station for emergencies. He noted the time. 9 p.m. From then until six in the morning, they would have the place all to themselves. They would just need flashlights so that they could keep all the lights off. And of course they needed Grigory to play his part and deliver the man at the other end of the line.

Grigory's mistrust of Anya did give Yuri pause for thought. But he was going into this with his eyes open. He was pretty sure he had the angle on everyone involved, their hidden agendas and what they were after. Everything seemed clear-cut. The safety net was that they all needed each other or else they wouldn't get what they wanted.

The weather front passed after three days and the next morning the town was greeted by mountains of snow, in all the wrong places. Anyone with non-essential tasks was given a shovel and set to work. Yuri and Catherine had to dig their way to the power station door, which was almost obscured from view. Heart-attack work. From the moment of her arrival, Yuri had noticed that she was in a bad mood. As much as he liked to see failure brewing between her and Timur, he did not like to see her unhappy. She attacked the snow with sharp jabs, like she wanted to hurt somebody.

'Slow down,' Yuri advised. 'Pace yourself.'

'I don't need to pace myself,' Catherine said. 'You just worry about yourself.'

When she was not looking, Yuri threw his next shovel-load at her head. It was a direct hit and some of it slid down the inside of her coat.

'Oh, you're in trouble now,' she said, and proceeded to bombard him with shovel-loads of snow.

'OK. OK,' he said, accepting defeat through a mouthful of snowflakes. 'Stop behaving like a child.'

'Me?' she protested. 'You were the one who started it.'

Yuri had to use his fingers to extract a compacted plug of snow from his ear.

Once they managed to get inside, they hung up their dripping coats to dry.

'Coffee,' offered Yuri. 'I think we deserve a break after that, don't you?'

'Yes, please,' said Catherine.

They warmed their red hands on the hot mugs. After a while, Yuri noticed that Catherine had fallen silent. He was about to ask her if everything was all right, but she spoke first.

'Could I ask your advice on something?'

'Sure,' he said.

'It's just I don't know too many people here, and I don't know who else I could talk to. You see, it's me and Timur. I know he's not your favourite person.'

Yuri tried not to smile as he hoped this would be the good news he had been waiting for – that they were finally splitting up.

'He asked me to move in with him, to his apartment,' she said.

This just kept getting worse and worse. It was impossible for him to feel any guiltier than he already did.

'I see,' said Yuri. 'And you're not sure?'

'Not sure. Yes,' said Catherine. 'Things are going well though.'

'Then don't do it,' said Yuri, knowing he was responding too quickly, but unable to stop himself. 'If you're not sure then that's always the best option, isn't it?'

Catherine was taken aback by his decisiveness. 'That's it? No discussion.'

'You asked my advice, and I gave it to you. Follow your first instincts. You're not sure. That says a lot to me. If it was the right thing to do, you would be sure.'

Catherine looked doubtful. 'I don't know if that's always the case.'

'Don't listen to me then,' snapped Yuri.

'Why are you getting annoyed with me?' she asked. 'I was just looking for your opinion. Nobody is asking for you to go and live with him.'

'I should hope not,' said Yuri, wondering how he could salvage something from the wreckage of this conversation.

'You've always been against us going out,' she said. 'Why is that?'

Yuri sighed. 'You're right. I don't like him. And I don't think he's good enough for you.'

'Well, I'm an adult,' said Catherine, 'and I'll decide.'

'Fine,' said Yuri. 'You do that.'

'You know, if I knew this conversation was going to go like this I never would have asked you. I should have known better.'

What an idiot I am, thought Yuri. He had just thrown away the opportunity to influence her decision. And now she might never confide in him again.

'What are you going to do?' he asked, in a calmer voice.

Catherine stared at him, with an angry expression.

'Either you care a lot, and you aren't saying,' she said, 'or else you don't care at all. Which is it?'

Yuri sighed and looked her in the eye. 'I do care.'

Catherine's anger subsided. 'Let me do this, OK? If I make a mess, then it will be my own fault, nobody else's. Back home, when you are my age and involved in protest politics, people treat you like you're some sort of a loon. But I'm no crazier than anyone else here, am I?'

Yuri smiled and shook his head. 'Saner than most.'

'So, I will make my own decisions, for myself. All right?'

Yuri reluctantly nodded his agreement.

Chapter 18

ON THE APPOINTED night for Anya to talk to her husband, the weather did not play ball. There was hardly a breeze in the air, and the moon and stars lit up the snow, meaning visibility was as far as the naked eye could see. Earlier, Yuri had taken the radio building key from the bunch at the power station. Now, he collected Anya from Paris. She looked nervous, and remained silent as they made their way to their destination. Grigory never tired of telling Yuri how big a deal it had been for him to set up this call.

Halfway there, they had to crouch behind a truck as they saw Timur walking across their path in the direction of the Gagarin sports centre. Many of the town's residents were already there for a basketball match. Yuri was happy to see the KGB man alone. It meant he was not with Catherine. For a moment, he was tempted to abandon his night's mission in favour of dispatching Timur from this world. They managed to stay out of sight until he was gone. As they drew nearer to their destination, Yuri kept his eyes fixed on the radio station building. It was in complete darkness, and he could see no movement inside or out. They stopped some distance away and waited, just to be sure.

'OK,' said Yuri, when he was satisfied. 'Just walk casually

up to the front door, like we're going about our normal business. If anybody sees us, we'll let them think we're just two lovers looking for somewhere new to make love.'

Anya smiled. 'We could come back another time, if you like? It's been a long time since we did anything like that.'

'Yeah, well let's just get through tonight first,' he replied.

At the front door, Yuri turned the key, while Anya scanned the streets. No one was around. They hurried inside and Yuri locked the door behind them. He clicked on his flashlight and led the way down the corridor. Once inside the radio room, he flicked a switch and the overhead lights blinked into life. There were no windows, so there was no danger of their activity being noticed from outside.

Anya looked at the large radio set with apprehension.

'What now?' she said.

'Now we wait,' said Yuri. 'It's arranged for twenty minutes from now. I'll get everything set up in the meantime.'

He pulled out a piece of paper with the radio coordinates Grigory had given him, and set the tuning dial to match. He sensed Anya behind him watching his every move. For now, there was only silence from the other end. He would prefer if it stayed that way, but then he would have to deal with Anya's disappointment.

'When it's all set, will I be able to speak to him in private? I'd rather you didn't listen in on our conversation.'

'Sure,' said Yuri. 'I don't know how many people will be at the other end, wherever that is. But I'll show you how to work it, and I'll leave you alone until you are finished. All right?'

She nodded, still looking nervous.

'Where will you be?' she said. 'In case I need you.'

'Outside in the corridor. Don't worry, I'm not going to run off and leave you.'

Anya folded her arms around her body.

'You're cold?'

'No, I'm fine. It's just been a long time. I can't imagine what this is going to be like.'

'Just relax,' said Yuri. 'You did the right thing by insisting on this.'

Anya nodded and stared at the radio set again.

'You sure you want to do this?' he asked. 'We can call it off if you want to?'

She paused and then took a deep breath. 'I'm sure. What harm can it do to talk? I can decide what to do afterwards. You'll help me then, won't you?'

'Of course,' he said. 'All right then. Come closer, and I'll show you.'

Yuri demonstrated how she should speak into the microphone and how to control the volume of what she was hearing back.

'I understand,' she said. 'Thank you for doing this.'

'No problem,' he said. He checked his watch. 'It's almost time. You'd better put the headphones on.'

She sat down in front of the radio set, adjusted the headphones over her ears and listened.

'You hear anything?' asked Yuri.

'No,' she said in a loud voice. 'Just some interference.'

Yuri hoped that her husband was at least going to fulfil his part of this bargain, and not let her down again. He could see in her eyes that Anya was thinking much the same thing. The fallout if she didn't get to speak to him, after all this anticipation, would be grim.

'Nothing's happening,' she said, with a worried expression on her face. 'There is no one there.'

'Wait,' he said. 'Give them a chance.'

He checked his watch once more. They were now ten minutes beyond the appointed time. He did not tell Anya that. Didn't her husband know it was rude to keep a lady waiting? After five years, ten minutes looked like the hardest part for Anya to bear. She put her hands up to the headphones, pushing them closer to her ears. Yuri saw her expression change and she turned and caught his eye.

'Yes, yes, I'm here,' she said, with a smile. 'Yes. I can hear you. I can hear you.'

Yuri could not hear what was being said by this man, but he saw her eyes turning glassy. She looked up at him, and he nodded and left her alone. He went out and sat on the floor in the corridor for a while but could not stay easy. He hoped Anya's husband was being nice to her. She deserved this much after everything he had put her through.

After pacing the length of the corridor a few times, curiosity got the better of him. Breaking his promise, he went into the smaller radio room next door, where he knew it would be possible to listen in. He told himself it was not spying; it was just to protect her. If he knew exactly how she had been treated on this call, it would be easier to deal with her afterwards. The rear room contained a smaller back-up radio, in case anything went wrong with the first. He plugged in a set of headphones, set the radio volume to barely register, and then he switched it on.

'I can't wait to see you,' he thought he heard her say. 'It's been torture, all this time. I am angry it has taken so long. I have told them.'

'Where will I be living?' Anya asked.

Yuri was confused by what he was hearing. Anya had definitely just spoken. But the first voice he had heard, a woman's, was not Anya.

'It's a little village,' said the first woman. 'They gave me a nice cottage. White, with yellow roses in the garden. There's a river at the back. It's beautiful. You'll love it.'

'In England?' Anya asked.

'Yes, yes, England.'

Another voice murmured something in the background at the other end of the line.

'Is someone there with you?' Anya asked. 'Who is it?'

'Yes,' the woman said, with a touch of remorse in her voice. 'One of the people who looks after me.'

'He's listening to us?' Anya said, annoyed.

'Yes. I had to agree to do that, or else they would not let me talk to you. I'm sorry. Is it OK?'

'It's all right,' Anya said, her voice calming. 'I understand. And what will I do there in England?'

Yuri had to stop himself from storming in there and asking her what the hell was going on. One thing was clear: there was no husband waiting for her in England. Anya had been lying to him all this time, and about more than that, it seemed. He was risking his own neck in order to reunite her with another woman.

'You can work with me again, of course,' the woman continued. 'And you could teach at university perhaps, like before, if you wanted. Oxford is only six miles away.'

For a moment, there was the man's voice again, mumbling in the room at the other end of the line, but Yuri could not make out any of what was being said. Even if he had been able to speak English, he was pretty sure he wouldn't have been able to pick out the words. He suspected that the speaker was placing his hand over the microphone before he spoke.

'I'm sorry, Anya, they want me to finish now,' the woman said. 'I love you, you know that, don't you? I've never stopped. Not even for a day.'

'I want to believe it,' Anya replied. 'I love you too.'

Yuri did not enjoy hearing her say that. She had never said these words to him. He turned off the radio set and went back outside to the corridor. After a few moments, the door of the main room opened and Anya walked out looking shell-shocked. Yuri had to make a quick decision, and he chose to say nothing about what he had heard, for the moment. He wanted to talk to Grigory first. That bastard must have been lying to him too. He was surrounded by deceivers.

'How was it?' he forced himself to ask.

'I feel like I've just spoken to a ghost,' she said. 'It doesn't feel real.'

'But you're happy?' he asked. 'You're glad you went through with it.'

'Yes,' she agreed. 'Let's get a drink. I need one.'

In a mischievous mood now, Yuri asked, 'How was he?'

'Fine,' she said. 'Sweet.'

'Is he the same man you remember?'

'Yes,' she replied. 'As far as I could tell, he hasn't changed too much.'

He guessed if he had not discovered the truth for himself, she would never have seen fit to tell him. It was tempting to keep asking her questions just to watch her lie over and over. But he was already bored with that.

He went back inside to check the radio room and put everything back as it had been when they had arrived. Then they made their way to the front door in darkness. Yuri checked up and down the street, and when he was satisfied that no one was around, he ushered her out the door.

'Thank you for doing that, Yuri,' she said, as they walked. 'I guess it must feel strange for you.'

'You've no idea,' he said.

'I don't think anyone else would have helped me the way you have.'

No, he thought, there are very few people as stupid and as gullible as me.

'Maybe not,' he said. 'Most people like to avoid trouble. I can't avoid it. It finds me.'

They crossed the street and made their way to the bar. To Anya's dismay, it was full after the basketball game. But Yuri was relieved. He really did not want to be alone with her, to have to talk, and pretend that he did not know anything. They sat at a table with some miners and he watched her gradually withdraw inside herself. But for once she seemed content. She had obviously gotten the reassurance she wanted from the phone call with that woman, whoever she was.

He made an excuse about having to do some late maintenance work, and walked her back home to Paris. She looked happier to be left alone too.

Then he made his way to the executive block. Using his own master front-door key, he let himself into the foyer. He knew Grigory's apartment, having been there as a guest several times over the years. He walked up the stairs to the third floor and rapped gently on the door. Timur's apartment was nearby, so he was careful not to attract unwanted attention.

Grigory opened the door, dressed in slippers and a dressing gown. He took one look at Yuri's expression and broke into a knowing smile. He opened the door wide for Yuri to enter.

'I was wondering how long it would take you,' said Grigory, waving for him to sit on the couch. 'You probably need a drink?'

'You knew about her, didn't you?' said Yuri. 'Who is that woman?'

'Yes, I knew,' said Grigory.

'Why didn't you tell me? I thought we were friends.'

'We are friends, really. But with something like that, I thought it might be best for you to find out for yourself. Though, I have to admit, it did take you a lot longer than I expected.'

Yuri took the tumbler of whiskey Grigory offered him, and knocked it back in one gulp.

'I've been racking my brain,' said Yuri. 'But honestly, I don't think there were any signs that I missed.'

'No,' agreed Grigory. 'She's clever that one. She keeps her cards close to her chest. If it's any consolation, I think she likes men too.'

Yuri shook his head. 'So it wasn't all a lie. Me and her. Just most of it.'

Grigory refilled his glass. 'What did she say to you? Why did she tell you now?'

'She didn't,' said Yuri. 'She doesn't know that I know. I found out by accident. I listened in to her radio conversation. She asked me not to. I can see why, now.'

'Ah, bravo. What a spy you are becoming. You are doing a lot of lying at the moment, wouldn't you say?'

'Spare me the lecture,' said Yuri. 'It's not what I need right now. You and me are risking our necks so she can go and live with this woman, whoever she is, in a little cottage with yellow roses.'

'What cottage?' said Grigory.

'That's what she said on the radio, white cottage, yellow roses, near a river. Who is she anyway?'

Grigory sat in an armchair and rested his head against the back.

'Quite the genius, I heard. Not Anya, the other one. Taisia. One of the stars of the third idea programme. A protégé of

Sakharov. So good that they let her get away with her affair with Anya, which is not usual, as you know. Anya managed to stay on the programme only because of her. And then word got out abroad about how good Taisia was. I can imagine how it went. Someone like me would have made contact. Sized her up, before making her an offer she couldn't refuse.'

'Is that what happened with you?' asked Yuri. 'An offer you couldn't refuse?'

'Unfortunately not,' said Grigory.

They both sat in silence for a moment, nursing their drinks. Yuri looked around the room. A lot of books on shelves. Framed pictures on the wall. Grigory with a woman and teenage children. He had never mentioned a wife. Then Grigory on the outer edge of a group photo with Brezhnev, almost falling out of the photo. Another on his own standing right beside Khrushchev. A handshake with smiles. Photos of a career that had been on an upward curve once, but had obviously stalled. His foreign handlers must not have been pleased with that. A man on the inside in the Arctic mining town of Pyramiden did not have quite the same value as a man inside the politburo.

'So, what now?' said Grigory, breaking the silence. 'Do we stand down because we found out she likes women just as much as you do?'

Yuri did not answer.

'Let me just say again,' said Grigory, 'if you're not doing it, then I'm out too. You don't owe her anything, you know. And I certainly don't. What do you say? Shall we abandon the little liar to her fate?'

Yuri sighed and shook his head.

'Since when did you get so soft?' asked Grigory.

'I said I would help her, and that's what I am going to do. This doesn't change that. And what's with you anyway? Didn't they give you this job, mission, whatever you guys call it? Won't you get into trouble if you don't carry it through?'

Grigory shrugged. 'I am more or less retired. They haven't asked me to do anything for a very long time. This one came out of the blue. I always wanted to go out with something big, but this is not quite what I had in mind. It's a domestic tale. Woman A left Woman B, and now Woman A wants B back. My advice, you want her, don't leave her behind in the first place. Simple, and a lot less grief for everyone else.'

Unlike Yuri's previous competitive relationship with Anya's fictitious male husband, thoughts of this woman, Taisia, wanting Anya did not make him feel angry or jealous. He did not know what to feel.

'Well, we're still going through with it,' said Yuri. 'We both are.'

Grigory sighed. 'I was afraid you were going to say that. Aren't you annoyed with her?'

'She is still leaving me for someone else. I already accepted that. Somehow it feels less bad that it's a woman.'

'But she's not worth risking our necks for. I would rather not spend my old age in a prison cell for her, if it's all the same to you. She would not do as much for you.'

'Nobody is going to prison,' said Yuri. 'Not us and not her. We're going to plan this until it's perfect. And then we are going to plan some more. All right?'

Grigory raised his glass in a toast. 'To prison.'

On his way down the stairs, Yuri ran into Timur coming up. The KGB man looked at him with suspicion, and stopped. Yuri was sorely tempted to lunge at him and push him over the railing, for a long drop to the foyer.

'What are you doing here so late?' Timur demanded.

'Some emergency maintenance for Grigory,' said Yuri, without stopping.

Timur looked like he didn't believe him but he let him pass.

'Must have been bad if it couldn't wait till morning,' said Timur, after him.

'No, it wasn't,' said Yuri. 'Grigory's getting fussy in his old age.'

Yuri looked over his shoulder and saw Timur smiling before continuing up the stairs.

As he trudged home through the snow and roadside sludge, he resolved that he would say nothing to Anya about what he knew. He would just get her away as soon as he could, and that would be the end of it.

However, when he opened his apartment door he found her lying in his bed. He had never thought in a million years that this sight could make him angry.

'I thought we were going to see each other tomorrow,' he said.

'We were,' she said. 'But I wanted to thank you for what you did. You deserve a reward.'

As much as he wanted a reward, he could not keep up the pretence any longer.

'I know you have no husband,' he blurted out. 'I heard you talking to her.'

Anya was momentarily dumbstruck before making a quick recovery.

'You listened?' she said, her face flushed with anger. She swung her legs out of bed and started to get dressed.

'Hey you,' he said. 'Don't even think about getting angry with me. On the scale of liars, I think you win hands down.'

Anya paused and let her anger subside as quickly as it had come.

'Keep your voice down,' she said.

She finished putting her boots on, but stayed sitting on the edge of the bed.

'No reward then?' said Yuri. 'How about an explanation? An apology? Anything will do. It's only me after all. Dumb old Yuri.'

He could see her temper flaring once more but she did not take the bait.

'Excuse me, Princess, I know you don't like to be criticised.'

She grabbed her coat from the end of the bed.

'Could you stop,' she said. 'Just stop. What would you have said if I had told you the truth? In case you hadn't noticed, loving a woman is not news you go broadcasting around our big backward country.'

'You were sleeping with me,' said Yuri. 'I am risking my neck to help you. And not just me. A little bit of honesty would have been a good thing.'

Anya sighed and nodded her head. 'All right. I'm sorry. Maybe I should have told you. I needed your help.'

'So you used me to try and get back with her. And that's all it was.'

'No. I like you, Yuri. It's been fun. And I wouldn't still be here if it wasn't for you.'

'But?' he said.

'But I love her. It's not important that she's a man or a woman. That doesn't matter to me.'

Yuri shook his head. 'Just a detail, huh?'

'Don't tell me you are afraid of gay people,' she said. 'You are, aren't you?'

'No actually, I'm not. You'd be surprised how many gay miners pass through here. I happen to like the opposite sex. Although my experience with you may make me reconsider.'

'Oh please,' she protested. 'Don't tell me you haven't enjoyed being with me.'

'I haven't.'

Anya looked away. 'I don't believe you.'

'You tried to kill yourself, remember that one?'

'You regret saving me now, is that what you're saying?'

Yuri shrugged. 'I haven't decided yet.'

Anya stood up and zipped up her coat.

'I'm leaving,' she said.

He guessed she would not walk out just like that. She still needed him. If she raised the subject now, he thought, it would be proof that he was just a means to this end. She reached out her hand but paused before touching the door handle. She turned to look at him.

'Does this mean you aren't going to help me?' she asked.

He smiled to himself, and did not look at her when he said, 'A promise is a promise. I will be in touch when it is time to go. In the meantime, please stay away from me.'

She stared at him, waiting for him to make eye contact. When he did not she nodded.

'Thank you,' she said, and left.

He could sell her out to Timur as fast as a click of his fingers. But it was not something he would even consider doing. The sooner she left the better it would be for both of them. And after that he thought he might like to stay single for several years. This one had not been worth the pain.

Completely exhausted, he undressed and climbed into bed. He tried to relax but something was annoying him. The pillows smelled of her so he flung them across the room. The sheets did too.

It was tempting to just put her in Pyramiden's helicopter

and fly her to Longyearbyen in the morning. And they could do whatever they wanted with him when he came back. But now he felt the same way as Grigory. He definitely did not want to go to prison for her.

He woke at six in the morning, feeling as though he had not slept at all. After making himself a coffee, he walked to the sports centre. There was no one else there as he changed into his swimming trunks. He dived into the pool and began to do lengths at a furious pace, one after the other, without stopping.

As he swam, he thought through a new plan, step by step. He wanted to be rid of her. He was not going to wait for the sun. Instead, they would go as soon as possible, when the weather forecast was good. Fifty miles, in the cold and dark, was going to be a challenge. It was not for nothing that every autumn they shipped in enough food to last till the spring. Even he was apprehensive about the trip. But she would have to endure it, if she wanted him to take her.

An imagined picture of Anya's non-existent husband had become so rooted in Yuri's consciousness that he found it hard to shake it off. He had no idea what this Taisia looked like. If only he could go back to the moment where it had all started. Anya standing outside London, waiting for him.

'Are you the one I'm waiting for?' she had asked.

'No, I am not. I hope you find him. Goodnight.'

Had it happened that way, he would not be where he was now, drained and depressed. He pushed himself to the bottom of the pool and held his breath for a full length. Breaking the surface at the end, he gasped for air.

When he could not swim any more, he pulled himself out of the pool. He showered, and dried, and managed to leave just as the early morning swimmers started to arrive.

In order for this plan to work, he would need to convince someone else to help him. This person had no reason to offer assistance; they were not even involved. But for him to be safe, there was no other option than to make this person complicit in what they were doing. And hope they would keep the secret.

Chapter 19

YURI SET THE trip for three days' time. Grigory advised against it, saying it was still too dark outside, but Yuri wanted the whole thing to be finished. Apart from Anya, only one person saw him every day and would notice his absence. Yuri feared that if Catherine did not see him for three or four whole days, she would raise the alarm and have everyone out searching the ice for him. He guessed she would not wait more than twenty-four hours before asking everyone she met if they had seen him.

It was difficult to gauge how she might react to what he had to say. Despite having gotten to know her well, and seen her strengths, in his opinion she still had a naive view of the world. He could not help seeing her as one of those western kids who thought that having the hammer and sickle on their bedroom wall equalled revolt. For Soviet kids it was western pop music and Levi jeans.

But he hoped that when push came to shove, she could discern what was really right from wrong in Anya's case. And she liked him. Or used to. He did not know how much that would count with her when she was faced with an ethical dilemma. There was only one way to find out. When they were alone at the power station he decided to take a chance on her.

'I might be gone for a few days,' he said. 'Do you think you can handle everything on your own while I'm away?'

She looked surprised. No one went anywhere for a few days at this time of year. No one came and no one left. Not unless there was a medical emergency that their small hospital could not handle.

'Where are you going?' she said.

'I am taking a trip with Anya,' he replied. 'It would be better if you didn't tell anyone about it.'

She paused and studied his expression. He tried to convey that this was something important to him.

'You are coming back?' she asked. 'You are not abandoning us?'

'Yes, I'll be back on the fourth day, at the latest.'

She could tell from his expression that it was not as simple as that.

'And Anya?' she asked. 'Will she be coming back too?'

This girl is far too smart for her own good, Yuri thought. Whatever the consequences, he did not want to lie to her again.

'Her trip will probably be one-way,' he said. 'Would it matter to you if she didn't come back?'

Catherine looked away for a moment, thinking this through. 'Not to me, no,' she said. 'But wouldn't you mind a lot if she didn't come back?'

'I've gotten used to the idea,' he admitted. 'I think it's probably the best thing for everyone involved. Including me.'

Catherine nodded. 'I see. So what is it exactly you want me to do?'

'Just do your work, as before, without me. And try not to draw attention to the fact that I'm not there.'

'I can do that,' she agreed. 'Will this thing get you into any trouble?'

'It shouldn't,' he said. 'It's not part of the plan. It's nothing I can't handle, no matter what happens. So you're OK with this?'

He saw her hesitate for a brief moment before she answered. 'Yes, I'm OK.'

'All right. I'll go through everything with you that will need to be done.'

'And if someone asks where you are? What will I say?'

They both knew he was asking her to lie on his behalf.

'If you're at the mine, say I'm at the power station. If you're here, say I'm at the mine. And if anyone is persistent, you could say I have a bad cold, and I'm staying in bed for a couple of days to shake it off. OK? I am sorry to put you in that position, but with any luck, no one will notice. Most of the time they only notice me when they need me to fix something for them.'

Catherine nodded. Dishonesty was not in her nature, and he felt bad about involving her. At least, being a foreign guest, she was unlikely to get into too much trouble if they were caught. He hoped he could count on her silence. He thought about asking for her word that she would keep this information between themselves. But he decided to make a leap of faith. She sat in silence, and he could see on her face that her mind was going over the implications of what she had just agreed to.

'If you need any help with anything while I'm gone, or you're not sure about anything, then Grigory will help you.'

She looked up sharply when he mentioned Grigory's name and he regretted saying it. She already knew far too much.

'Grigory knows that Anya is leaving?' she asked.

'Yes,' he replied. 'He does. You, me and him. And Anya of course. No one else needs to know.'

After a while, she said, 'You are definitely coming back?'

'Yes. I am,' he said. 'I promise.'

Again she was silent for a few moments, before she asked, 'Why? Why aren't you going with her? I thought you two were—'

'We were. But she needs to meet someone. Someone she was in a relationship with before we met,' he said. 'Then she won't need me any more.'

Hearing the words made him pause too. She really would not need him any more. It was true. Their relationship was based on her needs, and always had been. What he wanted was never part of the equation. And once he had fulfilled his part of their arrangement, he doubted she would spare him a thought for the rest of her days.

Catherine nodded as if she understood. She didn't ask who Anya was meeting, as if that did not matter to her. He was glad. If he had to explain who Anya was leaving him for, the conversation would get a whole lot more complicated. He wondered if she knew. If she could sense that Anya liked women too. Maybe everyone had known except him. It would not surprise him. These days he seemed to be the last person to know things.

Now that he had involved Catherine it could not be undone. He wanted this all to be over, so his life could go back to normal. All of this had happened because he had ignored every one of his golden rules. He had not kept his head down. He had trusted Anya. And he had not put himself first. She had her own agenda, and he had followed it willingly. No one had twisted his arm or held a gun to his head. Even now, he could turn his back on her and on the whole business. But he knew that really he was in far too deep to turn back now.

The success of their departure, and his return, rested on the shoulders of this young English woman. It was unfair to involve her, but necessary. He hoped he knew her as well as he thought.

'Any more questions?' he said. 'Now is the time to ask them.'

She shook her head.

'I appreciate this, Catherine. Thank you.'

He could tell she was uneasy about the whole business but it seemed this was not going to stop her from doing as he requested.

'And Timur?' he said.

'What about him?' she said, her expression and body language already shifting to defensive.

'If you could treat him like everyone else, that would be good. He doesn't need to know anything about this.'

'I won't mention it to anyone,' said Catherine. 'Anything else?'

Yuri smiled at her. 'Nothing. I think that's everything.'

He'd had little option other than to tell her about his trip. But if all went to plan, no one would be any the wiser. It would appear that Anya had disappeared in to thin air. And Catherine would be in the clear.

They started work, and did not speak of it again. He resolved to tell her all about Timur, and what he had done for him, once Anya was gone, even if giving her this information might mean the end of their friendship.

Grigory and Yuri went over the route several times. Neither of them had ever travelled by the land route in winter before. But judging by the information Grigory possessed, he had obviously spoken to someone who had. The Norwegian, Yuri guessed, before they had settled on a helicopter ride as the best way to get Anya out. A trapper like him would know all of the best paths to take. Not many men still followed the hunter's trade but there were a few still, who earned their living from the precious Arctic fox fur. They knew the island terrain like the back of their hands.

Time and the weather would be their enemies. Soon twilight would return, when the sun below the horizon would give them a little extra visibility. But that would not last long, and then they would be relying on a compass, the stars and the headlights of their snowmobiles. It would be slow going, and it was unlikely they could manage it in a day. To go too fast would invite disaster.

They would need to rest for a night, out in the harsh elements. Yuri planned to take a small tent and an oil heater. A strange way to spend their very last night, huddled together, fighting the Arctic cold. When twilight resumed the next morning, they could continue their journey. A mechanical failure or an accident, both strong possibilities, could allow any pursuers to catch up with them. But potential pursuers were not the biggest threat. If they got stuck out there on the ice and snow, too far away from real shelter, and with no way to contact anyone, then they might not come out of this alive.

The part that worried Yuri the most was not getting caught, or the weather, but that Anya was not physically up to the journey. She was underweight by Svalbard standards, and not in any shape for a gruelling, cross-country trip.

On the pretext of visiting the researcher's weather station, he took her out for a test drive on one of the snowmobiles. She quickly got into trouble and became frustrated. If it had been a straight, flat road the whole way there, she could have been fine. But nature had not made it so easy for them. On rougher terrain, she found it tough to control the vehicle underneath her. He was intimately acquainted with her body, and knew that she had little muscle to speak of, especially where it counted for this mode of transport, in the shoulders and arms. There was not enough time to build her up, even if she was willing. So he made the difficult decision that they would have to double up on one snowmobile. This would make them heavier on the snow, and slow them down considerably. But Anya greeted the news with relief.

'Will we still be all right?' she asked. 'We can make it that way?'

'We should be,' said Yuri, more in hope than certainty.

Anya shook her head. 'First I travelled thousands of miles, by plane and boat, to get here. Now I have to drive for two days across the frozen Arctic, in the dark. I bet they didn't put Taisia through so much trouble when they took her. She always got everything handed to her on a plate. People went out of their way to please her. Do you think they are making it as difficult as possible for me to come? Maybe they don't want me.'

Yuri had to agree. The scenario she had described made perfect sense. They were giving her almost no help at all. As if they wanted her to fail. Perhaps they were worried what effect her arrival would have on their prized possession. And if it all went wrong they could say they'd tried their best. Even put one of their most experienced agents on the job. If Taisia only knew it was Grigory, she would realise what a lie that was.

Assuming they reached Longyearbyen alive, they were to find the police station and ask them to contact the British Embassy in the Norwegian capital, Oslo, and they would take it from there. No doubt the Norwegians would not be too happy. They did not intentionally seek out problems with their giant communist neighbour, but they would have little option other than to help a genuine defector. They could always deny they had anything to do with it, if they wanted. Anya, if she even kept that name, was going to disappear into a world of safe houses and secret service minders. Once more to enter into the shadow of her more talented and sought-after girl-friend. Taisia must indeed be something special if the British were willing to even pretend to try to get Anya out. Anya obviously thought she was. She was willing to put whatever life she had left in jeopardy, in the attempt to be reunited with her. Despite himself, he was intrigued by this person he had never met. She seemed to be more of a manipulator than Anya. That was a scary thought. She had taught Anya well.

When they returned to town, Yuri went to find Grigory in his office. He looked up over his reading glasses as Yuri shut the door. The only light in the room was a lamp, illuminating the pages on the desk. Grigory was hard to make out in the shadows behind it.

'This operation they gave you—' Yuri began.

Grigory held up his hand.

'Not here. I told you, if you want to talk about that, we can meet in the usual place.'

'No,' said Yuri, tapping his finger on Grigory's desk. 'We'll talk about it now. It's designed to fail, isn't it? That's why they gave it to you. Some half-arsed semi-retired agent who has never done anything like this before in his life.'

Grigory looked hurt by these home truths, but then he nodded.

'The thought had occurred to me,' he agreed. 'I am, as you say, an unusual choice.'

'You might have mentioned this before now,' said Yuri. 'Instead of getting her hopes up. The way you waited months before revealing that you were her contact, whose idea was that?'

Grigory looked him in the eye. 'That was mine. The whole set-up made me nervous,' he said. 'Asking me in the first place. I wouldn't even pick me. And then her behaviour. I wouldn't have gotten involved at all, if she hadn't put herself in the hospital.'

'You think they don't want her?'

'I know they don't want her. You are the only one who wants her. And this girlfriend of hers. Everyone else rightly looks at her and sees more trouble than she's worth.'

'Then why bother bringing her here?'

Grigory shrugged. 'That's a good question. I wish I knew the answer to that one.'

'You think they want her to get caught?' asked Yuri.

The question worried Grigory. It remained unspoken but Yuri was sure that Grigory was thinking it too. If they did not mind her getting caught, then what about their own agent? How much did they care about him?

'Would they inform on us?' asked Yuri.

Grigory looked shocked at the suggestion. Watching him think it over worried Yuri even more.

'No,' he said. 'Anything's possible, but I believe not. They are making success difficult by their lack of material support, but if we succeed I think they are prepared to accept that outcome.'

'You think? If you had any doubts about their commitment, you should have warned me before now.'

'I have dealt with them for thirty years,' said Grigory. 'Up to this point they have treated me fairly, and honestly.'

'So what is it then? Are they just playing games with us?' asked Yuri. 'Rolling the dice and waiting to see which way they land.'

'That's one possible scenario,' said Grigory. 'One of several.'

'One of several!' said Yuri. 'I am not even going to ask what the others are. I don't like them. Please tell them that next time you are talking to them.'

'I will pass it on,' said Grigory.

The fact that the British did not seem to care if they succeeded made Yuri more determined than ever to see this to a successful conclusion. He did not care whether Anya and Taisia were happy together or whether they split up after one week. His only focus was on getting her to Longyearbyen. That would be the end of his part in her journey. And after that he did not want to know.

Yuri decided to discuss the risks involved with Anya again. He did not want her to suddenly change her mind when they were halfway across the ice.

'These are risks I am willing to take,' she insisted. 'If I stay I will be as good as dead anyway, so it makes no difference. At least by trying I will have a chance of a life.'

'Once we are out there, I am in charge,' said Yuri. 'You'll do whatever I say. If I decide we need to turn back, we will turn back.'

'Of course,' she agreed. 'You are the boss.'

'You may be willing to put your life on the line, but I am kind of attached to mine, and I'd like to hang on to it for a few more years.'

'After this, you should go back to Moscow in the spring,' she said. 'There is no future here for you in this place.'

'I met you here.'

'I'm leaving,' she said. 'What will you do after that? Wait for the next boat to see who it might bring? Moscow is full of interesting women. I think you'd be happier there.'

Yuri shook his head. 'No, I wouldn't.'

'What if I was there?' she said. 'What if I did not go to the west, and I went back to live in Moscow? What would you do?'

'Is that an offer? he asked.

'No,' she said. 'But if I was there, would it make a difference to you?'

Yuri thought about this for a moment. The answer was yes, it would make a difference, but he answered, 'It doesn't matter, does it, because you are leaving. And I am taking you.'

Chapter 20

WITH TWO DAYS to go, Yuri stopped sleeping. He had been over every detail many times in his head, and he could not foresee where it was going to go wrong. But he knew the unexpected was bound to happen. He could only hope that he would be ready for it, whatever it was.

At least this time he was in charge, not the Norwegian, or Grigory. And the fact that it was him had put Anya at ease too. The plan was simple enough. The distance they had to travel, in winter conditions, was the hard part. If they were careful, there was no need to worry about pursuers. No one would know they were gone for at least a day. There were no major storms forecast, and he was confident he could handle whatever the Arctic might throw at them. If he had any doubt that Anya would be in danger, he would have called the whole thing off. But so far things were going well, perhaps too well. And that's what worried him.

The idea that Yuri had sown in Grigory's mind, that the British might secretly desire this operation to fail, had made the party man angry. His professional pride was hurt, and for the first time he seemed to be personally engaged, and concerned for the success of their mission.

'It is too much to ask you to take this on alone. I could go with you,' Grigory whispered, over breakfast in the canteen. 'I could drive the other snowmobile.'

'Why would you do that?' asked Yuri.

He did not want Grigory to come along. It would leave him having to babysit two people who were not fit for the trip, instead of one.

'I don't know. In case something went wrong with your one.'

'Then there would be three of us out there, with one snow-mobile between us. What would we do then? Draw straws to see who stays behind to freeze to death?'

Grigory nodded his head. 'You're right. You're right. I hadn't thought of that.'

Grigory was tucking in to a plate of sausage and black bread. Whatever nervous nights he was having, it was not affecting his appetite. Behind Grigory, through the window, Yuri spotted a welcome event. The first faint halo below the eastern horizon that announced the beginning of the sun's return. Over the coming weeks, it would gradually rise a little more each day. Then one day, as if by magic, the town would wake to find that light had returned to the Arctic.

The party man sat silently, then he shook his head.

'I should be the one to go, not you. I should never have involved you.'

'You should never have involved me,' Yuri agreed. 'But you did and it's too late now. After the last disaster with your Norwegian, Anya will not go with anyone else now. Besides, who do you think has a better chance out there, you or me?'

Grigory looked defeated.

'You,' he said. 'The benefit of youth. But it was not always that way. Once, it would have been me. Unfortunately, those days are gone. It happens to us all.'

'You are not in a wheelchair yet,' said Yuri. 'Did you ever find out why your Norwegian didn't turn up?'

'No,' said Grigory. 'I have been trying to get in touch with him ever since but I have not had any reply. The last time I spoke to him was with you in the greenhouse. Not a word since then. It's not unusual for him. But he likes money, so I am surprised.'

'He obviously doesn't like money enough to risk his neck for it,' said Yuri.

Grigory shook his head. 'I really don't think it was fear that kept him away. He is not that type of man.'

'Then what?' said Yuri.

Grigory shrugged. 'I don't know. There is no point speculating, until I have the chance to talk to him.'

Yuri's favourite pastime was speculation. He did not care about the Norwegian. But he did want to know the reason for his no-show, in case it affected them.

'How about I go some of the way with you?' Grigory offered. 'Just to make sure you are not being followed.'

'Let's just leave things the way they are,' said Yuri. 'If we all go it will be more suspicious.'

Grigory nodded sadly, like a schoolboy who was not getting picked for the football team.

'Don't worry,' said Yuri. 'We will show the British how wrong they were.'

Grigory smiled but it did not last long. He stiffened as he saw Timur approaching their table.

'Morning, gentlemen. May I join you?' he asked.

Yuri could see that the party man was about to say no. Normally, he was diplomatic with everyone, no matter where they came in Pyramiden's pecking order. Those English spy handlers really had gotten under his skin.

'Sure,' said Yuri, though he wanted to say no too.

Timur spun a chair around and straddled it, resting his elbows on the back.

'What are you two talking about so quietly over here?' Timur asked.

'Chess,' replied Yuri. 'It's Grigory's obsession. Didn't you know?'

'No, I didn't,' said Timur. 'Perhaps you and I should play some time, Grigory. I am quite good, or so I am told.'

'He'd like that, wouldn't you?' asked Yuri. 'A new challenger.'

Yuri kicked Grigory under the table. He looked up and gave Timur a false smile.

'I'd love to. Any time,' said Grigory.

'It's good to see that you have other interests, Yuri, not just women,' said Timur.

The comment was not worth responding to so Yuri did not bother. Or maybe the man had intended it as a joke. It was hard to tell.

Grigory checked his watch and made a hasty departure, using the excuse of an imminent meeting in his office.

'I didn't know that you two had so much in common,' said Timur. 'Our friend Grigory always struck me as a solitary creature.'

'Oh, he is,' agreed Yuri. 'A proper grumpy old hermit. But he also likes to beat me at chess.'

For a horrible moment, Yuri thought that Timur was about to ask him to inform on Grigory. The man had done the same before with Semyon, and his curiosity about Pyramiden's resident party man had obviously not waned.

As Timur continued to talk, Yuri wondered again if he could have been the one to kill Semyon. The Latvian had been a good informant. Having read his file, it was clear he had applied himself to his task with enthusiasm and had done everything that had been asked of him. Why would Timur want to get rid of a good informant? There was no doubt the KGB man was physically capable of doing it, if he wanted to. Timur, while not a big man, was in good shape and had his KGB training to rely on. Yuri had felt the force of one of his blows himself. But he could not see a reason why Timur would have taken such a radical action. Where was the benefit?

'How do you find Grigory?' asked Timur.

'What do you mean?'

'I mean, would you say you know him well? I have always considered him to be one of the good guys. I think we are in excellent hands with him here in Pyramiden.'

'Very good,' agreed Yuri. 'If only all party execs were like him.'

Timur gave a half-smile, and let pass the implied criticism of all other party executives. Yuri could not tell if he was genuinely praising Grigory or not. It was more likely that he was fishing for something, as always.

'I am pleased you have gotten over our little misunderstanding about Catherine,' said Timur. 'I am very fond of her. And I want her to be happy. I believe it made her sad that our relationship disrupted yours with her. She is glad that you two are friends again.'

It pained Yuri to smile. He could not bring himself to add any words of agreement.

'It's a pity she's leaving so soon,' said Timur. 'But you never know what the future might bring.'

It took Yuri a moment to figure out what he was talking about.

'You mean a posting to London? For you?'

'Of course,' said Timur. 'I've been practising my English with Catherine. It's not so bad, if I do say so myself. And I've been in this backwater long enough. I never understood why they sent me here.'

So they did not have to listen to you talking about yourself all day long, thought Yuri. And Pyramiden was the furthest place they could find to send him. If they ever did decide to send communist colonists into space, he expected Timur's name would be top of their list.

'I hope you get it,' said Yuri, meaning every word.

The downside was that the KGB would inevitably send a replacement who was equally difficult to have around.

At work Catherine was quiet for most of the day, which suited Yuri as he was preoccupied with thoughts of the impending trip. He decided not to remind her about her role in his alibi. She had already agreed, and it was best to leave well enough alone. Since she had started seeing Timur, he had noticed that she had lost some of her bubbly nature. He blamed the KGB man for this. From what he could tell, there seemed to be no positive side for Catherine to their relationship. Other than the fact that she was in one, after such a long time. If Timur made her happy, Yuri might reconsider his opposition to their relationship. But from where he stood, it did not look like Timur was doing that.

At the end of the day, she put on her coat and walked to the door.

'See you tomorrow,' he said.

She nodded, without turning. 'Yes. See you.'

Yuri decided that once he had finished with Anya, he would apply himself to breaking up Catherine's relationship with Timur, by one means or another. He had no intention of playing fair. He would not get any thanks for it, but it was for her own good.

In the evening he visited Anya in her apartment. She was already a little drunk. Her eyes were bloodshot, and her cheeks were redder than usual. He looked around the room, and saw no bags packed. Her belongings were still in drawers or hanging in her wardrobe.

'We are going the day after tomorrow,' he said. 'Have you decided what you are taking with you?'

Anya shrugged. 'You told me to pack the last time and I ended up not going anywhere, just a trip to the weather station and back again.'

'Well, you are going this time. Definitely. So you better get organised.'

Anya nodded without enthusiasm.

'Look, it's happening. OK? Trust me. And no more booze.'

'Hey,' she protested, as he took the glass from her hand.

He also grabbed the bottle from the table, and poured both down the sink.

'You can survive without it for two days, can't you? When you get to the west you can drink all you want, all day every day.'

Anya looked up at him, then turned away.

'Taisia doesn't like me to drink. We had lots of rows about it. It drives her crazy when I do.'

Anya had not mentioned her name in a long time. Yuri did not like to hear her say it, and he had to remind himself that he did not care.

'That's something she and I have in common then. I disapprove of your drinking too.'

Anya smiled. 'You are not alike at all. Life with you is easier.'

'Easier?' said Yuri. 'Is that a good thing?'

'Yes,' she said. 'That is a good thing.'

'And life with Taisia?' he asked. 'What was that like?'

'Up and down,' said Anya. 'When it was up, it was fantastic. But at other times it was not so good. She likes to get her own way in all things. Not just at work.'

Yuri found it hard to imagine Anya allowing herself to be bossed around. This, he suspected, was where her depression pills came from. When she was in a vulnerable mood like this, he just wanted to wrap her in his arms. It was tempting to try again to talk her out of going but he knew he would be wasting his breath. She held up the possibility of them staying together like waving a stick to a dog. Only to squash his hopes almost in the same breath. He forced himself not to fall for it once more.

'I'm going,' he said. 'I'll check in with you tomorrow.'

'You don't have to leave.'

'I know,' he said. 'Sleep well. And please, do not go searching for more booze.'

He spotted a guilty look on her face. She had already been wondering where she could get some. He opened the door, and shut it behind him.

On his way home, he checked on the two snowmobiles in their covered car park. He did a quick check on their engines, and calculated how much extra fuel he would need to take. Enough for the return too, he decided. It would be better if he did not have to speak with any Norwegians at Longyearbyen. One of them might let slip that he had been seen in town with Anya. He doubted they would understand the consequences in store for him if such simple information was passed on to the wrong person. The KGB as a whole, and not just Timur, would be all over this when they figured out what had happened.

It did not matter what time of day they arrived in Longyearbyen. Darkness was still their companion twenty-four hours a day, apart from the halo below the horizon line on either side of sunrise and sunset. He would be able to drop her off without being noticed, and he could turn straight back around. Doing this would be risky for him. Double the journey, one hundred miles with no rest in between, would push his own body and the vehicle's engine to the limit. But overall, he considered it the safest option. When the alarm was raised that Anya was missing, he needed to be in Pyramiden. If he wasn't, then all the secrecy would have been for nothing. He would be considered guilty by everyone, and no matter what he said, he would not be able to talk himself out of it.

The next day, Catherine did not turn up for work at the power station. Yuri was not overly worried about her. She had seemed a bit down the day before and he expected that it was just this. Perhaps she needed some time alone. However, when there was no sign or word from her by six in the evening he decided to go and check on her.

Despite having been in Paris many times since Anya's arrival, he had never been to Catherine's apartment before. He knocked gently and after a few moments she opened the door a few inches. She did not seem pleased to see him but she walked back inside, leaving the door open for him. Scanning the room, he was not surprised to see a framed picture of Karl Marx hanging on her wall.

'Are you not feeling well?' he asked. 'Do you need anything?'

'I am not sick,' she said.

'Oh. That's good,' he said. 'You didn't feel like coming to work today? I know how that feels.'

When she did not respond, or even smile, he asked, 'What's wrong?'

'I have told you so much about myself,' said Catherine. 'Things I haven't told anyone else. But you keep everything from me. You asked me to be a part of this thing, without telling me what it's really all about.'

Yuri stared at her.

'She is a traitor, like her friend,' Catherine continued. 'And you're helping her. Which makes you a traitor too.'

'I am not a traitor,' said Yuri. 'I am doing it for her. She needs to go there, to the west. She has a chance to get her life back.'

Catherine avoided looking at him. 'You should have explained it to me, if you wanted my help. Don't you think I deserve to know, if I am to be involved in a crime?'

'Wait,' said Yuri. 'How did you know about her friend?'

Yuri's mind raced, trying to figure this out. He stopped himself from shouting at her, and demanding to know everything.

After a moment, she said, 'Timur told me.'

'What exactly did he say?' asked Yuri.

'He told me that her friend, Taisia, defected to the west five years ago.'

'What else did he tell you?

Catherine did not answer.

'Please, tell me, what else did he say? It's important.'

'He didn't say anything else,' replied Catherine. 'Just that.'

'When did he tell you this?'

'Two days ago.'

Yuri wondered when Timur had acquired this information about Anya and Taisia. And how?

'But he didn't know about my trip with her. Did he?'

Catherine turned away again.

Yuri tried not to, but couldn't help raising his voice. 'Did he know about that? You better tell me quick. If he did, more people than Anya will be in danger.'

Catherine looked up at him.

'No,' she replied. 'He didn't know . . . but he does now.'

'You told him?' asked Yuri.

'She won't be going anywhere after all, will she,' said Catherine, almost spitting the words. 'Except to jail.'

'How much did you tell him?' asked Yuri.

'I told him she was leaving. I didn't know she was planning to defect until he told me,' she replied. 'Don't worry. I didn't mention your name. I kept you out of it.'

Yuri went pale. He looked at her in disappointment.

'Why? Why did you do that? You said you would help me. I thought we agreed that you were not going to tell Timur anything.'

'I guessed there was more to it than you made out,' she said. 'You were not honest with me.'

'I did not want to involve you, that's all.' said Yuri. 'What did Timur tell you in return?'

Catherine was getting angry now. 'You did involve me. You didn't tell me she was a traitor. You didn't tell me that her friend had defected, and was working against the Soviet Union. You didn't mention any of those things.'

Yuri rested his forehead in one hand, trying to think. It did not make any sense.

'When did you tell Timur?'

'Two nights ago,' said Catherine.

'And you told him it was Anya?'

'Yes,' she said.

He had been with Anya yesterday, the day after Catherine had told Timur she was planning to defect. And he had already seen Anya walking around town that morning. If Timur knew about her planned trip, then why had he not done something about it? It should have been a big deal for an ambitious agent like him to catch a defector.

'What exactly did he say when you told him?'

Catherine shrugged. 'He didn't seem to care. He didn't look surprised, and he told me not to tell anyone else. He was most interested in how I knew all about it, but I didn't tell him that.'

'Come with me,' Yuri ordered. 'Now.'

'Where to?' she said, not budging from her chair.

'I need your help. Please,' he said.

She reluctantly got up and followed him out the door. Instead of heading down towards the exit door, he marched quickly up the stairs in the direction of the next floor.

'Where are we going?' she asked again.

'You'll see. By the way, now that we are being completely honest with each other, you and Timur have nothing in common,' said Yuri. 'He had me informing on you so he could find out all about you. He used that to make you think you were both interested in the same things. I doubt he's ever read Pushkin, or any poetry, in his life. He is certainly not your soulmate.'

It was not the most appropriate time to tell her, but he felt a great sense of relief about being truthful with her finally. He imagined she would not have given away what she knew to Timur, if she had understood what sort of a man she was dating.

'What! You spied on me!' Catherine said.

'For Timur, yes,' said Yuri. 'It's a long story. I'm sorry. I didn't want to. I don't do it any more. I'll explain it all to you another time.'

Catherine stopped halfway up the staircase. 'But how could you do something like that to me? To anyone?'

'He made me. I could have said no, it's true, but I didn't. But it's not me you should be angry with. I tried to warn you about him, didn't I?'

Catherine shook her head. 'I can't believe you. I thought we were friends.'

'We are,' said Yuri, pulling her by the arm. 'More than you know. Look, we can't talk about this right now. We'll get to it, I promise. But there are more important things happening.'

Catherine did not look as though she agreed anything else was more important. But she followed him in silence to the top of the staircase.

Yuri stopped outside Anya's apartment and knocked loudly on the door.

'Don't say anything unless I ask you,' he said. 'Just follow my lead.'

Chapter 21

A MOMENT LATER, Anya opened her apartment door. She smiled at first but stopped when she saw Catherine standing behind him. She looked at both of their expressions, and did not open the door any wider.

'What's wrong?' she said. 'Did something happen?'

'We need to talk to you,' said Yuri. 'It's urgent.'

Yuri pushed past her into the room. From the various items on the table, it seemed that Anya had spent the day making decorations out of plastic wiring, similar to what she had seen hanging in Yuri's apartment. Not the most obvious activity for someone who was planning to defect the next day. Catherine followed him inside, and shut the door behind her. She stayed put, hovering uncomfortably in the doorway. Yuri could see that she was not happy to be dragged in here. And she gave him a look to say he better have a damn good reason for it. Anya watched them both taking up positions facing her, and she walked nervously to the bed and sat down.

'Anya, you will have to get your things ready,' said Yuri. 'Something unexpected has happened and there's been a change of plan. We have to go today, not tomorrow. Tomorrow will be too late. So let's go. I'll explain on the way.'

Catherine turned to look at him with a surprised expression, but she did as he had asked, and said nothing. As Yuri had feared, Anya froze, and did not move a muscle. She just sat in the same position, looking confused.

'Why is she here?' Anya asked, pointing a finger at Catherine.

After betraying Catherine by acting as an informer for Timur, Yuri had hoped not to deceive anyone close to him ever again. But whatever he was about to do to Anya, it was probably nothing compared to what she had done.

'She's your contact, like you thought,' said Yuri. 'The English sent her. Come on, we're in a hurry. Get moving.'

Catherine was about to protest, but she stopped herself from interrupting. Her eyes could not have got any wider, as she took in the scene playing out in front of her.

'I can't go today,' said Anya. 'I'm not ready.'

'Why can't you go?' said Yuri. 'What else have you got to do? I am telling you if we don't go now, this might never happen. You'll have to trust me.'

'I'm not feeling well,' said Anya. 'I think I am coming down with something. A fever. I was going to tell you. Even tomorrow, I am not sure if I will be able.'

'But it's all arranged,' said Yuri. 'The English won't wait any longer. You don't want to miss the opportunity you have waited so long for. It might not come again. Isn't that right, Catherine?'

Catherine appeared to be angry with him for engaging her even further in his deception. But she dutifully nodded her head.

Anya stared at her.

'That one is not my contact,' she said. 'Why did you say she is? I am not a fool.'

'How do you know that?' asked Yuri. 'I am telling you, she is your contact. And we have to take you now, if you want to go. You don't look ill to me. You can see a doctor when you get to Longyearbyen.'

Anya still did not move. She seemed unsure what to do. But whatever she was thinking, she was not afraid.

'She isn't my contact,' said Anya. 'I know she isn't.'

Yuri shrugged. 'If you are so sure, then tell me, who is your contact?'

Anya looked away. 'I don't know, but it's not her. Are you going to tell me now?'

'No,' said Yuri. 'Definitely not now.'

He opened the wardrobe and started to pull out Anya's clothes from the shelves and hangers. He threw each one across the room on to the bed, beside her, and on to the floor at her feet.

'What are you doing?' she said, as they piled up around her. 'Stop.'

'I'm helping you,' he replied. 'It's too late to call this off.'

Catherine stared at Yuri. He could see she was having trouble holding back her questions.

'Come on,' he said, in a loud voice. 'What are you waiting for?'

'I am not going anywhere today,' said Anya, firmly. 'I'd like you both to leave.'

'I am afraid we can't do that,' he said. 'Can we, Catherine? Her bosses have promised to deliver you to your friend. She is expecting you. You don't want to disappoint her, do you? She has gone to so much trouble to get you back.'

'Why are you doing this to me?' said Anya. 'Please, can you just stop.'

Yuri stopped pulling her things out of the wardrobe and turned around. She looked up at him with watery eyes. A picture of innocence. If he had not known her so well, he might just have believed that face. He had once.

'Are you the one I'm waiting for?' said Yuri. 'That's what you said to me, remember? Is that what you said to Semyon?'

Yuri saw from her expression that Anya realised she had been caught. Catherine looked back and forth between the two of them, not understanding any of what was going on.

'You are the one in his notebook, aren't you?' said Yuri. 'Eagle.'

'What notebook?' said Anya.

She glanced towards the door, as though she might make a run for it. But Catherine was leaning against it, blocking her way.

'Before you say anything, please don't give me another lie,' said Yuri. 'I'm not sure I could take it. All right?'

Anya looked him in the eye, then turned away before she spoke.

'I am not the only one who has lied. Am I?' she said. 'He thought Semyon might be my contact. I don't know why. But that's why I asked him. I had already waited weeks.'

'Who are you talking about? Who is "he"?' asked Yuri.

'I think you already know the answer to that,' said Anya. 'Don't you?'

Yuri nodded his head, and glanced at Catherine before answering.

'Timur,' he said. 'He was the one who thought the contact might be Semyon.'

Catherine had been an objective observer up to this point, but now he saw her coming to the unwelcome realisation that she was involved after all.

'Yes,' said Anya. 'Neither of us could understand why the contact had not been in touch with me before then. They were the ones who arranged my trip here. So it was strange. At first we thought something had gone wrong. Then when the boats stopped coming, we thought it must be someone who was already here in Pyramiden. Semyon was working as an informer for Timur, but he didn't trust him. He said that anyone who was willing to inform for one side is capable of doing it for the other.'

'So you asked Semyon if he was your contact. And what did he say?'

Anya shook her head. 'He said yes, he was the one. He misunderstood. He thought I liked him.'

Yuri pictured the little Latvian standing in front of this beautiful woman, thinking all his dreams had come true at once. Of course, he had said yes. He remembered Semyon's file in Timur's office. All those reports he had gotten Semyon to do on Pyramiden's residents. He was looking for the contact, trying to figure out who it might be. The repeated and apparently innocuous conversations between Semyon and Grigory made sense now. Timur had seen something in Grigory that made him suspect him. Or perhaps he had wanted it to be him. The conversations between the two men had revealed nothing, so he had finally turned his gaze full circle on to his own informant.

'Let me guess, you arranged to meet Semyon at the whaling house,' said Yuri. 'Whose idea was it to go there?'

'How the hell did you know that?' asked Anya.

'I know a lot of things, now,' said Yuri. 'I am not as stupid as I used to be.'

'It was his idea, Semyon's. He said he used to go there sometimes to get away from everyone for a while. I can't see why. It's barely standing, and completely freezing.'

'All right, so you met him there. Then what happened?'

Anya made a face, as though the question brought back unpleasant memories.

'Then it all went wrong,' she said. 'Once we were inside he pushed the door shut, and then he tried to touch me. I told him to stop; that I had no interest in him in that way. He got angry, and started shouting. I said all I wanted from him was his help to get me to the west, as arranged.'

'I bet he wasn't expecting that,' said Yuri.

Anya nodded. 'No, he wasn't. He called me names. Said I was a traitor to my country. And worse things than that. He threatened to inform on me to Timur.'

'But that didn't scare you, did it?' asked Yuri. 'Because Timur already knew all about you, didn't he?'

Anya did not answer. She caught Catherine's eye, but they both looked away quickly. The English woman shifted her weight from one foot to the other, and looked even more confused.

'Did you tell Semyon that you and Timur were the best of pals?' asked Yuri. 'That would have made him keep his hands to himself.'

'No,' she said. 'I couldn't tell him. If he was not my contact, then I had already told him too much. I just wanted to get out of there. But he wouldn't let me leave. He said he was going to blackmail me . . . and not for money. He finally let me out when I promised to meet him again.'

Yuri's late-night conversation with the Lithuanians made sense now. They'd accused him of being the one that Semyon was trying to blackmail. They had gotten the wrong impression too; that the Latvian had come across some information that would enable him to extort money. But it was sex he was after. Semyon had not made a report to Timur, because he thought he could get Anya into bed by one means or another. Informing on her to the KGB man would have put an end to that possibility. He did not realise the game he was getting involved in was much bigger than that. It cost him his life. After hearing Anya's story, Yuri had even less sympathy for his former assistant.

'And is that why you killed him?' said Yuri. 'Because he was blackmailing you? Or because he knew too much about you, and you were afraid who else he might tell?'

'I thought that was an accident?' said Anya, her voice raised in indignation. 'How could you think that I did something like that?'

Yuri shrugged. Right now he did not know what she was capable of.

'He was killed,' said Yuri. 'I think because of what you told him.'

'Well, I did not do it,' said Anya. 'Thank you for thinking I did.'

'Timur then,' said Yuri. 'Did he do it?'

'I don't know,' said Anya. 'You will have to ask him that.'

Yuri caught a sharp glance from Catherine. She appeared shaken by the turn in the conversation.

'Semyon wasn't a spy,' said Yuri. 'He was just an ambitious little shit.'

Anya nodded that she knew this, and she appeared to feel some tinge of guilt over his death. Perhaps she had not drawn the short straw at the school after all, and had volunteered to attend his funeral.

'Did you really believe it was an accident?' asked Yuri. 'It was a pretty convenient one for you if it was.'

Anya shrugged. 'It seemed strange to me at the time, all right. But everyone said it had happened that way, so I thought that it must have.'

'Trust your instincts,' said Yuri. 'You will get into less trouble that way. I am trying to learn the same lesson. And then you thought your contact might be me. Let me guess – because I sabotaged my own system to keep my job.'

Anya nodded, and he thought he saw a flash of remorse in her eyes.

'It was Timur's idea. I just did what he told me to do. But with you, I thought he might be right. I'd seen you looking at me for weeks, like you had something to say to me. You even came into my classroom to fix something that wasn't broken.'

Yuri could see how they had gotten the wrong idea. It seemed he was not so different from Semyon after all; he was just trying to get her into bed too. He paused, trying to put all the pieces together. They still did not make sense.

'How long did it take you to figure out I was not your contact either?' asked Yuri.

'Not long. You made it pretty clear what you were after. Timur still believed it might be you, even though I told him I was sure you weren't the one. He made me put a listening device in your room. We have been giving him a good show for all these months.'

Catherine started coughing on the other side of the room.

'Where is it?' asked Yuri. 'The microphone.'

'In your radio,' she said. 'It's still there. Unless he took it. Then you said that the contact had spoken with you. Timur was angry with me because I couldn't find out who it was. But I said it was fine, that we should go ahead as planned. It did not matter that I never met him or her, whoever they are. As long as we got what we needed.'

'And did you?' asked Yuri. 'Did you get what you needed?'

Anya looked up at him with a cold look in her eyes.

'It seems that way,' she said. 'I am waiting to hear. We have given them enough time.'

'Hear what?' asked Yuri.

Anya almost answered him but then decided not to.

'You never had any intention of going, did you?' he said. 'All this time, you have just been stringing me along. I thought you wanted to be with her. Taisia. Was that not the whole point of all this? I don't understand why you came all this way if you were not going to go through with it.'

Anya shook her head. 'It was not a lie between you and me. I know you don't believe that right now. But it's true.'

'You're right. I don't.'

'She left me,' said Anya. 'Abandoned me, without one thought. Left my career in ruins. She took my whole life away. Everything. Then five years later she remembers I'm alive, and says "Sorry, I want to be with you after all." I don't want to be with her. I hate her.'

'So it was all an act,' said Yuri. 'All of it. The tears. The drinking. The suicide attempt.'

'No,' said Anya. 'Most of those things were real. I have nothing to go back to. I thought I had come here for nothing.'

'But you had, hadn't you?' said Yuri. 'If you weren't going to leave, then coming here was a waste of time. Why bother making her think you were going to join her in England? Was it just so you could stand her up at the altar? Is that all? I'm sorry, but I don't see the point. And what has Timur got to do with it? Why was he helping you to defect?'

Anya had a smug smile on her face. Then an idea came to Yuri, and he thought he had finally figured it out.

'They want you to go, and be an agent for them in England,' said Yuri. 'That's it, isn't it?'

Anya shook her head, and appeared to be bored with his lack of speed.

'No,' she said. 'They want the same thing I want. You really still don't get it?'

Yuri caught Catherine's eye. She was none the wiser either.

'A little village, six miles from Oxford,' said Anya. 'A white cottage, yellow roses in the front garden, a river in the back.'

'Oh no,' said Yuri.

He had arranged the radio call between them not knowing that Anya was looking for a way to kill her. He wondered if he could stop it now somehow. But there was no way for him to do it.

'Shouldn't be too hard to find her,' said Anya. 'Maybe they already have. They have been looking ever since I spoke to her. You know what they do to traitors.'

'Keep her here!' Yuri said to Catherine as he ran out the door. 'Don't let her leave.'

Chapter 22

YURI RACED FROM Paris, along the wooden walkway, to the administration building. He was going so fast that he skidded on ice at a corner and almost fell down on to the ground. He managed to right himself in time, and kept on going. He passed Igor on the way, but ignored the man's outstretched hand completely. Later, he would tell him that Timur had killed Semyon. It was unlikely he would be too surprised by that news. Knowing would not make much difference. Timur would never pay for the crime.

The sight of Yuri running down the administration building corridors drew a lot of attention from the clerical staff but there was no time for secrecy now. He burst into Grigory's office without knocking, and slammed the door behind him.

'What are you doing?' asked Grigory.

Yuri did not answer. He marched straight to the window, and looked out to see if anyone had followed him. He could not see anyone, but they knew. And not just Timur. This scheme to trap Taisia was way above his pay grade. It must have been set up well before Anya began her journey to Pyramiden. Yuri had been used as a pawn in a bigger game, and they had known everything, all along. Because Anya had been telling them.

But she did not know about Grigory. She couldn't. And suddenly he regretted coming here. If someone was watching him, perhaps he had led them straight to the inside man they were looking for. That's why they were still walking around free. An assassin had been dispatched to England to settle their vendetta against the betrayer, Taisia. But they wanted the contact too. Little did they know he was not much of a catch.

'Men are on their way to kill Anya's friend, if they haven't already,' said Yuri.

He saw the blood draining from Grigory's face. He had been right about not getting involved, thought Yuri. Always trust your instincts. Always. He should have walked away from Anya too, at the first sign of trouble.

'That's what this was all about,' he continued. 'From the beginning. They were after Taisia. Anya was too. She never had any intention of going to join her in the west. And when they send word that she's dead, Timur will be coming for you. We don't have much time. You have to get out of here. Now!'

'How do you know all this?' asked Grigory. 'Tell me. Is this another of your conspiracy theories?'

'No! There's no time for explanations,' said Yuri. 'You're going to have to trust me on this one, if you want to stay alive. I presume you would like to do that?'

Grigory didn't budge. Instead, he sat there looking confused.

'Let's go,' said Yuri. 'Come on.'

'I can't just—' Grigory was saying, before his mouth stopped in mid-motion.

'He's a clever boy, actually,' said Timur.

Yuri turned to see Timur standing in the doorway with his revolver trained on both of them. Once again, Yuri felt like the amateur that he was. Timur had tailed him all the way here without him noticing. They had waited patiently for him to give away the identity of Anya's contact. And of course, he had, because he was a fool.

'Too clever for your own good, Yuri. Should have stuck to your pipes. But then women always were your weakness. And you, Grigory, I had a feeling about you. And so close to retirement too. What a pity.'

'I don't imagine all this was your idea?' said Yuri.

'Not exactly. The plan came from Moscow, after Anya contacted them. But I'll be taking my share of the credit, don't you worry,' said Timur, smiling. 'Locating an important defector, and catching a veteran double agent, all in one week. I expect I'll be transferred back home within the month, with Brezhnev himself pinning the medals on my chest. It'll be a firing squad for you, Grigory, most likely. And as for you, Yuri, what are we going to do with you? A one-way ticket to Gorky perhaps, or worse, back to your old job at those uranium mines.'

'You killed Semyon,' said Yuri. 'Didn't you?'

Timur smiled. 'Poor little Semyon had no idea what he was dealing with. At first I thought he was the double agent. You know, trying to get you fired and get himself promoted. Standard spy tactic. You can see how I got confused. When Anya told me he was threatening to blackmail her, well I didn't need that. He was going to mess everything up. I followed him down the mine shaft that night. He thought we were having a meeting. It only took one hit with a lump hammer, and my Latvian problem was solved.'

'And you pulled the ventilation unit down afterwards,' said Yuri. 'And tried to blame it on me.'

Timur smiled. 'I did consider that. But then I thought you

might be the contact, Yuri. I sent Anya to talk to you that night. I didn't tell her to start sleeping with you. That was her own doing. She hasn't been easy to control, as you can imagine. But then it turns out it wasn't you or little Semyon, but dear old Grigory. The godfather of Pyramiden.'

Timur was so pleased with himself that at first he did not notice Catherine entering the room behind him. When he did, his smile disappeared. She looked at his gun, but he kept it pointed at Yuri and Grigory.

'Catherine,' he said. 'It would be better if you left now. I will explain all of this later.'

'I think you should go too,' said Yuri.

Catherine looked from Timur to Grigory, and then Yuri. She did not say a word. Just stared at them all in turn. Finally, her eyes returned to Timur.

'What are you doing?' she asked.

'These men are criminals,' he said. 'They need to face justice.'

'Like you gave Semyon,' said Yuri.

Catherine studied Timur's reaction, and then she looked over at Yuri again. He saw her glance at a typewriter on the table nearest the door. She turned and nodded to Timur, and walked towards the door.

Yuri dropped his arms.

'Hey,' said Timur. 'Did I say you could do that? Hands back in the air.'

Yuri did not budge.

'Did you hear what I said, hands up,' said Timur.

Catherine grabbed the typewriter and raised it above her head, before bringing it down hard on the back of Timur's left shoulder with one swift movement. Timur staggered sideways but didn't fall, nor did he drop his gun. He elbowed

Catherine in the face as she reached for his arm. Then he raised his revolver once more. The sound of a silenced gunshot was followed by an unnatural breath from Timur. Blood spread across his shirt, from a bullet hole in the dead centre of his chest. He dropped his gun first, then he followed it to the ground. Yuri looked from him to Grigory. The party man had impressed him with the speed with which he had retrieved his gun from the top drawer of his desk. He only had time for one shot, and he had not hesitated.

Catherine knelt down beside Timur and checked him for signs of life. When she could see there were none, she turned her face away.

'I thought you were not that sort of spy,' said Yuri.

Grigory laid the gun and silencer flat on his desk. 'I'm not. I've never killed anyone before. He is the first.'

Grigory rubbed his hands together. Yuri could see they were shaking.

'Hopefully, you will never have to do it again,' said Yuri. He turned to Catherine. 'You all right?' he asked.

She was standing now and seemed to be in a state of confusion.

'He would have done the same to us,' said Yuri. 'And he wouldn't have given it a second thought. One man is already dead because of him. And maybe one woman too.'

Catherine looked at him, and nodded her head. He could see there were tears in her eyes.

'Tell Grigory he'll be fine over there in the west. Won't he? He has to go, and today.'

He wanted her to lie to Grigory, whatever the truth was. Catherine hesitated a moment. She stared down at Timur's body again.

'Tell him, please,' Yuri repeated.

She pulled her eyes away and Yuri saw a coldness in them that he had never seen before.

'Yes,' she said. 'They will look after you, Grigory, I'm sure. You don't have to worry.'

'How would she know?' said Grigory. 'She doesn't know anything about these things.'

Catherine did not take offence, if she heard him at all. She turned her gaze away from the body of her former lover, and she did not look at him again.

'I am too old to be going to the west,' protested Grigory. 'I'm retired.'

'You'll be dead before the year is out, if you don't,' said Yuri. 'Is that what you want? Plus, they'll want to know everything you've done for the last thirty years, and they won't mind how they get that information out of you. You get the picture. It won't be pretty, Grigory. It's up to you.'

Grigory nodded reluctantly. He was trapped and he knew it, with only one way out.

'Same plan,' said Yuri. 'Except you're going, not Anya.'

He picked up the gun off the table and stuffed it into Grigory's pocket. 'Here, you might need to point that at someone.'

'What about him?' asked Catherine, nodding at the body on the floor. 'You're not going to just leave him here.'

Timur had become as much of a problem in death as he had been in life. Yuri turned to Catherine, and he saw that she knew what he was thinking.

'No,' she said, shaking her head.

Grigory looked confused. 'What is it?'

'The coal furnace at the power station,' he explained. 'It's the same as cremation. And he'll be gone in minutes. No evidence. No one will ever know what happened to him.'

'No,' insisted Catherine. 'We've done enough to him already. I am not doing that.'

Yuri was surprised to see that her feelings for Timur had been genuine.

'Besides,' said Grigory. 'There are people here old enough to know what that smell is.'

'Fine,' said Yuri, throwing his arms out. 'What then?'

'I'll take him with me,' said Grigory. 'I'll find a place to leave him on the way. Is that acceptable to you?'

Catherine nodded her agreement.

'How is that better?' asked Yuri. 'And it doubles our chances of getting caught.'

'It's decided,' said Grigory. 'As you said, there's no time to argue.'

Yuri accepted the will of the majority even though he thought they were both idiots.

Catherine kept watch in the corridor as Yuri and Grigory carried Timur's lifeless body out the office door. They rested him on the floor while Yuri opened the back window at the end of the corridor, and then they pushed him out. The corpse fell twelve feet and hit the ground with a dull thud, cushioned by a deep layer of fresh snow.

Catherine looked at them angrily.

'It's not hurting him now,' said Yuri.

Timur rolled once on the incline and Yuri saw that the snow was already stained red where he had landed. All traces would have to be removed before they moved on.

'Get whatever you need,' Yuri said to Grigory, 'and meet me out front in ten minutes. And remember, you need to stay light, so none of your books. I'll look after them.'

'What will I need, do you think?' asked Grigory.

'I don't know,' said Yuri. 'Imagine you are going on a two-week holiday.'

Grigory nodded. 'Thank you for this, Yuri.'

'My pleasure,' said Yuri. 'Doing this never made any sense to me until today. Now hurry.'

Grigory left, passing Catherine, who was still standing at the door of the office.

'I need you to do something else for me,' said Yuri. 'A last favour.'

'What?' asked Catherine.

'I need you to keep Anya out of the way. We can't have her talking to anyone else about this until Grigory's well away from Pyramiden.'

'I can do that,' said Catherine. 'But I get the feeling she's not interested in any of us.'

'You're probably right,' said Yuri. 'She never was. But just to be sure.'

No one would accuse Anya of doing what she did for ideological motives. It had been a purely personal revenge. So hopefully they could count on her silence about Grigory, since there was no benefit for her in betraying him.

There was no reason for anyone to walk through the thick snow behind the building. Yuri knew he would have some time to get organised. Just to be safe, though, he covered Timur's body in a tarpaulin. Then he piled snow on top of it. He kicked away the bloodstains where the body had hit the ground. When he was finished he walked around to the other side of the building. Catherine was keeping watch across the street. He waved to her that all was well, and she walked off to find Anya.

Yuri collected the keys to both snowmobiles. Luckily, none of the researchers had needed to take them out that day. He did not want to have to postpone Grigory's departure for any reason.

Grigory arrived looking ten years older and carrying too many of his belongings. Two coloured holdalls bursting with who knew what. Yuri made no comment, just handed him one set of keys. Together they drove to the rear of the administration building.

They strapped Timur's limp body to the back of Yuri's snowmobile and covered it with the tarpaulin. Yuri had zero sympathy for him.

'Why are you coming?' said Grigory. 'There is no need. And you should be here when they find out I am missing.'

'I'll see you part of the way,' replied Yuri.

Grigory was even more unfit than Anya. Too many big political dinners over the years. And since Yuri had known him, the only physical exercise he had engaged in was a game of chess. He let Grigory go ahead of him so he could watch his progress. They headed west out of town, with their heads and faces wrapped up against the cold. If anyone saw them, it would be nothing unusual. Everyone knew that he often accompanied the researchers on their field trips. And Timur's body was well hidden under the tarpaulin, and could appear from a distance as though they were carrying equipment.

Their headlights gave them a very limited field of view. However, the sun's halo, peeking faintly from below the horizon, afforded them at least some ambient light. As they passed the graveyard Yuri spotted a female polar bear heading towards the fjord, with her two cubs doing their best to keep up.

It took Grigory ten minutes to get into his stride. But when he did, he drove well and Yuri's fears began to subside. Yuri moved to the front and led the way for a further five miles.

When he spotted a copse of leafless trees up ahead, he slowed and pulled in.

They both dismounted and removed their goggles, and the scarves that were covering their mouths.

'What do you think?' asked Yuri, nodding towards the trees.

'As good a place as any,' agreed Grigory. 'Catherine would approve, I think.'

Yuri unstrapped Timur's body from the back of his snow-mobile. They carried him together into the trees. As they walked, Yuri looked down at the lifeless face of the man who had caused him so much grief over the past few months. There were no bushes under which to hide him. And burying him underground was not an option without digging equipment. They laid him on his side behind two trees, where he would not be easily visible if anyone passed in the spring. However, they both knew, but didn't say, that the body would most likely be scavenged long before that. An Arctic fox or a polar bear would be more than delighted to make an early spring meal of his corpse. Not to mention the birds. Yuri would not be pointing out this detail to Catherine.

'You want to say a few words?' asked Grigory.

'Not for him, no,' said Yuri. 'You?'

Grigory shook his head. They retraced their steps back to the snowmobiles.

'Maybe it's better not to have ambitions in this life,' said Yuri. 'Semyon and Timur had that in common, they were both desperate to get ahead. And it got them killed.'

'Funny how life works out sometimes, isn't it,' said Grigory. 'I never had any desire to go to the west, and now look at me. At my age, a most unlikely defector.'

'They owe you,' said Yuri. 'Make sure you remind them of that.'

'I will,' said Grigory. 'I will be a surprise package for them.'

He was in no hurry to depart, and Yuri hoped he was not having second thoughts. But they had time. No one knew that Timur was dead except Catherine. By the time someone decided to organise a search party, with any luck Grigory would be safe in Longyearbyen.

'What if Anya gets her wish, and they do find Taisia? Will you be in trouble?' asked Yuri.

Grigory considered the question.

'If it was the Soviet authorities, then yes, for sure. But with the British, who knows. I just did what they asked me to do. It's not my fault it went bad, is it?'

Yuri shrugged. 'You're right. You're lucky it was not a Soviet mission. Hopefully the British will be different.'

He pulled out a map of Spitsbergen from the inside pocket of his coat.

'Let's go over the route again.'

Grigory paid attention as Yuri went through it step by step, even though he was the one who had taught Yuri all of these things. Rocky ground and ravines to avoid. Stretches where he could go as fast as he liked, others where he would need to limit his speed.

'What if someone saw you leaving with me?' asked Grigory.

'Don't worry about that,' said Yuri. 'If anyone did, I'll make up something appropriate. Maybe we were paying our respects at the graveyard. And when my back was turned you sped away.'

Grigory frowned. 'Then as soon as you get back you must report it.'

Yuri shook his head. 'No. You'll need the time. At least a day before the alarm is raised. I'll think of something better on the ride back.'

Grigory nodded, his mind elsewhere again. Yuri folded up the map and handed it to him.

'Maybe I won't make it,' said Grigory. 'And you'll find me out here in the spring, like Timur.'

'You better make it,' said Yuri. 'I don't want to have gone to all this trouble for nothing.'

Grigory smiled. 'I will do my best, for you.'

Yuri offered his hand and Grigory shook it.

'Goodbye, my friend,' said Grigory. 'I left some things in my apartment for you. The chess set is one. You'll have to find yourself a new partner.'

'Someone I can beat,' said Yuri. 'And better-looking.'

'And you might consider actually fixing my bathroom plumbing while I'm gone.'

Yuri smiled. 'I will definitely consider it. But no promises.'

Grigory mounted his snowmobile and turned on the engine. After putting on his goggles, he waved once and drove off. Yuri watched him until he disappeared around the next hillside. Then he started his own engine, turned around and began the journey back to Pyramiden.

He made a mental note of all the people who saw him arriving back. As he drove slowly into town, he was seen by the principal of the school and some of the children in the playground. As he parked, he saw the Mongolian researcher looking at him out a window. He had the usual unreadable expression on his face. The man did not acknowledge him, just turned away from the window. The missing snowmobile would become a focus of the investigation as soon as it was discovered that both Grigory and Timur were gone.

A new idea had formed in Yuri's head on the ride home. If asked, he could say that he had seen Grigory and Timur together on the missing snowmobile. Two defectors, it would seem to anyone who did not know the truth. A partnership in crime. Who was to say that Timur had not made a pact with the double agent himself? Or perhaps Timur had also been a double agent all along. All of these theories would be hard to disprove without anyone to question.

There were only two loose ends as far as he could tell. Timur's body might be found in the spring. In which case the murder would be blamed on Grigory. So he and Catherine were safe in any event. The other loose end he would have to sort later that night. Timur's office and apartment would have to be thoroughly searched for any notes he might have kept. It would not be helpful for Yuri's name to feature prominently all over the dead man's writings.

However, that was a job for when everyone was sleeping. Right now, there was a more pressing matter to attend to. He made a beeline for Paris, where he hoped Catherine had been keeping an eye on Anya for the last few hours. He knocked on the apartment door. He heard voices inside, and a few seconds later Catherine opened the door an inch. When she saw it was him, she looked relieved. She opened the door wide to let him inside, and closed it behind him. Then she stood with her arms folded, barring the exit.

Catherine had evidently taken her task seriously. Anya was sitting sheepishly on the bed. On her face was the unmistakable early-stage colouring of a black eye.

'She hit me,' said Anya.

'I bet you deserved it,' said Yuri.

Catherine nodded in agreement from the doorway.

'She wouldn't even let me go to the bathroom,' said Anya.

'You can go now,' said Yuri. 'Just as soon as I'm finished with you.'

Anya slumped back against the wall with her arms folded.

'I thought you loved her,' said Yuri.

Anya looked at Catherine first, for her reaction, and then to Yuri.

'I did,' said Anya. 'That's the point. She was supposed to love me too. But instead, she turned my life upside down without a thought for what might happen to me after she was gone. It was typical of her, always putting herself first, before anyone else.'

Catherine had no idea what was going on. Anya turned to her.

'You think men are pigs,' she said. 'Try loving a woman.'

'But she wanted you to join her,' said Yuri. 'Didn't she? She wrote to you.'

Anya let out a laugh.

'You know why she did that, after five years?'

Yuri shook his head.

'I do,' said Anya. 'Because she's bored. That's all. She's bored and she thinks I'll make it better. Maybe it would be fine between us for a year or two, but then she'll find a way to leave me again.'

Catherine looked fit to burst with questions, but the answers would have to wait.

'So you wanted her dead, because of what she did to you,' said Yuri. 'Even before you came to Pyramiden.'

'She ruined me,' said Anya, almost spitting the words. 'I was somebody before she left. It wasn't my fault. She did it all. She turned me into a nobody in one day. And nothing can ever give me back what she took.'

'Maybe they won't find her,' said Yuri. 'Did you think about that?'

Anya looked up quickly. It was not an idea she liked.

'They'll find her,' she said. 'And when they do, she'll know I sent them. I want her to know that.'

She looked at her watch.

'Where's Timur?' she asked. 'He will be looking for me.'

Yuri caught Catherine's eye before he answered.

'He left,' said Yuri. 'With Grigory. Grigory was your contact, not Catherine. I don't think either of them is coming back.'

Anya looked down at the floor, gathering her thoughts.

'But why would Timur . . .?' she said.

'I think you may have put ideas in to his head, about going over to the other side. He was always an ambitious bastard, wouldn't you agree, Catherine?'

Catherine stared at him, wide-eyed, before nodding her head.

'You and Catherine have that in common now,' said Yuri. 'He didn't tell her he was leaving either. Not a word. Just upped and left.'

Anya turned her attention to Catherine. 'Is it true what he's saying?'

Catherine paused. 'Yes, it's true,' she said. 'And I don't expect to hear from him in five years' time.'

'See,' said Yuri. 'You are not the only one.'

Anya's head seemed to be spinning with all the complications he had suggested. Catherine too did not appear to be entirely sure of what was going on. Yuri pulled a chair near to the bed and sat down. Anya shifted nervously.

'Anya, I need to ask you to do something. Pretty soon, maybe as soon as tomorrow, people are going to come asking about all of this. And then after them, more people will come. Serious men. They will not be your friends or mine. When they talk to you, I'd like you to leave out Catherine's name, and mine. Will you do that? You can mention Grigory's name as often as you like. It doesn't matter now.'

Anya looked from him to Catherine. Then she nodded her agreement.

Chapter 23

I T WAS A full day before the alarm was raised. Two men missing. And not just any men. A thorough search was made of the town, but they were not found. In Timur's absence the accounts clerk was ordered to contact the Norwegian police at Longyearbyen to ask for help with a search party out in the countryside.

The Longyearbyen police informed her that there was no need to look for the former party boss of Pyramiden. Grigory Babkin had arrived in their town suffering from hypothermia, but was otherwise making a good recovery. When the accounts clerk enquired when she should send someone to pick him up, she heard laughter at the other end of the line. She was further informed that the new arrival had no inten- tion of returning to Pyramiden or the Soviet Union any time soon.

Yuri joined in the search party for Timur. He told anyone who would listen that he had seen the KGB man heading out of town, with Grigory, on a snowmobile two days previously. For appearance's sake, he drove his search team ever onward until they were exhausted and in danger of frostbite. By this stage, everyone had heard the story of Grigory's arrival in Longyearbyen. And no one really expected to come across

Timur alive and kicking. Yuri was forced to make speeches of encouragement in order to rouse some enthusiasm among his group.

On the third day, another search team found a helicopter not far from the weather station. Beside it, on the ground, was a bearded Norwegian man handcuffed to the landing rail. Frozen to death.

Yuri asked Anya if she had told Timur in advance of her planned trip with the Norwegian trapper. She admitted that she had. Their plan depended on her staying in Pyramiden until a way was found to find Taisia. Timur had told her that he would make sure, one way or another, that she did not have to get on that helicopter.

When the search for Timur was called off after five days, Yuri's was the loudest voice saying they should keep going.

The discordant sound of two helicopters making their way up the fjord was the first sign the heavy gang had been called in. Yuri watched four hard men disembark from each helicopter. These were not Norwegian policemen. They were KGB. Or something worse. A cloud of paranoia settled over the whole town. No one enjoyed having these men in their midst. Everyone was questioned about what they knew. And it wasn't long before two of the new arrivals came knocking on Yuri's door. He was jealous of how fit they looked. He suspected they did not keep in shape for health reasons.

They already knew a lot and were looking for more. The Mongolian had told them about his return on a snowmobile on the day of the two disappearances. What a pal, thought Yuri.

'What was the reason for your trip out of town?' asked the questioner.

The other man never said a word. He just watched.

'Paying my respects in the graveyard,' he replied. My assistant, Semyon, died a few months ago. Mining accident. He and I were very close.'

The mute one wrote down Semyon's name.

'And that was where you saw Grigory and Timur? At the graveyard? What were they doing there?'

'I was at the graveyard,' said Yuri. 'They drove past it while I was there. I waved at them but I'm not sure they saw me. They kept on going, in any case.'

'And Grigory, Comrade Babkin, was a friend of yours?'

The mute one looked up from his notes.

'No,' said Yuri. 'What makes you say that?'

'People tell us you played chess together. Regularly.'

My God, thought Yuri, tongues were certainly wagging around town. He supposed it was understandable that, when confronted by these men, everyone wanted to shift attention on to the next person. If too many people were mentioning his name, then he could be in trouble.

'That's right. We did play chess. Now and again. Not regularly. He wanted to learn. I was teaching him. He wasn't very good. But that was it. We weren't friends.'

The mute one wrote down a word. Yuri arched his neck but couldn't make it out. The man caught him doing it, and Yuri rolled his head to the other side as if he was stretching a pained muscle.

'And Anya, the former school teacher. You are lovers, isn't that so?' asked the questioner.

'Were. Until recently. Yes. Did she tell you that?'

The man ignored his question, as though it had not been asked.

'Why did it end between you two?'

'Why does any relationship end?' said Yuri. 'If I knew the answer to that I wouldn't go through so many.'

Yuri caught the hint of a smile from the silent one, and he began to relax a little. Anya had said nothing incriminating about him, he was sure. Otherwise this conversation would be taking an altogether different tack.

A day later, he was called to the mine director's office. The director and Yuri rarely had to deal with each other, except when there were problems on a large scale. And he made sure there were few of those. He made his way to his office with a sinking feeling. The subject of this chat was unlikely to be about a pay rise. When he knocked and entered, the director had his back to him, staring out the window. They now had a couple of hours of daylight each day. The sun, although it was not yet high in the sky, had already begun to have an effect on the ice-bound fjord.

'Sit down, Yuri,' said the director. His brow was creased with troubles.

Yuri sat stiff and upright, wondering if this was finally the end of his time here. The director sat and cleared his throat.

'A lot has happened lately,' he said, throwing Yuri an occasional glance. The rest of the time he stared down at his own hands. 'Most of it not good, I don't need to tell you.'

Yuri nodded, biding his time rather than opening his mouth and saying the wrong thing.

'Your contract is up with us when?' the director asked.

Here we go, he thought, time to start packing.

'Six months from now,' he said. 'End of September.'

'I see. And how long have you been with us, altogether?'

Yuri counted on his fingers. 'Six contracts. Minus six months. Eleven and a half years.'

The director raised an eyebrow. 'Really? Is it that long? You've been here almost as long as me.'

Yuri felt his pulse quickening. The director stood and looked out the window again.

'A bad business this, with Grigory and Timur. And that Norwegian pilot too. It's all very strange. They are saying now that Semyon's death might not have been an accident after all. They want to dig up the body. Grigory apparently is the chief suspect. They are calling him a traitor. I'm finding it all hard to believe.'

'They are wasting their time with Semyon,' said Yuri. 'I saw the autopsy report. Even if it did happen another way, there's no evidence to prove it wasn't an accident.'

The director nodded. 'They are going to do it anyway. I will let them. They can send him back to Latvia when they are finished. I never would have pegged Grigory for a traitor, though, would you?'

'You never can tell with people,' said Yuri. 'And do they have any idea where Timur is?'

'No,' said the director. 'That's even stranger. The man seems to have disappeared without a trace. No one has seen him since the day Grigory left.'

The director descended into a long, worried silence. The dark clouds forming above the glacier across the fjord seemed to match his mood.

'Was there something in particular that you wanted to see me about?' asked Yuri.

'What?' said the director, remembering that he was there. 'Oh, yes, sorry.'

Yuri took a deep breath.

'At unfortunate times like this,' said the director, as he retook his seat, 'what we need is stability. I need people I can rely on. Trust. Trust has been abused, by at least one among us, and we need to redress that. To be honest I am glad the bad apples are gone. We don't need them. Wouldn't you agree?'

Yuri nodded, only because this is what he guessed the man wanted from him.

'This contract of yours,' said the director, 'how about we extend it now for a further two years?'

Yuri made to speak but the director held up his hand to silence him.

'I know it's a lot to ask. Life in the Arctic is harsh. And there are probably loved ones back home you want to get back to. You know I'm sure we could arrange to bring them out here if that would help?'

Yuri thought for a moment. 'No. Thanks for the offer. But there's no one.'

The director looked surprised. 'I see.'

'Well, there is one,' said Yuri, as an idea formed in his head. 'I have a son. Perhaps you could find him a job here. If he was interested.'

'Yes, of course,' said the director. 'What are his skills?'

'I have no idea,' said Yuri, with no hint of embarrassment. 'I will write to him and ask. But isn't there a waiting list to come here?'

The director's face brightened considerably. 'Oh, don't worry about that. If he wants to come, then we'll find a way to make it happen. You are a family after all.'

Yuri smiled. They were not a family, and had not been for twenty years. But it was worth a shot to ask.

'So,' said the director. 'Are we in agreement? You will stay here until at least September 1980?'

Yuri paused, not wishing to seem too eager. 'My wages?'

The director frowned again. 'What about them?'

'Perhaps a raise is in order, given the length of my service. Not to mention the harshness of life here, as you said. Another two years would be a big sacrifice to make. I am willing to serve of course, wherever I am asked to. It is my duty.'

The director sighed. 'I am sure we can come to some arrangement,' he said. 'Another day?'

Yuri stood and offered his hand. The director did the same, and the deal was done.

Finally, spring and full sun returned. The first day when it rose high in the sky had a magical quality. There were droplets of water everywhere, sparkling in the light. Yuri sat outside the power station and let the rays fall on his face. There was little heat from it, but it felt good nonetheless.

For many reasons, it had been Yuri's hardest winter ever. He was not the same man he had been. And his relationship with this town had changed too. Things he had been certain about were no longer so fixed in his mind. Right now, despite his agreement with the director, he was not sure he could face the sun disappearing again. The sun was life. Darkness was sleep, and death. He chose life. But he decided he would look forward to the days to come. Spring, and summer after that. Right now, the next winter was a long way off, and any decisions about his future here could be put off for a while.

It would be a busy time too, with no space to dwell on these matters. The spring thaw would bring water, and lots of it. It needed to be managed so that it did not do whatever it wanted. Left to its own devices water was a destructive force. The ice on the fjord was the first to break up, separating into large floating blocks. These became smaller and smaller until, after a few weeks, they disappeared. Boat traffic would resume soon, and with it a changeover of staff at the mine as contracts ended and new ones began. The boats would bring new female faces, but he promised himself not to look. Although, he knew this was a lie. Look then, but don't touch, he thought. At least for a while.

He set about some spring cleaning in his apartment. The first chore was to empty the remains of any alcohol he had out the window. He set a target of two dry months. He knew it would not last longer than that, and perhaps he might not even reach this target. But his body would feel the benefit of even a fortnight of abstinence. His fiftieth birthday was looming in the not too distant future. If he wanted to see many years beyond that, he knew a change of lifestyle would be required.

His double bed remained. He had awoken many times expecting to find Anya there beside him. Unconsciously, he still slept on the same side of the bed, to give her room. He would get over that in time. Despite the raw memories it aroused, the bed was definitely staying, he decided.

One of the Lithuanian men who had helped him carry it was still in jail in Pyramiden. Jonas's name was top of the manifest list for shipment back to Russia. He had been questioned about the recent events, but he had the perfect alibi for all, except Semyon's death. The investigators had dug up the Latvian's body but found nothing that would cause them to change the autopsy verdict.

The first boat came, laden with oranges, and not a moment too soon. Their stores of fruit were long gone. As Yuri watched the crates being unloaded, a familiar figure arrived at the dock. She put down her two suitcases and walked slowly towards him. They had hardly spoken to each other since the day it had all happened, though he had seen her staggering out of the bar several times. He was surprised the KGB had not taken her back to Moscow. Perhaps they had not had room in their helicopters, given the number of men they had brought. Or perhaps they had left her as punishment for Timur's disappearance.

'Hey,' said Anya.

She smiled at him and he couldn't help smiling back.

'You're off then,' said Yuri.

'I am. Going home.'

'You'll be getting your old life back, like you wanted,' he said. 'I hope it was worth it.'

Anya shook her head. 'No, I won't. Nothing is changing for me. They are not happy with how things went.'

'They don't have to worry about Grigory,' said Yuri. 'He won't cause them any more trouble. He's retired. He's probably sitting on a beach somewhere. I hope he is. Although a library is more likely.'

'It's not that,' she said. 'She is still alive. Taisia, I mean. Did you know?'

'No,' said Yuri. 'I didn't know that.'

'Whoever was guarding her did their job well,' said Anya. 'The man they sent was the one who was killed. Her protector was a female agent. I heard she took a bullet for her. Typical of Taisia to have that effect on the women around her. I bet they were lovers. Do you think they were?'

Yuri didn't respond.

'They are not happy about that,' she continued, 'or about Grigory leaving and Timur disappearing. Too many questions without answers. I'll be lucky if they even let me teach kids again.'

Yuri was pleased about one thing. He did not care a jot for her former lover, but he was glad she was alive. He had no desire to be responsible for a stranger's execution. He had little sympathy for Anya's situation, yet he could see on her face that this is what she wanted from him. She would get none. She had lied to him about so many things. But he did not deny to himself that he still loved her.

'They can always send another assassin, without my help this time,' said Yuri. 'I presume they are not going to give up, just like that.'

Anya shrugged. 'I think they will never find her now. They will have moved her out of reach. And she will never get permission to contact me again. Not that she would want to now. I think she has gotten my message. Anyway, I don't care any more. It's over.'

Neither of them could look each other in the eye for very long. Behind them, the outgoing passengers had started to board. Yuri spotted the tall Lithuanian being led across the small gangplank in handcuffs.

'You want to teach kids again?' asked Yuri.

Anya shrugged. 'It's a job. I am going to need one of those.'

'You'll have to lay off the booze this time, if you do.'

He could see in her eyes that she had not been dry for quite a while. She made an expression of agreement but he had seen that one too many times before. The captain of the boat rang his bell to indicate an imminent departure. Anya appeared unsure about something and he worried for a moment that she was not going to get on it. He wanted her to leave.

The bell rang once more. Anya looked, and then turned back to him.

'You could come with me?' she said.

He looked up at her. Of all the things she could have said, he wasn't expecting that.

'We could start again, somewhere else. The two of us. We were good together, weren't we?'

He knew he would decline her offer. But despite himself, he did actually consider it for a moment as he remembered the sensation of her soft neck on his lips. He longed to feel that one more time. She was close enough to touch. And he knew that she would not object if he pulled her into his arms. Instead, he shook his head and smiled.

'Pyramiden still your home?' she said.

'Something like that,' he replied.

She took a step towards him but he kept his distance from her. Afraid that if he did hold her he might not let her go. It was ridiculous to even think about it. He would never trust her again. She had been wronged and she had wanted revenge. He was not so saintly that he did not understand those feelings. Yet, Semyon was dead because of her. He had not deserved that. Timur too was dead because of her. Perhaps he did deserve it. And she had abused his own feelings for her in order to set the whole chain of events in motion.

'So that's it then,' she said. 'Nothing more to be said?'

'Yes,' he agreed. 'Better that way.'

He wondered if, after all, she might feel an apology was necessary. But none came. He hadn't really expected one.

She looked him in the eye for the last time, and nodded. Then she turned on her heel and walked back to where she had left her belongings. As she struggled with the weight of the suitcases, a man offered to help her. She would not be short of admirers wherever she ended up. He decided not to stay and watch the boat depart.

He left the dock and walked back into town. He knew he would never hear from her again. He would have liked to know how Grigory was getting on. The unexpected defector deserved the red carpet treatment in the west. He was a resourceful old bastard, and Yuri was confident he would survive whatever life threw at him. Perhaps he was playing chess somewhere with a new challenger. Part of him was jealous.

A few days later, he sat with Catherine as they watched the melting ice-water rush down Pyramiden mountain. It had started as a slow trickle two days before and had gradually expanded to what it was now, a river. The falling water picked up speed on the slopes until it levelled off and bashed against the man-made dyke. This defence system was one of the last things Yuri had worked on with Semyon. For now, their hard work looked like it might hold.

'I think it's going to keep it back,' said Catherine.

Yuri was not so sure. The water level was still rising fast. It was easier for the river to flow straight through town. That's what it wanted to do. The dyke forced it to make an unnatural turn to the right, and on down to the fjord without troubling Pyramiden's buildings. But water preferred the easy route, and would take it whenever it could.

'We'll see,' said Yuri.

If the dyke was breached, they were in for a wet day's work putting it right.

'Can you swim?' he asked.

'Yes,' she said, laughing. 'You're not much of an optimist, are you?'

'These days I expect the worst.'

Catherine gave him a knowing glance.

'I suppose no one can blame you for that,' she said.

As they waited, the flow of water seemed to ease off.

'There, look,' said Catherine. 'Nothing to worry about.'

'I thought you were leaving in the spring,' said Yuri. 'Why weren't you on the first boat?'

'I am not leaving after all,' she said. 'They said I could stay as long as I wanted.'

Yuri turned to look at her, and she smiled.

'After everything, you still want to be here?' he asked. 'Why?'

'I like it here,' said Catherine. 'It's not without its challenges, I'll admit.'

'That's an understatement,' said Yuri.

'And you still need an assistant, don't you?' she asked.

Yuri grinned. 'I wouldn't say need, as such. But you're welcome to hang about, if you've nothing better to do.'

Catherine punched him hard on the shoulder. 'You deserve that. I work my ass off all winter and this is the—'

'All right,' Yuri interrupted. 'I need an assistant. I'd be very pleased if you stayed. Although you would have to be a bit mad to.'

'Pleased! That's quite the compliment coming from you,' she said.

'Yes, it is,' he agreed. 'Almost unheard of, and most likely never to be repeated.'

Catherine smiled. 'Going soft in your old age.'

They heard a loud noise above them on the mountain, and they looked up in time to see a large section of snow sliding off a cliff that had been supporting its weight.

'You miss her?' asked Catherine.

'No,' he replied.

'Sorry you met her in the first place?'

He pondered this for a moment. 'No. The sex was amazing. Really exceptional.'

'Hey! I don't need to hear details,' she said. 'And now we're both single.'

'Yes. And I intend to stay that way,' said Yuri. 'How about you?'

'Oh, we'll see,' said Catherine, looking away. 'Never say never.'

'It pays to check out the new arrivals off the boat,' he offered. 'Before the good ones are all taken.'

Catherine laughed. 'I don't think I'll be doing that, do you?'

Yuri watched the water level at the dyke rising as the newly fallen snow began to melt.

'You know I'm surprised you are staying on after everything that happened. I thought it would put you off us for life.'

Catherine became pensive. 'It certainly gave me pause for thought. As you said to me once, I had a picture in my head of what it was like here, and it turned out not to be like that. It's not so different from home after all. You had a workers' paradise, and you've all made a mess of it. Communism was supposed to put an end to personal ambition and selfish motives.'

'Was it?' said Yuri.

'Yes,' said Catherine. 'Lenin himself said . . .'

While she was talking, in a matter of seconds, the water level rose too high and breached the town's defences. The course of the river took a sharp turn to the left, flowing over the dyke. It flooded freely down past Lenin's statue, making a muddy mess of the town square and the Street for the 60th Anniversary of the Great October.

'Oh dear,' said Catherine.

'Come on,' said Yuri. 'We have work to do.'

Acknowledgements

Many thanks to Francine Toon at Hodder and Stoughton and
Caroline Wood at Felicity Bryan Associates. And to readers
Paul Fitzgerald and Jane Doolan.

While this story is fictional, Pyramiden does exist, and was a
functioning mine until the 1990s.

S.B. April 2017